Sweet Dreams

Merry Christmas
Marlene
What a thoughtful Son
you have
S Edwards
12/05

Sweet Dreams

D.L. Edwards

iUniverse, Inc.
New York Lincoln Shanghai

Sweet Dreams

Copyright © 2005 by D.L. Edwards

iUniverse books may be ordered through booksellers or by contacting:

iUniverse
2021 Pine Lake Road, Suite 100
Lincoln, NE 68512
www.iuniverse.com
1-800-Authors (1-800-288-4677)

ISBN: 0-595-34140-3

Printed in the United States of America

A heartfelt "thank you" goes out to all my wonderful friends and colleagues who have supported and helped me through this, but there are a few I'd like to mention personally—Scott and Dave for being the first ones to tell me to go for it, Amy for being my biggest cheerleader, Ashlee and Paula for their tireless proofing, Scott, the bartender, for helping me come up with the tacky name for my killer and Phil and Nicole, for not minding too much when this project took me away from them for hours on end.

Contents

▼

CHAPTER 1

▼

WEDNESDAY, JANUARY 14TH

✳   ✳   ✳   ✳

4:06 a.m.

The man stopped halfway up the narrow staircase and looked around. The only person in the lobby of the old hotel was a ragged, unkempt little man with his back to the stairs, absorbed in the wrestling match that flickered on the small TV screen behind the counter.

The woman he was following up the stairs, abruptly turned around and tapped the toe of one of her shiny vinyl black boots. She watched him for a few seconds, her fiery red hair shimmering in the harsh white light thrown from a bare overhead bulb, before she grabbed the grimy handrails on either side of her and swayed her hips into a squat just above him on the stairs. "Ain't no refunds, honey," she told him, offering him a good view of what he had paid for. "So, you comin' upstairs with me or not?"

The man's fingers tightened around the handle of the black briefcase he was carrying and, without a word, he followed her up to the second floor.

Using her key, she opened the door to room two-sixteen, turned around and crooked her finger at him. "Come on in, sugar." The hoarse croaking that spilled from her painted red lips was an ill match for the sexy body that housed it. "Don't want ya to waste a single penny of that fifty bucks."

She walked to the middle of the dark, boxy little room, slowly slipped off her once white fur coat and tossed it on the rickety old bed that sagged in the corner behind her. Her short, skintight black dress plunged deeply in the front, barely covering her small round breasts.

She smiled at him as he closed and locked the door before carrying the black case across the room with him. "So? Did ya bring some toys for us to play with, honey? You know, I expect a nice tip, if ya get too wild on me." She coughed out a hardy smoker's laugh.

Upon closer inspection, her face looked much older than her body. It was worn and hardened and there was no spark left in her almond-shaped green eyes. It was obvious that perhaps, not so long ago, she had been an extremely beautiful woman, but the time she had spent in her chosen profession seemed to have taken its toll on her. Her empty eyes told the tale of a rough life.

The man placed the case on the floor beside him and reached for the thin straps of her black dress. He slid them off over her shoulders and peeled the dress down to the floor around her ankles. Then his wrinkled old hands carefully began to examine his latest investment.

After a few minutes, she began to fidget and then after a few more, she sighed loudly. "Listen, honey, I ain't got all night."

Completely ignoring her, he slowly twisted fistfuls of her beautiful auburn hair into his hands and yanked both handfuls away from her scalp.

"Son of a bitch!" She stomped her foot and rubbed her head. "I told you I wasn't wearing a wig, damn it. Didn't you believe me?" Her faded green eyes narrowed for a moment, then suddenly her expression softened and a thin smile slid across her face.

"You like it rough, sugar?" She leaned forward and nipped his ear with her teeth. "Go ahead, honey, it's your nickel," her cracked, chapped lips whispered next to his ear. "Do whatever you like. I won't tell nobody. Whatever you want, baby. You paid for it. But let's just get going, huh?"

He nodded a couple of times as his fingers delicately made their way up her arms to her rounded shoulders. He kissed her left shoulder, then ran his thick, wet tongue up her neck and nestled his face in her hair. His nose immediately crinkled up. Her hair stunk of cheap perfume and even cheaper cigarettes, so he made a mental note to be sure and wash it real good when he got it home. Brushing the long red curls away from her face and neck, he studied her beautifully shaped shoulders. He felt a smile pull at his lips as he lifted his hands and wrapped his long fingers around her throat.

"You do like it rough, don't ya, baby?" She bit at his neck. "I thought so. I can usually tell. Well, don't be shy. Just tell me what you want me to do and I'll do it."

The man didn't answer, but his fingers tightened around her neck.

"Not quite so tight. Ok, honey?" She slid her hand down his chest to between his legs and squeezed him. "My, what a big boy you are. Can it come out and play now?" She looked up into his eyes and as his grip continued to tighten, panic slowly filled her face.

"Hey! You know what? That's....that's enough, asshole!" She slapped at him with one hand while the other tried its best to pry his fingers off of her throat. "I said, stop it," she croaked, clawing at his face and neck with her long, red, store-bought fingernails. She gasped for air while his large hands effectively squeezed the last bit of life out of her.

He seemed quite unaware of anything going on around him. Anything but how beautiful her red hair looked and how it sent tingles to his groin as it brushed against his hands and arms and delicately lay on her golden tan shoulders.

Her shoulders were a bonus. He had only picked her because he loved that long red hair of hers. It was beautiful the way it sparkled under the streetlights as she stood on the corner of Prospect and East 9th every night. It was exactly what he'd been looking for. But he just couldn't believe his luck when he saw what lovely shoulders and arms she had. He would take those, too.

With each passing second, the woman's pitiful attempt to stop him became less and less effective. Her once hard slaps became nothing but soft, weak touches before she stopped struggling altogether. Limp and motionless, her body looked not unlike a rag he twisted in his hands. Her bowels and kidneys spilled out over the light tan carpet just before her empty green eyes closed for the last time.

He held onto her neck, savoring the feel of every tendon, every muscle and vein crushing under the strength of his old, yet powerful hands. Finally, he released his hold and allowed her to gently fold to the floor.

The man stood there, above her, rubbing his chin as he analyzed the situation. Making up his mind about where to begin, he knelt down and opened the black case that had waited patiently on the floor beside him. Removing a pair of yellow, rubber kitchen gloves, he slid them over his hands and wiggled his long round fingers to check the fit.

He reached back into the black case, rummaged through it a bit, and pulled out a straight edge razor. Carefully unfolding it, he held it up to the light. The polished silver metal of the blade reflected the brilliant orange neon light that fell into the room through a small window. He studied the blade as he twisted it in the light. It needed to be very sharp to get every bit of that beautiful red hair. He had worked too hard finding it to leave any of it behind.

The first handful came off her scalp effortlessly. He held it in front of his face, fascinated by how the light danced off of it as he turned it in his hand. Beautiful and perfect. He put it to his nose and inhaled. It smelled awful! He couldn't wait to get it home and wash it in the shampoo she always used, then it really would be perfect.

Rubbing the silky lock of hair against his cheek, he felt the familiar twitching deep in his stomach and between his legs that he always got when he thought about her. But that would have to wait, he had work to do. Returning to his task, he shaved every last hair off of her head, leaving nothing but a bloody scalp behind.

Careful not to lose a single strand, he placed all the hair in a clear plastic bag, pinched it closed, and slid his fingers along the top of the bag, to seal it. He laid the bag in his case and patted it with his rubber glove, quite pleased with his newest acquisition.

He turned his attention back to the bald, naked woman lying on the floor in front of him and inspected her shoulders. Oh yes, they were perfect, too. He was so happy to have found them. Now he wouldn't even have to bother with that blonde receptionist who worked for his doctor. And that would save him some valuable time because he was, after all, in such a terrible hurry.

He wiped the straight edge off on the woman's black dress, folded it and returned it to his case. The metal instruments clinked out their objections, as he clawed through the assorted knives, blades, scissors and saws, until he removed an odd shaped hacksaw. Like the razor, he held it up to the light. Once he decided it would work just fine, he went straight to work.

*   *   *   *

4:52 a.m.

"No!" Megan screamed and bolted straight up in bed, trying to catch her breath as her eyes darted around the room. Jade green walls, black wrought iron nightstand, a flowered ivory comforter over her legs. A dark purple night gown, damp with perspiration, plastered to her body. She took a deep breath and closed her eyes. She was back in her own bed.

She held her hand over her chest in an unconscious attempt to keep her heart from pounding out of it. Whenever she had one of those nightmares, it was as if she were right there, living it, breathing it, watching it happen right before her eyes. Well, not exactly *her* eyes. She would see everything, but through someone else's eyes, the eyes of the killer. She was forced to watch, yet helpless to stop the terrible, awful things from happening only an arm's length away from her.

Megan put her other hand over her forehead and squeezed against the painful headache that had become a usual occurrence after one of the nightmares. Tears began to roll down her cheeks as she thought about the redhead and the three other women before her.

Shaking her head, she tried unsuccessfully to erase the hideous images floating around inside of it. Why was this happening to her again? What had she done so wrong to deserve having another maniac run around loose inside her head?

Nancy Montgomery burst into the room, tying her pink terrycloth robe as she ran. Falling on the edge of the bed, she swept Megan up into her arms. "It's ok. It's ok." Nancy patted her on the back and rocked her back and forth. "It'll be alright, honey." Her reassuring words were undermined by the panic in her voice, thinly masked by her warm southern accent.

Nancy was an older woman in her early sixties. Her long straight hair, which many years ago had been raven black, was now completely silver and pulled to the back of her head with a pink ribbon. She had a kind, round face with pale blue eyes that sparkled with laughter most of the time. Of course, there wasn't much to laugh about since Megan's nightmares had returned.

Megan hugged the dear old woman tightly. Nancy hadn't been the one who brought her into this world, but she was the only reason she was still in it. It was Nancy who had taken her into her home and truly loved her after Megan's parents were murdered fourteen years ago. It was Nancy who had saved her from life in an orphanage or worse yet, an institution, to be studied and researched like a laboratory rat. Nancy had stepped in and rescued her from the craziness her life had become, taking her away and hiding her, until eventually, she became old news.

"I'm so sorry, Nancy. I've been nothing but trouble to you."

"Don't you ever say that again," Nancy snapped. "I'd be all alone in this world if it weren't for you."

"And you'd be better off."

"Megan." The old woman pushed her away so she could look her in the eye. "You know that's not true," she scolded, then smiled and shook her head slightly. "You'll never know the joy you've brought to my life. So we happen to have a few tough times now and again. It's nothing we can't handle together. You know, a body can't fully appreciate the good times if there ain't a few bad ones thrown in just to show us the difference."

"But I think we've had our share of bad times, don't you?"

"Megan Marie Montgomery. Don't you ever let the good Lord hear ya talk like that! There are millions of people out there having it a lot worse than us. You just remember that, young lady. Why, anything we can walk away from stronger and smarter than before, well...well, you just gotta look at as a learnin' experience, that's all." A wide smiled stretched across Nancy's face and she winked. "With all you're learnin', you'll be one darn smart cookie when all's said and done, huh?"

Nancy's slender, knotted fingers pushed Megan's long, maple brown hair away from her eyes and hooked it back behind her ears. "I ain't ever seen anyone with such big blue eyes and long dark eyelashes before. You know, you've grown into such a beautiful young woman, it's hard to believe you were that scrawny little kid who lived next door to me." Nancy ran the back of her hand across Megan's high cheekbone. "You're still a little too skinny, if ya ask me."

Megan forced a smile onto her face that quickly fell back into a frown. "I just wish I knew why this was happening to me again."

"Oh, honey. I wish with my whole heart it *wasn't* happening again. But for some reason it is and we just gotta find a way to deal with it, that's all." Nancy was silent for a second and then looked Megan directly in the eye. "Actually, you gotta decide for yourself just what you're willing to do about it."

Megan was only eleven when she first started having nightmares, and once the killer was captured, they immediately stopped. She was terrified that it had been some sort of psychic awakening and waited for years with this suffocating sense of dread, holding her breath, helplessly waiting for the horror of it all to once again rear its ugly head. But nothing. Each passing year brought with it a growing sense of optimism and relief until eventually, weeks would go by without her even thinking about it. And that was a wonderful thing, because so much of her young life had already been consumed by it.

It had been almost fourteen years and the nightmares never returned. After all those years, there was absolutely no reason to think she would ever experience anything like that again. No reason at all.

Unfortunately ten days ago, another monster found his way inside her brain, bringing with him gruesome, horrible images of death. But there was still no reason to think of it as a premonition. No reason to think of it as anything other than what it was, a horrible nightmare. Looking back though, Megan decided she should have known. She should have done something, instead of denying the overwhelming sense of fear that nearly crippled her afterwards.

She had a second nightmare before finding out the first one had actually come true. But there it was, the images from her first dream plastered across the front page of every newspaper in town. And exactly as she dreamt it, every grisly detail ripped straight out of her nightmare.

Over a week passed without another dream or another murder. There was nothing at all on the news or in the papers about her second dream, so Megan tried to convince herself it was over, that it had been a fluke, a coincidence. But there was this sickening feeling in the pit of her stomach that told her differently. He was still there and she knew it. She could feel him somehow, the monstrous savage crouching somewhere in the darkness of her mind, searching for his next victim.

Then, a few days ago, it came. The third dream. She woke with screams and Nancy had been right there, holding her, trying, but unable to comfort her. The two of them talking through the night, deciding whether or not Megan should go to the police.

That's what she had done in Clarksburg and it had been terrible. She wasn't sure which was worse, the dreams or how the police and the press treated her once she finally did come forward. Was she ready to risk losing the quiet, ordinary life she finally had? Well, if it meant she could save a person's life, of course she would. She would risk everything, if that's what it took. But Megan never got the chance.

Sitting at the kitchen table with Nancy over warm cups of coffee and a box of Kleenex, she was trying to decide whether she should to go to the police in person or just try to call them from home, when they heard it. A news bulletin interrupted the music playing on the radio. Megan jumped to her feet and turned up the volume to hear a newscaster telling his audience the horrifying tale of what Megan had just seen in her third nightmare.

She dropped to her knees on the cold linoleum floor and wept for the woman who had been slaughtered. The woman she had failed to save, the woman who, because of Megan's indecisiveness, was now dead. If she hadn't been so reluctant, if she hadn't been so terrified to go to the police, maybe, just maybe, she could have saved her.

Well, now it looked as if the murderous beast who haunted her dreams had chosen his fourth victim, a victim he intended to kill tonight unless Megan did something to prevent it. Something that just might ruin everything she had worked for.

*   *   *   *

3:21 p.m.

"Earth to Miss Montgomery! Earth to Miss Montgomery!" A little boy's voice snapped Megan out of her daze. "Were you dreaming or were you in a coma?" The shaggy-haired boy's face was scrunched up with concern.

"Neither, you silly. I just didn't sleep too well last night. That's all." Megan tickled him in the tummy, making him squeal.

"Did you drink hot chocolate or pop before you went to bed last night? 'Cause you shouldn't drink any hot chocolate or pop right before you go to bed. My mom says they have caffanean in them and caffanean keeps you up all night. I'd like to drink hot chocolate or pop before I go to bed, but Mom won't let me 'cause she says caffanean is bad for you too close to bedtime. Did you drink something with caffanean in it before you went to bed last night?" Kyle finished, out of breath.

"Maybe that was the problem." Megan rubbed her chin, mocking deep thought. "Well, no more *caffeine* before bedtime for me ever again. Now, you need to get back to your seat and finish your math problems, young man." Megan leaned over and whispered in the little boy's ear, "By the way, thanks for waking me up." They both giggled and he hopped on one foot all the way back to his desk.

"Rough night?" Sue Johnson asked as she handed Megan the papers she had just finished grading. Sue was a third grade teacher at Fenwood Elementary School where Megan was doing her student teaching. Megan had been assigned to her class since September and although they didn't have much in common, except for their love of children and teaching, they quickly became good friends. Sue was a wonderful teacher with a lot of enthusiasm and a genuine concern for all of her students and Megan felt lucky to be learning the ropes from her.

"Yeah." Megan nodded.

"Another nightmare?"

"Yeah. And then I just couldn't get back to sleep."

"Meg, have you thought about seeing a doctor?"

Megan shot her a cold look and wondered if she was referring to a medical doctor or hinting at a psychologist. She hadn't told Sue what the dreams were about, only that they were horrible and that it was impossible for her to get them out of her mind once she woke up. If Sue only knew what was really going on inside her head, well, Megan knew there wouldn't be any doubt at all as to what kind of doctor Sue would want her to see.

"I'm serious, Meg," Sue continued, "you're starting to get bags under your eyes."

"Gee, thanks."

"You look like you haven't slept in a week."

The bell rang and twenty-two little third graders jumped to their feet in unison. "Have a great day," Sue yelled over the chatter and commotion. "But don't forget, your book reports are due tomorrow and I expect them to be neatly written. No sloppy copies."

"See ya tomorrow," Megan called out as the last of the students filed out of the room.

The two of them began stacking the little chairs on top of the desks to make it easier for the custodian to sweep and mop the floors. "Hey." Sue looked at Megan through the legs of one of the chairs. "The Blue Man Group is coming to Cleveland next month. The fifteenth, I think. I saw them in Chicago a few years ago and it was *wild*. Honestly, it's the closest you can get to being totally stoned out of your head without actually taking any drugs. Come with me. It'll be fun."

"Oh, I don't know." Megan crawled under a desk to reach a scrap of yellow construction paper left behind by one of the students.

"Come on," Sue pleaded, "you really need to get out more. That's exactly what your problem is, you know. You don't do anything but work and study. I mean, when was the last time you actually went out on a date?"

"You know how busy I am. I just don't have the time to devote to a relationship right now."

"Who said anything about a relationship?" Sue winked a big brown eye at her. "I was talking about getting laid."

"Susan Johnson! Shame on you."

"Oh, come on, girl. Don't tell me you don't think about it."

"No." Megan walked over to the trash can and deposited the scrap paper. "*I* think about finishing college and becoming a teacher because that, my friend, is the only thing *I* want right now. It's what I've always wanted since…since I can remember. I was so shy and terrified as a kid. My teachers were what kept me going, kept me sane. Without them or Nancy…. Well, if I were able to help kids like that, to be the reason they got up in the morning and wanted to do something with their lives…I mean, how great that would be."

"Yeah, it's great. But not as great as sex."

Megan walked back over to Sue and looked her in the eye. "Is that all you ever think about?"

"Yes, as a matter of fact." Sue slammed her hands on her rounded hips and her tight, curly black hair never moved as she bobbed her head back and forth a few times. "All the damn time." They both laughed out loud, but the smile on Sue's face quickly faded. "God, Meg, if I looked like you, I'd have guys lined up around the block."

"I thought you said I looked awful."

"I said you looked tired. Big difference." Sue smiled at her. "Really, look at you. You're gorgeous. Not one ounce of fat on your entire body. You got beautiful eyes, great legs and that wonderful perma-tan most you white girls would kill for. If I had all that going for me, I'd have a new guy every weekend."

"That's funny. I thought you already did."

"Not every weekend." Sue walked over to the emerald chalk board and began erasing the day's spelling words. "Honestly, I don't know how you can stand it. If I go more than a month without…." She turned around to look at Megan. "You know….it, I'm ready to pull my hair out. How long's it been?"

"Oh. I don't think about it much." Megan fiddled with a chair on the desk in front of her.

"Come on, fess up, sister. What's it been, really? Three months? Six months? A year? What?"

"Well…" Megan looked toward the ceiling and pursed her lips together, pretending to think. In truth, she hadn't had much of a sex life, certainly nothing to give that much thought to. In fact, there had been only one. "I had a boyfriend for a couple of months my freshman year of college. So that would make it……"

"What!" Sue's bottom jaw dropped open and stayed open.

"Better watch you don't catch any flies in that mouth of yours." Megan crossed her arms in front of her and shook her head at her friend's overly dramatic display.

"Get outta here! You're not serious. Your freshman year?"

"Don't act so shocked."

"No lie?"

"Well, not all of us are horn dogs like yourself."

"Horn dogs? Geeze O. Pete, Meg! My eighty-year old grandma gets busy more often than that."

Megan laughed.

Sue stood there, straight faced, shaking her head. "You really, honest to God, haven't had sex in over three years?"

Megan put her finger to her lips and rushed over to the door, looking down the hall for possible eavesdroppers before closing the door and putting her back to it. "Why don't you just announce it over the loud speaker?"

"Because no one in their right mind would believe me. I don't believe it. Please tell me you're joking."

"Well, actually he…it wasn't really that great anyway, you know. So it's not like I miss it much."

"Oh—My—God! I am *not* hearing this." Sue swept her hand through the air and bobbed her head. "I have gotta find you a man, girlfriend, and I mean fast."

"Oh, no. Oh, no you don't." Megan clenched her teeth and shook her index finger at Sue. "Thanks, but no thanks. I prefer it this way. Really, I do. A man would just complicate things and my life's complicated enough already."

"Liar! Don't you even try to tell me that if some hot, sexy looking man were to walk through that door right now and throw you down on my desk you wouldn't just melt like butter."

Megan closed her eyes, took a deep breath and threw her hands up in the air. "Ok. Alright, I give up! You found me out. I am a sex-starved nymphomaniac and I was trying really hard to control it, until *you…you* had to go and bring it up! Well, I hope you're happy. Because of you, my friend, the safety of every half-way decent looking man in the whole city of Cleveland is in jeopardy. I just hope you can live with yourself."

"Sorry." Sue snickered.

"Well." Megan plucked her purse out of the desk drawer, put it over her shoulder and, in a huff, flung open the door. "Now, thanks to you, I better stop at the store on the way home and buy some extra batteries or no man will be safe tonight!" Megan stuck out her chin and stomped out the door to the sounds of Sue's laughter.

*   *   *   *

4:16 p.m.

With her shoulders firmly set up under her ears, Megan clutched the steering wheel and stared out the windshield. She was so thankful for her dear friend, Sue, and the few minutes of laughter they shared, because in the last few weeks there hadn't been many reasons to laugh and it felt good. She missed feeling good.

Unfortunately, the good feeling didn't last long. Once alone in the silence of her car, the seriousness of what the next few hours held in store slammed back into her brain, causing a stabbing pain behind her right eye. A woman was going to die tonight if she didn't do something to stop it, and she had wrestled the entire day with how to actually go about doing that something.

She didn't want to miss school, she needed the hours to graduate this spring and she wasn't about to let the demon in her head take that away from her, too. He had taken so much from her already. But somehow she knew a few sleepless nights and some excruciating headaches wouldn't be the worst of it. No, the worst was definitely yet to come.

For instance, when she finally did tell the police, well, saying it wasn't going to be pleasant would be the understatement of the year. But she had to do it, she knew that. No matter how hard it was going to be, she had to do it. And calling the police from home won out by a landslide over actually going to the police station in person. She'd feel much braver on the other end of a telephone receiver, sitting in the comfort and safety of her own living room. And it was going to take all the courage she could muster just to pick up that phone.

There was really no reason why she couldn't just tell the police everything she saw in her dream right over the phone, without even giving them her name. They could catch the killer, save that redhead's life, stop her nightmares, and she could keep her life intact. Yeah, sure.

She pulled into the driveway of the white two-bedroom Cape Cod with burgundy shutters she shared with Nancy. It was a small house, but to Megan, it had seemed like a castle when they moved there from West Virginia twelve years ago, a pretty, burgundy and white castle that promised to magically keep her safe and locked away from the rest of the big, cold, dark world.

As the years slowly passed and she began to venture out of her shell, she never lost that sense of safety and security she first had when she walked into that tiny little house. Well, not until ten days ago when that monster broke in, crawled into her bed and forced himself into her dreams. Now there was nowhere she felt safe.

Nancy sold everything the two of them had owned back in West Virginia and moved them to Ohio to get away from the circus their lives had become and it had helped. It had taken awhile, but it had really helped. She legally adopted Megan and changed her last name to Montgomery so the researchers and newspaper headlines wouldn't follow her for the rest of her life.

Eventually Megan became old news and she found that old saying to be true, time really does heal most wounds. Nancy opened a little flower shop that was doing quite well and Megan was well on her way to becoming a teacher. Their lives were good here. Until the dreams started again.

Megan peeled her fingers off the steering wheel and watched her hands automatically ball up into fists. Taking a deep breath, she got out of her car and headed to the house, the cold air slapped at her face and stung her lungs. Once she closed the front door behind her, she hung her coat and purse on the oak pegged coat rack hanging by the door and slowly turned to look at the phone prominently perched on the desk in the living room. It seemed to have a spotlight directed at it, the way it glowed in the darkened room.

Megan stood in the hallway and stared at the thing as if it could, at any second, jump off the desk and attack her. "Not yet," she told it out loud and headed toward the kitchen. Grabbing a can of Coke from the fridge, she poured it and a little Bacardi rum into a glass of ice and drank it down in just two long swallows. It burned her throat a little, but she made herself another one, slightly stronger this time, and headed for the phone.

*   *   *   *

4:38 p.m.

Megan decided they had forgotten she was still on hold and was just about to hang up, when a man finally picked up the phone.

"Detective Stark." A deep, dark voice reached straight through the phone and grabbed a hold of her. Her body jerked straight up and a chill shot down her spine. The voice was strong, commanding and so incredibly…sexy that it caused something in her stomach to tighten.

"Hello?" The dark velvet voice caressed her ear and a shiver washed over her skin. "Hello?" He called out again.

Megan shook off the unsettling feeling that had come over her. "Um…yes…um, Detective Hudson said you were the one I needed to…um…speak to." She concentrated on keeping her voice as slow and controlled as possible, hoping not to sound as nervous as she really was.

"Detective Hudson sent your call to me?" Detective Stark looked over the paperwork loaded desks to where his new partner, Frank Hudson, stood in his old, rumpled brown suit and matching yellow tie. He was with two other detectives and all three of them were giggling like little school girls. Stark's eyes narrowed. "Well, Miss, I'm…I'm not exactly sure I'm the one you need to talk…."

"Oh, please. Please don't transfer me again," Megan pleaded, because if he did, she was going to hang up and forget about the whole stupid thing. This was crazy. She had already told Detective Hudson she had a dream about a murder and he instantly put her on hold to transfer her to this guy. This time she was going to play it differently, she wasn't even going to mention the dream thing unless she had to. "Listen, Detective Stark, was it? You're the fifth person I've talked to already. All I need is two minutes of your time, that's it."

The detective sighed as he leaned back into his chair, stretched out his long thick legs and propped his scuffed brown boots up on the top of his desk. He raked his right hand through his dark brown hair, unsuccessfully trying to tame an unruly curl that had flopped onto his forehead. Seven white buttons somehow managed to keep a blue denim shirt fastened across his chest while a black holster strap stretched across his wide back keeping a white-handled revolver firmly in place under his left arm and a shiny silver shield hung authoritatively from his front pocket. He rubbed his square chin and the scratchy sound of stubble could be heard working its way to the surface of his skin.

"Well…" Megan heard her voice begin to quiver. It was going to be a lot harder to tell this man with the incredibly sexy voice about her nightmare than she thought. "I'm…I'm calling about a murder."

The detective was picking at a small hole in the knee of his jeans, then immediately threw his legs down over the edge of the desk and leaned into the phone. He shot a confused look over at Hudson who was laughing with his buddies on the other side of the room, before he grabbed a pencil and held it over a piece of paper. "Ok. Ok. Just start at the beginning. Tell me everything."

"There's a woman with long red hair, I think she's a prostitute, and she's going to be murdered in a hotel in room two-sixteen. The killer is an older, white man, maybe in his fifties or sixties, I'd guess around six feet tall. He has rough, wrinkled old hands and wears a gold watch on his right wrist. It's going to be terrible. He strangles her with his bare hands and then cuts off all her hair and…"

Her voice trembled as it stumbled over the words. "Well, he…he cuts off her…" Tears began to sting her eyes. "He cuts off her arms, but leaves her hands." She could hardly finish her sentence before nausea flowed over her, causing an involuntary gag to lurch from deep in her throat.

"What? What do you mean, leaves her hands?"

Megan swallowed against the lump in her throat. "He only needs her shoulders and her arms. He already has the hands." She winced as the gory scene vividly flashed in her mind.

"Where are you? What time did you find the body? Miss, are you in any danger?"

"No, I'm alright." Now for the hard part. Megan took a deep breath, she could do this. It wasn't going to be easy to convince some tough cop she wasn't completely nuts, but she needed to try. She knew it was possible to stop that monster and maybe, with the help of this detective with the sexy voice, they could save a woman's life tonight, as well. At the very least, she was going to try.

She did nothing to save other women and the guilt consumed her, it kept her up at night and made her sick to her stomach. If only it were possible to have the last two weeks of her life back again, she would try to save them all.

She downed the last drop of artificial strength left in her glass and cleared her throat. "I...I don't know exactly which hotel it was. I just barely caught a glimpse of the front of the building as they walked in, but I know it has an orange neon sign on it. It was Saint something. I looked in the phone book and I think it's the St. John's Hotel on Prospect Ave. I did get a good look at the inside of the hotel, though. There's an old orange couch and a grandfather clock in the lobby. I could read the clock. It was three eighteen. I'm sure it was in the middle of the night. It was...I mean, it *will* be, dark outside.'"

Megan was good with the details. The last time it was the details that finally led the police to Peter Logan. He had been put away for life, but it had been a terrible experience, one that took a long time to truly put behind her. As a matter of fact, it had taken a lot of years just to feel normal again and here she was jeopardizing it all just by making this one phone call.

It was the last thing on earth she wanted to do. But she saw no other choice. She tried to ignore the other dreams, refused to believe it was happening to her again and now two women were dead, probably three. And that thought alone gave her the strength to continue.

"What? What do you mean?" The detective asked her. "I want to know what time you found the body?"

"It hasn't happened yet. I'm pretty sure it's going to happen at three-eighteen tomorrow morning at the St. John's Hotel on Prospect and the woman is a redhead about twenty-five or thirty and she'll be wearing a black dress and...." She figured if she spoke quickly, the detective wouldn't have the opportunity to interrupt her. She knew she had lost his interest now, but she would tell him everything. Give him all the information he needed to stop this one nightmare from coming true. What he did with that information would have to be up to him.

Detective Stark looked at his partner in the corner with a group that had grown into more than ten fellow detectives and sneered. The laughter that erupted from them was so loud, he had to put his hand over the phone receiver to keep the caller from hearing it. He rolled his eyes and shook his head at the hyenas bent over on the other side of the room.

"And she was…will be wearing black boots and a white fur coat. Did I mention it was in room two-sixteen?"

The detective looked down at the notes he had so carefully taken and threw down his pencil, bringing another roar of laughter from his colleagues. He shot them a nasty smile before answering her. "Why yes, Miss, you did actually." His once sexy voice had a patronizing ring to it now. "That was room two-sixteen at the St. John's Hotel tomorrow at three eighteen a.m." His jaw twitched as he leaned forward in his chair and spoke intently into the phone. "Ok, lady, now for the tricky part. Just how did you happen to come by this wealth of information, anyway?"

"Well…" Megan cleared her throat, wishing her answer wouldn't sound as crazy as it was going to. "I…I have these dreams…"

"Oh, but of course you do," he cut her off. "Well, I'd like to thank you so much for your call. I'll need to get your full name and address so we can send an officer over to take an official statement from you." A sneaky smile pulled across his lips as he spotted a rookie busy at his desk, one of the few officers in the room who appeared oblivious to the joke Hudson had played on his new partner.

"No! That won't be necessary. I've already told you everything I know."

"Oh, but I insist. You see, we're always very excited to meet the kind of person who actually gets off on wasting the valuable time of the Cleveland Police Department."

"But, I…"

"Listen, this is a serious case, lady. We have a monster on our hands and chasing after made up crap like this only keeps us from doing our real job."

Megan quickly hung up the phone and was immediately sorry. She knew this wasn't going to be easy, but the dreams weren't going to stop on their own. They weren't going to stop. Not until that madman was stopped and she knew that for a fact.

"Damn it!" She threw the phone off the desk and it crashed against the wall. She had let that asshole of a detective get the best of her, she had let him shame her into giving up.

But after stewing for a few seconds, she realized she had given Detective Stark all the information he needed to prevent this murder from happening, if he really wanted to. Still, she should have stayed on the phone and stuck to her guns, at least until he assured her that he would send someone to the hotel to check it out. Maybe just post someone there undercover until a redhead came in. It could be that easy, if he would just believe her.

That wasn't likely, the sexy sounding Detective Stark wouldn't even listen to her, much less believe her. No one believed her last time either. Not her parents, not the police, not until six innocent people were dead. And all because no one would believe her.

Megan's finger traced an ugly faded scar on her left wrist. The nightmares, the murders, the guilt and the thought of losing everything she had worked so hard for made her think about things she hadn't for many, many years. Things she had hoped she'd never think about again. She lowered her head into her arms on top of the desk and cried for the innocent woman who was going to die tonight.

*   *   *   *

4:46 p.m.

Not hearing the laughs that filled the room, David Stark looked thoughtfully at the phone in his hand and then slowly hung it up. He continued to stare at it as if somehow, someway, it could explain to him what had just happened.

He was nastier to the caller than he meant to be, but the frustration of finding out that this was yet another dead end, infuriated him. He was so sure this was going to be the first real lead they had on the so called Cleveland Cutter. That's what the papers had named him because of what the sick bastard did to his victims. David hated it. It was stupid, commercial and distasteful. But hey, they needed to sell newspapers and airtime. Who the hell was he to tell them how to run their business? Besides, now the cops were calling him The Cutter, too.

"Shit!" David whispered through his clenched teeth. After listening to her for just a few seconds, he was sure she was going to be the one who helped him finally catch that psycho and put him away forever. She was so careful with her details, so informative and he even got that familiar tingling in his gut that told him, this was it, that she was the key.

He only transferred to homicide a few months ago and still wasn't sure if he was happy about it or not. But it was a promotion, after all. It was what all good cops hoped for, to be a homicide detective. This was his first real case and it was turning into quite a doozey. If the call would have been legit, the prostitute would have been The Cutter's third victim in less than a month and there wasn't a single witness or even one solid lead. The Cutter was a psycho alright, but apparently, a very clever one.

Still, he wished he hadn't been quite so mean to the woman on the phone. She didn't sound crazy, well until she happened to mention that she dreamt it all. And he just didn't have the time for a wild goose chase now. He had no time for anything else but catching that son of a bitch before he killed again.

The bastard had killed, no, butchered two area women already and they didn't have a clue as to his identity or even his motive, except, of course, that he was seriously fucked up. That was David's own professional opinion and he didn't need much more of a motive than that.

But the woman who called didn't really sound like one of those phony psychics. They were after the attention and the publicity, weren't they? And she hung up as soon as he suggested sending someone out to take her statement.

Maybe it was worse. Maybe she really thought she was psychic. David shook his head, as far as he was concerned that put her at the top of his crazy list. Although he had heard of psychics helping the police, those cases were few and far between. More often than not, they were a waste of valuable time and money. But he should have listened to what she had to say and been more patient with her. She may have known something and was just using that dream story as a way to tell the police about it.

"Shit!" David banged his fist down on the desk. "I didn't even get her name!"

"Come on, Stark," Hudson yelled from across the room. "Ted just called. He's got something on that jogger he wants us to see."

David stood up and slowly crossed room.

Hudson threw his arm around his partner's neck and punched him lightly in the stomach. "Hey, don't take it personally. I was just busting your chops. Giving you a little taste of what we gotta put up with everyday here in homicide. Betcha didn't get too many of those kind of crackpots in vice, did ya?"

David absently shook his head.

"Oh, lighten up, kid. The call was just a joke. This isn't the fucking psychic hotline." Hudson laughed as they walked down the hall toward Ted Miller's office.

*   *   *   *

5:27 p.m.

How or why, for that matter, Megan dragged herself to class, she wasn't sure. Her eyes were still puffy from crying, but she had two classes that night, children's literature and art, and she couldn't afford to miss either of them with finals coming up. If she expected to graduate with honors, she needed to ace all her classes this quarter.

Besides, she didn't know what else she could do about it now anyway. It was officially out of her hands. She had done her civic duty and called the police. Now it was up to Detective Stark as to how pigheaded and narrow-minded he was going to be.

She planned to graduate next spring and had already put in her résumé at Fenwood Elementary. The principal, Mr. Temple, seemed to like her and Sue wrote her a great recommendation. At the very least, she was told she'd get a permanent substitute job there until a full-time position opened up. Her future, a future she had worked hard for and wanted with all her heart, was right there, within her reach. Who could expect her to do anymore than she had already done?

"Hi, Megan." A timid male voice pulled her thoughts back into the classroom.

"Oh, hi."

"You ok?" Bill Peak pushed his round, wire-framed glasses up his nose and studied her intently.

"Yeah, fine…fine. It's just been a really long day." Megan forced a smile at the man sitting at the desk beside her. He was doing his student teaching at the same school as Megan and he had been in a few of her classes over the years. She had noticed he seemed to be a little bit interested in her, but even though he seemed nice, she just didn't have the time or energy to devote to anything other than school and work.

To Megan, graduating and getting a teaching job was the most important thing in her life right now and, well, a man just wasn't part of her plan. Especially now, now that some demented psychopath had started haunting her dreams again.

"Well, if there's anything you need, or ever need, all you have to do is say the word." Bill narrowed his eyes and flipped his shaggy blonde hair out of his eyes. "You know I'd be happy to help you out with whatever it was you needed help with." He leaned forward, getting as close to her as he could without actually getting out of his seat.

"Thanks, but I'm fine. Really." Megan shot him a quick, polite smile before directing all her attention to the assignment on her desk.

"Sure, don't mention it." Bill's voice faded off as he slumped back into his chair and she could hear him sigh before he reluctantly looked down at the papers on his own desk.

CHAPTER 2

▼

THURSDAY, JANUARY 15TH

*   *   *   *

2:16 a.m.

Megan pressed her foot down harder on the gas petal. It was a little after two in the morning and she hadn't been able to sleep at all from worrying about whether or not Detective Stark took her seriously. A little less than an hour ago, she finally came to the conclusion that he hadn't. How could he really? She must have sounded like a complete nutcase on the phone and hanging up like some kid after making a prank, certainly didn't help.

So, Megan made up her mind that, by three o'clock, she would be at the St. John's hotel herself. Of course, the thought of actually seeing that monster from her nightmares terrified her, but if Detective Stark wouldn't believe her, she would be the one waiting for the killer…alone.

All she had to do really was make some kind of scene whenever the killer walked into the hotel with the redhead. She could do that, even though she had no idea what the man looked like, she got a very good look at the woman and would know her instantly. The killer certainly wouldn't hang around if some crazy lady in her pajamas was screaming bloody murder right there in the middle of the hotel lobby.

She couldn't catch him of course, but she could save that woman's life, and that was what was important right now. A lot more important than whether some sexy sounding cop thought she was a lunatic or not.

Megan had it all planned out. At exactly three-eighteen, she would be sitting on that ugly orange couch and when the redheaded woman walked into the St. John's Hotel, she would simply stand up and scream at the top of her lungs. The killer wouldn't hurt anyone out in the open. It wasn't his style. Besides he had the whole thing meticulously planned out, right down to the very last detail. If something were to change his plans, anything at all, she was positive he would panic and run out. Then all she had to do was to convince the woman to go to the police with the description of the man and have him arrested.

Megan's shoulders slumped. There was no way on earth she was ever going to talk a prostitute into going to the police and describing a customer who didn't even hurt her. That woman was never going to believe some crazy lady standing in the middle of a hotel lobby at three o'clock in the morning, in her jammies, screaming like a banshee. Megan shook her head. To top it off, the woman was probably going to be royally pissed off that Megan had just scared off her rent money. She'll never believe her life had just been saved.

Oh well, the important thing here was saving her life, whether she realized it or not. The plan wasn't without its flaws, but it could work and Megan smiled triumphantly as she turned her car onto Prospect Avenue. That's when she saw the lights.

Flashing red and blue lights slapped her across the face, stinging her eyes and the bridge of her nose. Her heart pushed its way up into her throat and she swallowed hard against it. "Oh God, please. No, no, no." Her breath caught in her chest as she watched an ambulance back up to the front door of the St. John's Hotel.

Tears were blurring the colored lights pulsating from the ambulance and police cars when she pulled into an empty lot across the street from the hotel and parked her car. "Oh no," Megan whispered to the dark and rested her forehead on the steering wheel. She knew she should just start the car and go back home. It was too late for her to help anyone now.

But something was wrong and she had to know what it was. Maybe that ambulance was for someone else. Maybe this wasn't even the right hotel and there was still time to save that woman. Whatever was going on here, there was no way she could make herself leave without knowing for sure what it was.

Megan got out of her car and slowly walked across the street. Three black and white police cars and two unmarked police cars were parked in front of the hotel, their lights silently screaming in the cold darkness of the January night.

Just as she made it to the sidewalk in front of the hotel, a young policeman in full uniform threw open the door. He was pale and had his mouth covered with one hand as the other one flailed about searching for something to grasp onto. He ran recklessly to the side of the hotel, bent over and threw up violently in the alley. He looked up at Megan with embarrassment and disgust in his young eyes before bending back over to throw up again.

She felt sorry for the young officer, because she knew exactly how he felt. It had sickened her too. People shouldn't see such horrible things. It wasn't right, it wasn't natural and it was the kind of thing that scarred a person. She knew that, because she was scarred, so much so, that she sometimes felt deformed. She could see the scars when she looked in the mirror. They were on her face and behind her eyes, and if anyone cared enough to really look at her, she was sure they could see them, too.

Maybe that's why she kept her distance from people. Maybe she was always afraid if she got too close to someone, they would see how badly disfigured she was on the inside. How messed up and bruised she was. But, unlike the young police officer bent over in the alley, it seemed she had no choice. She couldn't just quit and find a more pleasant profession. No. Her nightmares weren't going to stop, not until that madman was stopped. And then, how long would it be before the next madman found his way inside her head? Would she ever truly be free of it?

Another policeman came out to check on the young officer at the side of the building when he saw Megan and motioned for her to leave the area. She nodded, but as soon as his back was turned, she snuck under the yellow police tape and walked through the front door of the hotel unnoticed.

The lobby was deserted except for a policeman and an oily little man quietly talking behind the counter, but there was a lot of commotion coming from upstairs. The rest of the police and the paramedics had to be up there. And they were all in room two-sixteen, there was no doubt about it, this was definitely the place she saw in her dream. The same guy was behind the counter, the same dark stairway led upstairs and the same ugly, orange couch sat lazily in the corner.

And there, against the far wall, stood the old grandfather clock. She walked across the lobby toward the once magnificent timepiece. Its hands showed three-eighteen, but it wasn't even two-thirty yet. Megan's eyes scanned the scratched cherry wood cabinet and the dirty glass case beneath the face where the tarnished brass pendulum hung deathly still and her stomach instantly dropped.

It was broken. "Oh my God! The clock is broken," Megan's brain screamed the words while her lips moved silently over them. Her throat tightened and her heart pounded. Her legs strained to hold her upright. Why hadn't she notice it was broken in her dream? Why hadn't she notice the pendulum wasn't swinging? She had made a terrible mistake, a fatal mistake. One that cost the woman lying in pieces on the floor of room two-sixteen, her life. The lobby swam around her as guilt and grief washed over her. Megan stood there, frozen, holding her breath against the invisible assault.

*   *   *   *

Upstairs in room two-sixteen, Detective David Stark was disgusted. He just couldn't comprehend the sheer contempt for human life the psycho bastard he was dealing with had. It was times like these that made him really rethink his career choice.

"What kind of animal could do this to somebody?" A burly paramedic asked his thinner partner as they lifted the black body bag onto a stretcher.

David was wondering the exact same thing, standing there in that dirty little room, silently studying the grizzly scene in front of him.

The chief of police, Thad Banister, patted him on the back. "Sometime, Stark, you're gonna have to share with me just how you happened to be here at one o'clock in the morning." His lips stretched across his face forming two thin straight lines as he shook his head and left the room.

Good looking, tall and athletic with graying black hair, Chief Banister had aspirations of going into politics. He even considered running for mayor last year, but decided to wait one more term as he raised more money and support for his campaign. He was a good cop, a good chief and they had become friends over the years. Actually, he was the one who recommended David for homicide. David was going to miss him when he eventually left the force, but Banister was a fair, reasonable man and the city of Cleveland would be damn lucky to have him as mayor.

Banister walked down the stairs and tugged at his suit jacket, smoothing away any wrinkles in it as he prepared to deal with any reporters waiting for him outside. He was so concerned with straightening his dark maroon tie, he didn't even notice the petite brunette staring in disbelief at the broken grandfather clock with tears slowly rolling down her pretty face.

Ted Miller, the head of the forensics department, was there personally to make sure the evidence at the scene was collected correctly. This case required the best of the best to be working it and, although he wasn't exactly delighted when David called him out in the middle of this cold and snowy night, he got to the hotel in record time. Everyone wanted this nutcase behind bars, so if there was any evidence in this room to nail the bastard, David wanted to be sure that Ted was there to find it.

"So, what do ya think?" David asked after Ted approved the removal of the victim's body.

"Don't know." Ted shook his head and rubbed his chin. "There's skin and blood under the nails for sure. Especially that one you found by the door. Looks like our girl put up a bit of a fight. But from what I can tell, they look pretty contaminated. I'll know better when I get them to the lab. There's also traces of semen and evidence of vaginal bruising. Surprise, surprise. But if this was her third or fourth trick of the night….well then, who the hell knows what we've got."

"Well, if there's anything to find…"

"I'll find it." Ted finished David's statement, cracked his knuckles and got back down on his knees, to continue scouring the carpet for evidence.

David followed the paramedics down the stairs, leaving Ted and his crew busy doing their jobs, taking pictures, dusting for prints, taking fabric samples and whatever else it was they did. He looked over at the ugly, orange couch again. Everything was exactly like the caller said it would be.

David shook his head. Damn it, he really wished he had handled that call differently. He would do just about anything to get that opportunity back again. He didn't tell anyone what she said, because at the time he didn't think it was important. And now, now that he had blown it so badly, he certainly wasn't going to say anything. At least until he found the caller and figured out just what her connection was to the beast who had just mutilated the woman in room two-sixteen.

The caller had to know who was behind it and the thought was enough to make his blood boil. How in God's name could she just stand by and let that fucking monster do this to another innocent woman? Had she no conscience at all? Of course, she had tried to tell him. Damn! Damn! Damn!

The guilt he felt was horrible. He should have been able to stop this, save that woman's life. He followed up on the call. He had been the one who found the body. A lot of good it did that poor woman in the body bag.

David arrived at the hotel around one o'clock. He tried to sleep, but the caller's voice kept creeping into his brain. He couldn't stop thinking about what she had told him…the weird details she talked about. He didn't believe her story, but there was something about it that gnawed at his gut, something about it he just couldn't ignore.

Besides, it was the only lead he had and checking it out beat the hell out of lying in bed alone. So he made up his mind to be there waiting in the lobby of the St. John's hotel at three-eighteen, just in case.

When he got there, the first thing he noticed was the broken grandfather clock. It took a little coaxing, but David got the information he needed out of the greasy little hotel clerk. He told him there was indeed a redheaded working girl who lived in room two-sixteen, but she was in and out all the time with customers and he wasn't really sure who or even how many she had brought in so far that evening. The clerk repeatedly reminded him that it was part of his job not to notice too much.

Not wasting any time, David knocked on the door to room two-sixteen and after getting no response, gave the clerk a twenty to unlock the room with his master key. David slowly pushed open the door, his revolver drawn. But it was too late.

Pools of blood and human waste were on the floor surrounding the body and splashes of blood were on the walls and window. The woman's head had been shaved clean and was lying on the floor about three feet from the rest of her body. Her arms and shoulders were missing, but her hands were left on the floor beside her body.

The little weasel of a clerk ran off to be sick somewhere, ranting something about how they didn't pay him enough to clean up that kind of mess. And it *was* a mess, a disgusting horrible mess, and it was exactly like that woman on the phone had said it would be.

David called it in and tried to reach his partner, but got no answer at his home and an hour and a half later, Hudson still hadn't answered his page. David was actually a little relieved, he still hadn't figured out how to explain his being at a no-tell hotel in the middle of the night.

It was of little consolation that maybe tomorrow they'd have some real leads to follow up on. Maybe one of the guests could give them a description of the killer and maybe they'd find some fingerprints. Maybe the skin under the hooker's fingernails would give them the physical evidence they've been waiting for.

There were a lot of maybes, but it was a hell of a lot more than they had before and he was thankful, but he would gladly give it all up to bring back that woman being carried down the stairs.

David walked slowly down the steps and watched the paramedics load her body into the ambulance and slam the door on the last day of her life. By this time tomorrow, he would know just about everything there was to know about her. He would have to interview her friends and any family she had. And, like it or not, he would see her again, in the coroner's office and in the endless photos he would have to study. Yeah, he was going to become quite familiar with one Dixie Jones, victim number three.

David turned to take one last look at the broken grandfather clock and noticed a woman, in a long dark coat, standing with her back to him, looking up at the clock. After watching her stand completely motionless for nearly a minute, he took his hands out of his old, brown leather jacket and walked up behind her. "Excuse me, Miss. Just who are you and exactly how did you get in here? This area is off limits. Or couldn't you tell that from all the yellow tape out there?"

*   *   *   *

A booming voice jolted Megan out of her trance and she recognized it instantly. It sent the same chill down her spine as it had earlier that day on the phone. The voice belonged to Detective Stark. She closed her eyes and fought the overwhelming urge to run. She didn't want him to see the tears or the guilt in her eyes. It was all her fault the redhead was dead, all her fault they couldn't save her. It was all her fault she didn't notice that the damn clock was broken. She had screwed up and it cost a woman her life.

Well, there was no way out of it now. She had to face him and the fact that she had failed, failed to stop that evil monster from taking another life. She slowly turned around and saw, through her tears, the blurry image of a man who perfectly matched his voice.

"Who are you?" He asked again.

She searched her clouded mind for what to say, something, anything that made some sense out of what was happening. But her brain refused to work.

"Who are you?" His voice was turning angry now. His brown eyes were cold, hard and full of questions.

She cleared her throat to give her another second to think. "I'm…I'm Megan. Megan Montgomery. I…I spoke to you earlier today, Detective Stark."

He looked confused for a few seconds before realization swept across his face. "You…. you're the one who called me?"

She answered him with a slight nod of her head.

"Oh boy, do you have some explaining to do Ms. Montgomery." The harshness of his voice frightened her and she instinctively took a step back, knocking into the grandfather clock. She knew he wouldn't believe the truth, but she didn't expect the anger in his voice or in his eyes. A gigantic vein throbbed under the skin on the left side of his neck and he looked as if any second he would reach out and beat the hell out of her.

But even with her back up against the clock, she stuck out her chin, just a little. She couldn't let herself be afraid. She had to be tough, she had to stay strong and she had to make him believe her. It wasn't going to be easy, but maybe together they could catch the monster who had so brutally taken the life of the woman up in room two-sixteen.

"Yes. I do have a lot to tell you," she began in a tiny trembling voice that belied the courage her jutting chin was trying to portray. "I've been having these terrible nightmares…"

"Oh, don't you even start that shit with me, lady!"

Megan flattened against the grandfather clock, wishing somehow it was between her and the angry Detective Stark.

He pointed up the stairs and took a step closer to her. "I don't have the time or the patience for your little games right now! You see, I've just helped pick up pieces of a human being up there. So I want the truth and not some bullshit stories about your fucking dreams, you got it?" He poked his finger hard into her chest.

Good God, he *was* going to beat the hell out of her. Megan was terrified. Surely he had to realize just how hard it was for her to call him in the first place. He had to realize she was here tonight trying to save that woman's life, didn't he? She took a deep breath and held it, trying hard to fight the onslaught tears building up behind her eyes. But it was too much. Too much for her to take any longer. She buried her face in the soft red mittens on her hands and burst into tears.

*   *   *   *

David looked around the lobby. The officer and the hotel clerk were staring at him from behind the counter. He had to get this woman out of there immediately before any questions were asked that he just couldn't answer right now. He didn't want anyone to know who she was or how she had been the one who led him to the hotel and the body of Dixie Jones. At least not until he knew what the hell was going on himself.

"Come with me." He pulled on her elbow and escorted her out of the hotel. Once outside, he put his arm around her shoulders, trying to keep her face hidden from the waiting reporters as they headed for his car.

"Is this the work of The Cleveland Cutter?" One reporter yelled out.

"What did the killer take this time?" Another one asked.

"How are you going to stop him?" Snap. Snap. Snap. Over a dozen photos were taken of them in the time it took to get to his car.

"Get in," David barked, after opening the passenger's side door of his battered, green Chevy Beretta. She got in, without question, and he closed the door behind her. He walked around the car, pushing through the herd of reporters, and heaved himself into the driver's side. He started the engine and began driving without any thought as to where he was going to take her. He only knew he had to get her somewhere alone as soon as possible and get some answers out of her. There were so many questions, so many things he needed to know and she had to have the answers. She was the caller and he had found her. She was the key, she was the reason he had gone to the hotel and she was the reason a woman was butchered there.

He watched her silently drying her eyes. Well, at least she knew the reason a woman was butchered tonight. She knew the killer. She had to, it was the only explanation. And she could help him stop this from ever happening again. That is, if she would stop playing this stupid game of hers and tell him the truth.

David was determined to get some answers out of this woman, even if he had to shake them out of her. He pulled into the parking lot of his apartment building and slammed the car into park. He wasn't really sure how to play this. Should he be threatening? Hell no. She was barely on this side of a nervous breakdown as it was. He wouldn't get any answers out of a hysterical, blubbering female.

No, he had to be gentle, as gentle and compassionate as possible. That would be the way to get to the bottom of this, to get her to really open up and tell him the truth about tonight.

He turned to look at the woman in the seat next to him. "Let's go inside for a cup of coffee. We have a lot of things to discuss."

She nodded and, without a word, got out of the car to follow him into his building.

*   *   *   *

Detective Stark lived on the sixth floor of an older but nice apartment building downtown. "Sorry. The elevator's on the fritz. We'll have to take the stairs."

He turned his back to her and began to climb the wrought iron staircase. She watched his body move swiftly, taking the stairs like some ancient warrior invading his enemy's castle. With every step he conquered, she could see the muscles in his legs shift under his tight blue jeans. His shoulders were wide and almost completely filled the stairwell ahead of her.

He was quite incredible looking actually, in a rough and tough, cop sort of way that made her stomach tighten with feelings she had always thought she was immune to. Even before she had seen him, his voice had done more to turn her on, to stimulate her, than any other man she had ever met.

He probably had a different woman for every night of the week. She didn't notice a wedding ring on his hand during the drive over and she doubted very much he would bring a witness to his apartment if he had a live-in girlfriend. But then again, it was, after all, almost three in the morning. There weren't exactly too many places he *could* take her at this hour.

But what did it matter if he was married or not or whether he had a girlfriend or not? As a matter of fact, it wouldn't make any difference if he had a entire harem stashed away in his apartment because as far as Detective Stark was concerned, she was a nut or a witness or a suspect or…well, God only knew for sure what was going on in that gorgeous head of his.

The rattling of his keys brought her back and she shook her head to dislodge the inappropriate thoughts floating around inside it. This wasn't the time to think about that, even if it had been such a very long time since she was even remotely interested in a man, because this particular man, sexy as he was, had almost ripped her head off a few minutes ago. The attraction was not only ill timed, it was purely one sided.

The detective opened the door to his apartment and held it open for Megan. She hadn't said a word to him since the hotel. She was afraid to, really. He might start yelling at her again and then she might start crying again and that just wasn't going to get them anywhere.

Silently, she walked through the door and looked around his apartment. It was definitely a guy's place. And a guy who wasn't home much, either. There was mismatched furniture kept for the comfort factor alone. No pictures or knick-knacks of any kind hung on the off white walls or sat on the plain end tables. It was quite obvious he merely slept here and not much else.

Taking up most of one wall in his living room was a large sliding glass door leading to a small balcony that offered a fabulous view of the skyline of Cleveland. A beautiful view that was in sharp contrast to the ugliness they had just witnessed. Megan walked over to the glass door and looked out over the city.

He was out there somewhere, that evil man from her dreams, with the new additions to his awful collection. But, it was just a matter of time. She knew she could help Detective Stark stop that terrible monster before he did this again. She felt it in her heart that together they could and would finally stop him. And that feeling was what she needed to concentrate on, that small shred of hope that she never had before. That was what was going to give her the strength she needed to stand up to Detective Stark and make him believe in her.

She turned to watch him take off his coat and hang it on the back of a kitchen chair. The gun strapped to his side and the shiny metal badge hanging from his shirt pocket sent an involuntary shudder through her body as it reminded her of the seriousness of her situation.

He walked into his kitchen and started making the coffee. "Do you take cream and sugar?" His question finally breaking the unbearable silence between them.

"No." Megan cleared her throat. "No, thank you." She had no intentions of drinking it anyway. She was going to need something a little stronger than coffee to face this interrogation. Megan rolled her eyes into the back of her head and sighed. God, she wasn't ready for this. She needed some sleep. She needed a little more time to figure out just what to say and how to say it. What she needed was a drink.

Willing to risk the embarrassment of asking for some artificial strength to get her through this, Megan called into the kitchen, "Um…excuse me, Detective Stark, do you happen to have any rum? I could really use a rum and Coke instead, if you've got it."

Megan saw him raised his right eyebrow at her from the other side of the counter. "Uh, yeah, I…I think so." He opened his refrigerator door and looked inside. "How 'bout a rum and Diet Coke? That's the best I can do."

"That'll be fine. Thank you." Megan took off her coat and laid it across the back of his black leather couch. She looked down and realized she was still wearing the pink nightshirt she had gone to bed in. And either because of the cool temperature of his apartment or that short but vivid fantasy she just had of the handsome detective, garbed in armor and brandishing a sword, her nipples were straining against the silky material, making it quite obvious she had no bra on underneath.

She had been in bed when she got her brilliant idea about how to single handedly save the redhead's life and was in such a hurry, she simply threw on a pair of jeans, a coat, and dashed out the door. Never thinking she might end up in the handsome Detective Stark's apartment. She reached for her coat to put it back on as the detective walked out of his kitchen with a cup of coffee and a glass of rum and Diet Coke.

"Yes, please make yourself comfortable. I have a lot of questions for you and it's gonna take awhile." He handed her the drink.

She quickly crossed one arm in front of her breasts as she grabbed the glass and nervously took a large gulp. She watched his cop eyes as they studied her and made mental notes of her every move. She had every reason to be nervous. Detective Stark just might end up arresting her tonight.

He took a sip of his coffee and nodded his head toward his tiny dining room table. "Please, have a seat so we can get started." He couldn't possibly ever use the table for eating. A week's worth of unread newspapers and junk mail covered the tiny wood top. He moved a few envelopes to make room for his blue "World's Greatest Uncle" mug and with both hands swept up all the papers, envelopes and notes and dumped them into an empty chair. "Sorry 'bout the mess. I haven't been home much lately."

He pulled out another chair for Megan and took the chair right next to her. Why did he have to sit so close to her? Obviously it was some cop tactic to invade her space, keep her on edge, and to intimidate her. It was working.

She took another big mouthful of her drink and swallowed it down. At this rate she'd have an empty glass by the time he started questioning her, but she didn't dare ask for another. He already thought she was a nut or a liar. She didn't want to add alcoholic to his list.

The detective took a tiny tape recorder from his coat pocket and pushed a button before placing it in the middle of the table in front of her. She thought it was impossible to make her anymore nervous than she already was, but that little black box, pointed directly at her, was doing just that.

After a quick glance at his watch, he started, "Thursday, January 15th, three-eleven a.m. The questioning of Megan Montgomery." David turned his big, translucent brown cop eyes on her and she felt them stab into her flesh. "Ok, Miss Montgomery, tell me, from the beginning, how did you know about tonight's murder of Dixie Jones?"

Megan swallowed against the thick lump in her throat. She closed her eyes and took a deep breath, gathering the strength she needed to resist running out the door and down the stairs. She slowly opened her eyes and stared back at him. "I've had four dreams so far."

His shoulders slumped and disapproval immediately washed over his face, but she continued. "The first was just over two weeks ago. I don't know the exact date. But it was terrible. A man was walking on a sidewalk. There were streetlights, lots of streetlights. He was moving very quickly, trying to catch up with a lady who was on the sidewalk in front of him. It was pretty dark, kind of shadowy, even with the streetlights. The man had something black and heavy in his hand. A tire iron, I think, or a crowbar, something like that. He walked faster and faster. When the woman noticed him, she started to panic and began running from him. Then he started chasing after her."

Megan closed her eyes, trying to remember every detail. "He finally caught her and hit her on the head from behind. She fell to the ground. She was very pretty with shoulder-length blond hair and she was wearing a tight, short green skirt. She wears short skirts a lot, even in the winter. I'm not sure how I know that, but I think he's followed her before. I know he picked her because of her legs. He wanted her legs."

Detective Stark turned away for a second and then looked back at Megan, waiting for her to continue.

"The man looked around and didn't see anyone, so he picked up the lady and carried her into a dark alley beside a blue dumpster. He had his black briefcase already hidden behind the dumpster. He had it planned that way. He opened the case and took out a weird looking hacksaw and...and..."

She stopped. Was this doing any good at all? Her being here, telling him all this. Bringing it all back out of the dark places in her mind where she had tried so hard to hide it away. He had no idea how hard this was for her or that it was opening up old wounds, too. Ones that had taken such a long time to heal.

No, he didn't know and he didn't care and it didn't matter because there was no time now to feel the pain, no time now for crying. She had already wasted too much time on tears as it was. After this ordeal was over, she could cry her eyes out, if that's what she needed to do. But for now she had to be strong, because it was going to take everything she had to convince this mean, cynical cop that she wasn't completely crazy. And that's what she needed to do in order to stop this killer.

"Keep going," David urged her. "I need you to tell me everything."

She took another quick swig from her glass. It was difficult for her to put it into words. Her dreams were so graphic, so horrible. All the terrible things the man did to those women were burned into her memory forever. Just like the murders Peter Logan had committed all those years ago. Just like her parents' murder. She would never, could never forget them. Any of them. But, saying them out loud...well, it wasn't going to be easy.

"He...he cut.... he cut her legs off at the hips." She felt nauseous and cleared her throat. "He had a large black plastic garbage bag in his briefcase. He pulled it out and put her legs inside it. He wiped the hacksaw off with her skirt and put it back in his case. He tied the bag up, threw it over his shoulder, picked up his case and walked away. That's it. That's where the dream ended. I didn't see where he went or anything."

"Well, Miss Montgomery, that was the story they told in the newspaper," David said coldly. "That's not very helpful, isn't there more? Something, anything you can remember from your dream that the whole city of Cleveland doesn't already know?"

Megan could take a knife and cut through the sarcasm in his voice and the pulsating vein on the side of his neck contradicted his otherwise calm exterior. It was clear the man didn't believe a word she said.

"Well." She racked her brain, trying hard to remember every little detail about the horrible nightmare. There had to be something she could remember that would make him believe her. "Oh yeah, he has a pair of yellow rubber gloves that he wears. He wore them every time so far. He keeps them in his briefcase."

Megan leaned towards him. "Hey, there *is* something else. I don't remember him taking that iron thingy with him. As a matter of fact, I don't remember him carrying it to the alley at all. Did you find something like that by the sidewalk?"

*   *   *   *

David nodded his head slightly and watched Megan Montgomery sit back into her chair and cross her arms confidently in front of her. She seemed somehow proud of herself, like she had actually told him something important. Everyone in Cleveland who read the paper or watched the news knew those details. Everything she said had already been released to the press. Well, almost everything.

There was a black tire iron found about 100 yards or so from the body. It wasn't mentioned in the press release, because it wasn't the murder weapon. The blow to the head wasn't what killed Diane Long, a nurse at Metro Hospital. She bled to death.

David remembered standing over her body, wondering if she was conscious when her legs were severed, if not, wondering if she had regained consciousness before she died, and praying to God she hadn't. He also wondered if she would've lived if someone would have only found her sooner.

"So, did you happen to have a dream about the woman in the park?"

"Yes. Yes, I did. But I had it just a few hours before I heard about it on the radio. I saw a very pretty lady with short red hair jogging real early in the morning. It was still kind of dark outside and he was waiting for her behind a tree. He knew she would be passing him soon because she jogged that same path every morning at the same time. It was really too easy for him. He just reached out and grabbed her as she ran past and snapped her neck, just like that. Just like that, she was dead. He killed her because he wanted her…," she paused, apparently searching for the right word. "Well, he really liked her behind," she said, shrugging her shoulders.

"He had the case with him," she continued as David listened intently, not wanting to make the same mistake he had on the phone the day before. He would let her talk as much as she wanted to and then he'd make her talk some more. Sooner or later, she would slip up and the truth would come out. He just had to be patient and listen for it.

"It's a black case. Kinda like a briefcase and it's full of bags and saws and weird looking knives, razors and tools. Things I've never seen before. Oh, and those yellow rubber gloves, he keeps those in there, too. He checked to make sure she was really a redhead. You know." She made a few sweeping movements of her hands until he finally nodded his understanding. "Then, once he was sure, he cut her in half at the waist and then cut off her legs." She shook her head. "It was horrible."

Yes it was. David had seen it in person. That woman lying in the snow in three separate bloody pieces was sickening and it haunted him still. He had never seen anything like it before and hoped like hell he never would again. But sadly, what he saw a few hours ago in room two-sixteen was just as bad and he knew, in his gut, if they didn't find this guy fast, there'd soon be others.

She looked him straight in the eye and smiled. What the hell was she smiling about? Did she actually think he was buying her dream bullshit? Did she honestly think she was getting away with something? That this nightmare crap she was feeding him would somehow draw him off the trail? That woman was trying to put something over on him. But what?

David couldn't quite figure it out. Was she was covering up for someone? Could she really be in cahoots with that twisted butchering psychopath? David's contempt for her boiled up in his eyes and when she noticed it, her smile quickly faded.

"You already told me about the dream you said you had about tonight's murder." David could hear the disgust, thick in his own voice, and he refused to disguise it any longer. "Didn't you say you had a fourth dream?"

*   *   *   *

Megan nodded. God, he was never going to believe her. She was just wasting her time. Any delusions she had of their working together to catch the killer, evaporated in the anger she could physically feel radiating from him. She thought there for a second that he was starting to soften, that he was beginning to at least sympathize with her.

His expression had changed when she told him about the jogger and she thought that maybe he was beginning to realize how hard it was for her to tell him all these, these terrible, horrible things that had played out inside her mind. But the vein throbbing in his neck and the hatred she saw in his eyes told her differently. He was never going to trust her. It was no use to even try. "Actually, it was really the second dream I had. But it didn't come true. The others all happened right away, the very next day. So it must've just been my imagination."

This whole experience was wearing on her, twisting her guts into giant knots and she'd finally had enough. "Listen, it's been a really long, horrible day. Is there anyway we can finish this up tomorrow?"

"No, Ms. Montgomery, there isn't," the detective snapped at her. "We have to get to the bottom of this. I need to know just how you're involved. And why you know so damn much!"

"I already told you!" The venom she heard in her voice surprised her. "I had dreams about them. And that's it! That's all there is! I *am* trying to help, you know. I didn't have to come forward. I didn't have to call you."

The man just sat there and looked at her, contempt burning in his eyes.

"Look, Detective, I didn't choose any of this. If I had my choice of premonitions, don't you think I'd pick something like tomorrow's lottery numbers? I mean, women being brutally slaughtered right in front of my eyes is not exactly what I'd call a good time."

He still said nothing. A technique all cops used, she was sure. Just let your suspects talk and they'll talk themselves right into a confession.

Megan clenched her teeth as her nails cut into the skin on her palms. She knew she should just shut up and sit there, like a good little suspect. But he was driving her crazy, sitting there all smug, waiting for her to say something that he could misconstrue and use against her.

He crossed his arms in front of him and leaned back into his chair. Why wasn't he saying anything? It was infuriating!

"God! Can't you get it through your thick skull? I just want this to stop!" She grasped the arms of her chair as she leaned closer to him. "You have no idea how horrible this is for me, do you, Detective Stark?" She spit his name out of her mouth. "You may not believe what's happening to me is real…well, I wish to God it wasn't! You can't even imagine what it's like. I can actually feel those women through *his* fingertips and I can taste their lipstick when he kisses them. I can smell their perfume and….and the sickening sweetness of their blood when he cuts them. "

She stopped for a second to catch her breath and blink back the tears building up in her eyes. "And if that's not disturbing enough for you, detective, I can actually feel him get aroused when he finally takes what he's been looking for."

Megan looked at him. Nothing. No understanding, no trust, no compassion. Nothing but pure hatred in his cold brown eyes. This man despised her.

"You know, I just want it to all go away." She whispered the words so quietly she could barely hear them herself. "And I can't do it alone. I need your help. With your help, I think we can stop him."

The detective laughed out loud. "My help? Please!" He stood up and loomed over her, pointing his finger down at her face. "You, Miss Montgomery, are in a lot of trouble. Do you realize I could actually arrest you right now for withholding evidence and hindering a police investigation?"

Megan shot up to her feet. The rotten bastard! How dare he? She had, after all, tried to save that woman's life. How could he not realize that? How could he blame her? How dare he even think she was involved in something so repulsive, so wicked? Well, that's exactly what she deserved for thinking the police would help her.

Now, he thought she was an accomplice, he might even think she did it and the thought made her ill. This man had been nothing but spiteful and mean to her from the first moment he said "hello" on the phone and she wasn't about to take it for another second. Megan turned and headed for the door.

He followed her, grabbed her arm and spun her back around to face him. "And just where do you think you're going? We're not finished here. I want some answers and I want them now!"

"You asshole!" She raised her hand to slap him across the face, but he instinctively caught her arm in midair with one hand and pushed her shoulder to the wall with the other, effectively using his hips and legs to hold her firmly against the wall of his dining room. In less than a split second, he had rendered her utterly defenseless.

The only thing he had no control over was her mouth. "Just who in the *hell* do you think you are?" She glared up at him defiantly through thin little slits as she squirmed violently, pulling at his sleeve, trying to free herself from his trap. "You have no right to do this. Let go of me, right now!" She pushed and wiggled against him, but it was no use. Her struggling only caused him to tighten his hold on her.

He was over a foot taller than she was, but she hadn't noticed it until now, now that he was towering over her, looking like a giant madman with that vein in his neck about to explode and rage blazing in his eyes. In those big, liquid brown eyes that were piercing through her, burning themselves into her soul. She stood there, powerless against the steel of his unyielding body, trembling from anger, from fear and from something else. Something she didn't quite recognize. Something she felt slowly building inside her.

Megan's breath caught in her throat. A sensation, an ache really, began tingling deep within her where she had always, until tonight, felt nothing. It was a place inside her that had always before been numb, but was now prickling as it slowly and painfully came to life. All at once she became sharply aware of him, his warm, solid body pressing her firmly to the wall and for a second she unwillingly melted in his heat. Her body forming perfectly to his.

She was attracted to him, frightfully so, but he was so mean, so uncaring and accusing. Megan's teeth clenched in resentment and her anger quickly returned. "I said, let go of me!" Her body stiffened as she once again struggled to free herself from the cage of arms and legs and chest she found herself entangled in.

Despite her anger, she couldn't ignore the hunger growing inside her. He had unknowingly awakened a part of her she feared was dead, a part of her she thought she had killed and buried deep down inside her, a part of her that reminded her too much of her mother.

Megan inhaled and her nostrils filled with the smell of soap and clean laundry and spicy vanilla cologne and man. The smell of him was more intoxicating than the rum she had just swallowed and it made her lightheaded and weak as she stood there cocooned in the warmth of his arms.

His eyes had changed somehow when she wasn't looking. There was still an amber fire burning behind them, but the contempt and rage seemed to have been replaced by...by something else. Something Megan had never seen directed at her before. She held her breath and tried to control the intense trembling inside her.

Her hand, the one that was seconds earlier, pulling at his shirt sleeve, defied what little willpower she possessed and began exploring the muscles in his arm, discovering and memorizing every hard knot and bulge beneath his shirt.

Oh, God she wanted to kiss him. No. No, what she really wanted was for him to kiss her. That way she wouldn't be to blame. But what if he did kiss her? What then? There was no way she would just stand there or push him away. There was no way she wouldn't kiss him back.

She felt the last fragment of restraint slipping through her fingers. What was happening to her? Why were her knees and her brain turning to mush? This wasn't right and this wasn't at all like her. She had more respect for herself than this. She didn't do this sort of thing.

But in the dim light of his apartment and in the warm prison of his arms, Megan didn't care if being with this man was right or wrong. It became impossible for her to distinguish between the two. Her body had a mind of its own and she was incapable of fighting it.

Her eyelids began to flutter as the feel of him, the smell of him sent tingles flowing through her body. She could feel the physical evidence of Detective Stark's own desire pushing hard into her stomach and it made her drunk. Her brain didn't have the strength to fight, not when her whole body wanted him and had decided to mutiny against her common sense.

At this very moment, she didn't care about tomorrow, her reputation or if she was acting like her mother. Megan didn't care about anything but fulfilling her hunger for Detective Stark.

*   *   *   *

David looked down at her, noticing the redness building in her cheeks. Damn, she was beautiful. He noticed that right away. He was a man, after all, and she was an extremely sexy woman. But that thought immediately fled his mind as soon as he realized who she was.

She was the caller and all he could think about was how she must have the answers he needed to catch the sick son of a bitch who was terrorizing his city and how she was going to tell him everything even if he had to knock it out of her.

But now the only thing he could think about, focus on, was how fucking sexy she looked standing there against him, beneath him. Her long dark hair like silk brushing against his arm when she shook her head in a futile attempt to escape him. And her flawless bronze skin, so soft, so smooth, making his mouth water with the desperate need to taste it and feel it beneath his lips.

Her pink nightshirt was unbuttoned just enough so that from his vantage point above her, he could see the tops of her smooth golden breasts heaving with every breath she took and he could feel the tips of her hardened nipples pushing defiantly against his chest.

Of course, he had been a bastard to her. He had every right to be. It was a big case, and she was smack dab in the middle of it. She was his only lead and to top it off, he didn't believe a word of the bullshit she had just told him. But there was something else that pissed him off even more. He found himself actually angry with this woman for just being involved in this mess in the fist place.

Why couldn't he have met her somewhere like two normal people, buying groceries or walking in the park? He would have noticed her, he was damn sure of that. He would have asked her out, he was sure of that, too. So why did she have to be the one standing between him and his catching The Cutter? It wasn't like he believed she *was* the killer, but damn it, she definitely knew something she wasn't telling him, something that might help him stop that butcher before another innocent life was lost.

But all his anger and his questions had momentarily dissolved in the heady scent of ginger and flowers and woman that seared his lungs as he inhaled her. He couldn't concentrate on anything except how she smelled and how she looked standing there, trapped in his arms, staring up at him with those big shadowy blue eyes, the whites of which seemed to glow in the dim light of his apartment. There was something intense and unnerving about her eyes and the way she stared at him as if she could see right through to his soul. As if she could read his mind.

David wondered if she knew he didn't believe a word of her story and if she could tell that he knew she was involved somehow. Could she see that he was determined to find out the truth? Did she know how much he wanted her anyway and how very much he wanted to kiss her right now?

What in the hell was going on? This was wrong in so many different ways, he couldn't even count them all. Most importantly, this was completely unprofessional. Something like this could cost him his job, a job he worked way too hard for to throw away on some woman, especially one he just met. Even if she was the most desirable woman he believed he had ever held in his arms and even if her warm breath on his neck was causing his heart to beat wildly in his chest.

He had to stop this right now. Just let go of her and get her out of his apartment before he did something stupid. She was no doubt involved in this case, his case. She may even be an accomplice. But David believed that, even if his very life depended on it, he couldn't make himself let go of her, to free her from his trap against the dining room wall. Not until he kissed her, not until he, at least, tasted those full, wet, succulent lips.

David tightened his grip around her arm as his head slowly lowered to meet her lips. Damn, she tasted incredible. Warm, sweet, incredible. It took her a few seconds, but she finally kissed him back, timidly at first, but then, all of a sudden, with a passion that he was glad of, but did not expect. In truth, he expected her to haul off and slap him. He wished she would have, this was wrong and one of them should have enough sense to know better.

But instead, she kissed him back and her hand clawed at his shoulder, her fingernails biting into his skin as she pulled him closer, deeper into their kiss. He worked his knee between her legs and lifted her slightly off the floor, feeling the moist heat radiating from between her legs. She was readying herself for him and he could feel his stomach tighten into a knot.

He freed her arm from against the wall, placed it gently around his neck and reached around her waist, lifting her up into his kiss, while his hands explored the softness of the pink nightshirt that covered her back. One of his hands made its way under her shirt to explore the silky warmth of her back, from the waistband of her jeans up to the round firmness of her shoulders.

They emerged breathless from their first kiss. David wasn't sure how he could physically do it, but he was willing to stop, if he saw any indication in her eyes that he had made a mistake. But what he saw there was the same thing she must have seen burning in his own eyes. Raw need. Lust and want and need.

She clung to him as he kissed her again, his hungry lips working their way down her long smooth neck. And after every kiss, he found that he desperately needed at least one more, but her hands pulled his face away from her neck.

She kissed him on his cheek, on his lips, on his chin and then down to the opening of his shirt. David raised his head toward the ceiling and closed his eyes, allowing himself to get lost in the feeling of her wet tongue and velvety lips hot against his skin. She stopped suddenly and he looked down, afraid she had finally come to her senses, but a smile timidly played at the corner of her lips as she began to unbutton his denim shirt.

He felt drugged. So much so, that he would have actually been suspicious if she had been the one who made the coffee he just drank. He felt like he was in over his head, drowning in the murky blue depths of her eyes, unable to breath, unable to make a move to stop this, helpless to do anything but watch as her slender fingers worked to release one button and then the next and then the next.

His brain screamed out its objections. But right now it didn't matter if it was wrong. Nothing mattered except her soft warm body against his, her lips wet on his chest and his incredible need to be inside her.

David didn't know whether she was crazy or whether she was protecting someone or if she really was having some kind of psychic dreams about these murders. The only thing David Stark knew for sure was that he was going to make love to this woman. He'd worry about all that other stuff tomorrow.

*   *   *   *

Ring....ring. The telephone screamed into the silence and Megan's body jerked. She had the detective's shirt unbuttoned and pulled down around his elbows and was greedily kissing the skin just above the waistband of his jeans. She closed her eyes and let the reality of what was happening sink in. *Ring....ring.* She looked up at him from where she knelt on the floor until another ring of the phone brought her awkwardly to her feet.

Detective Stark offered his hand to help her up and then fumbled to pull his shirt up over his shoulders as he rushed over to pick up the phone. He cleared his throat. "Hello," he said in a husky, breathless voice that sounded nothing like the confident, determined man she had spoken to on the phone.

Megan turned away from him. Where had that come from? What had gotten into her? Was all a man had to do was throw her up against the wall for her to act like some kind of harlot? She cringed. She could only imagine what Detective Stark must think of her now. Oh, how she wished the floor would just open up and swallow her whole.

But for the first time in her life, she really, honest to God, wanted to make love to a man, not just sleep with him because that's what he expected her to do. No. She actually *wanted* to make love to Detective Stark. Make love? She wanted to have sex with him. Wild, crazy, passionate sex. Still did, as a matter of fact, as she watched him standing in the middle of the living room, listening intently to the phone call that had so rudely interrupted her from doing just that.

She felt heat, burning in her cheeks, either from the remnants of lust or the embarrassment she felt now, probably a little of both. Looking down, she saw her nipples pushing hard against her pink nightshirt with a need that wasn't going to be fulfilled tonight. She crossed her arms in front of her chest and searched for her coat.

*   *   *   *

David watched from across the room as Megan put on her coat. Her back was to him, but he could see that her shoulders sagged and she hung her head. Reading body language was second nature to most cops and he didn't like what he was seeing. She regretted what had just happened between them.

He, on the other hand, only regretted having to stop. He was so sorry that damn phone had to ring. So sorry he wasn't going to be able to have her tonight.

The skin on his stomach tingled as the wetness from her last kisses dried up and it made something inside him knot up. He wanted nothing more than to hang up that fucking phone, spin her around and let her know how hungry he was for her still. He wanted to rip off that coat, along with that cute little nightshirt of hers, and tell her, no, show her just how much he…David shook his head. What he *should* do right now was figure out why in the hell he ever let it get so far out of hand.

He held the phone to his ear with his shoulder and slowly buttoned his shirt back up as he listened to Hudson explain how Banister had finally gotten a hold of him and how he just couldn't wait to call with the latest details. David made a mental note to be sure and thank him later.

Apparently, there was a wealth of evidence gathered from the scene, skin samples from the victim's fingernails, semen, hair and fabric samples. And, even better, it seemed that one of the guests in the hotel saw an older white man leave a room on the second floor carrying a black bag. *A black bag.*

David shot a look at the woman across the room from him. She definitely knew something. He wasn't quite sure how she figured into it, but he was positive she was the key that would break the case wide open. He was also positive he had to keep his hands off her, at least until this was over.

But after what had just happened up against that wall, keeping his hands off Megan Montgomery was going to be a lot easier said than done.

Hudson wanted to meet for breakfast at a little truck stop off route 480, so they could go over a few things before they got to the station. "Ok, I'll meet you there. Seven thirty? Ok," David said into the phone as he finished tucking in his shirt.

Megan was standing by the door in her coat, looking down at the floor. He knew how she felt. As the thumping of his heart finally began to slow, he was also becoming more and more embarrassed by how he acted, by how easily he had lost it. As a matter of fact, he'd be damn lucky if she didn't file a complaint against him with the department. She should really. He was way out of line.

But it was obvious she had wanted him, too. And that's what he would remember about tonight. That's what he'd remember as he lay alone in bed tonight…that she had really, truly wanted him, too. A smile pulled at the right corner of his mouth when he thought about maybe someday, after all this nasty stuff with The Cutter was over, picking up right where he left off with the pretty Miss Montgomery.

"Listen," David said, trying to sound as professional as possible with the huge bulge still pressing hard against his jeans. "We can finish this up tomorrow. The questioning," he added quickly. He grabbed his jacket and opened his apartment door. "Do you have a car at the hotel?"

Megan nodded and walked out of his apartment, without looking up.

Not a word was spoken on the cold drive back to the St. John's Hotel. There were a couple of times David opened his mouth to apologize about what had happened, but every time he stopped himself, because the truth was, he was really only sorry that the phone rang.

The green glow from his dashboard illuminated her face. She looked so sad and so beautiful. Damn, he hoped she didn't have anything to do with those murders. But she had to. There was no other explanation for everything she knew.

This was his first homicide case and he had gone and let his dick do his thinking for the first time in his life. David couldn't blame anyone but himself if he fucked up the case or even lost his job over it, a job that was everything to him, all he had.

He had joined the Cleveland Police Department right out of college. It's what he had always wanted to do, since the time he was ten years old. That's how old he was when his father died in the line of duty. David didn't remember much about his dad, except for how proud he was of being a police officer and how people always seemed to respect him because of it. He remembered being hugged every night before he went to bed by his dad in his dark blue uniform. And he remembered how safe those hugs always made him feel and how much he missed them once they were gone.

After joining the force, David worked hard and followed the rules. It wasn't always easy, but he worked his way up and had just been promoted to homicide detective. He lived for his job, ate, drank and breathed it. Which was precisely why his wife, Sherry, left him.

After four years of marriage, she said she felt like he had no time left for her, that all his energy was spent on solving crimes and catching bad guys. She figured he didn't really need her, that he wouldn't even notice she was gone. But she was wrong. He noticed.

In fact, it almost killed him. He couldn't remember a time before he was in love with Sherry. They grew up just down the block from each other. She was his first and only girlfriend and, right after he graduated from the police academy, they got married. David had everything he had always wanted, a job as a police officer and his childhood sweetheart by his side. His life was perfect, for a while.

He was truly sorry for not realizing he was losing Sherry. He never really meant to take her for granted and he was sure he could have saved their marriage, if she would have given him the chance. But she was gone, just like that. Out of his life forever.

Last he heard she was living in Utah somewhere with her new husband, David's old tax accountant, and her two new kids, enjoying her new life. A life without having her husband called into work at two o'clock in the morning, a life without worrying every time the phone rang that someone would be on the other end telling her she was now a widow, a life without him.

He couldn't blame her really. Although his mother sure did. David's mom was furious when she found out Sherry had run off with some other man, leaving her only son devastated and heartbroken. David, however, blamed himself. He should have noticed. He was a cop, a good one, and she had totally blind-sighted him. She had fallen in love with someone else, right under his nose, and he never saw it coming. It served him right, as far as he was concerned. Of course, that didn't make it any easier to swallow.

He parked his car in front of the hotel and turned towards Megan. She was looking at the hotel and her eyes glowed an eerie orange from the neon light of the sign. "Hey, go home and get some rest," he said softly. "I'll get a hold of you tomorrow so we can finish up. Ok?"

Megan nodded and looked down.

"What's your phone number? And your address, I'll need that too." He took a piece of paper from a notepad attached to his dashboard and wrote down the information she gave him, but her eyes never once left the red knitted mittens resting in her lap.

After he folded the note paper and placed in his coat pocket, he watched her, silently studying the fabric that covered her hands until she finally turned to look at him. The longing he saw in the big, round, sad eyes looking back at him almost took his breath away.

Oh, God. He looked away, but could not get her face and those eyes out of his head. No one in the world would blame him if he took her, right now, in the front seat of his car. He tightened his grip on the steering wheel to keep his hands from reaching out to her.

"Ok. Tomorrow, then," she whispered and got out of his car, closing the door behind her. David watched her walk slowly across the street to the silver Sable waiting for her in the parking lot. She stopped when she got to her car and glanced over her shoulder at him.

"Oh, please, just get in your fucking car and go home," he said into the darkness of his car. He shook his head and took a deep breath. "You come back over here and…I…I won't be able to stop myself."

Man, he was losing it. It was taking every bit of willpower he had not to run across the street and take her into his arms. What the hell was wrong with him? She was just a woman. And he'd known a lot of women.

David suddenly felt completely drained from the incredible amount of energy it took just to stay inside his car. He was tired. So tired, he couldn't even think straight anymore. And he was horny. Tired and horny and stupid. That's all this was, that's what his problem was. He'd just relieve himself when he got home, get some sleep and forget all about Megan Montgomery, the woman, and focus only on Megan Montgomery, the informant.

He sat in his car, his knuckles turning white as his hands choked the steering wheel until, thankfully, she got in her car and drove away into the cold.

*   *   *   *

4:32 a.m.

Megan mechanically drove through the snowy, deserted streets thinking of only one thing, Detective Stark. What had happened was more like a movie than real life. This kind of thing didn't happen to her. Never. And now in the familiar surroundings of her car, she wasn't completely convinced it actually had. Maybe she dreamt it, too. Was her imagination, her overstressed brain, playing tricks on her, or was she really just seconds away from having sex with a man she didn't even know?

She'd had sex a couple of times before, but she had never once craved a man like this. Never once wanted and needed a man with every cell in her body the way she wanted and needed Detective Stark just a half an hour ago.

She could still smell him, on her clothes and in her hair, and she could still feel his warm, hard body pressing against her hers. She put her fingers to her lips. She could still feel his kisses, firm and hard, yet still tender. So tender, it surprised her, especially after the anger he had unleashed on.

But that anger had turned into a passion greater than any she had ever felt directed at her before. It was enough to take her breath away even now, when she was miles away from him. Maybe, if she hadn't locked away her heart, denied her needs as a real living, breathing woman, the detective's kisses wouldn't have effected her like they had. Maybe then, she would have had the power to fight it.

Megan closed her eyes, trying to recapture Detective Stark's image in her mind and the feel of his lips, wet and wonderful on her neck. She could feel a tingling in the pit of her stomach as she let her mind wander back to his apartment. Oh, if that blasted phone hadn't rung, she might be with him, right now, tasting him, holding him. It surprised her, how unfulfilled and how empty she felt now that there was no chance of having that incredibly sexy man inside her tonight.

Suddenly, she felt her car's tires slide off the side of the street. Her eyes flew open and her body snapped to attention. She instinctively turned the wheel and her car swerved, barely missing a mailbox, before it began fishtailing across the slick, snowy road. It took a few seconds, but she finally regained complete control of the car. She slowly exhaled the chest full of air she had sucked in.

Thinking about Detective Stark was going to get her into a lot of trouble and this was just a wake up call.

*   *   *   *

7:36 a.m.

Breakfast with Hudson came way too soon. David sauntered into Dad's Diner and asked a waitress for a cup of black coffee before spying Hudson at a corner booth with his nose buried in the morning newspaper.

David couldn't sleep when he got back to his cold and, after Megan left, lonely apartment. That woman had him so riled up, all he could do was lay there, staring at his bedroom ceiling, reliving their brief encounter over and over again in his mind.

It was eating him up inside that she had something to do with the case. He couldn't explain it, but his gut told him she was innocent and his gut was seldom wrong. His brain, however, was absolutely numb from the hours he spent trying to dissect the facts from the fiction in the story she had told him.

But, no matter how hard he tried to keep his mind on the case, his thoughts always ended up back against his dining room wall, with her on her knees in front of him about to…. Damn! He couldn't keep his focus, even this morning. No other woman had ever done that to him before and he was as mad as hell at himself for letting her do it to him now. He was letting his feelings for Megan Montgomery, whatever the fuck they were, interfere with his job and that was something he just could not afford to do.

David crossed the diner and dropped onto the light green vinyl bench across from his partner.

Hudson peeked over the top of his newspaper. "Man, you look like hell." He sounded more annoyed than concerned.

David ran his fingers through his hair. "Rough night."

"Yeah, no shit. Sorry I wasn't there to back you on it, partner. The damn battery's dead on my cell phone. But Banister got me at home about three-thirty and told me you were looking for me." He waited for David to say something, and when he didn't, Hudson continued. "So, you gonna tell me how in the hell you knew where to find that woman?"

"Here ya go, sweetie." An older blonde waitress sat a cup of hot steaming coffee in front of David. "Looks like you could use it."

"Rough night," Hudson offered his partner's excuse.

"The usual, Frank?" The waitress asked, pulling a pencil out of her frizzy hair.

"Yeah, that'll be great, Cindy. Thanks."

David looked inquisitively at his partner.

"I eat here a lot."

The waitress flicked some invisible crumbs off her yellow dress. "Too often if ya ask me. All this greasy food ain't good for his heart, ya know." She winked at David and then blew a kiss at Hudson. "But we do love him around here. And he tips pretty good, for a cop." She laughed and turned towards David. "Now, tell me, sweetie, what can I get for ya?"

"I'll have whatever he's having," David said, his eyes too tired for him to even think about looking at the menu.

The waitress threw her hand up in the air in mock disgust and shook her head. "Ok, but it's you guy's funeral." She walked back to the opening in the wall separating the dining area from the kitchen and slapped the order down on the counter. "Two big breakfast busters, extra cheese, extra onions, wheat toast."

"What the hell did I just order?" David asked between two giant gulps of coffee.

"A big ass omelet with everything and enough cheese to gum ya up for a week."

David shook his head. "No wonder you throw back those Tums like they're candy." He gulped down another big swallow of coffee and could feel the caffeine slowly starting to kick in to dissolve some of the cobwebs in his head.

"So?" Hudson leaned an elbow on the table. "You gonna tell me why you were at that hotel last night? How the hell'd ya know?"

"I didn't," David answered honestly. How was he going to explain this again? What had he decided to say? Damn, he wished he could have gotten some sleep last night because right now his brain wasn't quite working fast enough. "I just got this….." He stopped mid-sentence. If he said he got an anonymous phone call, Hudson would insist they check the recordings. If he told him it was on his cell phone, they could easily find out what number it came from.

"I was just there." David shrugged his shoulders, sorry he wasn't able to offer a better explanation than that.

"Really?" Hudson raised an eyebrow.

"Yeah, really."

"Business or pleasure?"

"It's not what you think."

"Oh, yeah? 'Cause right now I'm thinking you were there getting yourself a little pussy. Am I right?" Hudson leaned back in his seat, and eyed his partner.

David grimaced and looked around, hoping no children or little old ladies overheard his partner's crude remark. "Man, you really are a tactless SOB, you know that?"

"And, your point?"

David ran both hands through his hair to the back of his head and rubbed out some of the tension in his neck as he rested his elbows on the table. God, he didn't want Hudson thinking he was there banging some hooker, but that beat the hell out of actually telling him the truth right now. It wasn't going to be easy to tell anyone he followed some psychic's tip about a murder and before they even got the victim to the morgue, he's half naked with the prime suspect.

"Well. I told you I had a rough night, didn't I?" David looked up and offered Hudson a sheepish smile.

"Damn boy. I know you're ugly and all, but I didn't think you actually had to pay for it. This her?" Hudson slid the folded newspaper across the table. There was a small picture of David with his arm around Megan as he ushered her out of the hotel last night. It wasn't a very clear picture and it was in black and white but she looked so beautiful, standing there beside him. David could feel his stomach tighten as he remembered just how good she felt in his arms and how much he ached for her still this morning.

"Pretty classy lookin' for a hooker." Hudson pulled the paper back in front of him and studied the picture.

"She's not a hooker," David said into his coffee mug before downing the last sip. He searched through the crowd for their waitress and, after getting her attention, lifted his cup and pointed to it.

He hoped that was the end of the questions for now. He never was any good at lying, and besides, he wanted to tell Hudson the truth. Who knows, maybe the old man could help him make some sense out of this fiasco. But this truth was best saved for later, at least until after he found out a whole hell of a lot more about one Megan Marie Montgomery.

*   *   *   *

8:43 a.m.

"Girl, you look awful." Concern pinched Sue's eyebrows together as she watched Megan walk into the classroom. "Another nightmare?"

Well, it wasn't the truth, but there was no way she was going to tell Sue what really happened to her last night, at least not right now, so she simply nodded and closed her purse up in the desk drawer.

"Meg, you really need to see a doctor or something. I'd have already been, if it was happening to me. I mean, maybe at least they could give you some pills or something to help you sleep."

"I'll be alright. I'll catch up on my sleep this weekend."

"Well." A sneaky smile slowly crossed Sue's face. "Not tomorrow night, if I have anything to do with it."

"What? Why not?" Megan's left eye automatically narrowed. "Susan Johnson, what are you up to?"

"Well, you know that cute, blonde guy doing his student teaching with Dottie Langhall in second grade?"

"You mean Bill something?"

"Yeah, that's right. Bill Peak. You've noticed him, huh?"

"No. Well, yeah, I guess. I mean, not really. He's just in one of my night classes and I've talked to him a few times, but that's it. Why?" Megan wasn't in the mood for games, especially today. Her world was tearing apart at the seams and it had taken every last ounce of energy she had this morning just to fight the urge to crawl back into bed and hide under her covers. "What's this got to do with him? Sue? What's goin' on?"

"Well, we were all in the teachers' lounge this morning and he sort of asked me about you and I, of course, said that you definitely needed to get out more, and we sort of decided you'd meet him at O'Hara's tomorrow night at six for dinner."

"You what?"

Sue grimaced. "Well, it seemed like a good idea at the time."

"Oh, Sue!" Megan rubbed her fingers against the throbbing pain in her forehead.

"Sorry. I'm sorry. Don't kill me. He just seems like such a nice guy. And you really do need to get out more, I worry about you, ya know. And I warned you it was my number one priority to find someone for you, didn't I?"

"I really wished you hadn't done that. Not now."

"Well, he really seems taken with you. As a matter of fact, I think he likes you a lot. And if you ask me, you could use some attention from the opposite sex right now. Of course, as shy as you both are, it might take months just for you guys to hold hands."

A smirk played at the corner of Megan's mouth as she wondered what Sue would say if she saw her last night with that sexy Detective Stark.

"Please, say you'll go," Sue pleaded. "C'mon girl, it'll break that poor guy's heart, if you tell him no."

"You mean, if *you* tell him no."

"Well, ok. That's fair. I guess I'd have to tell him if you decided not to go out with him. But *puh-leese* go. It'll do you good to get out and have some fun. And I'm sure you don't really want me to crush him, do ya?"

"Oh, Sue. I really don't think I can. You know I've got a lot going on right now with my class work and working at the flower shop. Not to mention, these darn headaches and nightmares."

The school secretary, Mrs. Walker, opened the door and stuck her head into the classroom. "Excuse me, Ms. Johnson, Mr. Temple would like to see you for a moment."

"Oh, great, I wonder how much more trouble I can get into today?" Sue asked half laughing, but Mrs. Walker found no humor in it and just blankly stared back at her. "Meg, you mind covering the class for me if I'm late getting back?"

"Of course not, go on."

Mrs. Walker waited for Sue to walk out of the classroom and gave Megan a lingering look before closing the door behind her. Megan wondered what she had done to deserve that. Mrs. Walker wasn't exactly the friendliest of people, but Megan had been nothing but respectful to her. The other teachers, however, usually gave her a hard time. She was one of those humorless sticklers who made sure she knew everything that was going on in the school, whether it was any of her business or not. She wasn't a bad person, just not too often asked out to lunch.

Megan had the class going over the homework they were assigned the night before when Sue finally walked back into the classroom, the usual smile was missing from her face.

"What's wrong?" Megan asked.

"Class," Sue said, completely ignoring Megan's question, "please turn to page thirty-seven in your math workbooks and quietly work on problems one through ten." When she was satisfied her students were all busy, she grabbed Megan's arm and pulled her out into the empty hallway, closing the classroom door behind them. She looked at Megan, her jaw set firmly, but said nothing.

"What took so long?" Megan asked, ending the uncomfortable silence.

"Meg," she paused for a moment, "are you in some sort of trouble?"

"No. Why?"

"Well, some cop named Stark was just in the office asking a bunch of personal questions about you."

"What?" Megan stomach dropped. Well, so much for the salvia they swapped last night. This made it crystal clear she was back on the prime suspect list, if she was ever off it in the first place. She couldn't believe it. She had almost slept with a man who believed she could be guilty of murder. And not just murder, hideous *murders*, plural!

At least she didn't have to worry about what Detective Stark thought of her. That was pretty obvious now. She also didn't have to wonder whether or not they'd ever finish what they started last night up against his dinning room wall.

Her tongue slid across the inside of her lower lip. The soft skin was left cut and bruised under his hard, lusty kisses, like some kind of sick souvenir of their night together. But in a day or two it would be healed, leaving nothing but memories of how it felt to be in his arms.

Megan shook her head. "What kind of questions?"

"Stuff like who you hung out with and if I thought you did drugs or were in a cult."

"Jesus," Megan moaned.

"Yeah, I know. Crazy stuff like that." Sue hesitated for a moment. "But I got to tell you, girl, he was one fine looking man. I mean, like, drop dead gorgeous! I wonder what he wanted. You'd tell me if you were in any trouble, wouldn't you?"

Megan nodded and looked down the long deserted hallway. It was as empty as her life felt right now. "Sue, I thought about it and I think I will meet Bill for dinner tomorrow night." What did she have to lose? Any delusions she had about her and the 'drop dead gorgeous' Detective Stark had vanished in the morning light. And hey, maybe Sue was right. Maybe she did need to get out more. Maybe then she wouldn't fall head over hills for the first guy who threw her up against a wall.

"Great." Sue beamed with satisfaction.

"Just dinner, right? I mean, you didn't sign me up for a movie or the night in a motel, too. Did ya?"

"Of course not! Sex is strictly optional."

Megan rolled her eyes and shook her head. "Do this to me again and I'll rip your heart out."

Sue covered her chest with both hands, pretending to guard her heart from Megan's attack. "Never, never again. I swear to God. Even if he's as gorgeous as Brad Pitt and as rich as Bill Gates."

"Well. Maybe that one time would be alright."

"Good morning, Miss Johnson. Good morning, Miss Montgomery," a freckled faced little girl sang out as she skipped her way to the little girl's restroom, her pink hall pass flapping in her hand.

"Good morning, Nikki," the women said in unison.

After the little girl was in the restroom and they were alone again, Sue sighed. "You know, I'm not stupid, Meg. I know something's going on with that foxy cop."

Megan said nothing.

"It's ok. I know what a private person you are and I respect that. I've never pried into your life before, have I?"

Megan shook her head, sorry for not having the courage to tell her good friend the truth about what was going on.

"I know there's something you're not telling me. So, if or when you ever need to talk, I'll be here for you, ok."

"Thanks." Megan smiled at her good friend. "You have no idea how much that means to me." The two friends hugged tightly before heading back into their classroom.

＊　　＊　　＊　　＊

3:21 p.m.

"Well, Detective Stark, I think Meg's done pretty good for herself considering," Nancy Montgomery said, smiling at him from across her kitchen table as he sipped the hot chocolate she had made for him.

"Please, call me David."

"Oh, Ok, David. Not many kids orphaned at her age are so well adjusted, ya know. I'm really proud of her and everything she's accomplished. But these dang nightmares have really been hard on her. I sure hope you can catch this guy pretty soon and make 'em stop."

David hoped she didn't see him roll his eyes. He could tell by talking to her that she was as convinced as Megan was that there was something to these dreams and although he didn't want to offend the old lady, he wasn't quite ready to swallow the whole story just yet.

"She's too young to have all this sitting on her shoulders, ya know," Nancy continued. "By the way, did you say you were married?"

"No." David smiled at her, noticing the way her watery blue eyes twinkled merrily. She was quite a card. "Why won't Megan let you keep pictures of her mother in the house?"

"No, you aren't married or no, you didn't say if you were married or not?"

"No to both. Now tell me about Megan's mother."

Nancy started flipping through the pages of the old leather scrapbook in front of her. "It's a terrible shame really. You see, the defense attorney for Peter Logan brought up the fact that Debbie was quite the girl about town when she was younger. Like making a few mistakes when you're a kid is enough of a sin to deserve havin' some wacko kill ya." Nancy pointed to a clipping in the scrapbook. "Here it is. Here's Debbie." She turned the scrapbook around to show him a picture of Megan's mother that was cut out of a newspaper.

"Very beautiful," he said truthfully. It was in black and white and it had yellowed over the years, but he could tell how pretty she must have been, her long hair pulled loosely up on top of her head, her soft features, cute nose and full lips. "She looks just like Megan." David looked up and Nancy smiled at him.

"I know he was just doing his job," Nancy continued, "but that lawyer really shouldn't have said all those terrible things, especially in front of Meg. You see,

Meg, lost her mother twice. Once when she was murdered, then later 'cause of that terrible trial."

"The judge didn't allow it, of course, he had all of it stricken from the record, but he couldn't strike it from Meg's memory. It was too late for that. And from that moment on, she blamed her mom for her dad's murder. That night when we got home, Megan threw away every single picture and keepsake she had left of her mom. Of course, I got them all out of the trash after she went to sleep and hid them away, hoping one day she'd forgive Deb, but it don't look like that's ever gonna happen."

Nancy shook her head sadly. "I mean, here she was just twelve or so and hearing about how many men Deb had slept with, how many homes she wrecked and how many people could have wanted her dead. Well, you can just imagine how bad that hurt Meg. The sad thing is, Debbie hadn't been like that for a really long time. She was happily married to Gene and a good momma to Meg."

Nancy got up and refilled David's cup not missing a beat in the conversation. "Debbie was just a very pretty girl with absolutely the worst taste in men. I'm serious, the meaner they were to her, the harder she tried to please them. Oh, I know she did a whole lot of things wrong, but she did the right thing by Meg. She could of...."

Nancy laughed nervously and put the kettle back on the stove. "Oh, heavens, would you just listen to me go on? You come here to ask me a few simple questions and off I go on some tangent, wagging my tongue like a snake. You must think I'm somethin' awful."

"No, not at all." David smiled at her. "As a matter of fact, I really appreciate your taking this time with me." He turned the page in the thick scrapbook. "Please, tell me more about how Megan helped the police catch Peter Logan."

✳   ✳   ✳   ✳

Megan pulled onto Taylorwood Lane and her shoulders instantly slumped when she saw the green Berretta parked on the street in front of her house.

It had been a long night. She had to get ready for school just hours after she got home this morning and then go to a class at the college after that. Right now she was running on fumes and looking forward to grabbing a sandwich and crawling straight into bed. But there he was, in her house, waiting for her.

After spending the entire day questioning everyone she knew, he should have all the information he could possible need. She could only imagine what the principal was thinking, after some cop was asking crazy and personal questions about her. And who else had he talked to today? Who else was she going to have to explain things to? She was too tired to even think about that now.

Megan suppressed the impulse to keep driving. Detective Stark was the last person on earth she wanted to see right now and not only because of what happened between them last night, although that was a big part of it. Of course, she knew avoiding him wouldn't do any good either. He'd just hunt her down until she got this over with. Maybe, if she just answered all his questions, she'd never have to see him again and that would suit her just fine. She parked her Sable in the driveway and reluctantly walked to her front door.

She hoped Nancy hadn't tried to set them up on a date or anything. This situation was embarrassing enough already without her being in her usual matchmaker mode. Megan cringed at how embarrassing it would be for Detective Stark to hear about how nice Megan was and how smart she was. And especially how she really needed a nice guy, just like him, in her life. Poor guy. Nancy could go on for hours. Suddenly Megan's heart stopped.

Surely, she wouldn't have told him about Clarksburg, about her parents' murder, about....Megan nearly choked on the lump caught in her throat...about Peter Logan. The detective didn't need to know about all that. Not now, not when he already thought she was completely crazy.

Megan's hand was visibly shaking as she reached for the doorknob. Slowly, she walked through the door, closed it quietly behind her and tiptoed toward the kitchen. Detective Stark was sitting across the kitchen table from Nancy, hanging on her every word.

"We don't know what it is exactly," Nancy explained to him. "It's like Meg is this radio and she picks up certain stations that are on her same wavelength. We were hopin' it was just a fluke with that nasty Logan character 'cause it's been so long ago. But here we go again." Nancy tapped her finger on the big brown scrapbook Megan had happily forgotten about.

Detective Stark was wearing another pair of worn blue jeans and a red and white plaid flannel shirt that made him look more like a lumberjack than a police officer. He *was* incredibly handsome, she'd give him that. Too bad he thought she was a criminal or, more likely, after this enlightening little conversation with Nancy, a raving lunatic.

"Gee, Nancy. I hope you didn't leave anything out!" Megan shot her a dirty look from the doorway. "I'm not sure Detective Stark needed quite so much information." The detective looked up at her, his amber eyes studying her face as if trying to decide whether or not to call in the men in white coats to come and take her away.

"Oh, pooh!" Nancy threw her hands up. "This very nice and, if you don't mind me sayin' so…" She winked at David. "Very *handsome* young police detective is gonna help you stop those terrible nightmares. I can just tell he's gonna be your knight in shinning armor." Nancy smiled slyly at Megan. "And, by the way, he wants us to call him David. Isn't that a nice name?"

Nancy got up and pulled a red snowman coffee mug off a hook from under the kitchen cabinet and started to pour hot cocoa in it. "Oh, sit down, Meg. And don't get your panties in such a bunch."

Megan could see the detective blush before he looked down at his own cup. He was probably thinking about how close he was to actually seeing her panties last night. She was so embarrassed, she wanted to scream.

She took off her long black winter coat, hung it over the kitchen chair and sat down slowly, staring at the old beat up scrapbook David flipped through. All her dark, dirty secrets were in that book. It was all there, how Megan's parents were the first victims and how their poor daughter must have witnessed the whole thing.

The only thing not mentioned in the newspaper article was that Megan had actually dreamt it the night before it happened. She woke her parents with blood curdling screams and, as she wept, she told them everything. They dismissed it as only a bad dream and her mom even blamed her daddy for letting their little girl watch too many scary movies. They assured her everything was fine and Megan ignorantly believed them.

The next night, however, while she was sleeping at a girlfriend's house, her parents were brutally murdered. She told the police exactly what happened and it matched the evidence perfectly. They couldn't figure out how she could have known everything and because they couldn't explain it, they ignored it.

Megan had no other family and nowhere to go. That's when Nancy stepped in and became her guardian. Nancy had known Debbie and Gene Maxwell since before Megan was born and she loved them all dearly. She was already like a grandmother to Megan, so it was an easy transition for both of them, considering. But there was no possible way to prepare them for how rough the next two years would be.

Nancy was the one who called the police when Megan had another nightmare about a murder. It concerned a woman who lived alone in a trailer park in the next town over. The police didn't believe her, of course, but when it happened the next day, just the way Nancy told them it would, the police were everywhere. They questioned Megan and Nancy and actually arrested Nancy, until she could prove her whereabouts during the time of the murder.

Thankfully, the murders Peter Logan committed weren't as grizzly as the ones The Cleveland Cutter had a taste for, but to an eleven-year-old girl whose world was crashing down around her, they couldn't have been much worse. The nightmares, the sorrow from losing her parents and the guilt she felt for not having saved them tormented her. In fact it was so overwhelming, that at eleven and a half, she tried to commit suicide.

Megan was admitted to the psychiatric ward at Clarksburg General Hospital, which just added to the horror her life had become. Ironically, though, it was because of her time in the psychiatric ward that the police finally believed her premonitions.

She was in the hospital when she had the next three dreams. The doctors preformed hundreds of tests on her, from ink blots, to word association, to hypnosis and they documented every single detail she told them about her nightmares. She had an astonishing ability to recall even the smallest details from her dreams. The psychologists thought it was uncanny, but Megan found it impossible to *forget* any of the horrible images that flashed through her mind.

As awful as that experience was, if the doctors hadn't documented her nightmares so well, the police would never have followed up on the information she was able to give them, information that eventually lead to the arrest and conviction of Peter Logan, ending the murders and her nightmares as well.

That was a part of her life she wanted to forget, but there it was in black and white, pasted to the battered yellow pages of that old scrapbook Nancy insisted on keeping. A gut-wrenching feeling of vulnerability filled her as she watched the same hands that held her last night flip through the pages of her darkest, most painful secrets today. Secrets Megan wanted buried, forgotten, but there they were, out of their box and from under the bed, lying open, right on the kitchen table.

*   *   *   *

To call David confused didn't even come close. He didn't know what in the hell to think. He liked Nancy Montgomery a great deal. And how he felt about Megan, well, he didn't have that completely figured out just yet, but he sure hadn't been able to stop thinking about her since the second she drove out of that parking lot last night.

He was willing to jeopardize his career, his entire life's work, just to have her last night. And as he sat there watching her across that tiny, wooden table, all he could think about was how he wanted to help her, to stop the hurting he could see behind her sad, blue eyes. Eyes almost too painful to look at.

Could he help her? He didn't know. Could he stop the terrible nightmares that haunted her? He wasn't sure. But he decided right then and there, sitting in her kitchen, that he was going to at least try.

He wasn't sure he believed the whole thing, but he was convinced there was no way she could be involved, no way she was covering up for someone. He did a lot of checking up on her today. She didn't have so much as a speeding ticket and as far as hanging out with the wrong crowd, she didn't hang out with any crowd. She was a loner. Not many friends and no boyfriend, information which, not surprisingly, David was quite relieved to discover.

He had done his homework on Megan Montgomery, but that, in no way, prepared him for the story Nancy was going to tell him when he knocked on her door this afternoon. She told him the story of a little girl who witnessed the murders of not only her own mother and father, but of six other strangers, through her nightmares. A story of a little girl who had a curse, a curse that scarred her for life, a curse so terrible it had caused her to try and end her own life.

And after finally leading the police to the killer, the little girl was made to testify in the biggest criminal case ever tried in Clarksburg, West Virginia. And the trial had been a nightmare all of its own. David's heart ached for that little girl in the scrapbook and for the beautiful, haunted woman sitting across the table from him now.

Nancy sat a cup of steaming hot cocoa in front of Megan and filled David's cup up again, despite his objections. "Oh, have some more. It'll warm you up. Now I've got to get to the store. I'm terribly late already." She put the white tea kettle back on the stove and turned off the burner before wiping her hands off on a red and white dishtowel.

David stood up and shook Nancy's hand. "It was very nice meeting you, ma'am. Thanks again for your time."

"It was so nice meeting you, too, Detective Stark. I mean David. Please come back and see us again. I'm hoping we see a lot of you around here." She smiled and turned to Megan. "Remember this is my late night at the store. I'll be gone until almost ten."

"Thursdays are always your late night," Megan snapped.

"Yeah, I know, I just wanted to remind you." Nancy looked right at David and smiled.

Why that sneaky old woman. She wanted David to know the coast was clear. He felt himself blush under her long smile and hoped Megan hadn't noticed.

"Well, I'm sure Detective Stark won't be staying very long," Megan growled back at her.

'Fucking Asshole' could have replaced 'Detective Stark' and her tone would have remained exactly the same. He was sorry to hear the anger in her voice, especially after what happened between them last night. Even though he expected it, hearing it come out of those perfect pink lips, the ones that kissed him back last night, hurt a little more than he thought it would.

They silently sipped their hot chocolate until Nancy yelled a goodbye from the front door and was gone.

"I really don't know what to say." His words broke the silence as he patted the cover of the scrapbook with his hand.

"You don't have to say anything." Megan shot ice blue daggers at him with her eyes. "I'm fully aware you're investigating me for murder. I know you were at the school this morning. I hope you found out what kind of drugs I'm on and which cults I've joined lately. And I can only imagine what you're thinking now. Now that you know…everything." She flung her hand toward the scrapbook. "So? Are you ready to arrest me now or what?"

"It's not like that," he said calmly.

"It's not like what? Oh, maybe you're just going to toss me in the psycho ward instead? Wouldn't blame you. Been there before as I'm sure Nancy's already told you."

"Listen." David stretched out his arm and placed his hand on top of hers. "I'm really sorry I didn't take you more seriously last night. I want to help. I really do."

She shot a doubtful look at him.

"I know you don't trust me. And after how I've treated you, I don't blame you. But we need to work together if we're gonna stop this guy and your nightmares. We need to trust each other." His fingers curled under her hand and pressed into her palm while his thumb rubbed the top of her hand. "I'm willing to give you the benefit of the doubt. Are you willing to trust me?"

Megan bit her bottom lip and looked away.

"You can trust me," he whispered. "I want this to be over for you. For all of us. And I…I don't want you to hurt anymore."

*   *   *   *

Megan never heard anything so wonderful in all her life, if only it were true. She looked deep into the detective's transparent, brown eyes. Last night she could see the anger burning in them and later, the lust. Today she saw…. What? Concern? Yes, concern and kindness, too. How difficult it must be for him to do his job with eyes like that. She doubted he could ever lie to anyone and get away with it. For Detective David Stark, his eyes truly were windows to his soul.

Maybe he really was going to be her knight in shinning armor, just like Nancy said. And maybe he really was going to help her stop that madman who was running around rampant inside her dreams. She would owe him everything, if only he could. Tears of relief began to pool in her eyes.

He smiled at her. "I know it must be hard, but you have to tell me about your second dream. We only have three victims. Maybe she's going to be the fourth. Maybe together, she's the one we can save."

Megan shook her head and looked down at the thick dark liquid in her cup. "That's not the way it works. I'm afraid if the dream was true, she's already dead. You just haven't found her yet."

"And maybe not," he said, ignoring her pessimism. "Can you remember the whole dream?"

She stared at the wall behind him, trying to focus on that terrible second dream. Even though she had it over a week ago, the details easily flooded back to her. "She was a waitress in a little diner. I can't see the name of it and I can't tell where it's at. But he thinks she has the prettiest hands he's ever seen."

She saw David cringe and for the first time, she noticed the pain behind his eyes. It had been hard on her, these horrible dreams, but he had seen these women in the flesh. He probably had to study them in the morgue and maybe he even had to inform their families. Megan suddenly felt very sorry for the detective. He had treated her cruelly at first, but it was only because he wanted to put that madman away and stop the killing as much as she did. And now that he believed in her, maybe they could do just that.

She took a deep breath and forced her thoughts back into the dream. "The woman was in her twenties, I think, and had long black hair she wore up in a pony tail. She had on a yellow dress with a white apron and a nametag. Her name was Brenda."

"The man waited for her outside in his car. It was just barely light, but I couldn't tell whether it was late morning or early evening. She got into her car, a dark brown hatchback, and the man followed her. I couldn't see the outside of his car at all, but the inside was gray leather. It was an older car with one of those big, thin steering wheels. I didn't see a clock on the dashboard, but he never really looked at the dashboard much. I could see his hands on the steering wheel. They're old and rough and he wears a gold watch on his right wrist."

Sweat began to bead on Megan's forehead and upper lip, so she got up and pulled a glass from the cabinet, poured herself a glass of cold water from the refrigerator and took a long drink while David sat silently watching her.

"She pulled into the driveway of a little white house," Megan continued, after taking her seat again. "She got out of her car and walked up to her house. It had a big front porch across the whole front. She unlocked her front door and opened it, but just as she was walking through the door, the man pushed her from behind and slammed the door shut. She fell to the floor and tried to get up, but the man bent over and grabbed her head in his hands and smashed it against the hard-wood floor of her living room."

Megan propped her right elbow on the table and spread her hand across her forehead to cover her eyes. "He just kept doing it over and over and over and over."

David stood up and walked over to her side of the table. He crouched down beside her and put his arm around her shoulder. "I know it's hard. But you have to keep going," he said with the warmth of an old friend. "You have to tell me everything. I need to know everything."

Megan cleared her throat. "I know. I'm sorry." She nodded and took a deep breath, before using her bottom lip to blow the air up out of her mouth and move the hair out of her face. She had to pull herself together. It wasn't going to help anyone if she broke down every time she had to talk about the dreams.

"He killed her," she continued. "Then pulled that weird looking saw out of his case and...and cut her hands off just above the wrists. About here." She pointed to a place on her arm. "Then he put her hands in a big clear plastic bag, kinda like a freezer bag. Oh yeah, another thing. He wore those same yellow rubber gloves again." She wasn't sure how much that helped, but her job was to tell him everything, she'd leave its importance up to him.

"Do you think you could identify the kind of saw he used, if I showed you some pictures?"

"Maybe. I'll try."

"What about his car?"

Megan shook her head. "I don't think so. I'm sorry. I don't remember seeing it from the outside at all, only the inside, and not that good."

"Is that all of it? Is that when the dream ended?" There was no harshness in his voice today. No disbelief or ridicule, no suspicion. Today his voice and his eyes were full of understanding. He truly wanted to help her and she loved him for it. If nothing else ever happened between her and David Stark, she would always love him for that.

"No," she answered. "He got a drink of water, washed off his gloves and the saw in her kitchen sink and dried them with a towel that was lying on the counter and then he walked out the front door and locked it."

Megan leaned forward and put her hands on David's shoulders. "Oh my God! I saw the number on the house. I never realized it before, but I saw the number on the house. Two seventy-three."

"Come on, let's go." David stood up, grabbed her coat and helped her into it while practically pushing her out the door.

He helped her into his car and before she could even get her seat belt fastened, he was in the driver's seat, had the car started and was speeding down the street. He pulled a detachable siren from under his seat and put it on the roof of his car, then grabbed his police radio and began barking out commands in that strong, sexy voice of his. He was so in control, so gorgeous and he was sitting right next to her.

She watched the muscles in his neck flex as he turned the steering wheel sharply to the right and the memory of kissing those muscles and his bare flesh, hot against her lips, filled her with unexpected hunger. That man had wanted to make love to her last night and, at the very least, he wanted to help her today. Today, he wanted to save her.

Afraid he might see the heat she felt rising into her cheeks, she turned away and looked out the car window. It was one of those rare, beautiful January days in Ohio. The sun was shining brilliantly making the snow look as though it were scattered with millions of glimmering diamonds and the sky was a deep azure with big, white, puffy clouds in it that would look more at home in an August sky than one in the dead of winter.

It was sad really. Ohioans were only given a precious few of these magnificent winter days to enjoy and here they were spending it in search of a murder victim. She found herself actually jealous of the blissfully ignorant people she saw strolling the sidewalks, walking their dogs or playing with their kids, enjoying the wonderful day God had given them.

"This is Stark," David said into the piece of plastic he held in his hand.

A woman's voice broke through the static on the radio. "Lewis here. Go ahead Stark."

"Run this through the computer for me." David spoke so fast Megan wasn't sure how anyone could understand a word he said. "I need you to do a search. First name Brenda, living in the Cleveland area, drives a brown hatchback. House number two seventy-three."

He smiled over at Megan, silently thanking her for the tip. "Hang on," he warned her as he made another sharp right, sliding her closer to him.

"That doesn't give us much to go on, Stark," Lewis answered. "But, I'll do my best."

"Hey, Lewis, what truck stops or diners in the area have yellow uniforms for their waitresses? It's important!"

"No idea. Let me ask around."

"Where are we going?" Megan asked, one hand solidly planted on his dashboard and the other hanging on desperately to the 'oh shit handle' attached to the roof of his car, now knowing first hand exactly why she had always heard it called that.

David looked over at her and laughed. "Sorry. I'll try not to kill us."

It was the first time she had seen him really smile. It was such a big, bright, happy smile that showed off the deep sexy dimples in his cheeks not normally visible. It also softened that hard, tough, all business, look he had about him. It was the most infectious smile she had ever seen and she found it impossible not to smile back.

"I'm headed to a place called Dad's off 480," he explained. "I was just there this morning and I'm pretty sure the waitresses were wearing yellow dresses. So until someone has a better idea, that's where we're gonna start."

"Stark?" Lewis called out from the radio.

"Yeah, go ahead, Lewis."

"The DMV turned up 47 persons with the first name of Brenda who drive brown hatchbacks in the greater Cleveland area, but street address narrowed it down, big time. We have three with house numbers of two seventy-three."

"Write this down." David nodded toward a note pad and pen that were attached to his dashboard.

Lewis continued, "Brenda Thomas at two seventy-three East 22nd Street in Cleveland, Brenda Parker at two seventy-three Washington Court in Cleveland, and Brenda Davis at two seventy-three Milan Avenue in Lakewood."

"Thanks, Lewis."

"No problem. We're still looking for more matches. I'll let you know if I find anything else. By the way, O'Donnell thinks the girls at Dad's Truck Stop by 480 wear yellow, but he's not positive."

That must have been all he needed to convince him his hunch was right because he pushed the gas petal down to the floor, making Megan a little sick to her stomach. A few minutes later, David's green Berretta tore into the parking lot of Dad's Truck Stop and Diner with sirens blaring and stones flying.

He jumped out of the car, before it had completely stopped, and slammed the door behind him, leaving the engine running and Megan sitting in the car alone. Not sure what she was suppose to do, she jumped out herself and raced to catch up with him just as he bolted through the swinging glass door and ran to the nearest waitress.

"Is there a Brenda that works here?" He flashed his badge at the woman in the yellow dress and white apron standing behind the counter, coffee pot in her hand.

"No," she said. "Why? What'd she go and do?"

"Nothing. We have reason to believe her life may be in danger."

"Oh, God," the waitress gasped, putting her free hand over her mouth. "I knew something was wrong. Is that no good ex-husband of hers after her again?"

"After who?" David sounded annoyed. "Listen, Penny," he said, after reading her nametag. "Do you have a Brenda working here or not? If you do, it's imperative that I speak to her right away."

"No." The older, silver-haired waitress answered between chomps on her chewing gum. "Well, not anymore. Brenda Parker worked here for the past six months or so, but about a week ago, she just up and quit. Didn't even say goodbye to any of us."

David started running for the door, so Megan turned to follow him.

"Hey," the older waitress called after them, "if you see her, tell her she has to return her uniforms or we're gonna send her a bill for 'em!"

The ten-minute drive to Brenda Parker's home was silent except for the call David made to Lewis on his radio. "Send a back up unit and an ambulance to two seventy-three Washington Court and tell them to wait for me. I'm on my way."

A squad car was already waiting in front of Brenda Parker's house when they arrived at the scene. Megan got out of the car, knowing exactly what they were going to find, but praying to God she was wrong.

"You stay here, ok?" David told her.

Megan nodded and leaned up against his car.

She saw him say something to the two uniformed officers who had gotten out of their squad car. They both nodded and then one immediately went around to the back of the house, while the other one followed David to the front door.

David knocked on the door. "Brenda Parker?" He yelled through the door. "It's the police. Please open the door." No answer. He knocked again, then pulled a handkerchief from his pocket and tried the doorknob. It was locked.

David signaled toward a pile of mail and newspapers lying on the front porch with his head and asked the officer behind him, "Probable cause?"

The young officer nodded in agreement.

David shot a quick look back at Megan as he drew his weapon and turned to kick in the door. After it flew open, the two men slowly lowered their weapons. From where Megan stood on the street, in front of the house, she couldn't see inside, but she didn't need to. She had already seen it in her nightmare.

"Oh, Jesus," the uniformed officer exclaimed as David held the handkerchief he had in his hand over his nose and mouth.

Megan stayed outside by the car while David did his job, talking to neighbors, taking statements and supervising the five or six uniformed officers who searched the premises for clues and dusted for prints. The ambulance had already come and gone.

An older man, in a dark blue suit, stood on the front porch, eyeing her suspiciously. She didn't know who he was, but he gave her the creeps. He seemed to be more interested in her than in the murder that had taken place inside the house.

The sun had gone down and it was getting colder out. Megan was rubbing her frozen hands together and bouncing around outside David's car, trying to stay warm, when he finally looked over and noticed her. He whispered something to another officer, who nodded, strode over to his squad car, got in and started it.

David walked across the front yard towards Megan. "I'm sorry I didn't notice you were freezing out here. I'm going to have someone take you home. You should've said something."

"I'm fine," she lied. "I'm just sorry about her." Megan nodded her head toward the house.

"Yeah. Me, too." He leaned his back against the car and studied Megan with his dark eyes. "It's exactly like your dream." He paused, his brown eyes narrowed as he chewed at the corner of his lip thoughtfully and then he let out a long, tired sigh. "But you already knew that, didn't you?"

"Yes." She nodded her head and looked away. "I hoped not. But yeah, I...I guess I knew."

"Well, I don't mind telling you this is freaking me out a little, Megan. Um...you don't mind if I call you Megan, do you?"

She shook her head, no. Good Lord, last night she was licking his belly and today he's wondering if it's ok to call her by her first name. How on earth could David ever respect her after how she had acted last night? But somehow it felt *right* to be with him, to freely offer herself to him and to want him so much it hurt. Like it was hurting right now, standing so close to him, but not allowed to reach out and touch him, not allowed to kiss him, like she did last night.

David escorted her to the waiting police car and opened the rear door. "Go home, get warm and get some sleep. I'll call you later, ok?" He didn't wait for an answer, but leaned forward and kissed her on the cheek. It seemed like the natural thing for him to do at the time. A reaction really, something he didn't plan to do, just did, spur of the moment. But it completely caught Megan off guard.

Not knowing what to say, she simply nodded and got into the car. Their eyes locked for a long moment before David finally closed the door and hit the roof of the car twice to signal the driver that it was time to go. Megan turned around in the seat and watched him out the back window of the car, standing by the side of the street, the heat of his breath swirling around his head like a halo.

She watched him until he was out of sight and then turned back around to see the police officer watching her intently in his rear view mirror, probably as shocked by the kiss from Detective Stark as she was.

She turned away from the officer's questioning stare and looked out the car window. The beautiful day was over and the once blue skies had turned dark and grey. She hugged herself tightly to warm herself and to ease the pain of not having him near her, her arms, physically aching to hold him again and her mouth, longing to once more taste his hot, salty skin.

This was as effective a torture as ever devised. Like giving a person who's dying of thirst just enough water to wet her lips and remind her just what it was she was missing. David reminded her exactly what was missing from her life, passion, excitement, the love of a man.

But David Stark wasn't going to fall in love with some psychic freak, like her. Oh, he might indulge in some physical contact, that much was evident by last night's little episode. But he couldn't truly love her or want her to be part of his life, could he?

Today he was just being overly kind to her to make up for how rotten he treated her last night. He simply needed her help with this case and nothing more. And she could live with that, if he just kept his distance and stopped doing things like putting his arm around her and kissing her, even if it was only a peck on the cheek.

It was hard enough to forget about last night as it was, she certainly didn't need him standing so close to her, reminding her how wonderful he smelled, or how easy it was to get lost in those dark, velvet eyes of his or how hot his lips felt against her skin.

If Detective Stark wanted nothing more than her help, he was going to have to find a way to stop being so damn gorgeous.

*   *   *   *

David felt Hudson's eyes watching him walk back up to the front porch of Brenda Parker's home.

"Ok, who is she?" He demanded. "Isn't she the chick in the picture, the one from the hotel last night? And don't tell me she's your date. I'm beginning to realize what a romantic you are, Stark, but bringing your date to a murder scene is beneath even you."

"Well, that's kind of what happened, she was just with me." David still wasn't ready to admit to his partner that he was running around town, chasing after the bogeyman in Megan's dreams. He didn't think Hudson believed the lie he told him about the anonymous tip from the restaurant that led him to this house and the body of Brenda Parker, but it was the best he could do right now. And it *was*, after all, more believable than the truth.

Hudson's nostrils flared. "Damn it, Stark! We're supposed to be partners, or didn't you get the memo? This makes the second time in two days you were first at a scene. And I've been around long enough to know it's not by coincidence, either. You're fucking on to something and I wanna know what the hell it is!"

"I don't know what to tell you, buddy." David told the truth. "I've just been in the right place at the right..." He stopped, the rage and distrust he saw in Hudson's eyes told him the man wasn't buying a word. It was no use to even try. He was only making it worse.

"I don't know how you fellows in vice work, but in homicide, we work together, as a team. What is it? You afraid I'll steal some of your glory?"

"It's not like that."

"Then tell me how the hell it is, I'd really like to know. I'm not sure what it is you're keeping from me or why, for that matter. But it has something to do with her, doesn't it?" Hudson shot the question at him and didn't wait for an answer. "Do you have any idea how bad it looks for her to be with you today and last night?"

David shrugged his shoulders and shook his head. "Listen, when I can explain it better, I will, I promise."

"Not fucking good enough! Like it or not, we are partners and that's suppose to mean something." Hudson stomped off the porch, got into his car and sped away. The other officers who had stopped to eavesdrop on the argument quickly got back to work when David flashed them a stern look.

What the hell was the matter with him? First, he was lying to his new partner, then he's out running all over the city with this woman who somehow knows shit before it even happens. David's head throbbed. It was crazy.

He jammed his fingers through his thick hair and squeezed against the pain in the back of his head. How in the hell did she know? Right down to the last fucking detail. It went against everything he believed in, that someone could predict the future like this, to see thing through the eyes of a killer before it even happened.

And how could a beautiful woman, like her, be on the same "wavelength" as a slaughtering psychopath? It just didn't fit into his nice, neat understanding of the world. David Stark believed in God and in love, but other than that, he needed hard tangible proof. He never believed in things like psychics, mind readers, spoon-benders, or ghosts before. But he *was* beginning to believe in Megan Montgomery. It wasn't like he had much of a choice.

CHAPTER 3

▼

FRIDAY, JANUARY 16TH

*   *   *   *

8:36 a.m.

"Did you hear there's been another murder?" Sue gasped out the latest tidbit of gossip.

Megan nodded as she walked in and stored her purse in the desk drawer. Sue tapped her finger on her chin. "I think I'm gonna go out after school today and buy myself a dog for protection."

"What happened to Bear?" Bear was Sue's 4 year-old schnauzer that Megan had the misfortune of meeting a few times.

"You mean 'Horny the Dog'? The dog who goes around humping everything that doesn't move?"

"And even things that do."

Sue grimaced. "Again, sorry about that. I had him fixed over a year ago, but that still seems to be all he's interested in doing."

"No biggy. He's just got a sex drive like his owner, that's all. I am however a little disappointed he never called."

"That's exactly why I need to go out and get a new dog." Sue held her hands palm up in the air. "I mean really, what's Bear gonna do if The Cutter happened to break into my house, hump him to death?"

"Good point."

They were laughing when the first of the chattering children started filing into the classroom.

*   *   *   *

8:47 a.m.

Across town at the police station, David knocked on Ted Miller's office door and poked his head inside. "Morning, Ted. Chief says you got something back on the Jones woman."

"Yeah." Ted looked up from his desk and sighed. "A whole lot of nothing."

"Damn it! You're kidding me. You didn't find anything?" David walked into the office and slumped down on the top of a nearby desk, crossing his arms in front of him. He was exhausted and this was bad news. Everyone thought there'd be some solid leads from this one. It looked like she put up a bit of a fight and he was sure there'd be skin and blood samples under her fingernails, at the very least.

"Oh no, we found lots of stuff." Ted looked down on his desk and pulled out a file from underneath a neatly stacked pile of manila file folders. "Let's see. There were several different semen samples, none of which matched the sample found by the jogger's body. And we found skin and blood samples under her nails among other stuff."

"Well, that's great." David straightened up.

"Not really. We've come up with at least five different skin samples so far. Seems our girl scratched a few backs since her last manicure."

"Still, we should be able to separate the samples, if only to nail the bastard after we catch him, right?"

"Doubt it. The samples are so mixed up and contaminated…"

"Contaminated? With what?"

"Glad you asked." Ted flipped up a sheet of paper in the file and read from the list, "Semen, urine, makeup, fingernail adhesive, traces of cocaine, what appears to be egg salad and last, but not least, my favorite, human feces, not hers."

"What?" David made a grimace that made Ted laugh out loud.

"Guess our girl stuck her fingers up someone's…."

"Alright! I get it. You can stop right there." David held his hand up and closed his eyes. "Just tell me, do we have *anything* at all to go on?"

"Not really. Sorry, Stark. We can probably back up an arrest, but it'd be so flimsy, it would never hold up, even with a court-appointed clown as his lawyer."

"You know, buddy, that's all you had to say." David walked out of the lab, shaking his head. He wasn't any closer to solving this fucking case than he was when it was first assigned to him.

Defeated, he plopped down at his desk and went back to sorting through the piles of photos taken at the murder scenes.

A few feet away, Hudson stood beside a chalkboard covered with the facts of each victim listed in columns. Photos of the murder scene were taped above each column and below them, words were written in chalk: "Victim #1, Diane Long, Nurse, Jan. 4th, appox 12:30 a.m., Legs. Victim #2, Brenda Parker, Waitress, Jan. 6th, appox 3:15 p.m., Hands. Victim #3, Kim Jordan, Jogger, Jan.10th, appox 5:00 a.m., Lower Torso. Victim #4, Dixie Jones, Hooker, Jan. 14th, appox 11:30 p.m., Hair & Arms."

Hudson turned to look at his returning partner. "Well? Ted have anything good for us?"

"Nothing."

"Shit! There wasn't anything from that hooker?"

"Yeah. Shit, as a matter of fact." David's lips twisted into a frustrated smirk as he ran his fingers through his hair and rubbed the back of his neck. He was so tired he could barely keep his eyes open. "The hooker had lots of samples. Skin, blood, semen, shit, coke, egg salad, all mixed together."

"Cocaine and egg salad. The perfect diet for any working girl."

"How do you deal with it?"

"With what?"

"This!" David held up an 8 X10 color photograph of Dixie Jones's bald, severed head. "I've seen more blood in the last month, than I did my whole time on vice."

"A little too late to admit you got a weak constitution, don't you think?"

"No, that's not it. It's just...I don't know how you guys don't lose it. I mean, she was just doing her thing one day and then the next, we're picking up pieces of her strewn across the floor. How do you get to where that doesn't bother you?"

Hudson turned to look at the chalkboard again. "Well, ya know, that's the difference between us and you guys on vice. The second she died, she became part of the evidence, like fingerprints or tire tracks." He turned around and looked at David again. "And you better learn that quick, if you want to make it here in the big leagues, boy. There's no time to dwell on the sadness of it all. It'll drive you insane."

David nodded and turned his attention to the board. "Well, our man is obviously building himself the perfect woman and he's not wasting any time, either. The question is, why? What happened to him? Why does he need to cut up women to satisfy him? Why would he need to *make* a woman? Because no woman's ever wanted him. Maybe he's still a virgin or he can't get it up, so he needs to make someone who won't laugh at him."

"That's the vice cop in you talking. Not everything's about sex, my boy. The real question is, what's he missing?" Hudson tapped his finger on his chin as he studied the chalkboard. "He has the hair, the arms, the hands, the ass and the legs. That leaves a pair of tits and a head. At the rate he's going, he'll finish this little project before another week is out. If he don't screw up soon, we might never find him."

"So, you think it's a one time thing?"

"Yes. I do. I'll bet he's never done anything else wrong in his life. But for some reason, right now, he needs to do this. It's more than just a project to him, it's his obsession, maybe even his only reason for living. He has to finish it or it would all be for nothing. But once it's done...well, why kill again when you finally have the perfect woman at home?"

"Maybe 'cause the perfect woman starts to rot."

Hudson turned around and shot David a dirty look. "You just don't get it, do you?" He shook his head and walked down the hall to the john.

"Apparently not," David said to the empty space where Hudson had been standing and lowered his tired head on top of the photos of severed body parts and crime scenes that were on his desk.

He wasn't sure what he thought of his new partner, Frank Hudson. Not that it mattered too much. It was only temporary anyway. Hudson was retiring in less than a year. He had been a good cop, a great cop, actually, almost a legend on the force. In his prime, he had cracked some of the toughest cases the department had ever seen and word got around about it.

But less than a year ago, Hudson's wife of thirty two years died in a car accident and he all but lost it. Word got around about that, too. When Hudson's long time partner retired, four or five months ago, there was no one else who wanted to work with him. No one trusted him anymore. He had lost his edge, they said. And your edge is a dangerous thing to lose in this line of work.

Being the low man of the totem pole, David was stuck with him. Not that he wasn't a good guy, he was mostly. And he was smart, experienced, seasoned. In just the last month, he had already taught David a lot about how to process a crime scene. It was just that, until David got a new partner, he figured he was just going to have to watch his own back

*   *   *   *

Banister stuck his head out of his office. "Hey you two. Get in here."

David and Hudson wearily pulled themselves away from their research and strolled into the chief's office.

"Sit down," Banister directed. "Um, I wanted to be the one to tell you…The mayor, she called in the Feds in last night, right after you found that Parker woman's body."

"Shit!" Hudson stood up and slammed his fist against the wall.

"They'll be here any minute," Banister said. "Look you guys, I'm counting on you to do your best to cooperate. I need your support and input with this. I know how tough it is to work with those guys. Most of them think their shit don't stink. They fucking take over and push us out like we're incompetent assholes or something."

Banister clamped his jaw shut and took a deep breath. "Here I am asking you guys to cooperate when I want to lock them out of the station myself." He stood up behind his desk, his hands, flat on his desk, supporting him as he leaned over it. "I'm not looking forward to having this case ripped out of your hands. You guys have worked hard, given me everything you got. And I want you to know, I appreciate it."

When neither of them said anything, Banister continued. "They're gonna stroll in here, flashing those badges they're so damn proud of, step on our toes, and treat you guys like second-class citizens. Just don't let it get to you."

"Sounds like you've had the displeasure of working with them before," David said.

Banister nodded. "Just remember, despite how it seems, they *are* here to help us."

"Are you trying to convince us or yourself?" Hudson asked.

Banister walked from behind his desk. "Maybe this time will be different. Lord knows, we could use some help nailing the psychopath we're dealing with." He put a hand on David's shoulder. "Stark, when they figure it out, they're gonna give you hell about being the one who's called in the last two murders. If I were you, I'd get my ducks in a row."

Hudson shot David a dirty look from the corner of the room.

David pushed his fingers through his curly hair. Fucking great. He couldn't even explain what was going on to his own partner, much less a couple of federal agents. Hell, he could hardly believe the shit that was going on himself and he was living it. The Feds would have him slapped in a straight jacket, if he told them how he found those bodies.

David turned to look out the chief's window at the old, cluttered police station, when he saw two men walk into the room, being escorted by a pretty rookie, putting her time in at the front desk, greeting visitors and running mail. The men were Feds, no doubt about it. They were decked out in perfectly pressed dark suits with white starched shirts, dark ties and polished black shoes.

Oh yeah, they stuck out like sore thumbs around here with the jeans, flannel shirts and wrinkled, old, brown suits that screamed 'detective's salary'. A few of the old-timers, including Hudson, always wore suits and ties. Granted they were cheap and out-dated, but they *were* suits and ties. But those guys were the exception. Most of the other younger guys didn't care too much about dressing up for the drug dealers, thieves and murdering scum they hung out with everyday.

David, himself, owned only two suits. One for weddings and funerals and the other one for court and that's exactly how he liked it. Besides, he decided a long time ago that if the department expected him to work ten to fifteen hours a day, damned if he wasn't going to be as comfortable as possible.

Banister was really the only one around there that had any sort of fashion sense, always ready for an impromptu TV interview. But he was on the political ladder and knew his appearance was always under scrutiny. It wouldn't do for the next mayor to be seen wearing jeans to work.

"Th ey 're h e r e," David imitated a line from the movie "Poltergeist".

"Great." Banister's voice dripped with sarcasm. "Just in time for the line up."

"What?" Hudson asked. "What line up?"

"We got that witness from the hotel to come in," David answered him.

There was a man leaving a room on the third floor of the hotel, the night of the murder, and he was able to give the police a description of a man he saw on the second floor. The description was pretty basic and they knew it, but when straws are all you had to grasp for, well, you do just that. Anyway, they got a sketch out on the streets. Unfortunately, the sketch was so generic it could fit just about any white male in his fifties of average build and weight. But until they had better, they would run with what they had.

For the line up, they brought in two men who fit the description and had been in or around the hotel the night Dixie Jones was murdered. They also brought in a man they picked up in the park where they found the body of Kim Jordan and a man who worked as an orderly at the hospital with Diane Long and had harassed her on several occasions. And a couple other men that fit the description the witness gave.

"Get in the line up, Hudson," Chief Banister barked. "We need a cop in there."

"What? Why me, Chief? I had to do the last one," he whined. "You remember. The one for that eighty year old woman. I was in there for almost an hour! Come on, have somebody else do this one. Stark. How 'bout Stark, he *is* the new guy."

"Hate to tell you this, Hudson, but you're one of the only old farts I have left around here. Now get your ass in there, before I start to take out my lack of sleep on you!"

"Fuck," Hudson said under his breath as he reluctantly walked out of the chief's office and into the holding room with the men the police had gathered up.

Chief Banister invited the visitors in his office with more enthusiasm than David thought he would be able to muster and offered his hand. "I'm Police Chief, Thad Banister, and this is Detective David Stark. Stark, along with Detective Frank Hudson, has worked on this case from the beginning."

David shook hands with the men after Banister.

"Special Agent, Ronald Dotson and Special Agent, Charles Blackburn," the tall black man introduced himself and his partner. They both flashed their badges and David could see Banister cringe.

"You're just in time," Banister said quickly. "We have a witness from The St. John's Hotel who saw an older Caucasian male in his mid fifties on the second floor on the night of the prostitute's murder. So, if you'll follow me, gentlemen."

Banister left the room with David close behind. The Feds cut David off at the door and followed closely behind Banister. David held out his hand in mock politeness and then followed after the two men.

The four of them waited in a small dark room with a large glass window in one wall. An officer, by the name of Ed Martin, walked the witness, Willie Moore, into the room. Ed Martin had been the officer who interrogated Willie Moore the night of the murder.

Willie had been with a 'friend' who had a room on the third floor. When he was finished with his 'visit,' he started down the stairs and saw a man walk out of a room on the second floor. He wasn't sure which room.

He told Officer Martin that he didn't get a very good look at him because he was afraid the man was the private investigator his wife had hired to follow him, so he immediately ducked out of sight. As feeble as it was, he was the only witness they had from any of the murders.

The ten suspects were led into a well-lit room on the other side of the glass window. Each of the men stood under a number.

"Mr. Moore, this is a one way mirror so these men can't see or hear you," Officer Martin explained. "So, I want you to take your time and let us know if any of these men could be the same man you saw leaving the hotel the night of the murder."

Willie Moore carefully studied the faces of the suspects, pushing his glasses up on his forehead and back down over his eyes. Stark looked over at Banister and shook his head. This man's testimony would never stand up in court. But perhaps he could still give them the lead they needed.

After ten or fifteen minutes, Willie Moore shook his head and shrugged his shoulders. "Well, it was dark, ya know. And all I know fur sure is he was around fifty or fifty-five and white and carryin' a black bag." Willie scanned the suspects again. "But ifen my life depended on it, I'd say that number seven looks a lot like him but so does that number nine guy."

Number seven was Craig Freeman. The police had picked him up for questioning after a woman jogger had seen him masturbating in the same general area where the body of Kim Jordan was found. That was an interesting lead. Number nine was Detective Frank Hudson.

David stepped up beside Willie Moore. "Look closely, Mr. Moore. See if you can't narrow it down between the two of them."

After another minute of squinting and opening his eyes as wide as they would go, Willie Moore shook his head slowly. "Nope. Coulda been either one of those fellows. Or neither one, for that matter. Can't say fur sure. It was dark, ya know."

Banister looked at the two federal agents and when it was apparent they weren't going to add anything, he opened the door to let Willie Moore out. "Thank you for your time, Mr. Moore. If you think of anything else, please call us. Officer Martin will give you a card and see you out."

"Sorry I couldn't be of better help to ya. I was tryin' hard to stay hid, ya know."

"Well, if we need anything more, we'll be in touch." Banister shook his hand and turned back to David.

"Great," David said, after the witness left the room.

"Well, I believe that to be a dead-end, sir," Agent Dotson announced. "The man obviously doesn't have a clue. I'm not so sure he even saw anyone. Chief

Banister, if you would be so kind, my partner and I would like to have a private office and a copy of all the files from this case."

"Certainly," Banister said, walking to the door. "I'll see to it right away. Would you like to go over anything with Stark, here, or Hudson before you get started?"

"Not at this time," Dotson said, raising his chin a little higher than it already was. "My partner and I like to draw our own conclusions from the facts of the case. Maybe we will question your detectives later."

"If you think it'd be worth your time." David clamped his jaw shut and looked around. Had he said that out loud? He hadn't meant to, but now that it was out there, there wasn't a damn thing he could do about it.

Banister cleared his throat and opened the door. "Shall we?" He showed the Feds out of the room and tossed a stern look over his shoulder to David before closing the door behind him.

A few seconds later, Hudson opened the door to the small room and looked in. "So? Do we have our Cutter?"

"Yeah, you." David walked out of the room and Hudson followed.

"Shit, really? He gave us nothing?"

"Not necessarily." David's pace quickened as he continued, "Moore also fingered Craig Freeman, the guy they picked up whacking off in the woods where the jogger's body was found."

"There was semen found by the body of the jogger, wasn't there? All we have to do is match it up to his and boom….we got our man."

"I don't know, something doesn't jive. Why didn't he jack off by the other bodies? Why get all excited about the jogger and not the naked hooker or the nurse? No." David shook his head. "Doesn't make any sense."

"Oh, I'm sure that would be a first." Hudson threw his hands up in the air. "A psychopathic killer not making any sense."

"I just don't know."

"But if the semen puts him at one murder scene and this witness puts him at another," Hudson argued, "that's gotta count for something."

"This witness also puts you there, too. Don't forget that." David picked up the phone on his desk and dialed a number. "Hey, this is Stark. Can you get me a search warrant for Craig Freeman's home, pronto? Oh yeah, I need his rap sheet, too. Thanks." He hung up the phone, grabbed his jacket and zipped it up. "What do you say we pay our friend, Craig Freeman, a little visit?"

*   *   *   *

1:35 p.m.

It didn't take long to get a search warrant. Freeman had quite a record and this was such a high profile case, everyone was willing to jump through hoops to help out. The Feds stayed at the station to go over all the files on the case, while David, Hudson, Ted Miller and two other officers searched Freeman's apartment.

"Damn," Hudson said, flipping through the thick file folder in his hand. "The rap sheet on this bastard reads like a pervert's guide to Cleveland. He's been picked up everywhere. Hell, he's even been arrested once for jacking off at an Indian's game. He was doing it right there on the homerun patio!"

"That musta been back when they were good," David joked.

"Hey." Ted Miller stopped crawling around on the floor, gathering samples from Freeman's carpet. "Don't hold that against the man. I almost spewed myself when they won the pennant in '95."

"I'm pretty sure I did!" Hudson added.

David went back to searching Freeman's bedroom closet and came across a big wooden trunk pushed way in the back of it. He pulled it out into the center of the room, knelt down beside the chest and opened it carefully. "Well, would you look at this," he said, looking inside.

Hudson and Ted gathered around the open chest. The top tray was filled with gothic looking knives and swords. Ted motioned for a uniformed officer to bag the weapons so he could check them for prints and blood back at the lab. Once the top tray was empty, David pulled it out, revealing an interesting assortment of gadgets inside.

"Holy shit," David said, pulling out a weird looking sexual apparatus with his thumb and index finger. "What the hell is this for?"

"Where are you supposed to stick that?" Hudson asked.

"That, gentlemen, is what's known as butt beads," Ted offered. "Rather large ones, but that's what they are."

David grimaced. He looked at it and then at Ted. "You know, man, I'm not even gonna ask you how you know that."

Ted looked over David's shoulder. "Anything else in there?"

David dropped the toy back in the chest and stood up. "No way. I'm not touching anything else in there. Even with my gloves on. Damn! I thought I'd seen it all, but I couldn't even tell you what half this stuff is for."

Ted bent down and picked up a twenty inch dildo that was about three inches diameter and held it up. "Bet you know what this is for."

✳   ✳   ✳   ✳

3:27 p.m.

Banister called David and Hudson into his office as soon as they got back from Freeman's apartment. "Those two Feds are already driving me crazy," he said. "We gotta catch this guy, and now. Well? Get anything?"

David slid his fingers through his hair. "Not much, chief. He had some swords and knives we brought in. Ted's looking them over right now."

"Don't forget the chest full of toys," Hudson piped up.

"Toys?" Banister asked.

"Yeah," David explained. "The guy's a full blown perv, for sure. He had more gadgets than…Well, let's just say, he could open up his own shop."

"Well." Banister opened a file on his desk. "Our friend has an impressive record."

"Yeah, but nothing violent," David said.

"Maybe not yet," Hudson added.

Banister flipped through the file and pointed to a sheet of paper. "Says right here, Freeman was charged with, but never convicted, of fondling a woman at a movie theater. The woman didn't wish to testify in court, so the case was dropped."

Hudson stood up and walked over to Banister's desk. "You never can tell with these guys. One day they can just snap. And maybe he did."

Banister closed the file and hit it with his fist. "I want you two on him like white on rice. If he takes a shit, I want you to smell it before he does, got it?"

"Right, chief," Hudson said as he flew out the door with David close behind him.

*   *   *   *

6:16 p.m.

Megan sat in a cushy, purple booth in the corner of O'Hara's, waiting for Bill Peak to arrive. O'Hara's was an upscale restaurant just minutes from downtown. She'd been there once or twice before and enjoyed the food as well as the atmosphere. It had a contemporary decor with gold, dark purple and burnt orange textured walls and low hanging inverted cone-shaped lights glowing over every table. The place had a warm, soothing feel about it. But it was going to take a lot more than the color of the walls to calm Megan's nerves.

She ordered another rum and Coke and looked at her watch. Two minutes later than the last time she looked. God, she wished she hadn't said yes to this ridiculous date.

Sue meant well, but Megan still wanted to kill her. She looked at her watch again. Bill was sixteen minutes late and she had decided ten minutes ago that twenty minutes was a more than fair amount of time to wait before she made her escape. No one could blame her for not waiting more than twenty minutes. She'd even leave a note with the hostess, that way, if he finally did show up, he wouldn't think she had stood him up.

Suddenly a horrible thought entered her mind. Maybe she was the one being stood up. He had set this thing up, him and Sue, and now he wasn't even going to bother showing up. What was wrong with that man? And what did he think was wrong with her? She might not be the best looking girl he'd ever seen, but he could do a lot worse. What was she thinking? This was a blessing in disguise. Megan smiled and took another swallow of her drink. Bill standing her up wouldn't be such a bad thing after all.

"Hey," Bill said as he hung up his coat on the hook behind Megan's seat.

"Oh, hi." Megan sat up straight in her chair, wiped her sweaty palms off on her blue skirt and hoped Bill wouldn't notice the disappointment in her voice or on her face.

"Sorry I'm late. Traffic was horrible." He sat down on the bench across from her and let out a big sigh. "I allotted myself twenty-six minutes to get here, but the east side traffic was a nightmare. I mean, we get a little snow on the road and people turn into complete idiots. I really don't know how some people even get their driver's license at all. If they're gonna act like that when it snows, they shouldn't be allowed on the road again until spring."

Bill stopped, took a deep breath and smiled.

"Oh, that's ok, I haven't been here long." Megan mustered up a smile for him and tried to remind herself why she was here, but for the life of her, she couldn't remember. She wished it was David sitting across from her. Oh yeah, David. That's why she agreed to this date in the first place. To prove to David and to herself that she didn't need him, that there were plenty of other fish in the sea.

"Ready to order, now?" The waiter asked anxiously. Megan had tied up his table for almost twenty minutes waiting for Bill and it was cutting into his tip money.

"Sure," Megan said, happy to rush this date right along, too. "I'd like the blackened chicken with the house salad and ranch dressing on the side, please. And another rum and Coke, when you get a chance."

"And for you, sir?"

Bill picked up the menu and flung it open, obviously not happy about being rushed. After a few seconds, he ordered. "Smothered pork chop with a baked potato, just butter and an ice tea. And make sure there's just butter on the baked potato. Last time I was here, they put sour cream on it and I hate sour cream. Do you think you can see to that, butter only? If I get sour cream, I will send it back."

The waiter nodded. "Yes, sir. Butter only. I've got it. I'll be right out with your drinks."

Megan offered a smile as a silent apology to the waiter, hoping he wouldn't spit in their food, or at least not hers.

She sat there inspecting the flatware. This was torture, slow and painful torture. It would be different if this was a date with David. They probably wouldn't even be able to finish their dinner before they had to get alone. It was like that with him. Even with all the horrible things going on around them, whenever he was near her, she couldn't keep from thinking about how much she wanted to be with him. If they were standing in the middle of a burning building, her only thoughts would be of his dimples and his eyes and how much she wanted to kiss him.

It was sick, really. Not normal at all. But she had accepted it. She had gotten a small taste of what it felt like to be in his arms and she was determined to get herself back into them as soon as possible. Megan looked across the table at Bill and forced a smile. The poor guy didn't stand a chance with David Stark on her mind.

Bill wasn't a bad looking guy. As a matter of fact, he was handsome really, in a studious and tense kind of way. His sandy blond hair was cut short and tousled in the front. His complexion was light and at about five foot ten, he had a nice build. The funny thing was, she hadn't even noticed before now, even though he had sat beside her in class all semester.

David, on the other hand, demanded her full attention from the first second she saw him in the lobby of the St. John's Hotel. Honestly, even before that, when she had talked to him on the phone. Yeah, that poor sap across from her didn't stand a chance.

"So, how's your student teaching going?" Megan asked, trying to make small talk.

"Fine. Just fine. I enjoy it, enough. Though I wish I had a little more responsibility with the class. Sometimes I feel like I'm just an observer, an overqualified babysitter. I don't get to do as much as I'd like, but I guess that's what us pee-ons get. No respect, no trust. All we are to those teachers are..." Bill stopped and took a deep, calming breath. "How about you, Megan?" He smiled at her. "How's your student teaching going?"

Megan stared at him, her eyes dry from not being able to blink. Wow, where had that come from? "Um." Megan snapped out of her momentary daze and cleared her throat. "I...I love it, really. Sue Johnson is great and the kids are so much fun. I can't wait to graduate and have my own class."

"Yeah, like we could actually get our own class," Bill interrupted her. "You do know there's a waiting list of dozens of applicants at every school for every single position, don't you? Like we even stand a chance of getting a job. It's just a bullshit dream the college feeds us, so we keep on paying our tuition and the college keeps getting richer. We're no closer to getting a job than we were back in high school."

Megan looked around the restaurant, desperately trying to contact the waiter telepathically and beg him to hurry up with their food. Because the sooner the food got to the table, the sooner they could eat it and the sooner she could get the hell out of there.

Megan spent the entire dinner watching as Bill Peak would start talking about something, get worked up about it to the point of almost shouting, then calm himself down and change the subject. She could sense there was something bubbling up inside him, just beneath the surface. No matter what subject they discussed, food, the weather, his family, Bill would find some way to become angry about it. It would have been kind of funny, if it wasn't so scary. She was glad they hadn't become friends before. He was exhausting and more than a little creepy.

Mercifully, the waiter finally brought the check. Megan immediately turned it over and began searching her purse for her wallet.

"No." Bill put his hand over the bill and pulled it to him. "I've got it."

"No, really, let me get mine. This was just a friendly get together and I prefer to pay for my own."

"I couldn't. I could never let my date pay for her own meal. I mean, what kind of man do you think I am?"

That was a question Megan didn't dare answer. "But, really, Bill. It wouldn't be fair. My drinks cost more than your entire meal. Please, let me get it."

"*I.... said....no.*" Every word sent shivers down her spine and she decided it was best not to argue anymore. She wasn't about to be the one that sent that guy over the edge, which, she was sure, was just a matter of time before it happened.

He was like a volcano inside, simmering up and cooling down, simmering up and cooling down, until, when you least expected it, boom, a massive eruption. Megan didn't want to be anywhere near this guy when he finally blew and she hoped he wouldn't be responsible for a room full of children at the time, either.

"Well, thank you very much," Megan said, trying to sound as gracious as possible, while hiding the fact she wanted nothing more than to run screaming from the restaurant.

The waiter returned with the change and Bill pocketed every cent before standing up to get Megan's coat. She stood up and he helped her on with it. While he was busy putting on his own coat, she discreetly dropped a twenty on the table for the poor waiter who had to suffer through that dinner, too.

Bill placed a hand on her back and escorted her out of the restaurant. "What movie would you like to see?" He asked, standing unbearably close to her.

Megan backed away from him. "Oh, no, um, I...I can't really. I really need to get home now." She opened her mouth to offer some sort of excuse, but closed it again. She didn't really want to lie to the man and telling him the truth was just not an option.

"Come on!" Bill moved closer. "It's early and we're just getting to know each other. I've had a great time and I don't want it to end so soon."

Could he have possibly been on the same date as she was? There were a lot of words she could use to describe tonight, but 'great' was not one of them. And now that she could smell freedom and see her getaway car, there was just no stopping her. "I really can't," she said, more forcefully this time. "Thanks for the dinner, though. It was very....nice. Have a great weekend."

Megan started toward the crosswalk that led to the parking lot across the street, but Bill was right behind her. He grabbed her arm and spun her roughly around to face him. "I *said* I don't want it to end so soon." Then, with his free hand, he picked up a strand of her hair and put it to his nose, closed his eyes and deeply inhaled. "I love how you smell."

Ok, now she was worried. She felt a little nauseous in the pit of her stomach as her mind began to formulate her escape options. Could she outrun him to her car or should she make a break for it and run back into the restaurant to get some help? She tried to pull away from him gently, not wanting to upset him, but he pulled her closer to him.

The palms of Megan's hands were flat against his chest, pushing hard, trying in vain to widen the space between them when he leaned forward and kissed her, his tongue trying to force its slobbery way inside her mouth.

Megan clenched her lips and teeth together tightly and turned her face away from him. "That's enough. Please let go of me!" The slimy wetness on her face was making her ill and she just barely resisted the urge to gag.

"But I don't think you know just how I feel about you, Megan," he whispered in the ear she had turned towards him before sticking his tongue inside it, causing her to shudder and throw her shoulder up under his chin.

"Please, let go of me, right now."

His grip tightened.

"I don't want to make a scene, but if you don't take your hands off of me right now...I swear I will scream! You have exactly five seconds."

"Why, you little bitch!" He pushed her away, full force, and she stumbled backwards, nearly falling to the ground before eventually regaining her balance. She didn't say another word, only walked to her car as fast as she could without breaking into a full blown run. All the while, watching him over her shoulder, as he stood there, shooting daggers at her.

She opened her car door, got in and instantly locked the doors before wiping his disgusting saliva off her ear and mouth with her glove. She pulled out of the parking lot and left him alone, fuming on the sidewalk in front of O'Hara's. But before she went home and locked all her windows and doors, she was going to drop by Sue's apartment and give her a little piece of her mind.

*   *   *   *

7:59 p.m.

Sue opened the door to her apartment. "Well, I can see by your expression, you're not here to thank me for hooking you up with the man of your dreams."

"Not even close." Megan walked through the doorway, hands set firmly on her hips.

"Sorry."

"I know you meant well, but if you ever do this to me again, Susan Johnson, I will kill you with my bare hands!"

"That bad, aye?"

"Unbelievable. The man is a complete skitzo. I'm not lying, I was afraid he was going to…."

"Down, Bear!" Sue interrupted when she noticed her dog's instant attraction to Megan's right leg. "I'm sorry," she apologized, pulling the grey pooch off of Megan by his collar. The dog dug all four paws into the floor as Sue dragged him across the room. Folds of skin and fur pushed up over the red collar, distorting his face as he whimpered out his objections.

"Damn dog!" Sue scolded him and slammed the bedroom door, imprisoning her amorous pet. "I honestly don't know what to do with him. The vet said he'd grow out it, but I don't know." Bear let out a few doggy curse words before realizing in was useless and quieted down.

"I'm really sorry to bother you," Megan said. "I just didn't want to go home so early. You know Nancy, she was hoping I got lucky tonight."

"Me too." Sue smiled. "Come on, let's have some tea. I'm kinda glad you're here anyway. I've just been reading an article in the newspaper about The Cutter and it was giving me the heebie jeebies. So, I'm glad for the company."

Megan followed Sue into the kitchen and sat down at the small red and chrome table. "Looks like you were ready for bed."

Sue looked down at her red flannel pajamas and white fluffy slippers. "Na, just relaxing. No where to go tonight. I'm pretty bored, actually. Watching Bear molest my furniture gets a little old after awhile, ya know."

Sue filled a stainless steel kettle with water from her kitchen faucet. She turned a black knob on her old stove and the gas burner ticked a few times before a blue flame rose up. She adjusted the knob and sat the kettle on top of the flame.

"Name your poison," she said, opening one of the cupboards over her kitchen counter. "I got raspberry, lemon…" She moved a box of Corn Flakes. "Cinnamon spice and chamomile."

"Cinnamon spice sounds great, thanks."

She took the box from the cupboard, opened it and took a big sniff. "Ahhhh." After opening another cupboard, she pulled out two mugs, one with Christmas bears dancing around it and the other one covered with bright pink and purple flowers. She tossed a tea bag into each before turning to face Megan. "OK. Spill it, sister." Sue leaned her back against the counter and crossed her arms in front of her. "Tell me exactly what you think is wrong with Bill Peak."

"A lot of things. He tried to stick his tongue down my throat for one."

"Sounds like a successful date to me."

"You wouldn't say that, if you were there. It was gross, really. And he kept going off on these tangents. Getting all angry and stuff. Really freaked me out. The man's got issues, big time."

"I can't believe he's as bad as you're making him out to be. I mean, I know he's no Detective Stark, but...."

"What? Why would you say that?"

"C'mon, I'm not stupid. That cop was checking up on you because he's got the hots for you. Why else would he ask me if you had a boyfriend?"

"He asked you if I had a boyfriend?"

"Yes."

"Well, that doesn't mean he's got the hots for me." Or did it?

"Beg to differ with you, girlfriend. I could tell he did when I was talking to him. And you know what else? I think you got the hots for him right back."

"Sue. Don't be silly. I just had...I'm just helping him out on a case. That's all."

"A case?" Sue's eyes widened as she learned forward. "Like a police case? With bad guys and everything? How exciting!" She practically jumped in the chair across from Megan. "Tell me everything."

"I can't really talk about it right now."

"I promise, I won't tell. Who am I gonna tell, anyway? Come on, please, tell me."

"I can't. Not right now. Ok?"

"No, it's not ok," Sue pouted. "Nothing exciting ever happens around here. And when it finally does, I won't even hear about it until it's all over."

"Sorry," Megan offered her apology over the loud whistling of the tea kettle.

"It's not fair." Sue got up, turned her back to Megan and splashed some hot water into the mugs.

$$* \quad * \quad * \quad *$$

9:21 p.m.

Scheduling difficulties forced David and Hudson to pull double shifts in order to watch Freeman's apartment. So, instead of having both of them exhausted, David volunteered for the late watch. Hudson went home to get some sleep and then he would relieve David first thing in the morning.

It had been a long, hectic day, but once alone in the cold and quiet darkness of his car, David's thoughts rushed back to Megan. She was going to be his downfall, yet. He caught himself thinking about her more and more and it didn't always have to do with the case, either. He was going to have to have her soon, before it drove him completely insane. But things between them were complicated, to say the least.

When he was seventeen, he and his future wife, Sherry would spend an hour or two making out, before she'd have to be home. Then midnight would roll around and he'd be left, all horned up, alone in his car. That torment was nothing compared to what he was going through now. Taking Megan Montgomery into his arms and making love to her was becoming more important to him than sleeping or eating. And it scared the shit out of him.

David glanced at his watch. It wasn't quite nine-thirty, yet. He unclipped his cell phone from his belt and dialed Megan's number. When he last saw her at Brenda Parker's house, he told her he'd call her later and he really did need to follow up with her on a few things.

They had taken photos of the knives they found in Freeman's apartment and he wanted her to take a look at them. He also had a book of weapons, Ted had given him, and he was hoping she would be able to identify the weird looking hacksaw from her nightmare.

That would be his excuse for calling and it was a good one, it was legitimate. She wouldn't have to know how much he wanted to hear her voice again or how much he wished she was with him, right now, beside him, beneath him, holding him, kissing him, finishing what she started the other night in his apartment.

"Hello," Nancy answered the phone.

The vision of Megan licking his stomach scurried out of his mind. "Um, hi, this is uh, Detective Stark, David. I was wondering if I could please speak to Megan."

"Oh. I'm sorry, David, she's out. On a date."

"A date?" He hadn't meant to say that out loud or let Nancy hear all the shock and distress that came out with it.

"Why yes. Nice guy. Well, I haven't met him, yet, but he sounds real nice. Guess he likes Megan a whole lot. But who wouldn't?"

"Um, yeah, of course. Who wouldn't?"

Megan was out on a date? Shit! He had gotten the impression she didn't date. He had gotten the impression she was free and he was counting on that.

"But I don't know," Nancy continued. "I kinda got the feeling Meg had her sights on someone else, but I guess I was wrong. What do I know, anyhow? I mean, who could it be? There hasn't been anyone else around here. Besides, you, of course." She paused long enough for the words to sink in. "Oh, I don't know, maybe this guy will turn out to be the one for her. Unless, of course, that someone else lets her know he's interested, before it's too late."

What was that old woman babbling about? David's head was reeling. Megan was on a date...with a man. And she could be kissing him right now. And it could be with the same hot passion she kissed him with the other night. Well, why shouldn't she be? It wasn't as if she had any obligation to David. It was Friday night and she was a young, beautiful woman. A young, beautiful woman that he just might be in love with. Jealousy washed over him and heat rushed to his face.

"Detective Stark? You still there? David? Hello?"

"Sorry. My...my cell phone is fading in and out," David lied. "Um, well, tell her that I called and was just wondering how she was. I mean, I just wanted to know if she's remembered anything else. Oh, and I need to have her look at some photos for me. What time did she say she'd be home?"

"She didn't say, really. And if things are going well, they might not get home until real late. You know how it is with young people today."

"Um...yeah...I, I guess."

"Well, goodbye now," she sang out.

"Bye." David could have sworn he heard a muffled giggle, before he pushed the end button on his cell phone and lowered it into his lap.

He stared out the windshield of his car and pictured Megan in a sexy red dress, with the arms of a tan, blonde hunk around her. The guy probably seduced her with champagne and roses, because that's what a beautiful, sensual woman like Megan deserved. He would have kissed her, by now. And his kisses would have continued down her neck, down to her....

"Oh, damn," David said out loud and shook his head. "It's gonna be a long fucking night."

CHAPTER 4

▼

SATURDAY, JANUARY 17TH

*   *   *   *

3:30 a.m.

It wasn't daylight, yet, when Hudson jumped into the passenger's side of David's car. "Mornin' partner. Have some coffee." He handed David a large tan textured styrofoam cup with drawings of coffee beans on it.

David wrapped both hands around it and let the warmth seep into his frozen fingers. "Oh, thank you." He took a big whiff of the strong liquid energy. "I really needed this. The last hour's been murder. Man, am I glad you're here to take over. Another half hour and I'd be a goner." He tilted the cup and took a long swallow of the coffee and bit into the blueberry muffin Hudson handed him. "You are a life saver.

"Anything exciting happen?" Hudson motioned toward the brick apartment building across the street with his head.

David frowned. "Freeman hasn't moved all night. Well, except to walk down to the corner at about twelve-thirty to buy a T and A magazine and a bottle of 151. He went straight back to his apartment, probably to have some fun with his hand, since we took all his toys away."

"That guy's incredible for his age. Wonder how many times he gets it up in a day? He's a medical marvel, really. We should call Guinness and have him nominated." Hudson laughed at his own joke.

"Well, six straight hours of staring at the side of a brick building is about my limit, I'm outta here."

"Yeah, I'll take over from here." Hudson yawned. "Turner's gonna take over at nine-thirty and then I'll meet you back here at about…three-thirty this afternoon, right?"

"That's the plan."

"Good. Now go home, get a little shut eye and for God's sake take a fucking shower, would ya, pal?" Hudson winked at him and punched him in the right shoulder before getting out of David's car and walking back to his own.

David was heading home and straight for bed. He had to rest his brain, quit thinking for awhile. Because if he wasn't thinking about the case, he was thinking about Megan and both subjects confused the hell out of him.

*   *   *   *

9:21 a.m.

After only five hours of much needed sleep, David woke surprisingly refreshed. And he was glad, because he had a lot to do today. He needed to find Megan this morning and show her the pictures of the knives and swords they confiscated from Freeman's apartment. From what she had told him about the weapons she saw in her dreams, he doubted Freeman's collection was what they were looking for, but it was worth a shot.

Ted, the head of forensics, had also given him a thick book with pictures of all kinds of different tools and weapons to show her. Maybe there would be something in there that she could identify.

He also needed to get to the station. Sometime last night, while he sat alone thinking about Megan and the case, he decided to request some information on that Peter Logan character from West Virginia, the man she had helped put in jail. There were a lot of loose ends and questions when it came to Megan and her gift, or curse, or ability or whatever it was she wanted to call it. Maybe David could make some kind of sense out of the whole thing, if he just did a little research. Not likely, but also worth a shot.

David pushed the thick, blue and yellow plaid comforter off him and threw his legs over the side of the bed. He clasped his hands together and stretched them up over his head, trying to work out the kinks in his back and neck. Sitting in a car for six hours straight sure could take its toll on the old body and he wasn't looking forward to the six more hours he had to put in this afternoon. After stretching both his arms behind his back and rolling out the soreness in his achy shoulders, he pushed himself out of bed and wandered into the kitchen to start some coffee.

Once the coffee pot was loaded with the aromatic, black granules and switched on, he headed to the bathroom. David had been so beat when he got home, he just stripped and jumped into bed. A nice hot shower should do the trick, not only to warm him up, but hopefully help soothe his aching muscles, as well.

He twisted at the waist, first right, then left. He wished he had time to get to the gym today. He was abusing his body and it was definitely letting him know about it. David leaned over the bathroom sink and closely inspected his face in the mirror. God, did he look rough. He rubbed his fingers over his cheeks. He needed a shave in the worst way, but beyond that, he looked worn out, really tired.

He was glad his mother was in Florida for the winter, staying with his sister, Karen, and her family. Otherwise she'd be popping him so full of vitamins and herbal supplements right now, he would rattle when he walked. He smiled in the mirror at the thought of his mom. He missed her. She left town right after Christmas, like she did every year since she retired and wouldn't be back again until April.

His mom would like Nancy Montgomery. As a matter of fact, they'd probably get along great together. Yeah, he could see them becoming the best of friends, for sure. And his mom would like Megan, too.

Megan. He had to see her today and not just because he had questions for her or pictures for her to look at. He had to see her today, because he wouldn't be able to focus on anything else until he did. Of course, he wasn't sure seeing her would be a cure. Chances were it would only make matters worse.

If he hadn't kissed her the first night they met, if he hadn't gotten that tiny little taste of her, that little feel of her, soft and warm in his arms, maybe then he would be thinking straight, right now. Maybe then he wouldn't be spending so much of his energy trying to imagine just what would have happened, if Hudson hadn't called.

For a while, he was actually relieved the call interrupted them. He shouldn't have let himself get into that situation in the first place. But now, now he was consumed by his wanting her. It's not like he hadn't wanted a woman before, especially if he hadn't had sex in a while. But that was just being horny. Horny he felt in his dick. This…this was coming from somewhere else. These feelings he had for Megan were coming from deep inside his chest, his stomach, his gut.

Would it have helped, if he were able to make love to her that first night? He doubted it. For some reason he figured one taste of that woman couldn't possibly be enough to satisfy his hunger.

He looked down and saw what thinking about Megan was doing to him and wished she was there, so he could put it to good use.

*   *   *   *

10:15 a.m.

His first stop that morning was Megan's house. David knocked on the door and was just about to push the door bell, when Nancy cracked open the door and stuck her head through the opening.

"Oh, it's you, David." She opened the door fully and waved him in. "How nice to see you. Come in, come in. It's freezing out there, this morning." She bunched up her pink robe, tightly around her neck, and shivered. "It's not fit for man nor beast out there today."

He walked in and moved aside, so she could close the door. "I'm sorry to bother you so early on a Saturday. I hope I didn't wake you."

"Oh, good golly no." She motioned for him to follow her into the kitchen. "Meg opens the shop for me on Saturdays, so I can sleep in a little. Isn't she a dear?"

Realizing she wasn't going to continue until he answered her, he said, "Yes, she is."

"I never can. Sleep in, that is. But at least I get to be lazy and sit around the house drinking coffee and readin' the paper."

"So, she's not home?" David hoped she wouldn't pick up on the disappointment in his voice.

"No. We open the shop at nine, but she usually gets there by about eight. I didn't really hear her leave this morning. Come to think of it, I didn't hear her come home last night, either."

"Really?"

"Coffee?" Nancy asked cheerfully, holding up the pot.

"No, thanks." David smelled the sweet aroma of cherry tobacco and looked around the kitchen. "Oh, I'm sorry. You have company." He motioned to the lit pipe lying in a green glass ashtray in the middle of the kitchen table.

"No." She filled up her cup.

"It's yours?"

"Yes."

"*You* smoke a pipe?"

Nancy laughed. "No, I don't smoke it. I just light it, now and again. It was Elmer's, my late husband's."

"Oh. I'm sorry."

"It's ok." Nancy put her hand on David's shoulder. "It's not as pathetic as it sounds." She sat down at the table. "Well, I don't know, maybe it is." She laughed again.

David leaned back against the counter.

"Elmer died back in '83. Mining accident. But we were married fifteen wonderful years. We tried to have kids, but just weren't able to. So when Meg came along, we adored her. Spoiled her rotten, really. Elmer was there to see her first tooth and her first steps. Her first word was even "Mer." That's what she called him. Anyway, Meg don't remember him, 'cause she was just a little thing when he went home to glory." She put a finger to her chin and shook her head in disbelief. "Can't believe it's been over twenty years ago."

She was quiet for a few seconds and then took a sip of coffee. "Anyhow, we were so happy, I just couldn't bear packing up all his stuff and pretend like he never even existed. I love havin' some of his things around as kind of a reminder of him. I have this pipe and one of his old razors is upstairs on the bathroom counter. And the robe I bought him for his last Christmas still hangs next to mine on the back of my bedroom door," she said proudly. "That's about all that's left, now. But it's enough to bring a smile to my face, when I see 'em. Happy memories." She nodded her head thoughtfully before taking another sip of coffee.

David looked at the old woman and smiled. "You two must have been very happy."

"Oh, yes. Absolutely. It's a wonderful thing to have the person you love sharing your life with you." Nancy paused and a slow smile came to her lips. "Which reminds me, Meg is done at noon, that's when I take over. Why don't you stop over to the shop a little before twelve, so you two can have some lunch together? Wouldn't that be nice?"

David nodded and scratched his head just above his left ear. "But what if she already has plans?"

Nancy threw her hands up in the air, dismissing his question. "Oh, I'm sure she'd be just tickled to death to see you. And what would it cost you to find out? A couple of minutes?"

David shrugged his shoulders, she had a point.

"Do you know where the shop is?"

"No."

Nancy immediately jumped up, pulled a pencil and piece of paper out of a kitchen drawer and started scribbling down the address. This woman was good. Her middle name should be cupid. In a matter of minutes, she tried to make him jealous, as if he wasn't already, *and* gave him an excuse to go see Megan, as if he needed one.

"Here ya go." Nancy handed him the piece of paper.

"Thanks. I'll let myself out." David walked back down the hall to the front door.

"Sure you don't want a cup of hot coffee for the road, David? It's mighty cold out there this morning," she called out from the kitchen.

"No, thanks. I'm fine. See ya later."

"Bye, bye," he heard her say as he closed the door behind him.

The first thought that popped into his mind on the way back to the car was whether or not Megan even came home last night. The thought of her in another man's arms, another man's bed, was driving him crazy. Jealousy bubbled up inside him, as visions of her with that tan, blonde guy kissing her, holding her, making love to her, flashed in his brain.

He pushed the fingers of both his hands through his hair and squeezed the back of his head. He had to stop this. It was unhealthy. He had to stop obsessing over her and focus on his work. He had a case to solve. He would just have to deal with stealing her away from her hunky surfer boy later.

*   *   *   *

On his way to Nancy's flower shop, David passed a little shop on Euclid Avenue called "The Lights of Utopia." He'd seen the store before and knew it was one of those new age-witchcraft-UFO-past lives kind of stores, but he never gave it a second thought before today. Maybe someone in there could answer a few questions he had about Megan and her nightmares.

He parked his car and walked inside. As the door opened, wind chimes tinkled and the heady fragrance of incense instantly swallowed him. Crystals, tarot cards, books, wands, candles, little figurines and cups of colored stones filled every nook and cranny.

David brushed his hand across the massive collection of books covering one entire wall. There were books on everything from reading auras to discovering past lives. He snickered when he noticed the title of one book, 'How to Turn Your Ex into the Rat He is.'

"May I help you?" A woman behind him asked.

David cleared his throat, hoping she hadn't heard him laugh. "Oh, you know, I really don't think so." He was having second thoughts about this latest bright idea of his when he turned around to see a woman walk around the sales counter.

She was in her mid-thirties, with shoulder length, curly, brown hair, blue eyes and a warm friendly smile. The woman wore a pretty pink sweater with tiny pur-ple flowers, a pair of Levi's, white tennis shoes and dark framed glasses. The fact was, she looked more like a kindergarten teacher than someone who would work in an occult bookstore.

"Are you sure there's nothing I can interest you in? Some eye of newt or frog's tongue perhaps?"

David stared at her, but said nothing.

"Kidding." The woman laughed. "Your first time in a new age store, I see."

"Is it that obvious?"

"Yes." She nodded and smiled at David.

He smiled back.

The woman scratched her chin and thought for a moment. "You want to ask me some questions about a case, don't you?"

"Wow. How….how'd you know?"

"Well, I *am* a psychic. And I can see your badge through the opening in your coat. I'm pretty sure you're not here to buy a pack of tarot cards, am I right?" A big toothy grin filled her entire face. "Come on back." She motioned for David to join her in her office behind the counter. "This morning's been deathly slow and I could use the company. Have a cup of tea with me."

David followed her into her office. The room had bookshelves on all four walls and a big oak desk in the middle with a computer on it and three mauve wing-back chairs around it. "Sit down, um…" She waited for his name.

"Detective Stark. David Stark."

"Well then, sit down Detective David Stark. I'm Marsha Jones. Let me get you that tea." She poured two cups of tea and sat a delicate porcelain teacup on the desk in front of David without asking. "Drink up, it's echinacea with elderberry and reishi mushroom. Tastes like crap, but it'll keep you from catching a cold. And with this crazy Ohio weather, we can use all the help we can get. I mean, it was beautiful Thursday, the sun was shining and it got up into the forties. And today the wind chill's…what? Five, ten below? It's nuts. Anyway, drink up."

"Thanks." David hesitated briefly while he let his nose decide on whether or not to take a sip. "You were right," he said as the first mouthful slid down his throat. "It does taste like crap."

Marsha sat down, took a sip out of her teacup and scrunched up her nose. "Well, it's better than getting sick…I guess." She giggled. "So, what can I help you with Detective Stark?"

"Well." He wasn't completely sure why he had come here in the first place. "Ms. Jones…."

"Oh, goodness sakes, please call me Marsha. Mrs. Jones is my mother-in-law and if you knew my mother-in-law, you wouldn't call me that."

"Ok, Marsha. I met this woman who says she's having these graphic dreams about the murders a man commits, the night before he commits them."

Marsha put her hand up to her mouth and gasped. "Oh, God, someone is dreaming about The Cutter?"

"How did you…?"

"Well, I *am* a psychic. And I read the newspaper and have a scanner. I recognized your name. You're working on The Cutter's case and you did say 'murders'. Not too many mass murderers walking around Cleveland these days. Thank God."

"Maybe, I shouldn't have…" David stood up to leave, he had said too much already. This was all he needed. If his chief found out he was not only running around chasing after some woman's dream killer, but also consulting a psychic about the case, he'd be collecting unemployment before the day was out.

"No, sit down. I'm sorry, I talk too much." Marsha pulled on his arm and David reluctantly sat back down. "I won't say a word about your coming here. I swear. Now, how can I help?"

"I guess I just wanted to ask if you thought it was possible for someone totally unrelated to a case to be having dreams about it."

"Well, first of all, we are hardly ever unrelated to anything. There are so many connections out there, you wouldn't believe it." Marsha waved her hands around as she talked. "Like maybe she's met the killer without knowing it or bought something that belonged to him at a garage sale. Maybe she knows one of the victims or knows someone who is *going* to be a victim. She could have even been the mother or the father of the killer in a past live. You never know."

David rolled his eyes back into his head.

"Now, now, Detective Stark, you have to keep an open mind about this." Marsha shook her finger at him. "It's very important. See, lots of people are psychic, but just haven't developed it enough to control it. And one of the most common psychic abilities is to dream the future. For instance, Joseph, from the bible, you know, the one with the coat of many colors, he was a psychic who used dreams to predict the future."

"Yeah? Really?"

"Yeah, really. Did you ever have deja vue? Did you ever walk into a place you know you had never been before, but recognized it? Or were you ever in a conversation and realized that you've had that exact same conversation before?"

"Yeah, I guess."

"Well, the most common theory about deja vue is that it's actually you remembering parts of a dream you had in the past, about the future. It's usually not too important and we rarely remember the dream, until it happens. Then we just have this weird feeling that it's familiar, but we're not sure why."

"Oh, I don't know." David shook his head. "I just can't understand how she can dream about these murders in such detail and not be involved somehow."

"We don't choose this gift, Detective Stark. It chooses us. As a matter of fact, nine out of ten of us would argue that it's more of a pain in the ass than a gift."

Marsha looked away for a moment then looked back, directly into David's eyes. "When I was a little girl, every time I would touch my mom, I could see her having sex with a man, other than my father. It was awful and it upset me so much, I finally told my dad about it. He confronted her and it turned out, she actually had been having an affair. My parents got divorced over it and my mother blamed me. Still does. It was so bad, I even tried to kill myself over it."

Marsha pulled the neck of her sweater down to show him a faded scar around the side of her neck. "Luckily, my canopy bed gave way and I hit the floor. But while I was in the hospital, I met a nurse, who confided in me that she, too, was psychic and that she had learned a way to turn it on and off and control it, so it didn't control her anymore. She taught me and until about five years ago, I kept my abilities secret, too. Not even my husband knew about them."

The woman took another sip of her tea. "Eventually, I started this store. I've found real peace by helping others and teaching them how to develop and control their own abilities. So?" She smiled. "Have I freaked you out completely?"

"No," David laughed. "But you sure don't look the part."

"Most of the real ones don't."

"How does it happen? How does it work?"

"Look, you're a detective and you collect clues by sight, touch, smell, and I'm sure you have a gut feeling now and again, all good cops do."

He nodded his head.

"That's all this is. This woman, the one having those dreams, is getting clues, too, but from a different part of her brain. Why?" She threw her hands up in the air. "Who knows? Could be anything. Usually it's because there's some sort of emotional attachment, some kind of connection, but not always. That's why I thought it could be that she knew one of the victims or maybe knows someone who will be a victim. Maybe there's something about the killer. Hard to tell. It's not an exact science, by any means. I mean, people have dreams of plane crashes when no one they know is going to be on board. Maybe it's all just so horrible, she just can't help but get it caught in her brain. Does she have these kinds of dreams often?"

"No, I don't think so. I don't know, really. Maybe she does. I know she did. When she was a kid, she dreamt of her parents' murder and actually led the police to the killer."

"Oh, poor thing. How hard that had to be on her. I can't even imagine."

"Yeah," he said, remembering that Megan, too, had tried to kill herself because of it.

"Well, be very gentle with her, Detective Stark, remember she doesn't want this. She didn't ask for it. But she *is* stuck with it. It doesn't just go away." She looked at David. "May I?" Marsha asked, putting her hands on top of his and closing her eyes.

"Oh, I see," she said, after a few long moments. "You're in love with her. Did you know that?" She asked, not waiting for an answer. "But be careful. I can see that she *is* in danger. Either by her own actions or that of someone else's. I think, maybe both. Watch her closely, detective, because she *will* lead you to him, but be careful. The cost may be greater than the prize."

David heard the bells on the front door jingled. "Well, thank you very much for the advice and the tea. Mostly the advice." David handed her the nearly full teacup, before he got up to leave.

"Anytime. It was nice to meet you. And if this woman of yours ever needs to talk, have her call me." She took a business card out of a little wicker basket on her desk and handed it to him. David shook her hand and left.

*   *   *   *

11:45 a.m.

"How's that?" Megan asked, setting a clear glass vase filled with white marbles and ten green-stemmed pink tulips on the counter.

"Almost as pretty as you are," the customer said. He was a nice-looking older man, with big, sparkling blue eyes and a wide smile that lit up his wind-chapped face.

Megan cupped one of the large blooms in her hand. "Pink tulips are my favorite."

"I know. You've told me before. That's why I picked them." He smiled shyly.

"Well, I hope your wife knows how lucky she is. You come in here every Saturday, without fail, and pick out the prettiest arrangement we have. I only hope someday I'll get myself a husband that spoils me as much as you do your wife."

"Oh, trust me, with that angel face of yours, you will. But she's not my wife, yet. Soon though, very soon. And I can't wait." The man was absolutely beaming.

"That's so sweet." She gently wrapped a piece of green tissue paper around the flowers and stapled it closed. "Will there be anything else for you today?"

"No, thanks. This will be perfect." He reached into his wallet and laid a twenty on the counter.

Megan pushed a few buttons on the cash register. "That'll be $18.98," she said, picking up the twenty dollar bill. She pushed a few more buttons, the register dinged and the drawer flew open. Megan picked out the change and pushed the drawer closed again with her stomach. She turned to put the money in his waiting hand, and froze. Oh, God, his hand! His hand! Panic gripped her and she was unable to breath.

"Miss? Something wrong?" The man lowered his head so he could see into her face. "You ok?"

Megan shook her head. She was being ridiculous. "Yeah, I....I don't know what's wrong with me." She dropped the change into her customer's hand. "I just zoned out there for a minute. I'm sorry."

"Well, if you're sure, you're ok."

"Yes, of course."

"Ok. Thanks again." The man scooped up his flowers and headed for the door.

"Stay warm," Megan called after him.

"I'll try," he said over his shoulder.

David opened the door from the outside and held it for the man, before walking into the flower shop himself. "Hi, there," he said.

"Oh, yeah. Hi." She continued staring at the door, as David approached the counter.

After a few seconds, he turned his head and looked at the door and then back at her. "What's the matter?"

"Huh?" She shook her head and looked at him.

"What is it? What's wrong?"

"Oh, nothing. Nothing. I'm just losing my mind, that's all."

"What do ya mean?"

"Oh." Megan felt a little silly and was almost ashamed to tell him. "That guy. The one that just left. When I handed him his change….his…well, his hand kinda looked like the hand in my nightmares."

David didn't waste a second. He burst out the glass door and back out into the street, taking a few steps in one direction and then the other, before slowly walking back into the shop. "He's gone. What's his name? Where does he live?" David shot the questions at her.

Megan smiled at him. She enjoyed watching him in action. He was quite a sight in his nicely broken in blue jeans and his brown leather jacket. "Slow down, there, Detective Stark. That guy just happens to have the hands of every other white guy in his fifties, who works for a living. And you can't go after them all."

"But if you think his hands look familiar, I should check him out. Who is he?"

"His hands look familiar, because he's been coming in here every Saturday for…gee, I don't know…six months. You can't arrest the poor guy just because he's one of our best customers."

"What's his name?"

"My, my, you are the persistent one." Megan started fiddling around with another arrangement on the counter. "Come to think of it, I don't know what his name is. But I don't know a lot of our customer's names. We never delivered for him and he always pays in cash, so I've never had any reason to know his name. Trust me, he's really sweet. I guess I just haven't seen any old man hands since these dreams started and it kinda scared me. That's all. God, I hope I'm not developing a phobia."

She looked at David as she placed another yellow rose in the vase on the counter. "So? What brings you in here?"

"Well, I thought I'd ask you out to lunch."

"Really?" Megan felt herself stand a little taller and automatically push her shoulders back. Wow. He came here to ask her out to lunch. Maybe she *would* get the chance to kiss him again. Something she had been thinking about all day.

David patted a thick book he had tucked up under his arm. "I have pictures of some knives and saws. I want you to look through them and let me know if you recognize any of them."

"Oh." Megan's shoulders slumped forward. Ok, so much for the kissing. This was business and the sooner she learned to deal with it, the better.

"Why, hello, you two." Nancy walked through the front door, stomping the snow off her boots. "Ready for your big lunch date? You can leave now. I'm ready to take over the ship." Nancy smiled at both of them, before she walked into the back room of the store to hang up her coat and put away her purse.

"Let me guess." Megan eyed the detective. "Lunch was Nancy's idea?"

"Yeah." David ruffled the hair on the back of his head and avoided her eyes for a second. "But it was a good one. I haven't had a bite to eat since about three-thirty this morning. What do ya say? Will you please have lunch with me?"

"Gee, since you asked so nicely, let me get my coat. I'll be right back." She walked into the back room and shook her head at Nancy. "Would you just quit with the matchmaking, already?"

"Hey, what makes you think *I* did anything?" Nancy asked, doing her best to look innocent.

"Quit your fibbing. David told me lunch was your idea."

"Only 'cause I thought of it before he did, that's all. That boy called for you last night and then was at the house first thing this morning, looking for you. He's definitely interested in you. I can sense these things."

"Yeah, because he's a cop and I'm having nightmares about a serial killer. He *should* be interested in me."

"Well, Miss Smarty Pants, you didn't hear how whacked out he sounded on the phone last night, when he found out you were out on a date." She leaned forward and cupped her hand over her mouth. "I practically had to bite my tongue to keep from laughing."

"You told him I was on a date?"

"What did you want me to do?" Nancy threw up her hands. "Lie to the man? He's a cop, for heaven's sake. You want me to lie to a police officer?"

"Oh, Nancy. You are something else, you know that?" She hugged the old woman and kissed her on the cheek. "What am I going to do with you?"

"Don't worry about me, sweetie. If I were you, I'd get out there, before that cutie out there gets tired of waitin' for ya."

Megan put on her coat and mittens and walked back into the showroom where she found David inspecting a vase of white roses. "Ready when you are, officer."

He walked to the door and held it open for her. "What did you have a taste for?"

She waited for him outside on the sidewalk. "Um, anything really."

"What sounds good?"

"Well, there's a coffee shop just a block down." Megan pointed down the street. "They serve sandwiches and soup and stuff like that. Would that be ok?"

"Perfect."

They walked down the street together, exhaling white clouds into the cold afternoon air.

Megan stopped in front of a big window with snowmen painted on it. "Well, here it is."

David opened the door to the little coffee shop and the warm smell of freshly baked cookies invited them in.

"Mmmm. I'll have to have one of those," she told him and he nodded in agreement. They ordered at the counter and found an empty table by the fireplace to wait for their food.

"Well, here you go." David put the thick book in front of her, before reaching into the pocket of his coat and pulling out a white envelope. "Now, these are some weapons we took from a suspect's apartment." He opened the envelope and shook out fifteen or so photos onto the table. He stacked them and handed the stack to her. "Take a good look at them and tell me if anything looks familiar."

Megan carefully studied each photo and then laid it face down on the table. When she laid down the last photo, she looked up at David and shook her head.

"You sure?"

"Yeah, positive. I didn't see any of those things in my dreams."

"I didn't think so."

Megan handed him back the stack of photos and before he had them put away, she was already looking through the giant book of weapons and tools he had given her. A few minutes passed in silence as she flipped through the pages of the book.

"So. How was your date last night?" David asked, finally breaking the silence.

"What?" She looked up from the book. She had heard exactly what he said, she just wanted to see his face when he said it.

"Um...Nancy, she said you were out on a date last night, when I called." He leaned back in his chair, like someone working really hard to look relaxed.

"Oh," she said and went back to looking at the pictures of axes and machetes on the page in front of her.

After a few devastatingly quiet seconds, David cleared his throat and asked again, "Well? How did it go?"

Megan looked up and smiled at him. Was he jealous? Yes, she thought maybe he was. That gorgeous hunk of man sitting across from her was jealous that she went out on a date. "Well, if you must know." She hesitated for effect. "It was...terrible. The guy was a complete jerk. My friend, Sue, set me up with him. I should kill her, really. Oh, wait, I probably shouldn't say that in front of a cop, huh?"

"That's too bad." His words sounded genuinely sympathetic, but he couldn't seem to suppress the smile that played at the corners of his lips or the sigh of relief that escaped his mouth. Megan had to look down at the book to keep him from seeing the grin on her face.

When the waitress delivered the food to their table, Megan wasn't even half-way through the book. "There are some pretty interesting things in here," she said, putting a yellow paper with the descriptions of the shop's lunch specials in the book, to keep her place.

"Yeah, there's a million ways to kill somebody." David immediately offered her an apologetic smile.

"I guess your job brings you down a lot." She felt sorry for him. She had seen the way his eyes darkened over when she talked about the murder victims. And she felt the enthusiasm he had over thinking he could save Brenda Parker's life turn into frustration, when he discovered it was too late. She had also seen his face after they carried out the body of the redhead. Detective David Stark felt the pain of his job.

"Yeah, I guess so. I'm sorta new to homicide. My game was vice until just recently."

"Wow, what a case to cut your teeth on."

"Yeah, no kidding. If my partner didn't have so much seniority, I'm not sure I'd even be on this one at all. Anyway, I didn't mean to sound so callous, just then. I'm not really."

"I can tell you're not."

They finished their sandwiches and Megan was munching on her, still warm, chocolate chip cookie, when she went back to looking through the book.

"Hey," she said around the crumbs of cookie in her mouth, "this is the saw he uses. I'm sure of it."

David slid his chair beside her and looked at the photo of a saw that somewhat resembled a hack saw.

"It even had that same twisty piece of metal under the handle."

On the back of the yellow menu, David wrote down the page number and the words that were printed under the picture, '17 ½ in. Bone Saw'. "Keep looking," he urged her.

He didn't move his chair back to the other side of the table. She could feel the heat of his body and smell the wonderful soapy, fresh scent of him over the cookies as he looked over her shoulder and it made it impossible for her to concentrate.

She flipped a few more pages and pointed to a knife about three inches long that curved upward into almost a crescent shape. "This looks kind of like one of the knives I saw in his case. A whole lot like it."

It was labeled, 'Professional Skinning Knife' and David wrote down that information, as well.

"He just used a regular straight edge razor to cut that woman's hair off," she explained. "You know, the kind that opens up."

David pulled the book in front of him and flipped through the pages. After finding what he was looking for, he turned the book toward her. "Like this?"

"Yeah, that's it."

By the time Megan had finished going through the entire book, she had pointed out two more tools, one called a membrane separator and the other a fleshing knife.

David walked her to her car and waited for her to unlock it and open the door. "Thanks for all your help, Megan. I'm headed to the station right now to have my buddy in forensics take a look at what you picked out."

"I hope it helps." She couldn't take her eyes off his lips, wishing she had the guts to kiss him goodbye. "Thanks for lunch."

"You're welcome. Maybe we can do it again sometime, minus the weapons of death." He flashed that big, sexy, dimply smile at her.

"That would be nice." More than nice. "Well, I guess this is goodbye, then."

"Yeah, I got to get to the station. I'm on stake out duty with my partner in…," he glanced at his watch, "less than two hours, actually. So, I better get going. It was nice seeing you. Have a good rest of the day. You don't have another hot date planned for tonight, do you?" He asked and winked at her.

"Yes, actually I do."

His smile instantly dropped into a frown and his eyebrows squeezed together.

Megan couldn't help but giggle at the reaction she got out of him. "I'm going to the movies with Sue."

"Oh. Well…" David stumbled over his words as embarrassment reddened his cheeks. "In that case, have a good time."

"Thanks, I will." She got into her car and closed the door. There wasn't going to be a kiss on the cheek today, but she had more than that. He had been obviously bothered by the idea of her out on a date with another man. And that had to count for something. Megan smiled, as she watched him walk across the street. Yeah, that had to count for something.

*   *   *   *

5:27 p.m.

"What time is it?" Hudson yawned and stretched his arms out, as much as he could inside David's car. Hudson was relieved at about nine that morning and went home for a nap and a shower, before he and David took over Freeman's surveillance again at three-thirty this afternoon.

"About fifteen minutes after you asked me last time." David rolled his head trying to work out a kink in his neck. After he left Megan, he went straight to see Ted Miller, who had confirmed his suspicions. All the things Megan had picked out of that book were tools use by a taxidermist.

Neither David nor Ted knew the first thing about taxidermy, but luckily, Ted had a buddy who did it as a hobby. Ted called him and he agreed to meet them for a few drinks later that night to answer some questions.

"God, this guy leads a more boring life than I do." Hudson yawned again. "Well, except for the jacking off every ten minutes or so. That's pretty interesting."

"Who they sendin' down to watch Masturbation Man next?"

Hudson laughed. "I'm not sure. Smith and Thompson, I think." He leaned his head back and closed his eyes. "I'm really getting too old for this."

David sat up in his seat and watched Freeman close the door to his apartment. "Hey, look. Masturbation Man is on the move." Freeman walked down the sidewalk carrying a navy blue duffel bag.

"Didn't that witness from the hotel say the man was carrying a black bag?" Hudson asked his partner.

"Yeah." But more importantly to David was that Megan had said the killer carried a black case full of tools.

They quietly got out of the car and tailed Freeman, staying behind him by about a half a block. Freeman stopped at a hotdog stand and bought a dog and a soda. Hudson stopped to look in a store window and David knelt down to untie and tie the string on his boot.

Once he finished off his hotdog, Freeman began to walk again and the two detectives followed suit. After about ten blocks, he stopped at a phone booth and made a call. The call only lasted about a minute and after hanging up, Freeman stood by the phone booth, like he was waiting for someone or something. About five minutes had gone by when a blonde woman wearing a red coat, black boots and a black scarf walked past the phone booth, heading toward David and Hudson.

Freeman picked up his duffel bag and started after her, back the way he had come. He passed David and Hudson as they stood by a traffic light, pretending to be in deep conversation. The woman would glance behind her from time to time and Freeman would stop and try to look like he was doing something else. The woman seemed to sense danger and started walking faster as Freeman followed close behind her. After a few seconds, she started to run. Freeman ran after her and the detectives ran after him.

Adrenaline was pumping through David's veins as he raced down the sidewalk, weaving past pedestrians. Freeman had to be their man. But why hadn't Megan dreamt this last night? Could it be, because this was the one murder that doesn't happen? Could she be the woman he saved? And if she doesn't die, maybe Megan doesn't dream it. This was the murder he prevented. With that possibility, David's legs seem to carry him faster than he had ever moved before, leaving Hudson more than a block behind.

The blonde stopped at an apartment building, franticly opened up the door and tried to close it behind her, but it was too late, Freeman was right behind her. He pushed the door open and the woman cried out in fear as Freeman slapped her across the face. She fell to the ground, holding her gloved hand up to her face, trying to shield it from any more abuse. He dropped the duffel bag on the floor and looked down at her. "My, what beautiful lips you have."

David rushed through the open the door with his gun drawn. "Police, hands up." Freeman and the woman, both, immediately held their hands up in the air. David pushed Freeman up against the wall. He patted him down and cuffed him while Hudson, who had finally arrived, checked on the woman sitting on the floor with her hands held up in the air.

"Miss, it's ok, we're with the police. Did he hurt you?" Hudson crouched down to look at the red mark on her cheek.

The woman looked at Hudson and then at David. "Fuck!" The woman hit the floor with her fist. "I know you, you're vice. Look, man, I'm just tryin' to make a living here. Don't you cops have better things to do?" She got up and brushed herself off.

"Yeah, man, why you guys harassin' me like this?" Freeman asked, still up against the wall. "I got rights, ya know."

David knelt down and unzipped the duffel bag. He pulled out a pair of white latex gloves and a whip. There were also a few dildos and other toys in it that he wasn't about to touch with his bare hands. He zipped up the duffel bag, looked up at Hudson and shook his head.

David stood up. "Ma'am, we just picked up the pieces of a working girl in a hotel room a few nights ago. We're not too excited about doing it again anytime soon."

"Oh, God, I heard about that. I knew her, ya know. Dixie worked just a few blocks down from me." She looked at Freeman, spread eagle against the wall and pointed at him. "You don't think he....? Ha!" She laughed. "He's a perv alright, but he ain't no killer. He's been my six o'clock Saturday for over a year now."

"But he was chasing you," Hudson said

"Yeah, that's right. He chases me, I run to my apartment, he slaps me around and then I fuck his brains out. But he don't go around killin' nobody."

"Yeah, man, I'm no weirdo killer," Freeman piped up. "I like it rough, but, man, I pay for it. And I sure as hell wouldn't cut no girls up, man. I mean, shit, what the hell good is a pair of legs without a pussy. Know what I'm sayin', man? If you ask me, that Cutter dude is one sick mother-fucker."

"Well, I think you two should come downtown with us to write up a report," Hudson said, smiling at David.

"Shit! I'm on parole," the woman explained. "They'll throw my ass back in jail for this. Com'on you guys, cut me some slack. I'm not exactly dressed for the police station."

David and Hudson looked at each other as the woman unbuttoned her coat and opened it in front of the three men. She was completely naked underneath, except for the red garters belts that held up her silk stockings.

Freeman licked his lips and let out an, "Ooooo yeah! That's what I'm talkin' about!"

David pushed him back up against the wall. "Down, boy." Then David looked at the floor. "Ma'am, will you please button your coat back up?"

"Ya know, I could always arrange for you two to have a little freebee," the blonde said, slowly buttoning up her coat. "I could even do you both together, if ya like."

"Go on now, get out of here." Hudson tilted his head toward the door and the woman turned to leave.

"See you next Saturday, Craig."

David took the handcuffs off Freeman and the man rubbed his wrists. "You, too," David said. "Go home and try to stay out of trouble, would ya?"

As the two detectives walked back to their car, Hudson pulled a bottle of Tums out of his coat pocket and twisted off the lid. "Fucked up world out here, isn't it?" He asked, tossing a couple chalky tablets into his mouth.

"You got that right."

*   *   *   *

10:14 p.m.

"Hey, Ted, sorry I'm late." David shook Ted's hand and slapped him on the back.

"Stark, this here is Steve Lawson, a good friend of mine from way back. Played softball together."

"Before we got too old," Steve added.

"This is David Stark, the detective I was telling you about," Ted told his friend.

David shook Steve's hand and sat down across from him and Ted in a black vinyl booth at the back of Buddy's Bar and Grill. "Thanks a lot for meeting us here, Steve."

"No problem. I was glad to get out of the house. A little too much family time today with the wife and kids." Steve tipped a glass of beer to his lips and took a drink.

"Heard about you and Hudson's little excitement today," Ted said, grinning from ear to ear.

"What's that?" David asked.

"Heard you guys were offered a little ménage-a-trois." Ted could hardly contain himself as he and his buddy bumped shoulders and giggled like a couple of little girls.

"God, it didn't take that old coot long to tell everyone about that." David shook his head. "Steve," he said, wanting to change the subject. "Ted tells me you're a taxidermist."

"Yeah, I make a little extra money on the side, doing it out of my garage."

"I hope you don't mind me picking your brain."

"No, of course not. Anything to help." Steve downed the last drop of amber liquid in his glass.

Ted jumped up. "Name your poison, Stark."

"Sam Adams."

"You're drinking Coors, right?" Ted asked his buddy, who nodded. "Be right back." Ted walked across the sticky white and black tiled floor to the dark, maple bar and waited for a bartender.

"So, what do you know about taxidermy?" Steve asked.

"Not much, really. Just that, a hunter goes out and kills something and brings it back. Then a taxidermist stuffs it, so it can grace the wall of his den, forever."

"Well, you're close. But we actually don't stuff anything. That's a common misconception. Taxidermy comes from the Greek words, taxi, meaning to move and derma, meaning skin. So actually, it's the art of moving the skin of an animal over a mannikin, so it appears lifelike. The goal is always to make your mount look as natural as possible."

"So, in order to do a deer, you have to have a deer mannikin and to do a squirrel…."

"You need a squirrel mannikin." Steve interrupted. "That's right."

"What if you were doing something that you couldn't buy a mannikin for?" David asked.

"Well, they sell foam blocks you can use to carve out your own form. There's also this urethane foam you can buy. It's a powder that expands when you mix it with a certain liquid. It can actually be molded while it's expanding and still pliable. Then after it hardens you can cut it, sand it or carve it. They also have putty, an epoxy putty, that can be added to it to fix errors, add muscles, or cheeks bones, whatever."

"Have you ever made a mannikin before?"

"Hell no," Steve said. "You have to be a real artist to pull that off. Unless you're doing something easy, like a snake or something. No, I buy my mannikins from a magazine. Then all I have to do is sand them a little or do some minor carving. I'm only a weekend enthusiast."

Ted came back to the table with three glasses of beer in his hands and carefully sat them down on the table in front of each of the men. "Thanks," Steve said

David nodded at Ted. "Thanks, buddy."

"Not a problem," Ted said, downing a gulp himself.

"This is going to sound like a weird question." David quickly glanced at Ted.

"Shoot," Steve said, between sips.

"Could a person be done?"

Steve spit the beer in his mouth back into his glass and looked first at David and then his friend, Ted. "What?"

"Could a person be done?" David asked again.

"You're not serious?"

"Look, this is just a hunch I'm going on and it's important that it doesn't get out before I'm sure of what's going on. So, Steve, I need your word that you'll keep this under your hat for awhile. The last thing we need right now is more of a media frenzy than we already have."

"Is this about that Chopper or Cutter or whatever they call that guy who killed those women?" Steve asked with disgust on his face.

"Do I have your word you won't say anything about this?" David asked.

"Sure, no problem. I won't say a word."

"You can trust him," Ted added, unnecessarily.

"Well," David said, "I'm looking into the possibility that The Cutter might be a taxidermist and I just wondered what you thought."

"I think it's repulsive." Steve thought for a moment. "But, I guess it's possible. I mean, the man would have to be incredibly good to pull something like that off. Especially with all the different pieces. Unless he just doesn't care about all the seams."

"Seams?" Ted asked.

"Yeah." Steve let go of his beer glass to use both hands while he talked. "The cut on a deer, for instance, is made under the belly and you have the hair to hide it. But say, you were doing a fish, you would have to use hide glue to secure it to the form, and then suture it with nylon thread. If the seam showed, you could use a type of epoxy putty to cover it and then paint it."

"You guys use paint? What for?" David asked.

"Probably the same way undertakers do," Ted offered.

"Well, no, not really. We don't do people." Steve took a drink and David suspected he was probably sorry he ever agreed to meet with them.

"But, if you did do people, you would use paint the way an undertaker does, right?" Ted asked.

"Shit, Ted, I don't know. I guess it's something like that. I use paint and an airbrush a lot when I do fish and when I do mammals, I use paint around the eyes to cover the putty that holds the glass eyes in."

"I never thought about that. He would have to get eyes for this thing." David scratched his thumbnail against his chin. "Where would he get eyes for it?"

The two other men sat there silently, offering no suggestions.

"Hey, I got a question for ya." Ted turned to look at his buddy. "Doesn't the skin rot after a while?"

"Well, I personally use a liquid tanning agent on most things," Steve explained. "But some people like to use a dry preservative, like puffed or powdered borax. They just put the animal hide in a bag with the dry preservative and shake it up. They sell electric tumblers for that, but I don't do enough to buy one of those, yet."

"Ok," David said. "Let me see if I got this. Our guy carves out a mannikin of a woman. Then, let's say he cuts off a woman's leg. He takes it back to his place. Skins it?"

Steve nodded.

"Then he puts the skin in a bag and shakes it up with some borax powder," David continued.

"Or he could use a liquid tanner and soak the skin," Steve said. "There's a lot more to it than that, but that's the basic idea."

"Ok. Then he glues the skin to the mannikin and stitches it up."

"That's it." Steve downed the last drop of his second beer. "He would have to cover up the seams and then paint them and set some eyes in it. I hate to say it, but I guess it could be done."

The three men sat quietly, letting that comment sink in.

David pushed his glass away. "Two more questions, Steve. Did you have to go to school or take classes to learn how to do it?"

"No. All you need is the money to buy a kit. When I started, I bought a couple of video tapes, that's it, really. Anybody can do it."

"Do you have to get a license with the state?"

Steve shook his head. "All I did was stick a sign in my front yard."

"Thanks for your time, man." David stood up and shook Steve's hand.

"Stark, stay for another beer," Ted begged.

"Nah. My head's swimming right now. I gotta get some air. Next couple rounds on me, though." David put a twenty on the table. "Thanks again," he told Steve and walked out the door into the welcoming sting of cold air.

He unlocked his car door, then turned around and leaned his back on it. He needed a little more of the cold night air to clear his head. This new lead didn't help to narrow his search one iota. As a matter of fact, if what Steve said was true, anyone and his brother could set up shop in their own basement. This psychopath could just as easily be a full time pro or someone who bought a beginner kit on the internet. David jabbed the fingers of his right hand through his hair. He was getting damn tired of all these dead ends.

∗   ∗   ∗   ∗

David was almost home when he heard Sue Taylor's name mentioned over his radio. Her apartment had been broken into and her dog had been stabbed. Fortunately, Sue was unharmed. The dog had scared away the intruder, but not before the animal had taken the brunt of the intruder's hostility.

Megan was with Sue tonight. Had she been at the apartment, too? Was she safe? David needed to know. His heart was thumping against the inside of his chest, when he grabbed up the hand set and called out to the officer working the scene.

"Mayer, come in. This is Stark."

"Hey Stark," came a young man's voice from the radio.

"You at Sue Taylor's place?"

"No. Not anymore. I just dropped Miss Taylor off at her mother's house to spend the night. But the boys are still there, dusting."

"Was she about twenty-five or so, black, a school teacher?"

"Yeah. Pretty too."

"Is she ok?"

"Yeah, a little shaken up. And she was crying about her dog. They took him to the animal hospital down on 42nd, but it looked like it might be too late." Mayer paused then added, "It was pretty nasty, Stark. Whoever did that wasn't a well balanced individual."

"Was there anyone else with her?"

"With Miss Taylor? No, she was alone. She said a girlfriend had dropped her off at around nine-thirty and she was in bed by ten. The break in occurred between a quarter after ten and ten-thirty."

"He was watching her apartment," David said, thoughtfully, "waiting for her lights to go out."

"That's what we figure."

"It wasn't a robbery or he would have waited longer, until he was sure she was asleep. He was after her." David's skin crawled. "Thank God she had a dog. It very well, may have saved her life."

"Looks that way. Miss Taylor was pretty upset, but she doesn't believe anything's missing."

"Mayer, you got the phone number to her mother's house?"

"Yeah. Why? You know her?"

"She's a friend of a friend."

Mayer gave him the phone number and he jotted it down on the note pad on his dashboard.

"Thanks, Mayer."

"Um...hey, maybe you can put in a good word for me," the young officer said. "Later, of course."

"I'll do that."

"Thanks, Stark."

David immediately pulled his car over to an empty parking lot, flipped open his cell phone and looked for Megan's number. He wanted to tell her, before she heard about it on the news. Not to mention, he wanted to hear for himself that she was ok.

"Hello?" A sleepy voice asked.

"I'm sorry. You were asleep."

"Just," she yawned. "It's ok. What's up?"

"It's Sue. She's alright, but her apartment was broken into tonight and someone stabbed her dog."

"Bear? Oh, no. Is he dead? Was Sue hurt?"

"No," he reassured her. "Sue's fine. She's spending the night with her mother and the dog is at an animal hospital."

"Oh, my God," Megan said. "I just dropped her off a few hours ago."

"I know. That's why I called."

"Thanks. I'll call her, see if she needs me or if she wants me to do anything."

"I got her mother's phone number for you, in case you didn't have it. You have anything to write with?"

"Just a second." David heard papers rustling before Megan came back on the line. "Go ahead."

He gave her the number and waited while she wrote it down.

"Thanks. I'm going to call her right now. She's probably a nervous wreck."

"Well, you have my cell phone number if you need anything, right?"

"Yes. Thanks again for calling. I really do appreciate it."

"You're welcome." David paused for a second, wondering if he should tell her what he had learned from Ted's friend. "Hey, there's something I wanted to ask you. Do you know anyone who does taxidermy?"

"Um…no….I don't think so. No. Why?"

"Just wondering. Goodnight, Megan."

"Goodnight," he heard her say before the phone disconnected.

CHAPTER 5

▼

SUNDAY, JANUARY 18TH

*   *   *   *

1:34 a.m.

Megan's head pounded as she lay in bed thinking about all the terrible things going on all around her. What if something would have happed to Sue? She couldn't have handled losing her good friend, not on top of everything else.

Megan spent the last hour and a half talking to Sue on the phone. The poor thing was so distraught over what might have happened and about Bear, she couldn't stop crying. The dog was barely clinging to life at the animal clinic. They had him stabilized and sewn up, but the vet said it would be touch and go for the next few days. He had been stabbed twelve times. Twelve times. Megan couldn't imagine how anyone could do that. The animal was a hero. He probably saved Sue's life and it would be such a shame if he died.

It was really sweet of David to call her and let her know about Sue. He had acted jealous at lunch and worried when he called her a little while ago. There was definitely something going on between them. She just wished she knew what it was.

He had done something to her that night in his apartment that no other man had ever managed to do. He made her feel desirable and sexy and *normal.* The way he kissed her with more passion than she had ever felt before, the way he held her possessively in his arms, claiming her as his own, the way his hand explored her back, his warm fingers sending electrifying chills throughout her body as they touched her bare skin and most importantly, the way he hardened against her, physically demonstrating that he wanted her. *Really* wanted her.

She knew David needed her. Not the way he had a few days ago against his dining room wall, but he still needed her. She was his only link to the killer and he would have to use her to catch the monster. But the question that caused Megan to lie awake, staring at her bedroom ceiling, was whether she could ever make him *want* her again. Whether she would ever again be consumed by that passion that pumped blood through her heart for the first time in her life.

She closed her eyes and she could almost picture his face, his dark honest eyes and the sexy dimples in his cheeks. She could picture his thick solid arms and feel the strength of those arms. She could taste the delicious kisses that had stirred something inside her. Megan drifted off to sleep, thinking about making love to David Stark.

*   *   *   *

4:06 a.m.

Megan had the uncomfortable feeling she was being watched and opened her eyes. There was a figure of a man, standing in the darkness of her room. It startled her for a second until she realized it was David. He down sat on the edge of her bed and slid his arm under her back, pulling her up to him. "I couldn't stay away from you, Megan. I needed to see you tonight. I needed to be with you tonight." He leaned over and covered her mouth with his.

He withdrew from the kiss momentarily and brushed the hair away from her face. "I love you," he whispered, pulling her blue satin nightgown up, over her head. For a long moment, he sat there, his dark amber eyes drinking her in, before his eyelids fell and he bent forward to kiss her again. His kisses worked their way from her lips down her neck to her breasts, sending ice-hot tremors through her body.

She arched her back and closed her eyes. She had never felt this way before. So alive, so full of electricity. Her entire body tingling with sensations that, until now, were unknown to her. Suddenly, the kisses stopped and Megan opened her eyes.

David was gone and she was no longer in her bed. She was sitting alone at a table with a drink and a lit cigarette in an ashtray in front of her. Smoke from the cigarette swirled up around her head, burning her nostrils. There was a low rumble of music and people talking in the background. She was in a bar.

The background music stopped and the people around her quieted down as a woman, dressed in a tight, blue sequin-covered cowgirl dress, white fringed boots and gloves to match, strutted to the center of the stage and struck a seductive pose. A rowdy country song began to pulsate out of the large speakers and the chesty blonde began prancing around the stage, flapping and twirling her fringes as she danced.

She peeled off one white glove and then the other, throwing them to the floor. Turning her back to the crowd, she bent over and flipped her dress up over her back, exposing her bottom which was completely bare except for a thin strip of blue material running up the center. She stood up and pranced around the stage some more, before suddenly ripping off her dress, tearing it into two separated pieces and flinging them to either side of the stage. A roar of applause sounded from the crowd.

She had on only a tiny blue thong and her white fringed boots as she danced around the stage, shaking her head so her long blonde hair flew all around. She squatted at the edge of the stage, putting one hand on the floor behind her for balance and opened and closed her legs several times for the audience, before touching herself. The dancer then stood and shook her breasts at the crowd. She cupped one hand under her right breast and lifted it as she stuck out her tongue and licked at her nipple, sending another loud cheer through the bar.

Megan looked down and reached for the drink in front of her. The hand! The hand…. wasn't hers. It was the old, wrinkled hand of The Cutter. She tried to scream, to warn the blonde dancer, but nothing would come out. Again, she could do nothing, but watch.

The Cutter picked up the cigarette and put it to his lips. Megan tried to identify the brand, but the strobe light and flashing colored lights from the stage, made it impossible. She tried to look for the name of the club. The napkin under the drink was plain white, no name. No name or design was on the glass. No menu was on the table.

"Look around. Look around, you son of a bitch!" She screamed at him, but his eyes never left the stripper's full, round breasts. He watched her intently as she walked from table to table, collecting the ones, fives and tens the men were stuffing into her blue thong and Megan could feel the arousal tightening between his legs.

The dancer approached his table and shook her chest, back and forth, in front of him. He held out a twenty dollar bill and she squeezed her breasts together to grab it. He brushed his finger lightly across her nipple as he pulled his hand away and leaned over to whisper in a heavy, muffled voice, barely audible over the laughter and loud music. "There's more where that came from. I could use some company tonight."

"I can take care of that." She leaned forward, rubbing her breast across his mouth and Megan could taste the salty sweat of her skin. "Meet me out back."

"No! No! For God's sake, get away from him!" Why couldn't she hear? Why wouldn't she listen?

The Cutter got up and walked outside into the cold to wait for her behind the bar. There was no sign, no markings of any kind on the backside of the old, square, one-story concrete block building. Megan could see the parking lot. It was black top that had cracked and been repaired many times. She couldn't see if there was a building beside them, because no matter how much she willed him to, he would not look around.

Before long, the blonde walked out a brown steel door in the back of the building. She was wearing a tan overcoat and the same white boots she wore during her performance. The Cutter walked the woman to his car, which was parked beside the dark blue dumpster behind the club, and opened the door for her. The blonde sat down on the plastic covered front seat and waited for him to get in. Wasting no time, she opened her coat. Her boots were all she wore.

The Cutter's finger traced her puckered nipple before his hand kneaded her breast. It was important to him for it to be real.

"Is that all you're interested in?" She asked. "I've got a pussy, too, ya know."

Without a word, he violently elbowed her in the face with such force, Megan was sure it broke her nose, maybe even killed her. Blood poured from the unconscious blonde's face as her head slumped back against the car seat. The Cutter turned his attention back to her breasts. He leaned forward and kissed the warm flesh and sucked, hungrily, on her left nipple, until Megan could taste the blood that had run down onto her chest.

The Cutter wiped the back of his hand across his mouth, reached into his coat pocket and pulled out his yellow rubber gloves. He carefully put them over his hands, pushing the fingers of each hand between the other to ensure a perfect fit. He then reached under his front seat and retrieved his bone saw.

"Oh, God, please don't," Megan pleaded silently as the Cutter forced her to watch him add the next piece to his gruesome collection. He placed his prize in a black garbage bag, along with his bloody rubber gloves and tied the top of the bag, before putting it in his back seat. Then he carefully rolled up what was left of the blonde in the thick black plastic tarp he had covering his car seat and taped it closed.

The Cutter pulled the blonde's body out of his car and was about to lift it into the dumpster, when headlights lit up the dark parking lot. A man in a small blue car, a Ford Escort, Megan thought, pulled into a parking spot, not far from The Cutter's car. The Cutter awkwardly lifted the body up into the dumpster and hurried back to his car. He was scared for the first time and Megan felt his panic.

"Hey, what are you doing?" The man asked as he got out of his parked car.

The Cutter jumped into his car, started it and peeled out of the bar's parking lot, racing into the safety of the night.

*   *   *   *

6:21 a.m.

Beep, beep, beep. David Stark reached over with his eyes still closed and pushed the snooze button on his clock. Beep, beep, beep. He cracked open one eye and looked at the glowing red numbers. It was six twenty-one and it wasn't his alarm that was screeching in the darkness, it was his cell phone. He slapped blindly for it and after finding it, pushed a button and squinted at the piece of metal in his hand. Someone had left him a voice message.

He yawned and put his phone back on the nightstand. He and Hudson hadn't left the office until well after midnight, when they both agreed they were simply too tired to function one second longer. And after he finally got home and crawled into bed, his tired mind immediately started thinking about Megan.

At first, it was about the case and what questions he needed to ask her when he saw her again, but his thoughts soon began to wander back to his dining room and the night of lovemaking they were so close to sharing.

He should have gone to her house to tell her about Sue. He wanted to see with his own eyes that she was ok. He could have slept on her couch to guard her through the night. Oh, who did he think he was fooling? It had already taken what little willpower he possessed not to take her into his arms and attack her right there in the parking lot after lunch. He had to ball his hands up into fists and hold them tightly in his coat pockets, just to keep from touching her.

He was working a case and she was a lead. He had to find a way to get that through his thick skull and keep his hands off her, at least until the case was over. Then....then he could.... Thinking about then, hadn't helped him get to sleep. In fact, it had been nearly impossible to fall asleep with her on his mind, but he finally drifted off for what seemed like minutes before his damn cell phone started screaming.

David pushed himself out of bed and walked to the kitchen to start a pot of coffee, before he picked up the phone to retrieve his message. "Detective Stark, it's Nancy Montgomery. I'm real sorry to bother you at this hour, but I think you should come over here right away. It's Meg. She's had another one of those nightmares."

The coffee was still dripping into the pot when David slammed the door behind him.

The look on Nancy's face when she opened her front door, told him how relieved she was to see him. "I'm so glad you came, David. Meg's been trying to write down everything she can remember. And this one's a doosy. Let me tell ya."

David was sure he looked pretty rough. He only had about six or seven hours of sleep in the last two days and after he got Nancy's message, he just threw on a blue flannel shirt and his jeans. He brushed his teeth, but didn't take the time to shave, as a matter of fact, he couldn't remember if he even brushed his hair.

He was combing his fingers through his hair when he rushed into the kitchen to find Megan writing on a piece of white notebook paper. She turned to see him walk into the room and stood up. David threw his arms around her and held her tightly.

He heard Nancy clear her throat and he turned his head to see the old woman standing in the doorway. She raised an inquisitive eyebrow at him and smiled. Reluctantly, he let Megan out of his embrace.

"Um...can I get you a cup of coffee?" Nancy asked.

"Yes, please. Black, thank you." David sat down beside Megan at the table. "Tell me everything." He pulled his recorder out of his pocket and switched it on.

She told him about the dream she just had. About the stripper wearing a cowgirl costume in a bar she didn't recognize, The Cutter's old, silver car, the man in the little blue car who saw him dump the body.

"Do you think you can ID the car?" David asked. "If I got some pictures for you to look at, do you think you could ID the car?" This could be it. This could finally be the murder they prevent. The blonde could be the life they actually save. All they had to do was figure out which strip joint it was and wait for him.

There was no reason they couldn't catch this guy before he added the chest to his perfect woman.

Megan nodded her head. "I think so. I'll try."

"How 'bout the club? Would you know it again if you saw it?"

"Probably not from the outside. It was too dark and I couldn't see a sign or anything. But I know I could tell it from the inside. I'm sure if I saw that stage again, I'd know it!"

"Ok, go get dressed. We have a busy day in front of us, if we're going to catch ourselves a killer." David pulled Megan to her feet and practically pushed her out of the room.

Nancy put her hand on David's shoulder and nodded her head. "Thanks."

"You're welcome." He patted the old lady's soft hand.

"Take care of my little Megan."

"I will. I promise."

"I know you will." Nancy Montgomery smiled and went back to bed.

*   *   *   *

7:18 p.m.

Megan watched David's eyes as the ambulance pulled out of the blacktop parking lot of Fishnets Gentlemen's Club on Route 6 near Bay Village. They were in the North Olmsted area when they heard the dispatcher broadcast the news about a body being found in a dumpster behind the newly opened strip club up by Lake Erie.

David hadn't made a sound the entire fifteen minute drive to Bay Village. Actually, it had been almost an hour since he last said anything. Megan wanted to tell him it wasn't his fault, that it was her and her stupid dreams that were to blame. How could he expect to save anyone, when the place in her dream could have been anywhere in Ohio, or in the country for that matter?

It was her blasted nightmares that were giving him false hope, making him think there was a way to stop that monster. But he couldn't be stopped. And she realized that now. He wasn't meant to be stopped. He showed Megan these things, not to help anyone, but to torment her. And she in turn, was tormenting David.

They were parked down the street from the one-story brick building, watching in silence as the police secured the area around the club. She wondered why he didn't get out to help or let anyone know he was there, but she wasn't about to ask him about it. He was distant, in another world, sitting there with his jaw clamped so tightly shut, she wouldn't be a bit surprised if his teeth were to crack under the pressure.

He shouldn't be sitting there blaming himself. He had done everything humanly possible for one man to do. They had been on the road since seven o'clock that morning and hadn't stopped until they heard that a dancer's body had been found. Megan had no idea there were that many strip clubs in the Cleveland area. She knew about the ones on Brookpark Road, by the airport, but that was just the beginning. They were scattered everywhere, in every corner of every town, some, no more than a small private room in the back of a bar.

First they checked out the ones David knew about and being on the vice squad for as long as he was, he knew about a lot of them. Megan lost count somewhere after thirty four. Then they stopped at the police station and David had someone run off a printout of at least twenty more. They had worked their way all over Cuyahoga County and a good part of two other counties, but not one of the clubs they stopped at was the place she had seen in her dream.

David's cell phone rang, piercing through the silence in his car. He unclipped it from his belt and looked at the phone number flashing on the screen. Taking a deep breath, he flipped it open. "Stark," he said into the phone as he opened his car door and got out. Megan heard him say, "Yes chief," just before he shut the door.

David stood outside for at least five minutes, listening to the call. Every once in awhile, she could see him nod his head and open his mouth to say something, but apparently he'd get cut off, because he'd immediately shut his mouth and listen again. He finally slapped the phone shut and just stood there a long while, looking down the street at the club.

As she sat there alone, smack dab in the middle of the incredible mess she had found herself in, she wished, with all her heart, she had never made that damn phone call in the first place. If there was anyway she could go back and undo it, she would have. It hadn't done any good. It hadn't helped anyone. As a matter of fact, it looked like David was in a ton of trouble over it.

He got back in the car and started it, but sat there for a minute, his hands on the wheel, staring out the windshield.

Megan's heart was breaking. He was hurting and it was killing her. "David. You can't blame…"

He turned to look at her and the enormous amount of pain she saw in his eyes, silenced her. She reached out her hand to touch his cheek and then slowly leaned forward to kiss him. Just a soft, tender kiss to let him know that he was not alone, that she, too, felt his pain.

David turned his head to look back out the windshield again and, without a word, drove her home.

*   *   *   *

11:17 p.m.

There was a soft knock on David's apartment door. "Go away!" He yelled. He saw the doorknob turn and heard the door slowly creak open. Light spilled in from the outside hallway, flooding the dark room where David was hiding. He looked up from where he was sitting on the floor and squinted against the harsh brightness of the light. The silhouette of a woman stood in his doorway, silver white light outlining her body. David slowly lowered his head back into his arms.

He heard her close the door and felt her eyes watching him as he sat in the middle of his living room floor, grieving for the woman he had failed to save. The guilt he felt was unbearable and the thought of The Cutter being so easily permitted to add another piece of flesh to his sick puzzle, made him furious. The only suspect they had, Craig Freeman, was at home, quietly whacking off, with two police officers to back up his alibi.

After he dropped Megan off at her house, he headed home to take a long, hot shower, in hopes that it would somehow ease the pain in his head. It didn't. And neither did the three beers he poured down his throat since he got home. In fact, it still felt as though his head could split wide open at any moment, spilling his brains out onto the floor, but at least that might bring him some relief.

Why was she here? He didn't want her here. He didn't want Megan to see him like this, a broken man, a failure, a fucking waste of a cop. He wrapped his arms up over his head, trying to silence the voices—the dispatcher announcing that a body had been found in a dumpster behind a strip club only minutes away from where David was—his chief demanding answers after he found out David had spent the entire day searching clubs and warning blonde strippers to be on the lookout—Megan describing every hideous move the killer made with only enough details to make him think he had a chance to stop it, but not enough to actually do any good—and The Cutter laughing at the inept homicide detective who was always just one step behind him.

Eventually, Megan crossed the distance between them and knelt down beside him on the floor. Her arms, still cold from the January night, wound tightly around him and he clung to her, allowing himself to get lost in the soft, comforting arms of the woman he loved. "Please, David," she whispered in his ear, her voice, hoarse and strained. "Please. Stop blaming yourself. You tried. We both did."

David kissed her concerned forehead and stood up, pulling her to her feet along with him. "I'm ok. I was just so sure we were going to save that girl's life. You know she was only seventeen?"

Megan shook her head. Her eyes were red and her lips twisted into a heart-breaking frown.

He gently pinched her chin and forced a smile on his face. "I'm sorry I let you down, Megan. I…" He stopped when he felt a stinging pain behind his eyes and across the bridge of his nose.

David had a lot of explaining to do tomorrow. Banister had made that very clear. He still wasn't sure what he was going to tell them or if he would even have his job by this time tomorrow. But he decided he'd worry about that in the morning. Because tonight, he had the woman he'd been dreaming about standing right there in front of him. And making love to her was the only thing he wanted to think about.

✳   ✳   ✳   ✳

Megan found it impossible to stay away from David. He had been completely devastated when the dancer's body had been found. He seemed so angry with himself that she felt compelled to come here and check on him. Just to make sure he was alright. Even though her being there was probably making things worse, seeing as she was the cause of all his problems.

"Can I get you a rum and Diet Coke?" David asked, on his way to the kitchen.

"Yes, thank you."

He returned to the living room with a bottle of beer and a glass of rum and Diet Coke. "Here," he said and handed her the glass. Eyeing her, he took a long swig of his beer before walking over to the stereo. "Do you like The Dave Matthew's Band?" He asked and knelt down in front of a wire rack that held his CD collection. Megan watched him, searching through the plastic cases. He was wearing an old Browns T-shirt and a pair of jeans with one of the knees ripped out. His damp hair was tousled, dark brown curls twisted in every direction all over his head. He was barefoot and he was gorgeous.

"Yeah." Megan pulled her eyes away and walked over to the sliding glass, patio door to look out over the city she had grown to love. "He's out there somewhere, right now, adding a new piece to his collection," she whispered, mostly to herself.

After sliding a CD into his stereo, he walked up beside her. "And there doesn't seem to be a damn thing I can do to stop him." He took another long swig of his beer. "Do you have any idea how fucking frustrating that is?"

"Yes," she answered simply. Megan was aware he had turned to look at her, but she refused to take her eyes off the downtown skyline, embarrassed by the tears she was unable to control. He must hate her right now, her and her stupid dreams, giving him only enough information to tease him, but never enough to change anything.

David sat his beer on top of the large stereo speaker behind him and reached out for her. His hands cupped her face and gently turned her toward him. "Don't cry, Megan. Don't let that monster make you cry, again." His thumb slid over her cheek and brushed away a tear. "You're not alone anymore, remember that. We're in this together, now. You and I."

He smiled at her then and she caught a glimpse of the deep dimple that cut into his left cheek. It was such a pity really, that they only showed up when he smiled, because in the short time she had known him, David Stark had very little to smile about.

He leaned forward to kiss her on the forehead, then pulled away to look into her eyes. What was he searching for? She had no more answers than he did.

He slowly rubbed his thumb across her lips, sending goose bumps down her neck and arms. Lifting her face with his hand, he bent down to touch his lips to hers, so gently, it was just barely a kiss at all. She felt his tongue lightly trace her bottom lip before it entered her mouth to entwine with her own.

It finally registered in her brain, that he was kissing her. David Stark was kissing her again. She threw her arms up around his neck to kiss him back and accidentally spilled her drink down his back.

He jumped away from her and arched his back. "Whoa, that's cold," he yelped before a broad dimpled smile stretched across his face.

"Oh, God, I'm so sorry!" Megan put her hand over her mouth.

"Now look what you did," David laughed, pulling his T-shirt up over his head and shaking it at her. "I'll have you know, lady, this is a classic Bernie Kozar T-shirt. They just don't make these anymore."

"I like you better without it." Did that actually come out of her mouth? Apparently so, judging by the way David was looking at her, eyes narrow and intense.

A week ago, she would have never said anything like that. A week ago, she would have stayed home after he left her standing in her driveway. But as she showered off the sticky smoke and stench from the dozens of nasty bars and strip clubs they were in, all she could think about was being with him. As the steamy water caressed her body, she had decided it didn't matter whether he wanted a long-term relationship with her or just a one-night stand. All that mattered was being with him, making love to him and feeling him inside her, at last. Even if it was only this one time.

Because the reality of it all was that after this case was over, she might never see him again. She might never get the change to know how incredible it would be to be with him, to have him take her. To have him want her.

Megan didn't care what the morning brought with it, because tonight she was going to have the man who had brought her to life.

David tossed his shirt to the couch, took the empty glass out of her hand and sat it on the speaker, beside his beer. As soon as he turned back to face her, Megan leaned forward and planted a kiss on his bare chest. She loved his body. Hard and tight, but covered with smooth, silky skin that tasted clean and fresh.

He smiled and slipped his hand under her chin, tilting her head up as he bent down to kiss her on the mouth, a real kiss this time, but with a playfulness that had been missing from their first night together.

Megan ran her hands over his smooth, firm shoulders and she smiled under his kiss. He was beautiful, perfect and it felt so good to be touching him again. Her fingers traveled through the few crispy black hairs on his chest and pressed into the tight, solid muscles beneath.

David's hands were busy, too, pulling her lavender sweater up and over her head, tossing it to his left, not really caring if it made it all the way to the couch or not. He looked down at her breasts, confined by only a wispy, white lace bra. His eyelids lowered as he took in a deep breath and leaned forward to kiss the soft mounds of flesh spilling out over the top of the delicate fabric.

His hands found their way to her back and deftly unhooked her bra. She felt his fingers follow the straps up her shoulders and slowly slide them down her arms, letting the lacy garment fall to the floor between them.

David held her hands in his and lifted them up to his lips. He kissed her fingers and the backs of her hands before turning them palm-side up. Both of her wrists had a faded scar across it, left as a reminder of what her last nightmares had led her to do. A constant reminder of how weak she had been and of how little her life had meant to her. Embarrassed by his obvious interest in them, she tried to pull her hands away, but David held on tightly as his right thumb traced the path of one scar.

Looking into her eyes, he gently kissed both scars and placed her arms up around his neck. He wrapped his arms around her waist and pulled her close to his chest, their bare bodies touching for the first time. "My heart aches for that little girl," he whispered into her hair, "and for the beautiful woman in my arms who's still haunted by her dreams."

The sexy, soulful ballad drifted up from the speakers while they stood there in front of the glass door, their skin pressed together, kissing and touching and finding comfort in one another.

David must have read Megan's mind and been more than willing to oblige her, because he abruptly swept her up into his arms. She wrapped her arms around his neck and kissed him, pulling his bottom lip into her mouth. She needed to have this man, the one who hadn't escaped her thoughts since the first night they met. And she needed to have him now, before this night, this opportunity was lost forever.

David kicked open the door to his bedroom with his bare foot. His room had a bed, a simple dresser and plain white walls with no pictures or decorations at all. He pushed the rumbled clothes off his bed, before setting her down and kneeling on the floor in front of her. He kissed her and she kissed him back, her hands on the back of his head, pulling him deeper into their kiss as their tongues danced together.

David unzipped her jeans and she stood so he could easily pull them down her legs and help her step out of them. He lifted each leg and kissed each knee as he pulled off her socks and threw them behind him. He was kneeling in front of her, his mouth just above her belly button and his hands on her back, pulling her to him, as he nibbled on her stomach. His fingers hooked under her lacy white panties and slowly pulled them down her legs, leaving her completely naked and feeling vulnerable, standing there in front of him.

He reached up to her and gently pulled her down to the bed, her legs hanging over the edge as she lay on her back. He lifted her left leg and ran his hands down its length, before placing it on top of his shoulder. His hand reached up to her stomach and then up to her breast, circling her nipple with his finger for a moment before lifting Megan's other leg and putting it over his other shoulder.

"I love the feel of you, Megan," he said, sliding a pillow under her to give him a better angle, "and I'm sure I'm going to love the taste of you." Her stomach was already doing flips before David started at her knees and kissed his way up to her inner thigh and, at last, to the center of her desire. She twisted and jerked from the intense pleasure he brought to her, his tongue and fingers leading her to a place she had never before been. A white hot burning was quickly building inside her and every flick of his long thick finger, every lick of his wet tongue added another flame to the fire.

With building intensity, all her energy and sensations seemed to converge in that one special place between her legs. She wasn't sure if it started at her toes and shot upwards or if it was the other way around, but in a split second, a wondrous explosion ripped through her, causing blinding lights to flash behind her eyes and the folds of skin between her legs to pulsate uncontrollably. She squeezed her eyes shut and tears fell from the outside corners of her eyes as waves of excruciating pleasure shook her whole body.

She could barely breathe as David continued his magnificent torture. Unable to stand another second of it, she sat up and threw her arms around his neck. He held her trembling body, soothing her with warm, gentle kisses on her neck and shoulder. Once she regained control over her breathing, she kissed him and could taste herself on his lips. She pulled away, a little surprised by it. But then she kissed him again, this time with such appreciation that David laughed out loud.

"Why, you're welcome," he said, looking at her from under his hooded eyelids.

Megan stood up on wobbly legs. She wanted him inside her, but just the thought of that right now was enough to cause her to scream. She needed a few minutes to calm her heart and get her body back under control. Pulling him to his feet, she started at his neck with delicate wet kisses before moving down his shoulders and his chest, stopping momentarily to playfully bite one of his erect nipples. She heard him suck in his breath and hold it.

Megan continued her kisses down to his flat, hard stomach. She knelt in front of him and slid her tongue along the waistband of his jeans before she unbuttoned them and slowly pulled his zipper down. He looked at her and took in another deep breath, holding it as she pulled his jeans down his legs, letting them pool around his ankles.

She made up for her lack of experience with the incredible craving she had for the man in front of her, taking as much of him in her mouth as she could with such enthusiasm and gratitude that it made David lose his balance and teeter backward. He reached his hand out for her shoulder and looked up at the ceiling as a long moan escaped his lips.

She was doing this to him. She was causing this strong, tough man to stagger and cry out. She smiled as she continued working her mouth back and forth over the satiny skin.

It wasn't long before he stopped her and pushed her off of him. "Wow." He closed his eyes and exhaled loudly. "You have no idea what you're doing to me." He shook his head, smiled at her and pulled her up from her kneeling position. "If you keep that up much longer, it'll all be over."

He kicked his jeans off his ankles and put his arms around the small of her back, kissing her lips and her neck, his hand moving smoothly down her back to cradle her bottom. He gently laid her back on the bed and positioned himself above her.

"Oh, wait," he said. "I should get something." He stumbled out of bed and over to the dresser, pulling open the top drawer and flinging clothes to the ground. "Got it!" He smiled and held up the little square orange piece of plastic.

David ripped open the package and pulled out the rubber disc, carefully rolling it over his hardness before crawling back onto the bed. He kissed her a few more times before carefully entering her. She shuddered as her tightness devoured him. He pulled out slowly and then gently forced himself into her a little deeper with every thrust until, at last, she stretched enough to allow all of him inside her.

He slid into her fully, his hips solid against her, before pulling back out to repeat it over and over and over again. She squirmed beneath him, until the power of his actions finally built up inside her and she shook from the release of reaching her climax, bucking and moaning in unbearable ecstasy and then shivering as waves of delight flowed through her jelly like body.

Her insides pulsated around him, squeezing him until he, too, started to come. He plunged himself deeply inside her once more and stayed there, his eyes squeezed tightly shut as he trembled above her, his face twisted as if in pain.

David eventually pulled out of her and rolled off onto his back, his thick chest heaving as he lay there beside her. After a few seconds, he pulled her still quivering body into his arms and she clung to him, slowly coming down from where he had taken her.

"Incredible," he whispered, watching her in the light streaming in from the bedroom door. He leaned forward and kissed her on the lips. "That was well worth the wait, don't you think?" Not waiting for an answer, he kissed her again and brushed her long brown hair out of her face.

Megan smiled and nodded. So, he had been thinking about it, too.

David got out of bed, washed up and crawled back into bed. He held her in his arms and pulled a blanket over them.

So exhausted from the last couple of days, it only took a few seconds for her to be lulled by the soothing sound of David's heartbeat, keeping perfect time with the music that crept in from the living room stereo. Megan fell into a deep, content and peaceful sleep, safe in David Stark's arms.

CHAPTER 6

▼

MONDAY, JANUARY 19TH

*   *   *   *

6:58 a.m.

There was a loud knock at the door. "Stark, you in there?" It was Hudson. David rolled over and looked at Megan. She really was there beside him, he hadn't dreamt it after all. He shifted himself up on his elbow and looked down at her. The blanket was just under her right breast and her pink nipple was pulled tightly into a cold little point. Her leg had wrapped up around the edge of the blanket and he could see the side of her rounded hip.

She was beautiful, soft and golden, and he smiled, remembering the great sex they had the night before. Brushing some stray hairs out of her face, he kissed her softly as she blinked her eyes open and smiled up at him.

Hudson knocked louder. "Get your ass out of bed, Stark! Chief wants to see us in an hour!" Hudson yelled through the door, obviously not caring whether any other residents in David's building were sleeping or not. "Stark. Stark. Your damn phone's off the hook!"

A big smile slowly pulled across Megan's lips. "You. You took the phone off the hook, didn't you?" David nodded and she wrapped her arms up around his neck, letting the blanket fall, uncovering her down to her waist. "Why, you sneaky little devil, you."

Her big blue eyes sparkled and David couldn't help but kiss her. Last night he had made sure that no one or no thing stopped him from having her. He only wished there was something he could do about today. But there was nothing he could do to protect them from what was going to happen today.

If only there was some way he could freeze this moment and stay here in the warmth of his bed and the softness of her arms, instead of doing what he'd been dreading since he first got that anonymous phone call about a murder at the St. John's Hotel. If only he could stay in this bed and make love to her just two or three more times.

He smiled at her, regret filling his chest. "I'm glad your here, Megan. Last night was wonderful. I just don't..."

"Damn it, Stark. Wake up or get your ass off the john and open this door!"

"You stay here and I'll get rid of him. I'm not quite ready to subject you to my partner's total lack of charm, just yet." David got out of bed and kissed her softly on the cheek. "Coming!" He yelled over his shoulder and grabbed his jeans, winking at Megan as he closed the bedroom door behind him.

David knew Hudson wanted some answers and apparently he wanted them right now. "You're leaving me out in the dark, damn it. And I don't like it one bit. You fucking know something and for some reason you're intentionally keeping it from me!"

David watched his partner pace back and forth through his living room as he racked his brain for something sensible to say. But nothing made sense. Not one damn thing that had happened made any sense at all.

"What's your angle, Stark? What in the hell do you know? And why the fuck aren't you telling me about it?" Hudson crossed his arms in front of his chest and glared at him before shaking his hands in the air. "I can't, for the life of me, imagine what could be so fucking secret that you can't even tell your own partner about it. You *knew* about the last three victims, didn't you? It's like you're fucking psychic or something."

Well, there it was. Psychic or something. How in the hell was he going to tell his partner, that's exactly what it was? That there was a naked woman lying in his bed right now who was psychic. David shook his head and walked into the kitchen to start the coffee. There was no easy way to do this. He'll be damn lucky, if they didn't end up throwing him off the force or worse yet, lock him in a padded cell.

"Um…hum." Hudson cleared his throat as he walked into the kitchen with a lacy white bra hanging from his index finger. He took a long whiff of the lacy material. "Smells like you've changed your cologne, buddy." Hudson shook his head. "You got something you want to tell me?"

David snatched the bra out of his hands. "No."

"She's here isn't she? That girl from the hotel. I *knew* she had something to do with this. But if she's your source, kid, why are you keeping her under wraps? And why in the hell are you sleeping with her? Have you lost your fucking mind? You know, those Feds are gonna be all over your ass when they find out and if you're not careful, boy, they could have your badge over this."

"How 'bout you getting out of here and I'll meet you at the office in an hour?" David held the bra behind his back as he walked to the front door and opened it. "I'll explain everything to you and Banister then."

Hudson walked out the door and into the hall. "This is some serious shit, boy. You know that, don't you?" He turned to look at David, distrust and suspicion in his eyes. Then he shook his head and headed for the stairs.

Damn it! He'd really fucked up this time. David slowly closed the door. He should have just told Hudson everything, right from the beginning. This thing with Megan had snowballed into such a gigantic mess that coming clean now might just be too little, too late. The damage, he feared, had already been done.

"Is it safe?" Megan walked out of the bedroom in her jeans and a white, long-sleeve shirt she had gotten out of David's closet. "I hope you don't mind." She pinched the collar of the shirt that came down to her knees.

David shook his head and released the death grip he had on the door knob. Silently he walked back into the kitchen to get a cup of the coffee that was beginning to fill the room with its rich aroma. Megan walked up behind him with her hand out. He looked at her, then at her hand, not understanding what it was she wanted until she walked closer to him and took her bra out of his hand.

"Oh," he said, snapping out of his daze. "I'm sorry. I think your sweater's on the couch. Want a cup of coffee?"

"No, thank you." Megan walked into the living room. "So. What are you going to tell them?" She asked. "They're gonna want to know everything."

"I really don't know what I *can* tell them."

"How about the truth?" Megan was in the living room with her back to him, as she unbuttoned his shirt and laid it on the back of the couch. David's mouth began to water as he admired her smooth golden skin, the curves of her back and the outline of her breast. He watched her work to put her bra on and longed to make love to her again. If only things were different, if only he wasn't standing there deciding how to handle a situation that was probably going to destroy his career, his reputation and, not to mention, any chance he had of a real relationship with Megan. Today everything was on the line.

David pulled his eyes away from her. "Oh sure. Right. I'll just waltz into my chief's office and tell him I'm chasing after your bogeyman. Bet he'll get a big kick out of that!" He slammed his fist down on the kitchen counter. "Damn it. There's no way I can make them understand this." He leaned over the counter. "Hell, Megan, I don't even understand it! It's hard enough for me to believe it. How can I expect them to?"

He paused for a second and stared at her. "How in the *hell* can you possibly know what's in that monster's mind?" He practically yelled at her. He wanted to scream at her for being part of this, for not simply being the woman he could come home to and sleep with at the end of the day.

How she could be on the same "wavelength," as Nancy called it, with a complete psychopathic murderer just didn't make any sense to him. What was the connection? He believed she really was having dreams about it. There was no way he could deny that, now. But how? Why?

Those were the questions he needed to find the answers to. Was there a connection to the murders back when she was a kid? Or was it just a coincidence? Some kind of high energy thought pattern she tuned into? Or was it like Marsha Jones had said and Megan was somehow connected to The Cutter or one of his victims. God! All this hocus-pocus bullshit was driving him crazy. How could anyone make sense out of something that just didn't make any sense?

"I could go with you," Megan said, and then looked as though she instantly regretted her offer. "I don't want to. But if it will help, I will. Besides, maybe coming from both of us, it'll be easier for them to believe it."

David bit his bottom lip and quietly nodded. He was hoping she would say that. He didn't want to walk into his boss's office alone and tell this ridiculous story without her there to back it up. But he didn't want to be the one to suggest she go with him, either. Because chances were, it was going to get pretty ugly.

Hey, who knows, maybe she could tell her story and with him there to verify it all, the chief would have to believe them. Aw, who the fuck was he kidding?

*   *   *   *

8:32 a.m.

After a quick shower, they drove to the police station together. Megan was already regretting her decision, when they walked into the crowded building. Hudson and Chief Banister were waiting for David in Banister's office.

"You better wait here." David winked at her and pointed to an empty desk across the room from the office. "Let me brief them on what's been going on. I think it'll be easier that way."

Banister had a large windowed office, where he could sit at his desk and see the entire room and, from David's desk, Megan could easily see the three men behind closed doors. David talked for about five minutes, before Banister stood up from behind his desk and animatedly hit the desk with his fist as he yelled something. Hudson threw his arms up in the air and paced back and forth across the office, like a caged tiger.

Suddenly, both men turned in unison and looked at Megan. She wanted to crawl under the scratched metal desk, but instead, she forced herself to pull her shoulders back and sit up as straight and as tall in the chair as she could.

The men went back to yelling at David, each taking his own turn. But David remained calm, talking only after the other men had their say. Hudson must have heard something he especially didn't like, because he exploded out of the office, slamming the door behind him. He stopped and glared at Megan, his eyes, nasty little black slits, before storming out the front door of the station.

The normal din around her stopped and there was a few seconds of uneasy silence throughout the office as everyone tried to figure out what the latest drama was all about.

Megan watched David, looking very much like a little boy in his principal's office, hands in his front pockets, eyes cast down and looking...guilty. He was probably still blaming himself for not being able to save that dancer's life the night before and it wasn't right. It wasn't his fault. If it was anyone's fault it was her's. The sight of him taking the brunt of all this alone was breaking her heart and she couldn't stand to see him take anymore of this abuse on her behalf.

She walked across the room and knocked on Banister's door as she opened it. "May I come in?" She asked, walking through the door and closing it behind her, before anyone could answer. "I think I may be able to help you better understand what Detective Stark is talking about. If you'll just hear me out."

Banister was instantly the gentleman in front of Megan, as she knew he would be. "Yes, of course. Please sit down, Miss Montgomery, isn't it?"

Megan nodded and took a seat in front of Banister's desk.

"Detective Stark tells me you say you're having dreams that could be connected to The Cutter…"

"Could be?" David started to voice his objections, but a quick, nasty glance by Banister, stopped him.

"And that is how he has known the whereabouts of the last three victims," Banister continued. "Is that right?" The chief's voice was calm, but his face was still red and sweaty from the screaming he did just moments before Megan walked in.

"That's right, sir." Megan wiped the palms of her hands on her jeans and told him her story, starting with what happened in Clarksburg and ending with the murder of the dancer last night.

Chief Banister sat in his chair, his hands clasped together under his chin, politely listening as Megan told him everything. After she had finished, he sat back in his chair, crossed his arms in front of him and rocked a few times, while chewing at the corner of his bottom lip. "Well, Miss Montgomery," he finally said, "we certainly do appreciate your coming forward with this information. However, you must understand our department's policies regarding psychics."

Megan winced at the name Banister had just called her.

"It has never been the practice of The Cleveland Police Department to follow leads that have no basis in fact."

"No basis in fact?" David barked. "How in the hell can you say that, Chief? Her dreams were the reason I found Brenda Parker and the body of Dixie Jones and she is the only reason I was almost able to prevent the murder of Jamie Standen last night!"

"Almost," Banister shot back at him and Megan could see the pain that word caused him. "I'm not saying you haven't given Detective Stark a lot of information about The Cutter, Miss Montgomery." Banister stood up behind his desk. "It's obvious you have. I'm just questioning your source."

Megan stood up. "Well, then. May I please have my one phone call now before you throw me in jail for being stupid enough to think I should try and help?"

"Now, Miss Montgomery. I don't think we need to go that far." Banister walked around his desk and put his hand on her back. "But I would like to have you give us an official statement. I'll get Officer Simons to take it." David opened his mouth, but before he could object, Banister held up his hand and silenced him. "Stark, you stay right here. I'm not quite finished with you, just yet."

David reached his hand out and put it on Megan's arm. She knew he was sorry, but she also knew there was nothing he could do about it. It was out of his hands now.

Banister escorted Megan out of the room and through the sea of desks to an interrogation room with three blindingly white walls and one dark mirrored wall where she could be watched from another room. There was a black video camera hanging from the ceiling in one corner, and it was pointing directly at a table in the center of the room with a chair on either side. It was just like in the movies and it made her feel sick to her stomach.

"Don't let the room scare you, Miss Montgomery," Banister said with a smile. "You're not being interrogated. I just want an official statement taken and this is the only private room we have available, right now. I'd like very much to keep this situation quiet. I hope you understand my predicament. I don't think the newspapers would be very kind to either of us, if this got out."

He pulled out a chair for Megan and pushed it back in, after she sat down. "I hope I have your cooperation in keeping this little..." he searched for the right word, "this information you have out of the papers."

Megan nodded and rolled her eyes when he walked out of the room. What did he think she was going to do? Sell her story to The Inquirer, so it could really ruin her life? Sure, why not? Why should she care if the entire world thought she was a freak who was dreaming about a serial killer? That would look great on any résumé. What mother wouldn't want Megan teaching her seven-year-old?

*   *   *   *

David sat alone in Banister's office, leaning his pounding head on the back of the chair, as his fingers massaged his temples. But his massive headache was nothing compared to the pain in his chest. Knowing what Megan was going through in the other room was making him ill. He should have never let her come down here with him. He knew what was going to happen.

Maybe he should have just lied. But lied and told them what? There was nothing. No lie, no truth they would believe. He hated the trap he had led Megan into. David shook his head and closed his eyes. Things were quickly going from bad to worse.

Banister returned to his office and closed the door behind him. David opened his eyes and watched his chief walk to the front of his desk and sit down on the corner. "Ok, Stark, how do we know *she's* not The Cutter?"

"Oh, come on. For Christ's sake!" David threw his arms in the air and rose up out of the chair. "I told you, she was with me the entire day yesterday, searching for the strip joint she saw in her dream." David walked around to the back of the chair. He didn't want to be too close to the man he had just gotten the sudden urge to punch in the face.

"She was in the car with me, when we heard the call about the stripper's body being found." David put his hands on the back of the chair and leaned forward. "She even told me about the man in the blue Escort yesterday morning! Fourteen hours *before* it happen."

"You know, there's only a hand full of guys I wouldn't have thrown out of my office by now and you're one of them. But a psychic? I just don't know. It's....."

"Fucking nuts?" David finished Banister's sentence for him. "Why the hell do you think I waited so long to tell you about this? To tell anyone about this. You saw the way Hudson ran out of here. I knew no one would believe it. But she's for real, man. I didn't believe it at first, either. I wanted to be damn sure, before I said anything."

"And?"

"And *now* I'm damn sure."

"Doesn't make any sense." Banister shook his head.

"You're telling me?"

The phone on Banister's desk rang and he reached around behind him to pick it up. "Banister," he said and listened. "What? Aw, fuck! Ok, listen, I want you to keep them outside and tell them we will have a statement for them in a few minutes. Nothing more, you got it? Do you know who tipped them off?" There was silence. "Ok. Just get out there."

"Son of a bitch!" Banister slammed down the phone and stood up. "Someone's tipped off the press that we have a psychic in here helping us on the case."

"Oh, shit," David said, thrusting his fingers through his hair. "It's gonna turn into a fucking circus. Who spilled it?"

"Could be anyone. With Hudson's mouth, the whole city probably knows by now."

*   *   *   *

"That's her, Harry! Snap it now!" A reporter pushed his photographer at Megan as she walked out of the police department, escorted by the officer who had taken her statement. The camera flashes and the stampede of reporters startled her, causing her to lose her balance on the slick concrete steps. Officer Simons grabbed a hold of her and held her arm until she regained her footing.

Simons was to drop her off at her car because she was told David had other things to take care of. She shook her head and sank into the policeman's arms. It was Clarksburg all over again and if she thought the press had been rough on her when she was eleven, she couldn't even imagine how horrible this was going to get.

She wished David was the one holding her now. She needed him, he was her strength and his belief in her was what was going to get her through this. But right now, he had his own problems to deal with.

Within seconds of walking out the door, swarms of flash bulbs, microphones, TV cameras and questions bombarded her.

"Miss Montgomery," there was a hush over the sea of reporters as a young, black man asked his question. "I've been told you're a psychic who has come forward to help the police capture The Cutter. Is that true?"

The words were like a starter pistol, signaling to every other reporter to begin his or her own line of questioning.

"Can you tell us when The Cutter is going to strike next?"

"Did the police call you in?"

"Can you tell us who The Cutter is?"

Megan shook her head as microphones were jabbed at her face and flash bulbs exploded in her eyes. She put her hands over her face, trying to hide as she and Officer Simons fought their way through the crowd.

"Do you use a crystal ball or Tarot cards?"

"Can you go into a psychic trance for us now?"

The ridiculous questions swirled around her, making her dizzy and disoriented. She pushed her way down the steps, leaving Simons to fight off one especially rambunctious reporter who had tried to grab Megan by her hair.

Suddenly, the attention on the stairs turned away from Megan and focused on David and Chief Banister as they opened the door and stood on the top step of the old government building.

Megan looked up the stairs and took a step toward David, longing for him to save her, to protect her, but he simply stood there beside Banister, intentionally diverting his eyes away from her.

"Your attention please," Banister yelled over the rumbling of the crowd. "Your attention please. This is Detective David Stark. He is in charge of this investigation, along with his partner, Detective Frank Hudson. He has prepared a brief statement."

David looked straight ahead and cleared his throat. "We have several witnesses who have come forward from last night's murder of Jamie Standen and there's not much doubt that the suspect you call The Cleveland Cutter is the culprit. As soon as we have gathered and verified all information regarding last night's horrendous act of violence against Ms. Standen, we will call a press conference. Thank you." David turned quickly to escape the thousands of questions exploding from the horde of reporters.

"Is it true, a psychic is helping you with the case?"

"Did Megan Montgomery lead you to the victim?"

"Is it true, she dreams about the murders, before they happen?"

Banister put his hand on David's shoulder and he turned back around to face the press. "It is the opinion of The Cleveland Police Department," David spoke, as if reading from an invisible script, "that Megan Montgomery has nothing to contribute to this investigation. She has given her statement and we thanked her, but it has been decided that the information she gave us does not warrant our wasting the department's time or the public's money chasing after her imaginary phantom." David's eyes looked directly at Megan as his words ripped out her heart.

"Detective Stark, is it your opinion that Megan Montgomery is a fraud?" One reporter yelled out.

"Um, I, uh." David stumbled over his words and then cleared his throat. "Yes. Yes, it is."

Megan stood there for a second, staring in disbelief at the man she had given herself to so completely the night before. The man who had kissed her and touched her where no other man ever had. He was to be her strength, her backbone, her rock.

She thought she loved him and this morning she actually thought he might love her back. But that man was a stranger to her now, standing up there, telling the world she was a fake and denying the fact that she had even helped him, at all.

It shouldn't have surprised her. It's what they had done to her in Clarksburg. Used her and discarded her, leaving her to pick up the pieces of her broken life.

But they hadn't used her the way David had. He had used her in ways she might never be able to recover from. Not only had he just publicly denounced her, he had broken the heart she had, for so long, kept safely locked away.

She closed her eyes and felt warm tears rolling down her face as she turned and raced down the rest of the steps, to the sidewalk and down the street. She ran, not knowing where she was headed and not caring. She just needed to get away, as far away from the reporters and David Stark as she could get.

After a couple of blocks, the yells and the pounding footsteps faded. The only noises she heard were the sounds of tires rolling through the snowy slush, an angry car horn and the crackling of frozen icicles hanging from the building above her.

She stopped and wiped her eyes with the scratchy, black wool gloves on her hands and took a quick look behind her. The press had given up on the chase and David was nowhere to be seen. She was glad because she never wanted to see his face again. She walked up to the next crosswalk and looked behind her again. Why hadn't he followed her? She really thought he would have. He should have, after what he had done to her.

She knew Banister was behind it. That he was the one that made David say those things. Because there couldn't be any doubt left in his mind that her dreams were for real. But that was beside the point. He *did* say those terrible things. They came right out of his mouth and there was no gun to his head. More importantly, he had broken the promise he had made to her.

He had lied to her and she felt more alone now than she had since she sat in that cold, silver, metal chair in that scary mental hospital all those years ago. While all those doctors, with their long, white coats and their prying eyes, watched her every move and jotted down her every word on their little brown clipboards.

After aimlessly walking around for what had to be over an hour, a blast of January wind reminded Megan how cold it actually was and she finally decided to hail a taxi to take her back to her car. The sooner she got her car, the sooner she could get home, crawl into bed and forget all about The Cutter, the police, the reporters, and most importantly, Detective David Stark.

A green and white taxi pulled to the curb and stopped. She got into the back seat and gave the driver directions to David's apartment building. When the taxi pulled into the building's parking lot, she saw David, leaning up against her car.

What was he doing there? Did he actually think he could apologize for what he had done to her? What was he hoping for, another tumble in bed, maybe? Did he think she was stupid? Apparently so. But the truth was simple. He had deserted her, turned his back on her when she needed him most.

If he wanted her forgiveness, he could forget it. It wasn't happening. Because if there was one thing she was for sure, it was a quick learner. And she had learned the hard way that Detective Stark was a cop, plain and simple. A cop who obviously had no qualms about sleeping with someone just to keep the information coming. And as far as Megan was concerned, he could go to hell right along with The Cutter.

"Can you just circle around please and take me across town to Taylorwood Avenue?" Megan asked the driver. He nodded and drove past David on his way around the parking lot. Megan watched out the back window of the taxi as David ran after them, waving his arms and yelling something. "Just keep going, please," she whispered, turning back around in her seat and closing her eyes.

Detective Stark better have enjoyed last night, because she'd be damned if it was never going to happen again.

*   *   *   *

12:51 p.m.

David slammed the door to his apartment. He was absolutely frozen through to the bone. He'd been standing outside in the snow for almost an hour, waiting for Megan to come back and get her car.

He threw his jacket over the back of his couch and rubbed his hands together, trying to bring some feeling back into them. He missed her already. He wanted to have her with him tonight. He wanted to make love to her, to fall asleep to the sound of her breathing and to wake up with her in his arms. But as he plopped down on the couch, he knew that wasn't likely to happen again anytime soon. It was obvious she wasn't even going to give him the opportunity to explain.

He was sorry he didn't get the chance to talk to her before the press conference, but he would have done the exact same thing again. Banister had made a deal with him. If David could stop the press circus before it got totally out of control, he would allow him to secretly work with her on the case. He was actually intrigued by what David had to say about her dreams. He just didn't want all of Cleveland and most importantly, the mayor and the Feds, knowing that one of his detectives was working with a psychic.

But the facts spoke for themselves. He had known David a long time and he trusted him. So if David thought Megan could help him find The Cutter, well,

Banister decided he was going to give him the opportunity to prove it. The fact of the matter was, whether Banister believed the story or not, he was willing to give David the benefit of the doubt.

They both agreed they wouldn't get anywhere with the press hounding Megan and reporting every step she made. But what really had David worried was if The Cutter believed she could identify him, her life would be in danger. So, in one brief statement, David tried to make sure the reporters wouldn't spend too much time on her and The Cutter wouldn't consider her a real threat. But just in case, David had already posted a man outside her home, to keep an eye on her.

The plan was for Simons to quietly get her home and David would say his little piece and head for Megan's to tell her what was going on. But the reporters were like hawks, swarming around her as soon as she walked out the door. He felt bad, but he figured he'd be able to talk to her and straighten things out as soon as she came back to get her car. If she would have just given him a fucking chance!

Women! David hadn't planned on her being so pissed she'd rather leave her car there than to talk to him. He saw the look on her face through the back window of the taxi. She was mad. Real mad. It was going to take some time for her to cool off enough for him to even get near her, much less get her to listen to anything he had to say.

He'd give her time, if that's what she needed. He had to get back to work anyway. There were a lot of leads to follow up on. The man in the blue car who had surprised The Cutter in the parking lot didn't get a decent look at The Cutter's face, but he was able to give the police a very helpful description of the car. And it matched that of Megan's. A silver or white 1980 something Oldsmobile. It wasn't much, but it was a hell of a lot more than they had before.

The police had the DMV looking statewide for anyone with that type of car. Hopefully it wouldn't be long now. Soon these clues would lead them to The Cutter. But there was a lot of work to do before that happened and he just didn't have the time to wait around for Megan to forgive him.

She really had no right to get that pissed off at him. If she would have just stopped for a second and thought about it, she would know that what he had done was for the best. Why should he even have to apologize? He had done the right thing. And he did it for her own good. Couldn't she see that? Couldn't she understand he had done it all to keep her safe?

Well, if that was true, why did he feel so damn bad? Why did his chest ache every time he remembered the look on her face? And why did it fucking bother him so much that she was across town, hating him right now?

He put his arm up to his nose and inhaled. Yeah, that's what he thought. It wasn't all in his head, he could still smell her on his shirt. She looked so good standing right here just a few hours ago, taking off this shirt. She was definitely something he could see himself getting use to.

*   *   *   *

1:24 p.m.

"What in heaven's name happened?" Nancy demanded as soon as Megan walked through the front door.

"I really messed up." Megan sat down on a little wooden bench and pulled off her shoes. "I went with David this morning to the police station and I told them everything. They didn't believe a word I said. They called me a fraud. David called me a fraud. He told everyone I was lying."

"Yeah. I know."

"How? How did you…."

"You've been on the television all afternoon, honey. The phone's been ringing off the hook." When Megan stood up, Nancy took her into her arms and hugged her. "I heard everything he said and I'm so sorry, pumpkin, I thought he was different. I really liked him. I thought he was going to help you."

"Me, too."

After Nancy made her eat a little something, which was more like a five course meal, she went back to work, but not before Megan had to swear on a stack of Bibles that she was alright.

It felt good to be alone. She took the phone off the hook and walked into the kitchen to make herself a drink. As she poured the clear Bacardi rum into her glass, she decided she didn't need him. That one night of sex, no matter how fabulous, didn't really add up to much in the long run. It obviously meant nothing to him. It was just sex. It had served its purpose and now it was over.

And she was fine with that. She was probably better off, actually. Men were trouble, too much work, like vampires draining a woman of all her energy and focus. There was a good reason she had decided to avoid them until after her career was on track. And if only she had stuck to her original plan, she wouldn't be standing here with a broken heart.

But she had to admit, last night was incredible. More than incredible, to her anyway. Probably nothing more to him than another notch in his holster. This shouldn't be such a big deal really. After all, she had just met the man. She had gotten what she deserved for jumping into bed with a complete stranger. What did she expect? The situation was just so intense, she'd simply been swept up in the madness of it all. It wasn't as if she was in love with him or anything.

Megan laughed under her breath and took a drink. If she was trying to make herself feel better, it wasn't working. She *was* in love with the jerk and that was just too bad for her. She'd have to get over it, that's all. And as impossible as that seemed right now, she knew she eventually would. "Life goes on," she told her empty glass as she placed it in the sink and dragged herself up the stairs to her room.

It seemed unbelievable that just the night before his arms were around her and his kisses covered her entire body. Unbelievable that just this morning she woke up in his bed with that perfect, hard body of his hovering over her. Megan took a deep breath and closed her eyes. And it was unbelievable how incredible he made her feel.

She crawled into bed, pulled her flowered comforter up over her head and, in that warm cocoon of blankets, felt more and more alone with every beat of her heart.

CHAPTER 7

▼

TUESDAY, JANUARY 20TH

*   *   *   *

5:10 a.m.

The morning paper landed on David's desk with a thud. "Wake up, sleeping beauty," Officer Thomas said, passing in front of David as he threw a copy of the newspaper on the top of everyone's desk.

David yawned, scratched his head and squinted at his watch. "When did I crash?"

"Huh?" Hudson peeked around his computer screen at David, looking half asleep himself. "What'd ya say?"

"I must've fallen asleep. You want some more coffee?" David pushed himself up out of his chair, stretched his arms and yawned again.

"Hell, no," Hudson yawned back. "If I drink one more cup of coffee, my eyes will turn as brown as yours. I'm already gonna spend the rest of the day pissin' as it is." Hudson leaned back in his chair and stretched so far, he almost tipped his chair over. "What time is it anyway?"

"A little after five." David poured himself a cup of coffee, gulped down the caffeine and ran a hand through the mop of hair on his head. "You know, I'd like to open a little pizza joint, someday. My mom has this killer recipe for sauce that's outta this world. That'd be the life, alright. Think about it. No more all-nighters, no more perverted sickos, no more hacked up corpses. Just nice regular people and nice regular hours. I could have a life, too. Maybe get married again, have a couple kids and actually be around to watch 'em grow up. I heard somewhere there were people out there who actually did that sorta thing."

"You'd die of boredom after the third day," Hudson said. He opened his desk drawer, pulled out a bottle of Tums and twisted the lid off. He shook two tablets into his hand, tossed them in his mouth and chewed them up before throwing the bottle back into his drawer. "Sleep, I need some sleep. I'm gettin' too old for this." Hudson stiffly stood up and headed to the restroom. "I'm gonna spend the first two weeks of my retirement, in bed."

"As sad as that is, it sounds pretty good right now." David dropped back down in his chair with his cup of black coffee and picked up the newspaper. Right there, on the front page, was a big color picture of Megan underneath the bold printed caption, 'COPS CLAIM PSYCHIC A FRAUD'. David visibly winced. That sure as hell wasn't going to help Megan forgive him anytime soon.

The picture was taken in front of the police department when the press had surrounded her. She looked frightened and trapped. He studied her picture, the soft curves of her face, her big, round, startling blue eyes. She really was beautiful.

He sat back in his chair, still holding the paper in front of his face, and felt sick to his stomach. Shit. He hoped he hadn't done something that couldn't ever be undone. He hoped he hadn't done something that she could never forgive him for.

David started missing her again. He had tried to call her at least two or three times since he got back to the station, but she had taken her phone off the hook. And now he was going to go home soon, to an empty apartment and sleep in an empty bed. A bed in which, just yesterday, he had made love to the beautiful, sexy woman in that picture.

He wanted her lying there beside him. He was too tired to do anything but sleep. But he still wanted her close to him, to know she was safe in his arms, to know he *could* make love to her, if he just happened to be so inclined. But there seemed to be no chance of that anytime in the near future.

David decided the best thing to do was to give her some time to cool off. He was busy right now, anyway. But once The Cutter was behind bars, he'd get her to forgive him. He'd do whatever it took. A smile pulled at the corners of his lips at the thought of having her back into his life, back into his arms and back into his bed.

"Oh, lover boy." Hudson returned from the bathroom just in time to interrupt David's little daydream by grabbing the paper out of his hand. "Well, she may be a loony tune, but she's a beautiful loony tune. Kinda looks like Michelle, when she was younger. Except for the hair." Hudson mumbled something else David couldn't quite make out as he grabbed his keys off his desk and walked out of the office without taking his eyes off Megan's picture.

David sat up straight in his chair. *Red hair!* Hudson's wife had beautiful long red hair. The picture on Hudson's desk came sharply into focus. It was a picture of his wife Michelle about a year before the accident. She was a very pretty, well endowed woman in her early fifties with fiery red hair, down past her shoulders.

David didn't like the thoughts that were beginning to fill his mind and he shook his head to sort the allegations building against his partner. There was no ignoring the fact that things were starting to add up.

The witness from the hotel picked him out of the lineup and Hudson certainly could fit Megan's description. Of course, so could every other fifty to sixty year-old white male with rough old hands. Not much to go on there.

But, there was something about the way he talked about The Cutter's collection that had unnerved David. At the time, he just chalked it up to the numbness policemen feel after too many years in the field. All cops got that way after awhile, it was an occupational hazard.

But why had he become so furious when David told him and Banister about Megan's dreams? Granted, it wasn't like David expected him to embrace the idea with open arms, but he was a little surprised at Hudson's overly irate protest to Megan's help with the case.

Oh, for God's sake, what was he suggesting? There had to be a thousand old men in the Cleveland area who like redheads. And as far as using Megan's dreams as a lead in the case, hell, it took David awhile to really believe it. He remembered how angry he was with Megan that first night they met and he felt ashamed he was so quick to even think such a ridiculous thing.

"Here's that info you wanted on Peter Logan in Clarksburg, West Virginia," a woman said, handing David a thick manila folder.

"Thanks, Laurie." David smiled at the young officer who filled out her dark blue uniform better than anyone else in the department. The pretty blonde returned his smile as she backed away slowly without taking her eyes off of him. She bumped into a nearby desk and giggled nervously, trying to hide the blush that filled her cheeks as she hurried back down the hall.

David turned his attention to the file in his hands. He had put in a request with the research department for all the information they could get him on Peter

Logan right after he talked to Marsha Jones at that new-age book store. He was wondering if there was some kind of connection, something that he was over-looking, and judging by the thickness of the file, there was no lack of information on the subject.

David read through the scores of newspaper clippings, police reports, trial highlights and interviews with the mass murderer from his prison cell. Logan was only nineteen when he murdered Megan's parents, Debbie and Gene Maxwell. They were his first two victims. The third victim was a woman who lived in the trailer park where Logan lived with his mother, before she died. The fourth was a woman who worked the late shift at a liquor store. And the fifth and sixth were a couple that were out for a late night walk.

The would-be seventh victim was a woman who worked at a grocery store in town. Luckily, with the details Megan's doctors gave the police from a dream she had while in the hospital, the police knew the exact place and time Logan would strike next. This time, however, instead of the grocer, Logan found an under-cover cop behind the counter and it had been an easy bust.

Peter Logan was convicted on six counts of first-degree murder and sentenced to six consecutive life sentences, but his motives were never really explained. There were no signs of robbery at any of the scenes and no apparent connection between the victims. Logan used the same gun to kill all of the victims and it was the same gun he carried into the grocery store when he was busted.

He didn't testify on his own behalf to shed any light on his motives, it just seemed like the kid snapped after his mother died. The prosecution painted a pic-ture of Peter Logan as an insensitive killing machine with little to no regard for human life and they didn't need any more of a motive than that.

Take out the whole psychic dream stuff and it was a pretty cut and dry case. The only thing that really stuck out was an article reporting that on the day of his conviction, as he was being led away, Logan yelled to reporters that he hoped his father was happy.

David pulled that news report out of the file. "Hey, Matthews. Can you get me the West Virginia State Penitentiary on the phone, please?"

"Sure, honey, hold on," answered the older woman sitting at the main desk by the door.

After a bit of a runaround from the warden, David was finally given permis-sion to speak to Peter Logan at noon later that day. He looked at his watch. It was almost seven. "Well, I guess that will have to do. Thanks for all your help," he said, sounding more sarcastic than he meant to, and hung up the phone.

He closed the hefty file on Peter Logan and stretched. He yawned and rested the back of his head on his chair while his thoughts immediately rushed back to Megan. He had to see her today. This was crazy. He couldn't stop thinking about her. Besides the fact that she was smack dab right in the center of the biggest case he had ever worked on, he was in love with her.

It wasn't exactly what he wanted right now, as a matter of fact, the timing couldn't be worse. But that didn't change the fact that he had, against his wishes, fallen hopelessly and madly in love with her.

"Hey, why don't you go home and get some rest?" David looked up and saw Chief Banister walking over to his desk. "You look terrible, Stark. Have you been here all night?"

David nodded and combed his fingers through his hair.

"You know you won't do us any good, if you're too tired to think. I need you and Hudson to be on top of things, now more than ever. The press is eating us alive and the commissioner is about to serve my head on a shiny silver platter to the mayor. And, of course, let's not forget those two Feds, on me like flies on shit. I got to get them some answers and I mean in a hurry!" Banister looked around, then leaned forward and whispered, "Has Miss Montgomery given you anything more we can use?"

"No, not really," David said, unwilling to tell his boss they weren't exactly on speaking terms at the moment.

"Did Hudson come up with anything on the car?"

"I don't think so." David stood up and walked over to Hudson's desk. "He was so tired, he left without even turning off his computer. I think I'll enlarge the search and see if I can't come up with something."

"Not too long, ok? You got to get yourself some sleep. And that's an order." Banister turned and headed for his office.

"Yeah, ok," David muttered as he sat down in front of Hudson's computer and began typing in a new search for the DMV on the Internet. He requested a statewide list of 1970 to 1990 Oldsmobiles, any color, with current or expired tags.

Hudson had been looking for a 1980 to 1989 silver or white Olds with current tags. Neither Megan nor the witness in the blue Escort had seen a license plate and in the dark, in a split second or two, they could have guessed wrong on the year and the color. Anyway, it couldn't hurt to check it out.

The harsh white light glowing from the monitor's screen was causing his already tired eyes to burn as he blinked at the endless list of names scrolling down the computer screen. He had just about talked himself into heading home for some much needed sleep when something caught his attention. Light blue, 1978, Oldsmobile Cutlass Supreme. Title held by one Michelle Hudson of West 22nd Street, Cleveland, Ohio.

In the dark, under parking lot lights, a light blue car could have looked silver. Why hadn't Hudson said anything about Michelle's car? Why would he have? He probably didn't even have it anymore. But what if he did?

David didn't like it, but suspicion started filling his head again. Evidence was piling up and it was pointing directly at Hudson. He leaned forward to take a closer look at the computer screen and his mind raced. Could it possibly be true?

No. No! He refused to believe it. There had to be some other explanation. But there was just a little too much to ignore. First the line up, then the redhead thing, and now the car. And perhaps more importantly, was the motive. He could be building a new Michelle to replace his dead wife. The clues were all pointing in one direction and David didn't like it one little bit.

He had to be real careful about this. Police officers don't go around accusing other police officers of murder, unless they have rock solid evidence. Not to mention, Hudson was his partner and a good cop with a lot more pull around here than he had. David had to be one hundred percent sure before he did or said anything.

His brain felt like mush. He was too tired to think anymore and to sick to imagine the possibility, so he printed the screen and shut down the computer. He was going home to take a long shower and a short nap. Then, with a clearer mind, he could figure out what to do next. He would decide what was the best way to go about getting some psychical evidence to support or, hopefully, disprove his theory about Hudson.

David pulled on his jacket and prayed to God he was wrong.

*   *   *   *

8:46 a.m.

Megan arrived at Fenwood Elementary School looking forward to getting back to some normal routine and talking to Sue. She wanted to see how she was holding up and how Bear was. And after school today, she was going to take Sue out for a drink and tell her everything. Everything about the nightmares, about The Cutter and about David Stark.

The last few days had been crazy, almost surreal. She felt like she had been on a rollercoaster that she couldn't get off of. What she needed now was to throw herself back into her work and forget about everything else.

When Megan walked into the classroom, Sue nearly jumped out of her seat, ushered her back out into the hall and closed the door to her classroom. "What the hell is going on?" She whispered.

"What do you mean?" Megan had never seen Sue so serious and upset before. "Is this about the break in? Is Bear ok?"

"Meg! Your picture's on the front page of the paper this morning. Someone said you were even on the news last night. That cop that was here asking a bunch of questions about you the other day, it was all about your dreams, wasn't it?"

Megan nodded, her eyes beginning to sting a little.

"Mr. Temple's been in here twice already, looking for you. He wants me to send you down to his office as soon as you get here. What's going on, honey? Those nightmares you've been having, they're not really about The Cutter, are they?"

For some stupid reason, Megan thought the insanity from yesterday would somehow fail to penetrate the thick, red brick walls of her sanctuary here at school. She had hoped to come in here just like every other day and do what she normally did and forget all about how out of hand her life had gotten and about how easily David Stark had shattered her heart into pieces.

Megan felt her chin begin to quiver. She shrugged her shoulders and nodded her head, afraid to open her mouth in case cries would escape instead of words.

"Oh, honey." Sue put her arm around Megan's shoulder.

Megan pulled away. It was taking everything she had to keep it together and a hug from her best friend right now just might send her over the edge. There was no way she would be able to stop the tears, once they started. Megan cleared her throat and stretched her neck up as high as it could go. "What does Mr. Temple want?"

"He wouldn't tell me anything, but you better go see him before he has a nervous breakdown. Want me to come with you?"

Megan shook her head and turned to walk past the brightly colored pictures of snowmen lining the hall to the principal's office. The secretary, Mrs. Walker, looked up from her computer. "Go right in, Miss Montgomery. He's expecting you." Megan felt her judgmental eyes following her across the room.

She knocked lightly at the door and opened it. Mr. Temple was sitting at his dark wooden desk with his head hung over the newspaper and his hands buried in what little hair he had left. "You wanted to see me?" Megan asked, trying to keep her emotions in check. It wouldn't do for her, hopefully, future employer to see her breakdown in front of him. She needed to show him that she could handle this, that she wouldn't crack under the pressure. Even if she wasn't quite convinced of it herself.

Philip Temple jumped from his seat and motioned to her to sit in the oversized, brown leather chair facing his desk. "Please sit down, Miss Montgomery."

After she settled into the chair, he sat down on the corner of the desk nearest her and fidgeted with his hands. Then he scratched his chin and rubbed his nose before saying anything. "Miss Montgomery, you have done a great job with Miss Johnson's class. Sue has nothing but wonderful things to say about you. But..." he hesitated for several seconds and then cleared his throat before continuing. "I'm afraid that in light of what happened yesterday..." He reached behind him and held up the newspaper on his desk.

Megan stared at the paper in Mr. Temple's hands. There, plastered on the front page of the paper, 'COPS CLAIM PSYCHIC A FRAUD' printed in big bold letters over a giant picture of her looking like a frightened child. Shame and embarrassment washed over her, as she fought the onslaught of tears, just behind her eyes. Her secret was out again and she knew, as sure as she was sitting there, she could never get things back to the way they were. She would never have a normal life again. Not here anyway.

"Maybe you should take a few days off. Let's say a week or two. You can always come back once this thing's blown over. Look, Megan, I'm sorry." He laid the newspaper on the desk behind him. "I really am. It's just that parents get very nervous when the people teaching their children are in the news, no matter what the story's about. I've already gotten four phone calls from concerned parents this morning and one from a member of the school board." He stood up and put his hand on her shoulder. "Listen, you can come back as soon as this is all over. Promise. OK?"

Megan nodded her head, stood up and turned to leave.

"I'll personally call your professor today," he called after her. "I'm sure, under the circumstances, he won't hold this against you."

Without a word, she walked out of his office, out of the school and through the parking lot to her car. She dug in her purse for her car keys and, after finding them, tried to unlock the door. After a couple of frustrating tries, the key finally slipped into the lock. Once the door was open, she threw her purse and her books on the passenger seat and jumped in, slamming the car door behind her.

She took a few deep breaths to try and calm her nerves, but the pain inside her head just wouldn't go away. Violently, she shook the steering wheel, hoping to rip it from the dashboard, and screamed. After letting out the pain and frustration she had bottled up over the past few days, she rested her forehead on the cold steering wheel and closed her eyes. She could taste the salty wetness of her tears pool in the corners of her mouth.

She needed to keep it together, not let this get the best of her. She would survive this, too. And the surviving started right now. She put her fists to her eyes, dug out any remaining tears, slapped her cheeks a few times and took a deep breath. She let it out slowly and then took another and then another.

She stared the car and drove to the flower shop. She needed to keep busy, keep her mind off what was going on. But when she turned onto the street the flower shop was on, she felt her chest implode. When she finally caught her breath, she pulled into a parking spot just down the street from Nancy's shop.

There were cars and news vans everywhere. And a group of at least a dozen reporters with cameras and tape recorders were standing in front of the shop.

Megan closed her eyes and remembered how the press had surrounded Nancy's home, back in Clarksburg, hoping to get the chance to take a picture of the psychic little freak inside. It had been so bad during the trial that they actually had to get a hotel room, just to hide from them.

Megan drove around the block and pulled in behind the flower shop and went in through the back door unnoticed. Inside, Nancy looked frazzled. She was holding the phone to her ear and shouting at someone on the other end of the line. "She's not here, I told you. She doesn't do interviews and she's not interested in doing a 900 number thing! Do not call back!" Nancy hung up the phone and a split second later it was ringing again. She picked up the receiver, immediately hung it up, and then banged it against the top of the desk two or three times before finally leaving it off the hook.

Nancy looked up when she noticed Megan standing in the back of the store. "What are you doing here?" she snapped.

"The principal sent me home. He told me not to come back for a week or two."

"Oh, Meg." Nancy rushed over and took her into her arms. "I'm sorry. It's been awful here today, too. I didn't mean to take it out on you. I just haven't had a real customer in here all day. That media circus outside is scaring everyone off."

"I'm so sorry."

"It's not your fault, honey."

"It's so awful."

"Yes. Yes it is. And I don't know what I'm gonna do." Anger and frustration was thick in Nancy's voice. "I'm too old to start all over again."

Just then a loud murmur erupted outside as one of the reporters shouted, "There she is. She's inside the store." The reporters and cameramen pushed their way into the flower shop and the store lit up from the explosion of flashbulbs.

"When will The Cutter strike next?"

"Will you put a curse on the police force for calling you a fraud?"

"Are the police considering you a suspect?"

"Miss Montgomery, are you covering up for someone?"

"Get out! Get outta here, right now!" Nancy had to scream to be heard over the questions. "Get out, I said, before I call the police on all ya'll." She shoved and pushed at the mob, then closed and locked the front door. Nancy turned around. "Please go home, Megan. Just go home."

Megan pushed her way past the reporters who had discovered her car at the back of the shop. Hands were grabbing at her and blinding flashes were going off in her face, but she didn't stop until she was safe inside her car. Reporters stood in front of her car, trying to block her exit, but she slowly pulled out of the parking lot, slicing thru the sea of reporters, and headed for home.

Home was worse. Even with the wind chill in the single digits, there were people camped out all over her front lawn. Only the thought of jumping into her own bed, kept her from driving off to find a safer haven. She took a deep breath and opened the car door to get out. They swarmed around her like a bunch of hornets, buzzing with questions from every direction. She slowly made her way to her front door.

"Have you given the police the whereabouts of The Cutter?" A lady reporter in a long navy blue coat asked before jabbing a microphone in Megan's face. Megan put her hand between the microphone and her face and walked around the woman.

"We would like to write an article about you," a young man with thick glasses and greased back hair told her as he held up a magazine with a photo of a UFO on the cover. Megan shook her head and kept walking. She could see the walkway to her porch just a few feet away.

"Can you give our viewers a description of The Cutter?" A man with a video camera on his shoulder asked. Megan pulled the lapel of her jacket up to partially hide her face.

"My husband's run off again. Can you tell me if he's having an affair?" An angry voice called out from behind her.

A haggard looking woman with frizzy black hair stepped forward and pressed a little pink nightgown into Megan's hand. "My little girl is missing. Please, Miss, can you help me find her?"

Megan looked down at the satiny garment in her hand and then at the desperation in the mother's pleading eyes and her heart ached. "No," Megan whispered and handed the tiny nightgown back to the woman. "I wish I could. I'm so sorry. It just doesn't work that way." Megan looked away. The pain in that woman's eyes was more than she could bear. She put her head down and fought her way through the rest of the crowd.

She made it to the door and struggled to get the key into the door knob. "Just leave me alone," Megan yelled at a man who had followed her onto her porch. "Please, go away." She opened the door and slammed it closed behind her, locking it against the assault.

Megan leaned her back against the door, ready to give into the overwhelming urge to burst into tears. She had ruined Nancy's career, as well as her own. And for what? She hadn't saved anyone. The redhead and the dancer were dead anyway. The police weren't any closer to catching The Cutter than they would have been without her. She hadn't helped anyone and now her life was flipped upside down.

Where could she run and hide this time? It was true. Nancy was too old to start over again. She had spent years and worked hard building her little business and in one afternoon, Megan had destroyed it.

A hard pounding on the door almost sent Megan out of her skin. Another firm knock followed. "Go away," Megan yelled through the door. "Just go away."

"Megan Montgomery?" A deep, male voice called from the other side of the door. "We need to have a few words with you."

"I said, go away, or I'll call the police."

"I'd open the door if I were you, Miss Montgomery. We are with the Federal Bureau of Investigations."

She didn't answer. She couldn't, she was in shock. Did she hear him correctly? Did he say he was with the Federal Bureau of Investigations? The FBI?

"Miss Montgomery," he called out again, "we could break down the door, if you would prefer."

Megan cracked the door slowly and squinted against the camera flashes. Two tall men with dark suits and dark sunglasses stood with their badges held out in their hands, making an excellent photo op for the news hungry reporters on her front lawn.

"Miss Montgomery, I'm Special Agent Dotson," one of the men said, "and this is Special Agent Blackburn. May we come in?"

"Yes. Yes, of course." Megan opened the door fully and moved to one side, allowing the men to enter. She then closed the door to the shouts coming from her yard. "How can I help you?"

The men stood uncomfortably in the foyer, as if waiting to be asked inside the house. When they weren't, the man who was introduced as Special Agent Blackburn began talking, "Miss Montgomery, we are working with the Cleveland Police Department and the chief of police, Thad Banister, tells us you have been feeding the department information about five murder victims and about the person who has committed these murders. Is that correct?"

"Yes. I guess it is." Megan looked at the tall redheaded man with fair skin and piercing grey eyes. "I mean, I've tried to give them as much information as I could."

"That's where we are a little confused, Miss Montgomery," the other agent continued the conversation. "The detective in charge of this case believes you know more than you are telling them. That you could, in fact, be protecting the murderer."

Megan's heart dropped. Her knees felt weak, her vision blurred and her chest tightened. She felt dizzy and unable to breath.

"Miss Montgomery? Miss Montgomery?" One of the agents grabbed a hold of her arm just before she crashed against the wall and helped her over to a chair in the living room. "Can I get you some water?"

"I can't believe David thinks..." She cleared her throat. "That the police think I'm covering up for that...that monster." The two agents exchanged glances and she was sure they were wondering why a suspect was on a first name basis with the head detective on the case.

"Ma'am, you're not officially a suspect, yet," Blackburn said, towering above her chair.

Yet? Did he say, yet? Oh, God. The FBI was in her living room telling her she's not officially a suspect, yet!

"But we are very curious about your connection to this case," Blackburn continued. "We would like to understand how you knew so much about these murders before they happened, if that is indeed what is going on here."

"Here is my card. It has my cell phone number on it." Dotson pushed the card into her hand and she weakly closed her fingers around it. "Call us, if there is anything you need to tell us. It will be much easier on you, if you come to us and not the other way around. We'll see ourselves out." The two men turned to walk out the front door.

Dotson turned back to look at her again. "Oh, and Miss Montgomery, I shouldn't need to advise you not to leave town. It wouldn't look very good if we had to hunt you down." The door closed and the men left.

Megan wasn't sure how long she sat there looking at the card in her hand, willing herself to wake up from this nightmare, before she realized she never was going to. If she just hadn't been so stupid to think she could actually save that woman's life. If she could only turn back time and have it to do over again, she would have never made that damn phone call.

It was less than a week ago, yet it seemed like a lifetime. In fact, it was a life-time ago. Last week she had a normal life with a wonderful career in front of her, doing what she loved and Nancy had a thriving business that made her happy. Last week there weren't a hundred people standing on her front lawn and last week the FBI wasn't in her living room, ready to arrest her for murder. It was amazing how a little thing like a phone call could change everything.

Megan let the card slip from her hand and fall to the floor. She got up and walked into the kitchen to pour herself a drink before climbing the stairs to the bathroom.

✳   ✳   ✳   ✳

11:23 a.m.

David was back at the station before noon, refreshed by a hot steamy shower and four hours of uninterrupted sleep. He decided the best solution was to wait until Hudson was back at the station and then get away to check out his house.

The first thing he needed to find out was whether or not he still even had Michelle's car. If he did and it was the car Megan saw, there would have to be bloodstains somewhere in it. The dancer's death was a messy one. There had to be something he could find that would once and for all either prove Hudson's guilt or, hopefully, clear him of the suspicions running rampant inside David's head. As much as he wanted to stop The Cutter, this was one lead he hoped would *not* pan out.

"Stark, you have a call from the West Virginia State Penitentiary," Officer Segal called out from his desk across the room.

David had completely forgotten about Peter Logan. "I'll take it over here." He pointed to the phone on his desk and franticly searched for the notepad he had scribbled down the questions he had as he read through Logan's file.

Peter Logan was very cooperative, considering the fact he had nothing to gain or lose from his talking to an Ohio policeman. At this point in his life, Logan probably just wanted someone to talk to, someone to tell his side of the story to. The first couple of years he spent in prison, he was a celebrity of sorts. But now he had long been forgotten, left to rot away in prison with absolutely no hope for parole.

"What did you mean when you said you hoped your father was happy?"

"Well," Logan began in a slow southern drawl, "when I was 'bout ten, Dad left Momma and me for some whore he met in a bar. It hurt Momma real bad. He was even gonna marry that bitch, if you could imagine. But they split up beforen the year was out. Dad left town after that. Ashamed, I guess. Never did hear from him again."

Logan was silent for a moment and David was just about to ask his next question when Logan erupted angrily, "I didn't have a daddy all 'causen of that Maxwell whore! Momma had to work two jobs just to feed us. We barely had a pot to piss in. We cursed that bitch every day and I promised...I promised Momma on her death bed that I would see that whore in hell."

"Ok. But why did you kill the others?"

"Well, that bitch's husband had to go 'causen I didn't want no witnesses," he said calmly. "That Simmons woman was next. No wait. It was Jane Dempsey, the woman who ran the trailer park where me and Momma lived. That bitch tried to evict us two times. She was a mean, nasty old hag. I doubt anybody in that whole trailer park was sorry to see that witch go. Probably had a party. Then that Simmons woman. She worked at the liquor store. Threatened to turn Momma over to the cops for writin' bad checks. Only a couple of them was bad and she was gonna make 'em good."

It sounded like Logan took a long drink of something before continuing. "Dick Martin dated Momma some years after Dad left us. The rotten son of a bitch broke Momma's heart. He made Momma cry a lot. She loved him, but the second he found out she was a sick, the bastard took off. I found him out with some other woman and I killed 'em both."

"And Lori Fines," Logan gushed. "Over at the Shop and Save, wouldn't let Momma charge no more groceries. Momma always made her payments, when the government checks came, but that woman embarrassed her right in front of the whole store and made her put her groceries back. She cried all the way home."

"So. You killed all those people because they hurt your mother?"

"I didn't kill Lori Fines. The cops were a'waitin' for me 'causen of that Debbie Maxwell's daughter." Logan's voice was cold and hard. The years he spent in prison seemed to do nothing to rehabilitate the man. "My lawyers told me all about it. She was havin' dreams about me or something. The damn freak. Can't believe the cops actually listened to the freak. Well, I guess the joke's on me 'cause they shure enough got me. But if I ever get outta here, I'll personally see to it that Megan Maxwell meets her momma in hell."

David sure hoped the security at the West Virginia State Penitentiary was top notch because Megan would be in some serious danger, if Peter Logan ever escaped. He understood now why Nancy had her named changed and moved her away.

"Why didn't you say any of this during your trial?" David wondered why his lawyers didn't have him plead insanity. It seems he could have easily been sentenced to a maximum security mental facility, where he could get some help. And after talking to the man for just a few minutes, it sounded like he could really use some help.

"The bastard lawyers they gave me wanted me to. They wanted me to pretend I was nuts," Logan explained. "But I wasn't fuckin' nuts, I was fucking pissed. Those people killed my momma. They deserved to die. I got friends and family. I didn't want 'em to think I was nuts. I couldn't live with that. So I passed all their silly little tests and there wasn't nothin' they could do about it."

David shook his head. "One last question, Logan. Why didn't you kill your father? It seems to me, he's the one who hurt your mother the most."

"I would of, ifen I coulda found him."

David slowly hung up the phone. The answers he got only gave him more and more questions. He needed to talk to Nancy. She was there. She should be able to answer some of the questions he had about Peter Logan's father and Megan's mother. It all happened before Megan was born, so she couldn't help him, even if she was talking to him. Nancy Montgomery would have to fill in the blanks for him.

*   *   *   *

12:22 p.m.

Megan turned on the hot water and let the bathtub slowly fill as she got undressed. Closing her eyes, she lowered herself into the warm soapy water and stayed submersed under the bathwater for as long as she could hold her breath before slowly raising her face out of the water. She could hear the commotion outside. The reporters' voices and the noise of the traffic were hauntingly distorted by the water sloshing in both her ears.

As she lay there, she realized this was kind of how she felt most of the time. Like everything around her was fuzzy, muttered and muffled. Everything except for her own thoughts and lately, those were kind of muffled and distorted, too.

The only time she felt really connected to what was going on around her was when she was teaching. She loved the children, with their inquisitive little faces, asking questions and soaking up the answers like little sponges. That's when she felt most alive, teaching and being with David. But now both those things seemed lost to her forever.

She had made so many mistakes in the last week. She had gone to the police and it ended her career, not to mention the irreversible damage it must be doing to Nancy's flower shop. Small businesses can only survive minimal down time before they fold, it happened every day.

And she had trusted David, slept with him, fell in love with him and he had used her. He seduced her to gain information, kept her close to catch her in a lie. It made her physically ill to think about how she had given herself so freely and so completely to a man who could use her so ruthlessly.

And there was that thing about her being psychically connected to a hideous, perverted monster. How could she forget about that? How could she forget that every time she closed her eyes, he could be there waiting for her? Eager to show her things no one should ever have to see.

Megan sat up in the tub and lowered her aching head into her hands. She was mentally and physically exhausted. Just breathing in and out was becoming a chore. She wasn't sure how long she could keep going when simply being alive was wearing her out.

She lifted her head and studied the faded scars on her wrists. The whitish lines puckered unevenly across both wrists. They had been really nasty looking when they were fresh, but over the years, they had become less and less visible. In fact, if her skin tone hadn't been so dark, the scars probably wouldn't even be noticeable at all. She held one wrist up out in front of her and wondered if the world wouldn't have been better off, if her attempt had been successful all those years ago.

It had been easy the last time, a lot easier than living, actually. Living was the hard part, waking up every morning to look in the mirror at the face she hated because it looked so much like her mother's. The mother she had warned, but couldn't save. The mother who had caused a sick young man to go on a killing spree and take her father away from her.

Megan looked around the bathroom and noticed Elmer's old razor on the edge of the sink. She leaned up out of the tub and reached for it, dripping water on the floor. The razor was something Nancy kept around to remind her of her late husband. It had been on their bathroom counter ever since she could remember. Nancy cleaned it often and it looked like new, even though it was practically an antique.

Megan slowly twisted the handle and watched, fascinated, as the top of the razor spread open like wings, revealing a double-edged blade inside. She carefully took out the blade and studied it the way she had seen The Cutter study his weapons in her dreams.

She placed the razor on the edge of the tub and lightly traced the scar on her left wrist with the blade, feeling the cold thin metal against her warm skin. She traced the scar again, this time applying a little more pressure, and felt the blade just barely slice through the top layer of her skin. There was no pain, just the cold of the blade and the warmth of her blood as tiny bubbles of it began to ooze out of the thin cut.

Her hand began to tremble as if what she was doing registered in her hand before it did so in her brain. She dropped the blade on the floor beside her and it made a tiny tinkling sound as it hit the tiled floor. "Oh, dear Heavenly Father, please forgive me," she whispered, wiping the droplets of blood from her wrist.

She pulled her knees up to her chest and wrapped her arms around her legs, rocking herself back and forth as she cried, "Oh, God, please help me."

*   *   *   *

1:33 p.m.

"Mrs. Montgomery," David said as Nancy unlocked the door to the flower shop. "Thank you for seeing me right away. I realize I'm not your favorite person right now. And you have every right to be mad at me." He was genuinely sorry he had fallen out of favor with Nancy and especially with Megan.

"Well, you can't really blame me, now can you?" Nancy's nasty tone betrayed her friendly southern accent. "Shame on you, Detective Stark. I really trusted you. Meg and me both did. Then ya go and treat her like dirt. Worse than dirt. Calling her a liar like that."

"But I…"

Nancy walked behind the sales counter. "My shop's been surrounded all morning. Reporters from every newspaper and TV station in the state of Ohio are out there." Nancy's voice grew louder and her sagging cheeks were turning bright red in front of his eyes.

"Nancy, please, just hear me out."

"There's nothing you can say…"

"I did it for Megan."

"Oh, please." She threw her hands up in disgust. "That's exactly what I'd expect you to say. Well, Meg and me can do without your kinda help, thank you very much."

"Will you just let me explain?"

"Come on. Did you know she's been kicked out of the school she was teaching at? Are you trying to tell me that it's in Megan's best interest to have all those people at her school and those reporters out there and everyone else in town thinkin' she's nuts and that you guys don't believe a word she's sayin'?"

"Yes! That's exactly what I'm trying to tell you!" David could feel the vein in his neck begin to throb. "You tell me, Nancy, what do you think that murdering son of a bitch would do to Megan if he knew she could lead us to him? Huh? Tell me that?"

Nancy stared back at him, her face suddenly long and expressionless.

"Do you really think for one second he would just sit around and wait for her to have another dream? Or do you think maybe he might make sure she never dreamed about him again?" David knew he'd gotten through to the old woman by the look of panic that had crept over her face, so he continued in a calmer, softer tone, just to drive the point home. "Now Nancy, I may not be the greatest detective in the world, but I'm quite sure The Cutter would have no problem with using his hacksaw on our little Megan. Do you?"

"I never thought about that." Nancy put her hand up to her face. "I should have thought of that. I would have never let her go to the police, if I'd only just thought about the danger she'd be in." She looked David straight in the eye. "This has all been a big mistake. You've been a big mistake. She shouldn't ever see you again."

"Why would you say that?"

"I only want what's best for Megan, and quite frankly, Detective Stark, I don't think you're what's best for her."

"Is it best for Megan not to tell her about Wayne Logan?" David shot back at her. "That her mother and Peter Logan's father were lovers?"

"She already knows that. That's no secret. It all came out during the trial. That's one of the reasons she hates Debbie so much, she blames her for getting her daddy killed."

"Don't you mean her stepfather?"

"What? What are you talking about?"

"Do you ever intend to tell her that Wayne Logan is her real father?"

Nancy's eyes widened. "No," she whispered. "How? When did you...? Oh, dear God, Megan mustn't ever know." All the blood drained from her face and the suddenly frail woman fell back onto a small bench behind her.

David rushed around the counter and knelt in front of her. He hadn't been sure, but the timing made it possible, so he decided to take a shot and Nancy's reaction told him his hunch was dead on. But he still wanted to be sure. "Wayne Logan is Megan's father?"

Nancy nodded, looking straight through him.

"That would make Peter Logan Megan's half-brother?" David whispered the question, already knowing the answer.

Nancy nodded again and slowly put her worn old hands over her face. "This will kill her."

"Nancy, I need to know everything. It's the only way I can really help her."

Tears were glistening in the old woman's eyes when she lowered her hands and looked at David. She swallowed and nodded slowly. "I know. I know your right. I guess I was just hoping this day would never come. But I guess it's time to fess up. I just love her so much. The kid has had enough hard knocks as it is. She don't need this on top of everything else."

"I care about Megan, too. A great deal, actually. And, like you, I want what's best for her. But I think it's best she knows the truth, don't you?" David hesitated for a second and then looked the old lady in the eyes. "Living a lie is no way to live at all."

Nancy nodded in agreement and opened her mouth, but it took a few seconds before any words finally came out. "Debbie, Meg's mom, when she was about twenty or so she got herself messed up with a married man."

"Logan?"

"Yeah." Nancy nodded. "He left his wife and their little boy to move in with Debbie for awhile. They seemed happy enough, even talked about gettin' married when Wayne's divorce was final. But one day Debbie met Gene Maxwell and it was love at first sight for those two. She told Wayne and asked him to move out. It literally broke his heart 'cause he was so in love with her. I felt right sorry for the man. Except for his leaving his wife and kid, he seemed like a nice enough guy. Always very pleasant to me, a hard worker and good to Debbie. Worshiped her, really. Treated her like a princess."

"Ugly scene, it was," she continued. "The poor guy begged Debbie to take him back. Gene and him even got into a fist fight over it. Broke Gene's nose and sent him to the hospital, but when Wayne finally realized she wasn't 'bout to change her mind, he took off. Don't know where to, but nobody saw or heard from him again. The man was devastated. I figured he drove off the side of a cliff or something. There's a million places up in those mountains where you'd never find a body."

Nancy stood up and walked into the break room in the back of the shop and David silently followed her. She pulled two mugs out of the cabinet and poured coffee into both. She handed one to David, without even asking if he wanted it. "Gene moved in right after Wayne left. They were as happy as can be. But one day, a couple months later, Debbie came to see me. She'd been crying all night. She was pregnant and she was sure it was Wayne's baby. She asked if I would drive her to the clinic, so she could have one of them there abortions. She didn't wanted Gene or Wayne, neither one to ever find out about the baby."

"I told her I was dead set against it, but she was hysterical and she begged me. I didn't want her taking a bus or being alone, so I took her. Well, when we got there, they showed us this movie about how they were going to suck the baby out of her and I was a'cryin' and Debbie was a'cryin' and thanks be to God, she just couldn't go through with it. I drove her home and she told Gene everything."

"Well, he was a real prince and married her two days later in the gazebo in my backyard. He raised Meg as his own little baby and couldn't have loved her any more, ifen she was. Even though every time he looked into her eyes, he could see her real daddy looking back. Meg's got his eyes, ya know."

David shook his head and slowly raked his fingers though his hair. "Logan never knew?"

"No. Deb didn't know 'til after he'd already took off. And besides, I think she actually tried to convince herself that Meg was Gene's. I think I was the only other person on earth, besides them two, who knew the truth. I never even told Elmer about it and Debbie's own momma went to the grave thinking Gene was the daddy. It wasn't like the secret was hurting nobody. It was for the best really."

David's mind raced. This had to be why Megan had those dreams as a kid. Of course. That was the connection. It all made prefect sense now. Well, as much sense as that crazy stuff could. He sat down his full coffee cup on the gray Formica counter. "You need to have a long talk with Megan today. I don't think you want me to be the one to tell her." David turned and headed for the front door.

"No," Nancy said numbly, mostly to herself, "I...I guess not."

David got in his car and slammed the door. His brain was reeling and he felt sick for Megan. She *was* getting it put to her from all angles. He wanted to be there when Nancy told her. He wanted to take her into his arms and love her pain away. But this was between her and Nancy. Megan knew his number. If she needed him, he could be there, by her side, in minutes. He rested his head on his steering wheel. Unfortunately, he had become part of her problems and chances were slim he'd ever get that phone call.

He sat there with his head on the steering wheel, wondering what in the hell to do next, when he noticed the white sheet of paper in the seat next to him. It was the DMV listing of Michelle Hudson's light blue 1978 Olds. David started his car and headed to Frank Hudson's house.

David pulled over to the curb and parked his car on the street in front of his partner's brown two-story house. He was in luck, Hudson's truck wasn't there. That should give him a little time to snoop around. He got out of his car and walked down the gravel driveway to the garage, about twenty-five feet behind his house. The windows were dirty but he could definitely see a car inside covered up with a blue tarp.

He checked the door, locked. He went around to the back and found an unlocked window. The cold had chased even the most avid outdoor types inside and a quick glance around hadn't turned up any snooping old women at their windows, so he slid through the small opening in the back of the garage.

The car had been driven very recently. There were puddles of melted snow around the car tires and a grey residue on the bottom half of the car from the rock salt the city puts on the roads to melt the snow and ice. He ran his finger across the font fender. The grey grime came off easily with his finger, telling him that it hadn't been there long.

After he pulled the blue plastic tarp off of the car, he looked through the windshield at the front seat. According to Megan's dream, the stripper was killed right there. She had said the front seat was covered with black plastic, but it was such a vicious murder, he figured there had to be a good chance blood had splattered somewhere inside the car.

He took a white handkerchief out of his pocket and tried the car door, it opened and he looked inside. Everything appeared clean, no noticeable stains on the seat or floor, nothing on the dashboard or windshield. As his trained eyes searched every inch of the car's interior, he noticed something. A dark red, almost black, spot about the size of a dime was on the passenger's side door near the floor.

He reached into his coat pocket, pulled out a clear plastic bag and out of his jeans' pocket, a pocketknife. Carefully he scrapped a portion of the dried red stuff into the plastic bag, sealed it and stuffed it back into his pocket. "Could be ketchup," he whispered to himself. There was nothing else on the carpet or under the seat, so David quietly shut the car door and covered it back up with the blue tarp.

Once he got back outside, he walked around the perimeter of the Hudson house, looking for anything that seemed out of the ordinary. The basement windows were filthy and yellowed with age, making them almost impossible to see through. He was just about to check if the door was unlocked when a red pickup truck pulled into the driveway.

Hudson hopped out of the Ford F150. "To what do I owe this pleasure?" He pulled two brown paper bags of groceries from out of the front seat. "Well, since you're here, why don't you make yourself useful?" Hudson threw a bag of groceries into David's arms as he walked by him on his way to the house. He wrestled his keys out of his coat pocket. "Well?" Hudson unlocked and opened his side door. "What's up?"

"I…I've been…Oh, I don't know! This case has me so fucked up, I don't know what in the hell to think anymore." David was disgusted with himself. It had been much easier to think his partner was capable of these horrible crimes when he wasn't looking him straight in the eye. Hudson was no killer. Much less a vile, sadistic mass murderer like The Cutter.

"You've been working too hard, son." Hudson shook his head and climbed the three steps to his green and apple red kitchen. He sat his bag of groceries on a little square table against the wall and turned to look at David. "Maybe you should take some time off, buddy. I think that psychic girlfriend of yours has filled your head with so much bullshit, you don't even know your ass from a hole in the ground anymore."

David shook his head. "You just don't get it."

"What? Don't tell me you honestly believe that crap. You don't really think she's dreaming about those murders, do ya?"

"Yes. I do."

"God, boy. You're more fucked up than I thought, if you think she's gonna help you catch The Cutter." Hudson laughed. "That's what I told those Feds. Of course, *I* was joking."

"What?" David shot at him.

"I told those guys they were just wasting their time. That you were gonna solve the whole thing single-handedly by sleeping with a psychic."

"Screw you!"

"Screw yourself." Hudson turned his attention to the brown grocery bag on his table and stuck his hand inside.

"I can't believe you think she's lying."

"I can't believe you don't!"

David glared at the old man. "She's for real, Hudson. It all can't be a coincidence."

"No shit!" Hudson pulled his empty hand out of the bag. "That's what I've been trying to tell you, boy. I think she knows the bastard. She's probably just using you to throw us off his trail. Ever think of that, partner?"

David shook his head. "No, that's not...

"How the fuck do you know that's not *exactly* what's going on here?" Hudson's face was becoming blotchy and red. "How long have you known her? I mean really, Stark. Is she that great a piece of ass, she's made you forget you're a cop?"

David said nothing. What could he say? He couldn't think of anything to say or do, but stand there in the middle of Hudson's kitchen with a bag full of groceries in his arms.

"Well, since you can't seem to see past that pretty little face of hers, Banister has those two FBI agents looking into just why she happens to know so much."

"Banister?"

"Yeah, the chief told them everything and they..."

"Son of a Bitch!" David threw the bag of groceries he was holding down on the table. The brown paper bag fell over, spilling some of its contents across the table and onto the floor. David's jaw dropped. Lying at Hudson's feet were two bottles of Tums and a box of yellow kitchen gloves.

"There they are." Hudson bent down to pick up the items off the floor. He tossed the gloves and one bottle of antacids on the dark green countertop behind him. Twisting the cap off of the other bottle, he ripped through the foil seal, and stuck his finger in the bottle to fish out the wad of cotton. He shook out two yellow tablets into his hand, popped them in his mouth and chewed them ferociously on his way to the trash.

"What the fuck's your problem, Stark?" Hudson followed David's gaze to the box of gloves on his countertop. "Ya know, if you ever cleaned your own fucking apartment, you'd use them, too. Maybe next week, I can introduce you to a toilet bowl brush."

David never told Hudson or Banister about the gloves. But there they were. Right out of Megan's dreams. He felt ill, sick to his stomach, his brain went numb and his heart raced. He had no idea what to do, but he knew he couldn't stand to be in that room with that man for another second. David turned, without a word, and headed for the door.

"Hey." Hudson bent down to pick up the rest of the groceries off the floor. "Thanks for all your help, asshole!"

*   *   *   *

3:26 p.m.

"Have this analyzed," David ordered, slamming the plastic bag down on Ted Miller's desk.

"Well, hello to you, too. What? My day? Why, it's been fine, thanks so much for asking. How about yours?"

"I think it's blood and I think it might match the stripper's." David turned on his heels and walked back out the door.

Ted sat straight up in his chair and held the plastic bag up to the light to examine the contents. "Holy shit," he said just before David closed the door.

David marched down the long hallway, getting angrier with every step he took. He exploded through the door of Banister's office and slammed it behind him.

"Can I help you?" Banister looked up from a file on his desk.

David braced both hands on the desk and leaned forward, only inches away from Banister's face. "Our friends with the FBI just asked me if I was sleeping with our prime suspect."

"And? Are you?" Banister rose to his feet, his eyes glued to the throbbing vein on the side of David's neck.

"Fuck you! What about our deal? You promised me you'd keep her out of this and let me handle her."

"Yes. And it appears you are handling her in more ways than one."

David's eyes narrowed. "You know she has nothing to do with the killer. How could you fucking throw her to those sharks? You know, as well as I do, how these guys handle shit. Shoot first and ask questions later. They'll have her in cuffs before they bother to know the whole story."

Banister sat back down in his chair. "Well, she *is* our number one suspect, Stark."

"How can you sit there, look me in the eye and say that?" David's fingers coiled into tight fists. "She's given us the only leads we've had on this case."

"Exactly my point." Banister nervously wrung his hands. "You've got to admit how suspicious that is."

"I thought you believed in her."

"Oh, come on, Stark. How do you think all this looks?"

"I don't give a shit *how* it looks." David pounded a fist on the desk, causing Banister to jerk back. "She's done nothing but try to help us. She doesn't deserve the hassle she's getting from those two pricks….or from you for that matter."

"Whether she deserves it or not, I don't really give a rat's ass. I gotta think about how this looks for the department."

"You mean how it looks for you, don't you?"

"It's easy for you to be so self righteous." Banister stood up and looked out his office window, his hands clutched tightly behind his back. The officers who had stopped to watch him and Stark go at it, scurried around, trying to look as if they hadn't noticed a thing. "*You* don't have to worry about every move you make or every word you say ending up on the front page of the fucking newspaper or on the eleven o'clock news."

David stood up straight and stared a hole through Banister's back. "You know, I remember a time, not so long ago, when you didn't worry about anything else but doing your job. Do you even remember why we're here? Something about protecting the innocent and catching the bad guys. You use to be good at it."

Banister turned and looked at him, but said nothing.

David shoved his hand into his front jeans pocket, pulled out a crumbled twenty dollar bill and slapped it down on the desk.

Banister looked down at the wadded up twenty on his desk and then up at David. "What's that for?"

"Consider it my contribution to the "Thad Banister for Mayor" campaign, because you've officially started acting more like a politician than a cop." David stomped to the door and flung it open. He turned back to look at his boss. "By the way. Just in case you were wondering, that's *not* a compliment." David slammed the door behind him.

$$*\qquad*\qquad*\qquad*$$

10:02 p.m.

David jumped out of the shower, trying to reach his phone before the answering machine picked up. Soaking wet, he grabbed for a towel as he ran, dripping water through his bathroom and then through his kitchen. The recorder announced that he was out and to please leave a message as he frantically searched his apartment for the receiver to his cordless phone.

"David," a tiny quivering voice called out. "I need to talk to you. It's Megan."

"Damn." He dropped his towel and used both hands in the search, throwing dirty clothes, newspapers, and McDonald's wrappers aside in a desperate attempt to find the phone. She sounded as if she'd been crying. Nancy must have told her about her real father and she was calling him. She had turned to him. This was a good sign, a very good sign. Now he could explain everything to her and she would forgive him, maybe she already had.

"I just got home from the hospital," Megan's voice continued. "It's Nancy. She...she had a heart attack this afternoon." Her voice cracked and she hung up.

Within minutes, David was dressed, out the door and on his way to Megan's house. Her car was in the driveway, but when he knocked on the door there was no answer. He tried the door knob. The door was unlocked, so he opened it slowly and walked inside. "Megan?" He called out through the darkness. "Megan? You home?"

Closing the door behind him, he waited a few seconds for his eyes to become accustom to the dark before walking down the hall. Megan was sitting at the top of the stairs, her head hanging over the drink in her hands. David rushed up the stairs to her side. "Is she ok? Is Nancy ok?"

Megan looked up at him and opened her mouth to speak, but then simply nodded her head instead.

"Thank God." David sat down on the top step beside Megan, put his arm around her and rubbed her back. "Tell me what happened?"

"It's my fault," she sniffed. "It's all my fault."

"No. It's not your fault." He pulled her closer. "I'm sure it's not your fault."

"Yes, it is. I yelled at her. I got her all upset. I screamed at her." She began to sob. "I almost killed her and she's all I have."

David felt something inside him deflate. It hurt to hear her say that. On the drive over, he figured that since she called him, he must not have screwed things up too bad. He figured she had forgiven him and that there was still a chance he could be part of her life. He had even started thinking flowers, cakes and white dresses. No woman he had met since his divorce had him thinking about that.

"Tell me what happened?" David asked once more.

"Nancy told me that my dad...that my dad wasn't my real dad. And she knew about it all along. She always knew it and she intentionally kept it from me." Megan hesitated.

"Go on."

"I was so mad at her. I mean, why would she keep something like this from me? My whole life…My whole life has been nothing but a lie."

"That's not true, Megan. You are exactly who you were this morning and who you'll be tomorrow. Nothing can change that. Nothing can change the fact that your parents loved you and that Nancy loves you." He wanted to add that he also loved her, but it just didn't seem like the right time to bring that up.

"You don't understand. It's worse than that. Much worse. That disgusting man in West Virginia who killed all those people, he's….he's….he's my brother." Disdain curled the corner of her lip as the statement hung in the air around her.

"I know."

"What!" Anger flashed behind the tears in Megan's eyes. "Jesus! Does everyone know about this but me?" She pushed David's arm off her shoulder and stood up. "I…I just can't believe this. How did you…?" She hesitated, then threw back the last bit of her drink and slammed the empty glass down on a little table in the hallway. It took her a few seconds to finally let go of it before turning her attention back to David for his answer.

"Well. I called Peter Logan and talked to him." David got to his feet and stood in front of her. "He doesn't know about you're being his…well, being related, but he does know that his father left his family to be with your mom. Nancy told me the rest."

Megan turned her back to him. "It *was* all her fault she and Dad were killed."

"No!" David grabbed her upper arm and turned her around to look at him. "Logan is a psychopathic, cold-blooded murderer who killed a lot of people just because he thought they hurt his mother. Your mom made a mistake, that's all. She shouldn't of had to pay for it with her life."

She closed her eyes and turned her head against his words, but David continued, "Listen to me, Megan. Your mom did the right thing by you. She was strong enough to have you and to make a good life for you. And she loved you, didn't she, Megan? Can't you *ever* remember her loving you?"

David watched a big round tear slowly roll down her cheek. If there was anyway he could take her pain away, to stop her from hurting right now, he would do it. Anything. But all he could think to do was to hold her.

He started to pull her against him, but she flung her arms and took a step back. "You!" She cried out. "You have caused me nothing but pain."

The words cut into him like a knife.

"Get outta my house and stay away from me! I don't need you and I don't want you near me ever again. Just go away! Go away."

She couldn't possibly mean what she was saying. There was no way she would ask him to leave, if she knew how much he loved her. Or how good they were going to be together once all this was over. She had been drinking and she was upset, hysterical really. She was only lashing out at whoever was closest, which just so happened to be him. She wouldn't have said those things, if she knew how those words were ripping out his heart.

He stepped forward and wrapped his arms tightly around her shoulders and pulled her close to his chest.

Megan beat her fists against him with all her strength and rocked her shoulders back and forth, trying to escape his embrace. "Let go of me. Let go of me." She struggled for about a minute before calming down and eventually melting into his arms, her face resting against his chest and her hands on his back.

He lifted her chin with his right hand. "I can't let go of you and I can't stay away from you," he said softly. "Because I need you, Megan. And I want you with me always." He leaned forward and kissed her, his hand on the back of her head, gently pulling her into his kiss. It took a second or two, but, to his relief, she eventually joined the kiss.

*   *   *   *

Megan felt David's fingers intertwine with her long, brown hair, as he pressed his body firmly against hers. His hair was wet and clean. The strong scent of soap and shampoo filled her nose.

Maybe it was the two drinks she just had or maybe it was because earlier today she felt her life was no longer worth living and making love to David was the surest way she knew of to feel alive again. Or maybe it was because she felt her body was the only thing she had any control over and giving it to David, or better yet, using it to possess him, was the only thing at this moment that made any sense to her.

What had he said? She tried to concentrate over the deafening sound of her heart beat. It was something like, he couldn't stay away from her, he needed her, and he wanted her near him or with him. And he had said, 'always.' She heard him. He didn't say he loved her, but he said he needed her and wanted her, *always*. And that was something. That was something more than she had ever had before.

She realized it was possible he was lying to her, but she didn't care. At least not right now, not tonight while she was safe and alive in his arms. And if it was the last time she would ever feel the warmth of his body against hers or the last time she would ever savor the taste of his lips and his skin, well then she was determined to make it something worth remembering.

And if he was still just using her, she was going to see to it that the memory of this night would burn in his mind for years. If she couldn't have his love, she would, at the very least, have his body tonight.

She kissed him harder. David pulled away from the kiss, touched his lower lip and looked at the smudge of blood on his fingertips as his tongue quickly assessed the damage. He looked deeply into her eyes and then, as though he could read her mind, he took a step toward her, pulled the back of her hair and lifted her face up towards him before he devoured her lips with a hunger that nearly matched that of Megan's.

She tore the soft, leather jacket off his shoulders, down his arms and threw it to the floor. Her fingernails, piercing the tense muscles in his arms, as she pulled him deeper into their kiss. Her kisses traveled from his firm lips to the stubble on his square chin and then down his neck.

She violently tugged on his blue t-shirt, her mouth unable to wait for the taste of the warm hard skin beneath. The cotton fabric strained and she heard the seam at the top of his shoulder surrender and rip open allowing her access to his nipple. Taking it gently between her teeth, she alternated between sucking and biting at it before her tongue slid through the crispy black hairs on his chest to find the other nipple anxiously waiting for her.

Apparently, she bit it too hard, because he jerked away and pushed her off him. He looked at her as if she were a stranger, as if he had no idea what had gotten into her. And that was understandable, because she had no idea what had gotten into her, either. All she knew was that she wanted and needed him more than either of them could have ever imagined.

Instead of the numb, dullness she lived with most of her life, she felt truly alive when she was with David. Yes, alive. He added so much to her life that had been missing, vibrancy, passion, excitement. Even if the sharp, excruciating pain of a broken heart went along with it, at least now she could truly feel.

But what about Nancy, alone in that hospital bed? The doctors said she would be fine, that it was only a mild heart attack brought on by stress. Stress *she* had caused her. *She* had sent Nancy to the hospital and, only a few hours later, was seducing a man in Nancy's house. Guilt began to dull her senses again.

She should ask him to leave. And she should never see him again, if every time he got this close to her, she wanted to tear his clothes off and throw herself into his arms. That's what she should do, but her body wasn't about to let that happen. Her hands reached out for him, she couldn't let him go now. Not when she was so close to having him and his strength to help her through the night. Not when she was so close to having him bring her back from the dead.

David stood there in the dark, silently studying her, his hooded brown eyes, devouring her with his gaze. He pulled his gun out of its holster and laid it beside the empty glass on the hall table and slowly slipped the black straps of his holster off his shoulders.

He was just about to lay the holster on the table beside his gun, when Megan stretched her arms out in front of her and wound her wrists up in the black leather straps. She thought that maybe, if she were to be his captive, it would lessen the guilt that was eating at her. Maybe then, she wouldn't be at fault for feeling so alive while Nancy lay in the hospital. And maybe then, she wouldn't be the one responsible for what they were about to do.

He pulled up on the strap, raising both her arms up over her head and held them against the wall. With his free hand, he ripped open the dark olive green blouse she was wearing, sending several buttons flying and bouncing across the carpet below. One more forceful tug on the flimsy material left it hanging open to reveal the silky green bra that covered her breasts.

Her nipples pushed against the thin material, eager to be touched. Touched by the man who had stolen her heart, her mind, her body. Not wasting the time to find the hook, he pushed the bra up over her breasts and immediately lowered his head to hungrily suck on one.

Megan's eyelids fluttered as a throaty moan, she didn't recognize, unwillingly escaped her lips. Her knees went weak and she felt a delightful tightening in the pit of her stomach as her entire body ached for him. She needed him, right now, inside her. Another second was much too long to wait.

She bent her head to kiss his cheek and then ran her tongue over to his ear before taking his earlobe gently between her teeth. Her teeth scraped across his flesh as she slowly pulled away. "Fuck me, David," she whispered into his ear.

The words caused his body to stiffen and he immediately stopped what he was doing to look at her. His eyes widened and then immediately narrowed, his nostrils flared and his chest heaved. He resembled a bull ready to charge and Megan was the red blanket.

He firmly pulled the holster strap to the floor, bringing her along with it and took two steps down the stairs before grabbing her by her ankles. He dragged her towards the steps and her blouse bunched up by her elbows as she slid across the floor, the rough pile of the carpet scratching her back. David yanked her slacks and panties off in one swift motion and threw them up over Megan's head to the hallway floor. He then unzipped and stepped out of his jeans, leaving them to roll down a few steps. Then he lifted his ripped t-shirt up over his sculpted chest and flung it down the stairs.

Megan marveled at the perfect man standing between her legs as she lay on the top step with her legs dangling down the stairs, her hands tied and arms up over her head. Her bra around her neck and her green blouse bunched up somewhere between her wrists and her elbows.

What was he waiting for? Why wouldn't he take her? She lifted her hips and squirmed on the floor beneath him, until he finally granted her unspoken plea and entered her at last.

✳   ✳   ✳   ✳

David leaned over Megan's back, one hand on her hip and the other on the rocker's armrest, trying to catch his breath. God, she was phenomenal. The most sexy, passionate, incredible creature he had ever met.

She practically attacked him in the hallway. Of course he knew she was only using him. Making love to him the same way he used a punching bag to alleviate stress. That's not to say he wasn't happy to oblige her in anyway he could. His only fear was that she would regret it later. Wake up in the morning and be ashamed of how wild and uninhibited she had been, or worse yet, be sorry she had chosen him to be the one she unleashed her enthusiasm on.

He had hurt her and he was sorry. More sorry than she could ever know, but she had to finally realize that he had done it to protect her. She had to know he would never intentionally hurt her, he loved her. Surely she had to feel it. She had to know how much he cared for her. And maybe she would wake up in the morning, with his arms around her, and come to love him, too.

Megan was on her knees in the rocker, her hands were still fisted around the spindles on the back of the chair and she was trembling. He wrapped his arms around her, bringing her upright with her back flat against his chest, hoping the heat of his body would stop her from shaking. She leaned against him and rested the back of her head on his shoulder. After the stairs, she had brought him into her room. But instead of climbing into bed, she crawled up into the rocker and waved her exquisite ass in the air until he slid into her, giving her what she seemed to want.

Wow, she was unbelievable. He could spend all day just looking at her body, it was beautiful. She was beautiful. But to have the kind of reckless need and enormous drive she had, well, she was the proverbial dream come true.

Her hands were on top of his as they ran over the swells of her breast and the curves of her waist. Man, he wished he had one more go left in him, but he felt like he had been chewed up and spit back out. He needed a couple hours of sleep, then he'd be able to go again in the morning.

Megan took the holster strap that was still tied to her right wrist and tied the other end of it around David's left hand before she backed up out of the chair. She led him to the bed and pushed him down so he fell on his back.

How sexy she looked, standing there over him, her big round eyes, a deep dark blue. And those lips. Full and swollen, pouting at him. He wanted to. God, did he want to, but it was too much to ask of his worn out body. Maybe if he hadn't pushed himself so hard over the last few weeks, or maybe if he had gotten just one full night of sleep in the last month.

"You know," he sighed, "I could use a little break. The equipment needs to recharge."

"Oh, really?" Her eyes narrowed and she stared down at him. "You think you got nothing left?" She crawled over top of him, kissed his face, his chin and his neck. Her kisses, inching their way down his body, until a soft wet kiss landed on the tip of his penis. "I'm not quite done with you yet," she told it before sucking the limp appendage fully into her mouth.

"Oh my God," David said to the ceiling. Every flick of her tongue was sending volts of electricity through his body as she quickly brought him back to life.

"I thought you said you needed break." Her sparkling blue eyes looked up at him as she sucked him into her mouth and pulled him back out again. "He doesn't seem to agree with you." A deep giggle left her throat before she took all of him into her mouth again.

David groaned out in an insane mixture of pleasure and pain that left him dizzy. "God. Are you trying to kill me?"

She sucked hard as she slowly pulled him out of her mouth and then smiled up at him. "You know, I don't think I could ever get enough of you." She carefully straddled his waist and slowly lowered herself over him before lifting up again and lowing back down in a slow and sensual sequence that tortured David with her every movement.

With the fingers of their tied hands laced together, she used his strength to help lift her up, while her other hand was flat against his chest, helping to keep her balance. She flung her head back and her long silky hair swept back and forth across his thighs. David watched in awe as Megan made love to him.

He felt it building up inside him, filling him, overtaking him. Unable to hold back any longer, he put his hands on her hips and bounced her on him quickly several time until he came with such intensity, he felt as if it was being ripped from his toes. He cried out as she tightened around him and ached backward, biting her bottom lip. Suddenly she bucked forward, tossing her soft hair onto his face. She wailed, trembled violently, and then fell onto his chest, wonderfully wasted, and exhausted.

He kissed the back of her neck, leaned his head back into his pillow and closed his eyes. That was, by far, the most intense orgasm he had ever experienced. Never had he felt this way with a woman, not his ex-wife, not even the horny cop groupies he had occasionally picked up.

With his free hand, he pulled the soft ivory blanket over them and held her close to his chest, the fingers of their bound hands interlocked. He could feel her body rise and lower with every breath she took, until eventually, her breathing slowed to a deep steady rhythm.

"I love you," he whispered into her hair, not knowing why he waited until he was sure she was asleep to say it, because it was true. He was utterly, hopelessly in love with her and, as he lay there with her naked body sprawled across his chest, he made up his mind to tell her so just as soon as she woke up.

C H A P T E R   8

▼

WEDNESDAY, JANUARY 21ST

*   *   *   *

6:21 a.m.

David was awakened from the most peaceful sleep he'd had in months by a tiny whimper. He opened his eyes and a wide smiled stretched across his face when he realized he was in Megan's bed.

Wow, what a night! She had given him the most incredible night of sex he had ever known. He stretched his arms, pulling her hand along with his, and when he noticed the black holster straps still tied to their wrists, his penis twitched slightly. Maybe he would wake her and they could go a few more times this morning before he had to get back to work.

He leaned over to kiss her when she let out another whimper, mumbled something unintelligible and violently tossed her head back and forth. Her eyes were tightly shut and there was a panicked look on her face. He instinctively reached out to wake her, but stopped. She could be having another nightmare about The Cutter.

A strange excitement filled him as he waited anxiously for the information she was sure to wake with. But watching her beautiful face distort in fear and hearing her little cries for help was starting to tear him up inside. If only he could see exactly what she was seeing right now, if only he were the one taking on this terrible burden instead of her.

It took every ounce of determination he had not to rescue Megan from witnessing whatever horrible things were flashing inside her brain. He hated himself for sitting there and not stopping it, when he could, with only a touch of his hand. But he knew, in order to truly save her from the phantom inside her mind, he would need all the clues she would have for him when she woke up.

He would be right there, waiting to take her into his arms and kiss her pain away, but more importantly, he would be right there, waiting to learn how he could stop The Cutter from claiming another life. And maybe this would be the time she gave him enough information to finally nail the bastard.

Suddenly, a terrible look of absolute horror washed across her face, her body tensed up and then she violently bolted upright as she let out a blood curdling scream. Beads of sweat covered her forehead and her upper lip. "He found a face," she whispered, gasping for air. Her eyes were wide and wild and she looked straight through David, as if he wasn't even there. "He found a face. He found a face."

David didn't say a word or move a muscle. He was afraid she might still be asleep and he didn't want to interrupt. Maybe she was still seeing through the killer's eyes. Maybe she was seeing something right now that would tell her who the animal was.

She blinked her eyes several times and then looked at David like she was surprised to see him in her bed. "David?" She blinked a couple more times. "He found a face, David. Mine."

He pulled her into his arms and held her tightly as the walls closed in around him. What had she said? That it was her face The Cutter had been searching for? That she was next? Was this why she dreamt it all along? Was this the connection that woman at the bookstore was talking about? Could it be that Megan was the last piece of that butcher's puzzle from the beginning? Or had The Cutter changed his mind and picked her because he thought she was a threat? The questions spun around inside of David's head like a tornado.

"Don't let him kill me." She burrowed deeper into his arms.·

David stroked the back of her head and wondered just how in the hell he was going to stop him. The Cutter had always been one step ahead of him. Always, just out of his reach. And now, Megan's life depended on his cracking the toughest case he'd ever had. But he would think of something. He had to. He had no other choice.

*   *   *   *

Megan told David everything she could remember about her latest nightmare. The Cutter would be waiting for her at the college, eager to add her face to his macabre collection.

Seeing the dream, as usual, through the eyes of the killer, Megan had watched the whole thing not knowing she was his intended victim. She watched as he followed a woman through the deserted campus. She watched him chase her and finally catch her. Not until he lifted his hacksaw, did she actually see her own head being cut from her body.

David had gone downstairs to call the station and start some coffee while she jumped into the shower. Unfortunately, it did nothing to alleviate the chill that had settled into her bones and she was still trembling as the steaming hot water cascaded down her body.

She was so glad David was there. It had been terrifying enough to wake up from that nightmare with David by her side, if she had been alone, well, she wasn't sure what she would have done.

But as scary as it all was, it had finally started to make sense to her now. This had to be why she was having those dreams in the first place. They were some kind of warning. "And why bother warning me, if there's nothing I could do to stop it, right?" Her unanswered question echoed against the shower walls. That had to be it. Some kind of power in the universe was warning her. God was warning her.

She got out of the shower, toweled off and got dressed. She opened the bathroom door and found David standing in the hall, waiting his turn. "There's a towel and a washcloth on top of the hamper for you. And there's toothpaste and a box on the sink with a new toothbrush in it. Nancy buys everything in bulk."

"Thanks." He kissed her on the forehead on his way to the shower.

She could smell the coffee brewing and hear it dripping into the pot as she made her way into the kitchen. Her mouth watered as the strong aroma began to clear her head. Pulling two mugs from the cabinet, she sat them next to the coffee pot and then went to the phone. After looking up the number to the hospital, she dialed it and asked for Nancy's room.

"How are you?"

"Can't complain," Nancy said, in her usual merry tone.

"Well, you sound great."

"Can't wait to get outta here, I'll tell you that."

"But you need to…"

"You should see the garbage sitting in front of me that they have the nerve to call breakfast. I wouldn't feed this junk to a dog."

"Oh, come on, it can't be that bad."

"Well then, little lady, *you* come down here and eat it!"

"Has the doctor been in to see you, yet this morning?"

"No, but my nurse said she thinks I should be able to go home tomorrow."

"The insurance company's idea, no doubt. I can't believe you had a heart attack last night and they'd send you home tomorrow." Megan threw her hand up in disgust.

"*Mild* heart attack, Meg. I'm fine. Besides, you'd wanna get outta here to, if you were the one trying to sleep on this two inch thick mattress."

"Probably so. Hey, do you want me to bring you anything when I come see you?"

"Don't you have school? Oh, I'm sorry." Nancy hesitated and then said, "Oh, I know. You could bring me the book that's on my nightstand. I was just gettin' to the good part. And a couple pairs of underwear and my gown. This thing they got me in has air conditioning all up the backside. And if you wouldn't mind bringing me something to wear home, please. Anything. Thanks, honey."

"No problem. I'll be there in a little while."

"Ok. Bye bye."

"See ya." Megan slowly untwisted her fingers from the cord, hung up the phone and stood there chewing her index finger. She knew she couldn't tell Nancy about her nightmare, but she hated keeping it from her, too. Whatever the outcome, she knew it wouldn't help to tell Nancy about it. She heard David's footsteps galloping down the stairs before he walked through the kitchen door, rubbing his hair with a purple towel.

"I just called the hospital. Nancy's doing really well. She may even get to come home tomorrow."

"That's great." He hung his towel on the back of a kitchen chair.

She felt heat rise up into her face at the sight of him standing there in his torn t-shirt and his shoulder holster resuming its intended position stretched across his back. Not wanting David to see her blush, she quickly turned to the coffee pot and started pouring the rich brown liquid into the cups on top of the counter.

She couldn't believe she had done that. What in the heck had gotten into her? The man probably had bite marks under his shirt. She felt a tingle of excitement flow through her and then immediately put it aside. There were more important things to think about right now, like the fact someone was going to try and kill her before the day was over.

David walked up behind her, put his hands on her hips and kissed the side of her neck before smacking her playfully on the behind. "You wild little animal, you."

"Coffee?" She turned and offered him a cup, hoping to change the subject.

"Thanks." David took the cup and leaned up against the kitchen counter beside her.

"I'm going to the hospital to see Nancy this morning."

"I really wish you wouldn't."

"She'll think something's wrong, if I don't."

"Something *is* wrong, Megan. Terribly wrong." His amber eyes were cold and hard as they looked at her.

"I *am* going and I want you to promise me you won't tell her about any of this. The last thing she needs right now is to worry about me."

"I'll worry enough for the both of us." He took a swallow of his coffee and hesitated for a second. "Alright. But you're not going anywhere without me or the two officers I called in this morning. They're already on their way here."

She shook her head. "It doesn't happen at the hospital."

"Maybe not, but I'm not taking any chances. Someone will be with you twenty four seven until we catch this creep. You got it? And I don't want any argument from you, either."

"Fine. As long as Nancy doesn't see them." She took a sip of her hot coffee and felt its warmth flow down her throat and into her chest. "I just don't want her to worry." She took another sip and then looked up at him. "I thought about it. And I think I should go to the college tonight."

"Absolutely not! Are you crazy?"

"Probably. But he's after me, right?"

"Yeah! Which is exactly why you are *not* going to the college tonight."

"Just hear me out. I think...."

"No. Under no circumstances. Absolutely not. It's too dangerous, Megan. Way too dangerous."

"But listen. If he's after me, he won't stop just because I'm not there tonight."

David looked down into his coffee cup and said nothing.

"You know that as well as I do," she said. "So why not take advantage of our knowing he'll be there tonight?"

"No. It's too risky." He shook his head. "No."

"I might not have a dream about the next place he'll be waiting for me. And I refuse to spend the rest of my life, looking over my shoulder."

"But we're bound to get him sooner or later and then it'll all be over."

"Come on." Megan put her cup down on the counter. "You don't believe that and neither do I. David, we know too much this time to pass up the chance to catch him."

"Do you forget what happened the last two times we had a chance to catch him?" His eyes darkened and the left corner of his mouth pulled downward.

"But this time is different."

"Yeah, this time's different because you're *not* going to be there."

"No. *This* time is different because we know the where, the when *and* the who. This time is different because, this time we'll get him."

He shook his head.

"You know I'm right. Admit it. This is our best chance to end it once and for all."

"There's no way I'm going to let you take this chance. This is your *life* we're talking about. You realize that don't you?"

She frowned and crossed her arms in front of her chest. "Yeah, that's right. *My* life. And you know as well as I do, he won't stop until we either catch him or he finally gets me. And like I said, this might be our best and only chance." Megan leaned forward and crooked her neck to look up into his eyes. "I'm right, aren't I?"

"Do you understand how dangerous this is? *He* will be there. Waiting for you."

"Yeah, but he doesn't know that you and I know that. He doesn't know that you will be there waiting for *him*."

David ran his hand through his wet hair and fluffed it up in the back. "Why do I feel like I'm going to regret this? You know, I won't get any more help from my chief or the department. I'm not even supposed to be here with you. The only reason I got Smith and Thomas is because they're on my team. And I'm gonna catch hell about it as soon as Banister finds out."

"What about your partner?"

David clenched his jaw and then took a long swallow of his coffee. "Megan, there's something I have to tell you." He took another sip of coffee. "I...um...I want you to be very careful about who you trust." He sucked his lower lip into his mouth and scraped his teeth across it. "What I mean is, don't go off with anyone but me and the two officers on their way here. No one else. Got it?"

She looked at him and pinched her eyebrows together. "What are you saying?"

"I think my partner, Hudson…Well, I think he might have something to do with this." David sat his cup down firmly on the kitchen counter he was leaning against and slid both of his hands through his dark curly hair. He took a deep breath and noisily pushed the air out of his mouth. "You saw him. Could he be the man in your nightmare? Could he be The Cutter?"

Megan thought for a minute. She had only seen Hudson twice and not real close up. "I…I don't…I don't know. Maybe. I mean, I guess he could. Oh!" Megan turned away from David and slammed both of her hands down on the counter top. "These stupid dreams! They haven't helped at all. It's frustrating as…." Megan stopped and turned back around. "Like the stupid clock and only seeing the inside of the club, not having any idea where it really was. I am sorry. I'm so sorry I even dragged you into this."

"Megan, you didn't drag me into this. I was already knee deep in it myself. But now, now we're in it *together*." David put his hand on her shoulder and looked down at her. "I'm sure Hudson isn't…I mean, I hope he couldn't possibly be. But…just in case, stay away from him. Until I know for sure, just stay away from him, ok?"

Megan nodded her consent.

"Promise me," David demanded as the dark blue vein in his neck started to swell.

"Ok. Ok. I promise."

His big hands cupped her face and tilted it up toward his. "If anything happens to you…" David's voice trailed off and he swallowed hard. Lowering his face to hers, he kissed her with a warmth and tenderness that made Megan's insides tremble.

It was something Megan had never felt before, even with David. Something much more intimate than the great sex they had shared last night. Did he love her? How could he kiss her like that, look at her like that, and not love her as much as she loved him?

But a tiny voice inside her head reminded her that if they couldn't outsmart The Cutter tonight, it wouldn't really matter very much whether he loved her or not.

✱   ✱   ✱   ✱

8:05 a.m.

David wasn't comfortable leaving Megan's side. Even though Smith and Thomas were with her, watching her every move. And even though nothing was supposed to happen until after dark, he couldn't ignore the strangling fear that gripped him as soon as she was out of his sight.

But he couldn't take her with him and he really needed to get to the station. Ted was supposed to have the lab report on the stuff he found in Hudson's car on his desk first thing this morning. He also had someone checking on the where-abouts of Wayne Logan, Megan's real father.

Seems Mr. Logan was quite the rolling stone. They had traced him from West Virginia to Georgia to a small town in Florida. He was a drifter with no real profession or home. He just moved from one odd job in one small town to the next odd job in the next small town. The only police record they found so far was from when he had been in a drunken bar fight somewhere in Georgia back in 1989. He was released as soon as he slept it off.

The last known job they found for him was at a little construction company in the Florida Keys. The research department was still trying to get a current phone number and address for him. It probably wouldn't lead anywhere, but Logan was a loose end and David hated loose ends. Besides, once the initial shock wore off, maybe Megan would eventually want to get in touch with her real father.

David's biggest concern, however, was what he was going to do if the stuff he found in Hudson's car turned out to be blood and the same type as the stripper's. He had no idea how he was going to go about accusing his partner of murder.

He wanted to have more hard evidence against Hudson before he talked to Banister. Unfortunately, getting more proof would take time and time was a luxury he didn't have. Megan was The Cutter's next target and David only had until sundown to catch him or she was going to use herself as bait. But no matter how desperate he was to see The Cutter behind bars before the sun went down, he prayed to God he was wrong about his partner, Frank Hudson.

David found a lab report waiting for him, on his desk. He picked it up and looked around. Hudson was nowhere to be seen. Opening the envelope carefully, David read the words, 'Blood. Type A negative.' He sat down and pulled out his file on the dancer. Flipping through the papers, he found the sheet he was looking for. 'Blood type: A negative.' He slammed the file closed with his fist.

Of course, they would have to do DNA tests. That would take about a week, but David was convinced. The car, the lineup, the redhead, the yellow rubber gloves, now the blood. It was all too much to ignore.

Now his only obstacle was to try and convince Banister his suspicions concerning Hudson were at least worth investigating. David laid his head down on the file. He would have given just about anything for this not to be true.

*   *   *   *

"Are you out of your fucking mind?" Banister stood up and twisted the rod connected to the blinds that hung on his office window. Once the blinds were completely closed, he turned to look at David. "Did your psychic girlfriend tell you that, too?"

David was leaning forward in the chair, his hands on the back of his head and his elbows on his knees. He shook his head without looking up.

"I thought I made it clear, I didn't want you seeing that woman again. You're lucky the Feds didn't follow you there. You know what? They probably did. And the reporters. Shit! Did any reporters see you there? Am I going to see your picture plastered all over tomorrow's paper?"

"Did you even hear a fucking word I just said?" David looked up at him. "I come in here to tell you I think my partner may be a serial killer and you're fucking worried about whether a reporter took my picture or not."

"Oh, I heard you alright. The question is whether you actually believe what you're saying. I can't even imagine how twisted that girl has to have you around her finger, for you to be in here accusing Hudson of being a sadistic mass murderer. Tell me, Stark, are you actually *trying* to get yourself suspended? 'Cause you're doing one hell of a job."

David knew Banister wouldn't be interested in the yellow gloves, the old wrinkled hands, the gold watch or anything else that had to do with Megan's dreams. But David, on the other hand, had no doubt whatsoever in the validity of her nightmares and that…Well, that terrified the shit out of him, because he also had no doubt whatsoever that someone was going to try and kill her tonight. And it looked to him like Hudson might be that someone.

"Just forget about her. She has nothing to do with it," David lied. "There's more than enough incriminating evidence on Hudson without even bringing her into it."

"Enough to ruin a good cop's reputation?"

"If Hudson's innocent, this won't hurt him at all."

"I wasn't talking about him. I was talking about you."

David leaned back in the chair and combed his fingers through his hair. Banister was right. Cops who accuse other cops of jaywalking, much less murder, better be damn sure and David was only pretty sure, at best.

But today he had to play the hand he was dealt, because tomorrow might be too late for Megan. Whoever The Cutter happened to be, planned on adding her face to his collection tonight. And that just didn't give David enough time to be damn sure.

"You were there at the line up, chief. The witness from the hotel fingered Hudson."

"And Freeman," Banister added.

"Yeah, but Freeman has a water tight alibi for the night the stripper was killed. The witness at the strip joint saw The Cutter's car. And Hudson has a similar looking car parked in his garage with A negative blood in it. Which just so happens to be the same type as the stripper's. It all adds up."

"I've known Hudson a long time. I even worked with him on a couple of cases back when *you're* biggest problem was which cheerleader to bang on Friday night. I just can't believe he could do anything like this."

"Prove me wrong. Please! For Christ's sake, prove me wrong! I'd like nothing better than to be wrong about this." David stood up and paced the floor, his right hand rubbing the back of his neck. "But we have to check it out, don't you think?"

"Why would he do something like this?"

"I told you, I think he's building a new Michelle."

"Nah, I don't buy it. It's insane."

"Oh, and mutilating women to collect their body parts isn't?"

"You've got a point." Banister scratched his temple.

"Michelle was chesty, with red hair and dark skin. It all fits."

"And we couldn't find him for hours the night that hooker was killed, remember?"

David rubbed his chin. "Yeah, that's right. I forgot about that." They both were silent for a few seconds before David spoke up again. "You know, if we had all this on *anyone* else, we'd bring him in, right now. No hesitation."

"But he's one of us." Banister plopped down on the corner of his desk.

"Why do you think I've waited this long? I needed to be sure."

"And? Are you? Are you sure?"

"Hell no!" David threw his hands up over his head and turned away from Banister. "I'm not sure of anything..." David turned back around and looked

Banister straight in the eye. "Except that we *have* to check it out. There's one more piece missing to The Cutter's puzzle and I *am* damn sure someone else will die, if we don't end it now."

David squeezed his eyes shut, fighting to put the image of Megan's headless body lying on the ground in a pool of blood out of his mind. He swallowed against the bile that began to rise up from his stomach. He knew he should go get her right now, put her on a plane and get her as far away from here as he could.

Why had he agreed to let her go through with this? He sure as hell didn't feel right about it. Any of it. And he sure as hell didn't like the feeling of helplessness that suffocated him.

"You know, I think you might be right, Stark." Banister stood up and walked around to the back of his desk. "A few too many things do point to him, don't they?"

David nodded.

"Well, I don't want you on this at all." Banister sat down in his chair and pulled a piece of paper out of his drawer. "I'm going to send for a search warrant for Hudson's house right now, but I'm gonna get Harris on it. You're too close to it."

Banister waited for David to object, but he didn't. He didn't want to go to Hudson's house and he didn't want to be at the station when Hudson walked in. All he wanted to do was get to Megan's side as soon as possible and stay there until this whole thing was over.

"As a matter of fact," Banister continued, "why don't you get outta here and I'll keep you posted. I want to talk to Hudson alone when he gets in and I want Harris and his team to be at his house while he's here. Just in case."

"Have Ted go, too," David suggested. "He'll make sure it's handled right."

"Yes, of course. I'll take care of it. But you...you get going. The last thing I want in here is a huge scene. I'll try to be as discreet as possible. I don't want it getting out to the press, until we've had a chance to check it out."

David shook his head. Forever the politician. David had just accused one of his best cops of murder and Banister was worried about the fucking press. "Maybe I *should* talk to him. Try to explain myself..."

"Later," Banister snapped. "Not here and not now. Go on, get lost. That's an order. I'll call you later with an update." Banister picked up the phone and held it to his ear with one hand and pointed to the door with the other.

David slowly walked out the door and left the station without a word to anyone. When he got to his car, he kicked it, leaving a dent in the lower panel and barely resisted the urge to punch his clenched fist through the driver's side window.

He let out a low growl that started deep in his stomach, then opened the car door and threw himself inside. His fingers curled around the steering wheel, squeezing it until he felt his palms bruising.

What kind of man was he? Accusing his own partner of this, this horrible thing and then leaving someone else to do the dirty work for him. Not even being man enough to accuse him of it to his face. But the thought of seeing Hudson being led away in handcuffs was almost too much to bear.

What if Hudson was innocent? David prayed that he was, but if he was, how would he ever be able to look him in the eye again? Or anyone else on the force for that matter.

Well, the damage was already done. It was over. There was nothing he could do about it now. What was done could never be undone and things would be forever changed because of it.

*   *   *   *

12:04 p.m.

Megan was sitting in a chair next to Nancy's bed, listening to her complain about the low cholesterol diet the doctor had put her on, when David walked into the hospital room. She practically jumped out of her chair and into his arms.

"Oh, I'm so glad you're here," she whispered in his ear. "I was starting to get a little nervous." A little nervous? Who did she think she was kidding? If she was anymore nervous, she'd be in the bed next to Nancy with her own heart attack.

David kissed her on the cheek and wrapped her up tightly in his arms.

"Ah, hum," Nancy cleared her throat and raised her eyebrow as they walked, hand in hand, toward her bed. She seemed to be waiting for an explanation, but Megan had none to offer.

"How are you, Nancy?" David put his hand on her arm.

"Good, good." She patted his hand with her own. "You can't keep a good woman down, ya know. But I must say, I am gettin' a little tired of being poked and prodded every few minutes. You'd think these nurses would have enough people to pester that they could leave me alone for an hour or two and let me get some sleep."

Her southern accent made her complaining sound somehow sweet and endearing. "They keep telling me to get some rest and then they're back in ten minutes to take my temperature or my blood pressure or to throw another horse pill down my throat."

David laughed. "I see this hasn't taken any of the fight out of you."

"Still as ornery as ever," Megan added.

"Hey, don't you have class tonight?" Nancy's eyes narrowed as she looked at Megan. "Don't you think for one minute I'm gonna let you use *me* as an excuse to skip your classes, young lady. Oh no. I can't wait to see you handed that diploma, you've worked so hard for it."

Megan tried to smile, but the thought of being in the same place she *knew* that butcher from her nightmares was going to be was beginning to terrify her.

"I'll be fine," Nancy said, "you go on and get ready for class now and don't you dare worry about me."

Megan squeezed David's hand. God, how she dreaded the night ahead of her. She had felt so brave this morning when she insisted on going to the college to trap the killer. But as it got closer to the time when she'd actually have to go through with her plan, panic slowly began to replace her bravery.

David must have sensed the fear building inside her, because he pulled her closer to him and squeezed her hand twice, like a signal reminding her that he was there, right beside her and she instantly felt calmer. She gave him an appreciative smile and let go of his hand to lean over the rail on Nancy's hospital bed and give her a big kiss on the cheek. "I love you," she said, hugging her tightly.

"Oh, my goodness." Nancy patted her on the back. "Come on now. You're acting like you might never see me again. I'm not going anywhere, Meg. I told you, the doctor said I'm fine. So stop all your worryin' and git. Maybe David, here, can take you to get some lunch before you have to head off to school."

David nodded. "Sure."

Megan let go of the old woman and started to walk out of the room. As she walked into the hall, she heard Nancy talking to David. "Will you please tell her I'm fine? She doesn't seem to believe me."

"Don't worry, I'll take care of her," he told Nancy before turning to follow Megan into the hall. Once the door was closed behind him, he immediately pulled her into his arms. "You ok?"

She nodded against his chest. The two police officers who had brought her to the hospital were watching them, until David flipped his head and they quickly turned around, trying their hardest to look interested in something at the other end of the hall.

"You don't have to go through with this," David said into the top of her head. "As a matter of fact, I wish you wouldn't. I have a bad feeling about this."

She peeled herself off him and shook her head. She felt better, almost as if she had magically absorbed some of his strength. She could go through with it now, now that David was by her side. Besides, it was best to take care of this tonight because she knew, in her heart, she was right about The Cutter not stopping until he had her.

If not tonight, he'd be waiting for her another night, another place and David couldn't always be there to protect her. This was something she had to do, no matter how terrified she was. "I'm fine. Really."

"You sure? 'Cause you don't have to do this."

"Yes. Yes, I'm afraid do." She felt her chin quiver just a little, so she held her breath and mentally commanded the muscles in her chin to hold still. She didn't want him worrying about how scared she was. He had much more important things to worry about, like catching a killer.

David leaned forward and kissed her on the forehead. "Let's go get some lunch. We need to talk." He held her hand in his as they walked over to the other officers who were trying their best to ignore them. "How 'bout you guys meet us at the Applebee's by the college? We need to talk some strategy." The two officers said nothing until David added, "My treat."

"Yeah, sure," Thomas piped in.

Smith shrugged his shoulders. "Hey, man, you're the boss."

They silently rode down the elevator together then separated in the lobby to head for their own cars.

She watched the two men who, along with David, were to be her protectors tonight. They looked ordinary, which, she decided, should be very helpful. The last thing she wanted was The Cutter scared off. She wanted him caught and she wanted this over, tonight.

Officer Smith looked to be in his mid-twenties and was dressed very casually, like David. He would blend right in with most of the older students that took night classes at the college. The other man, Officer Thomas, was in his early to mid-forties and wore a navy suit. He could easily pass for a professor.

David, on the other hand, would have to be careful. He'd been on TV and in the paper talking about the case. His picture had been on the front page, right along with Megan's. The Cutter had to know him and, if he were to see David there, he would certainly pick another night to do his business. He had proven more than once, he wasn't a stupid man.

As they walked to David's green Beretta, she suddenly realized, The Cutter wasn't going to be there wearing a lighted sign, flashing the words, 'HERE I

AM'. She hadn't really thought about it before, but in order for them to catch that monster, he would actually have to approach her and try to…

Oh, God, there went all the strength she had borrowed from David, every ounce of it. She felt drained, scared, sick to her stomach and she held on tight to David's hand, as they walked through the hospital parking lot.

There were going to be three policemen around her at all times. Three of them. But David would have to be out of sight and that wasn't a very comforting thought at all. She wanted him right beside her, holding her hand, but that wasn't going to happen. It just couldn't work that way. She was sure those two other guys were good cops or David wouldn't have picked them, but David made her *feel* safe. Whether or not she *was* safe, was something she refused to worry about right now.

She took a deep breath, before letting go of his hand when he opened the car door for her. She got in and watched him walk around the front of his car to get to the drivers side. He was wearing his dark brown leather jacket, jeans and a black t-shirt. She hadn't noticed until know, but he must have gone home and changed. He couldn't very well have gone to the police station this morning in the shirt she had ripped and stretched out of shape.

She thought about how wonderful and fulfilling last night had been and how much she had really needed him, holding her and loving her. And she thought about how much she'd rather be doing that again tonight, instead of what they were about to do.

He climbed into the car and sat down beside her. There was complete silence in the car for a long time until he finally turned to look at her with his sad brown eyes. He pulled her into his arms and held her close to his chest, mashing her cheek against his neck and crushing her hip against the consol between their two seats. She could feel his pulse beating against her face and his breath, warm against the side of her head, as he talked into her hair. "I hated being away from you this morning."

Megan's fingers dug into the cold leather of his jacket, feeling the strength slowly returning to her body. With him by her side, she could do anything, she was sure of it. He kissed the side of her head and then tilted her face up and kissed her on the forehead, on the cheek and then on the lips. His kisses were warm, tender and caring, much different from the all-consuming, hungry kisses from last night.

After a few seconds, he tore himself away from her and started the car. "I have something I have to tell you before we meet up with the guys. They've been with you all morning, so they don't know yet."

Megan waited a few seconds, but he wouldn't elaborate. "What? What is it?"

"Well. It looks like Hudson may be our man after all."

She noticed his hands, tight around the steering wheel, as he drove out of the parking lot.

"He has a light blue Oldsmobile and I found blood in it," he continued.

"I don't think it was blue. I…I think it was silver."

"It's *light* blue and we found blood in it, Megan. The same blood type as the dancer's." He looked forward and stared out the window, his jaw tightly clenched. He swallowed and then added, "They're checking out his house now."

She looked at him. The poor guy was dying inside, she could tell. He looked like the weight of the entire world was on his shoulders. She reached out and put her hand on his arm. "Does he know that you…." She wasn't quite sure how to ask him if his partner knew that he was the one who had turned him in.

"Yeah, I think so." A muscle in his jaw jerked as he stared out the windshield and drove silently to the restaurant. They pulled into the parking lot and he found an empty space behind the building. He turned off the car and looked at her. "I'm still not letting you out of my sight."

"Good," she said and smiled at him.

"But what if we fail, Megan? What if it's not Hudson? And what if I don't stop him?"

"You will. I trust you." She meant that as a compliment, but he looked as though she had just slapped him across the face. "It'll be alright, David. Really. It was my idea and you're obviously unaware of how incredibly smart I am. I would have thought by now you'd know how completely brilliant I am."

He half smiled at her, apparently not very amused by her weak attempt at humor.

They got out of the car and walked over to the front door of the restaurant where Thomas was smoking a cigarette.

Smith cracked open the heavy leaded glass door and stuck his head out. "Hey, they got us a booth ready."

"Take her in and I'll be right there," David said. "I gotta call Banister and check in."

The three of them were seated and gave their drink orders to the waitress. They sat there in the uncomfortable silence that hung over their table, waiting for David. She wasn't sure how much they knew, so she decided to say nothing. She'd let David do all the talking. Maybe he'd come in and tell her it was all over. That Hudson had confessed and it was over. Wouldn't that be wonderful? They would have their man and she wouldn't have to go through with this, after all.

"We ordered you a diet Pepsi," Smith told David as he walked over to their booth. "Don't have diet Coke."

He sat down beside Megan and put his arm around her shoulder. "That's fine." He looked at her and shook his head. Didn't seem like he had the news she was looking for. It wasn't over and she'd still have to risk her life tonight.

David had her draw a map of the college campus on the back of a paper place-mat and chart out her entire night. He wanted to know exactly where she was going to be and when. She had two classes that night, children's lit at four in the language arts building and art for the elementary school child at five-thirty in the arts and human development building. Then after that, she had an appointment to meet with her professor regarding her being dismissed from her student teaching position at Fenwood Elementary. She wasn't looking forward to leaning that she might not be able to graduate this spring.

Megan watched in fascination as David and his fellow policemen worked on the details for the evening. They decided who was going to be where at exactly what time. Smith was to be inside the class with Megan, hanging around in the back, blending in with the other students. Thomas was to be directly outside the classroom door to watch everyone, coming in or out.

But David, much to her disappointment, would be the farthest away, being that he was the one who was most identifiable. But from his vantage point he could oversee the entire operation. He would have her in his sights when she was outside the buildings. The three officers would have constant radio contact with each other. And David assured her, that he could be inside the building within seconds.

She watched the other men shovel food into their mouth as they listened intently to David's instructions. How could they eat like that? Weren't their stomachs tied up into knots, too? Of course, it wasn't their neck on the line.

She turned over a piece of lettuce with her fork, half listening to them going over the plan for what seemed like the tenth time, and wondered why she had even ordered anything to eat in the first place. Surely she would gag, if she even thought about putting that food in her mouth. She looked down at David's plate. He hadn't touched a bite of his food, either.

"Got that?" David asked her.

Megan sat up and looked at him. "I'm sorry. What?"

"You know where to meet us, if something happens and we get separated?"

"I'm sorry. I…I didn't catch that part. I was thinking about something else. I'm sorry."

"Megan, this is important. Please, please pay attention. You are to meet us here." He pointed to a building on her map. It was the student center in the middle of the campus. "Right in front of the book store. Got it?"

She nodded her head. "Got it."

"It's very important. The second you don't see at least one of us, you head straight for it and we'll do the same."

"Ok."

"Alright," David said to his troops. "Let's do this."

$$* \qquad * \qquad * \qquad *$$

3:57 p.m.

She made it to her first classroom without incident and slowly released the air she had held in her lungs since the second she let go of David's hand in the parking lot. Wow, that was scary. Her muscles almost ached from her being so tense. She had to calm down or she'd never make it though the night. David had it all under control. There was no need to panic. Panicking would just get her into trouble.

She walked over to her desk and dropped her books onto it. She took off her coat and watched the door. Where was Smith? He was supposed to be right behind her. Ok, there he was. She draped her coat over the back of her chair and smiled at him, as relief washed over her. The feeling, however, didn't last long because walking in the room, right behind Smith, was Bill Peak.

Oh, darn, she had forgotten all about him. She turned around and fell into her chair. She put her elbow on the desk and her hand up on the side of her head to hide her face. Having two psychos to deal with in one night was a little too much to ask of anyone. Maybe he'd leave her alone. He should be embarrassed and ashamed of himself. Maybe he wouldn't even say a word to her.

No such luck. "Megan, I need to apologize about the other night." His voice was steady and monotone.

She rolled her eyes back into her head before looking at him through her fingers. Oh, why couldn't he have just been the weasel he was and completely ignore her? "Don't worry about it," she said. "No big deal."

"Really. I'm sorry. I was way out of line. I just wanted to make a good impression on you."

Oh, he made an impression on her alright, the creep. "No big deal." She turned her attention to the books on her desk and rearranged them for no particular reason.

"I was hoping, maybe, you could give me another chance."

Megan's eyes flew open. Was he serious? She turned her head and looked him in the eyes. He was serious.

She figured she had two choices. She could tell him, hell no, not even after the two or three years of intense therapy he needed or she could tell him that, while she appreciated his offer, she was currently involved with someone else. And after the wild, hot, incredible sex she had participated in last night, that seemed to be, not only the nicest thing she could think of to say, it also seemed to be the truth.

She cleared her throat. "I'm sorry, Bill, I'm...I'm sort of seeing someone now."

"What?" He practically screamed at her. "You went out with me while you were seeing someone else?"

She saw Smith, out of the corner of her eye, straighten up in his seat and crane his neck to look around the student sitting in front of him. "No, no. Not exactly," she said, extremely sorry she hadn't chosen the 'hell no, you're a nut' answer.

"What do you *mean*, 'not exactly'?" Bill raised his voice, causing not only Smith, but half of the class to stop what they were doing and stare at him.

Megan wanted to crawl under her desk. "I...I just met him a week ago and now...now we're....sorta seeing each other."

"Seeing each other or sleeping with each other?" His angry whisper and wild eyes scared Megan. The volcano she knew was inside Bill Peak looked like it was just about to erupt.

"Listen. I don't think I have to explain *anything* to you."

Bill leaned over his desk as far as he could without actually getting out of his chair. "The hell you don't! Who the fuck do you think you are, toying with me like some heartless whore?"

Megan shrank back into her chair and looked around the room. Everyone in the class was dead silent and staring in disbelief at their usually quiet and shy classmate. She saw Smith stand up in the back of the room and discreetly whisper something into the hidden microphone on his shirt.

Bill took a deep breath and leaned back into his chair. His angry eyes softened and he looked at Megan as if he might cry. "I really thought we had something together."

"What?" She had to fight back a laugh. "Are you serious?"

The professor walked into the room and dropped his black portfolio bag on his desk in the front of the class. He opened it and pulled out a stack of white papers. "Hope you all took the time over the long weekend to read "Peter Pan" in its entirety, because tonight we shall have a test on that very subject."

A collective "Awe" came from the class.

"I knew you'd like that and that is precisely why there is room on the back for your thoughtful comments on whether Peter went back to Neverland or if he stayed in London with Wendy and why. And let me tell you, watching the cartoon before class isn't going to help you with *this* test." The professor smiled and handed a stack of tests to each of the students sitting in the front row.

Megan took a sheet of paper and passed the rest to the girl behind her. She had actually done the assignment, but found it impossible to concentrate. She found she had to read each question at least three times before her brain would even register the words.

She glanced over her shoulder at Officer Smith who was staring at the piece of paper on his desk like it was some kind of dead animal. He looked up and gave her a reassuring smile. She then turned back around and noticed Bill shooting daggers at her from his desk. It had to be her imagination, but she could swear there was steam rising off of him. His face was red and his hands gripped the sides of his desk so hard, his knuckles were white. Well, at least she wasn't the only one in the class failing the test.

Megan sat through class with the uneasy feeling that at any second Bill was going to jump out of his chair and strangle her right in front of the other students, making her all but forget that someone else outside this classroom also wanted her dead.

The professor looked at this watch and stood up from behind his desk. "Ok. Please put down your pencils and pass your papers to the front. Please, read chapter eighteen in your textbooks about Jakob and Wilhelm Grimm. And I want a two hundred word essay on my desk Monday, comparing one of the Grimm fairytales to the Disney treatment of such. Have a nice weekend."

Most of the students were whining as they passed their papers forward, but not Megan. She'd consider herself quite lucky to even be around next Monday to hand in a paper. She passed the last of the test papers to the guy in front of her and stood up quickly to put on her coat, not once looking in Bill's direction. She grabbed up her books and bolted out of the room, glancing at Smith as she walked by.

She was out in the hall, looking for Officer Thomas, when Bill grabbed her arm from behind and spun her around to look at him. "You have some explaining to do."

"No. You're absolutely wrong." She jerked her arm out of his grip. "I have nothing to say to you, except, keep your hands off me!" She noticed Thomas just down the hall with his hand over his ear, like he was listening to a transmission.

"You are such a bitch!" He slapped her across the face causing a white light to flash behind her eyes.

She fell back against the wall and held her hand over her cheek. "You hit me. You bastard! Don't you ever hit me again."

Bill walked closer to her and looked into her eyes. "You teased me, Megan and made me fall in love with you and then you dump me like I'm nothing but garbage." He hung his head, his shoulders sagged and he looked like he was crying.

Megan shook her head. That man needed some serious help. "Look, Bill, I'm sorry if I ever made you think there was anything between us. I never meant to hurt you. I thought it was only a friendly dinner, that's all."

"You can't tell me that when you kissed me, you didn't feel something. Something very special."

She couldn't believe her ears. "Listen to me. I *never* kissed you. *Never*. You kissed me."

"You fucking whore!" Bill shoved her against the wall before leaning forward and mashing a kiss down, hard on her lips. She used her books to push him off her, but he still stood only inches away from her face.

"I would have showed you just how special being with me can be," he whispered, "if your fucking dog hadn't got in the way. How is the old mutt, anyway? Dead, I hope. The bastard bit my leg before I stabbed him. But next time you won't be so lucky." He licked his lips. "Next time I'm gonna...."

"There won't be a next time, scumbag." David grabbed Bill by the shoulder, ripping him away from Megan and knocked him up against the wall.

"David," she said, trying to catch her breath. "He's...he's the one. He's the one that broke into Sue's apartment." She wrapped her arms around herself to stop from shaking. "He's the one that stabbed Bear. He's the one. He just told me. Oh, God, he must've followed me to Sue's apartment." She closed her eyes and shook her head as the thought of what he might have done to Sue, if Bear hadn't stopped him, exploded in her brain.

Bill made a feeble attempt to escape and David shoved him up against the wall again. "Don't even think about it, punk." Officers Thomas and Smith were blending in with the crowd of curious onlookers, waiting to assist David, if he were to give them the signal.

"Stay right here," David told her and pulled Bill by the back of the neck over to where Thomas was standing a few feet away. "Take him downtown. He's the one that broke into that Johnson woman's apartment and stabbed her dog."

"No shit? I heard about that." Thomas looked at Bill, disgust curling his upper lip.

"I want you to take him in. The last thing we need is a bunch of uniforms here, if this hasn't already scared him off." David looked around. "If he was watching her, it's probably over."

"No problem. Consider it done."

"Nice collar, Thomas." David slapped him on the back.

"Really? Thanks, man." Officer Thomas grabbed Bill by the arm and pulled him down the hall.

David walked over to where Smith was standing and whispered something to him. He nodded and walked down the hall, out of sight. David looked around again and then at his watch. He slowly walked back over to where Megan was standing by the wall.

"You ok?" He gingerly brushed his fingertips across her cheek.

She nodded.

"Good thing I came along when I did."

"Yeah. Hard to tell what he was going to do." She put her fingers to her cheek and moved her jaw back and forth, it was already sore.

"No. I mean, if that's the kind of boyfriends you're use to….I must seem like Prince Charming." David flashed his beautiful dimples at her.

"Let's not get carried away, now." She smiled back at him.

"Well," he said, the smile leaving his lips, "this really screws things up."

"What do you mean?"

"Well, if our man was watching you, which he probably was, he's gone now. Chances are, he wouldn't stick around after that little episode."

She looked around and cringed, not liking the feeling it gave her to know a mass murderer might be watching her at this very second. She leaned forward and whispered, "Do you think he knows you guys are policemen?"

"Maybe. Maybe not. I tried to be as discreet as possible. But if he's watching us now, he probably knows who I am."

Megan looked around again. Everyone who had been standing around watching had lost interest and gone on. No one was even looking in their direction, anymore.

"Thomas is out. That only leaves me and Smith. You don't have to go to the next class. What do ya say, I take you home right now?"

She slowly shook her head. "No. He'll just try again later. And what if next time, you aren't there?" She swallowed hard and looked at him, trying to read his amber brown eyes. "What do *you* think I should do?"

David closed his eyes and shook his head. "Don't know. I just don't know. I didn't want you here in the first place and now with only two of us…"

"Do you think I'm right? That he'll just try again."

David nodded his head without looking at her.

"Then we have to do it." Megan took a deep breath and pushed her shoulders back. She stood up on her tiptoes and kissed him on the cheek. "Wish me luck."

"I wish this night was over."

"Not any more than I do."

"I'll bet." He took her hand in his and pulled it up to his lips and kissed it lightly, his eyes silently reassuring her. "Smith is waiting for you right outside. I'm going to wait here until I hear Smith has you in his sight. Then I'm going out the opposite way. I'll be waiting right outside the art building before you even get there."

Megan smiled at him and nodded. She squeezed his hand tightly and then let it go, as she turned to walk away. She could feel his eyes watching her as she walked out the door into the snow.

✳   ✳   ✳   ✳

Megan looked for David as soon as she walked out of the art building. Now that both her classes were over, all she had left was her appointment with the professor in charge of her student teaching. If The Cutter was still there somewhere waiting for her, he would have to strike soon. Most of the other classes were over and a lot of the students had already left for the evening. The campus was eerily deserted. It was dark and the snow was beginning to cover the freshly shoveled sidewalks.

She noticed David leaning against the wall of the science building about 70 yards in front of her and Officer Smith was only about 20 yards or so behind her.

"Good," she whispered, as the overwhelming urge to run across the campus dissipated. She walked slowly but decisively toward David and the science building. Her professor's office was two buildings past that. She saw David rise up from the wall, tilt his head to the right and look past her. He held his hand up to his ear. She could see his lips move, but couldn't make out what he was saying. She watched him take a few steps in her direction, before she sensed someone behind her.

She figured it was Officer Smith, until she glanced back and saw a man in a long dark overcoat rushing toward her. She quickly turned back around and looked at David, hoping he would somehow tell her what she should do. She felt her heart beating against her chest, as panic seemed to spread, like an infection, through her body.

She wasn't sure if she was still walking or if she had stopped and was just standing there watching David move towards her. She hugged her books to her chest and listened to the pounding of heavy footsteps behind her. They were muffled by the snow, but she could hear them getting closer and closer.

She could feel his presence behind her at the same time she noticed David, running towards her. She closed her eyes, took a deep breath and braced herself for the attack that was coming.

She felt the contact of his body, hard against her back, knocking her forward. Her heart stopped. She held her breath.

"Excuse me," the man said, over his shoulder, as he hurried past her, practically running to the science building. Megan exhaled loudly and leaned forward, putting a hand on her knee. She shook her head and laughed at herself for getting so worked up over nothing.

Smith gave her a quick glance as he rushed past.

"Check it out," David told him as the two passed each other on the sidewalk, just in front of Megan. Smith nodded and followed the man into the science building. David gave her a wink and slowly walked by her. "Just keep walking," he said out of the corner of his mouth. "I'm going to go up this way a little bit and turn around. I'll be right behind you." Megan gave him a quick nod and headed to her appointment.

A class had just let out and several dozen students poured out of the doors to the science building. She zigzagged through the chattering crowd until she reached the other side of the building. Once the crowd had thinned out, she noticed a man, all alone, leaning up against a tree beside the sidewalk in front of her. He lit a cigarette, shook out the match and then threw it down into the snow beneath him. He looked as though he was watching her. She walked past him and got a good look at his face. It was Frank Hudson.

Cold icy fear slithered inside her. She turned her head just enough to see him out of the corner of her eye. He had started to follow her. She walked a little faster and reminded herself to stay calm. David was right behind her and he'd take care of it. She just needed to stay calm.

She looked over her shoulder. Hudson was just a short distance away. She stretched her neck, trying to look beyond Hudson. Where was David? She couldn't see him anywhere. Had he lost her in that group of students? She should have walked slower. She had walked too fast for him to keep up with her. She had lost him. How could she have been so stupid? Oh, God where was he?

Hudson was gaining on her. The heck with remaining calm, she began to run. Her brain wasn't working. Where was she to go if they got separated? There was a check point. But where was it? Where? In front of...in front of the bookstore. That was it. She needed to head for the bookstore. It was well lit and at this time of night, the area would be more populated than the rest of the campus. But the checkpoint was back there. She'd have to turn around and run right past Hudson. There was no way she was doing that. Forget it.

Wait! She could run around one of the buildings and head back to the bookstore that way. But David had insisted that she stay on the main walkway. Well, she couldn't do both. So she would just have to hope that David had seen her run. He couldn't have been too far behind her. Maybe he saw Hudson, too. Maybe David had already apprehended him. Maybe it was already over.

She was terrified of turning around because it would slow her down, but she needed to know for sure. She needed to know if Hudson was still chasing her. At a full run, Megan quickly turned her head. A split second later, her left foot caught on an uneven paving block in the sidewalk and it sent her, headfirst, to the ground. Instinctively, she dropped her books and held out her hands to keep her face from smashing into the pavement.

She quickly stood up, forcing herself to ignore the shooting pain coming from her right knee. She looked back. He was almost on her now. She took off with every bit of strength she had, pumping her arms as she sprinted around the side of a building.

When she reached the back, she tried the door. The handle rattled, it was locked. She ran to the next door and nearly fell inside as it opened easily. The lights had been turned out, but she could see a red exit sign glowing at the other end of the hall. She raced down the hallway, the pounding of her footsteps echoed hauntingly through the building. She stopped when she heard the metallic squeak of the door she had just come through opening slowly. Quietly, she tiptoed to the side door and left the building.

She had to lose him and get back to the check point. David or Officer Smith was probably waiting for her there. She ran, full speed, to the rec center. If she got to the other side of it, Hudson wouldn't see her when he came out the door.

As she turned the corner to the backside of the building, she ran into someone, nearly knocking the breath out of her. "Oh, thank God," she gasped, looking behind her. "You gotta help me. Someone's chasing me."

She felt the person's hands tighten around her arms. She turned and looked down at their hands. Her entire body immediately went numb. She tried to scream, but fear had squeezed her throat closed. Yellow…. rubber…. gloves. All went black.

*   *   *   *

Megan felt a sharp pain in her neck and it jerked her back into consciousness. Her eyelids fluttered open. She was lying on her back in the snow and someone, a man, was kneeling over her. Just then, someone jumped him from behind and they both went tumbling against the building.

Hudson stood up and lunged at the other man. The man swung his blade at Hudson, cutting him on the cheek. Hudson returned with a right hook, up under the man's chin. The man staggered backward and then came at Hudson, kicking him between the legs. Hudson doubled over and the man used the handle of the saw to hit Hudson in the back of the head, sending him to the ground. The Cutter grabbed his black case and fled into the night.

Megan tried to sit up, but she was dizzy and lightheaded. Hudson recovered and crawled to Megan's side. "Don't try to get up. You've lost a lot of blood. You'll be ok, just stay still." He checked the wound on her neck. "You'll be ok, it's not too deep."

He took a handful of snow and held it firmly to her neck while he pulled a cell phone out of his pocket and flipped it open with his free hand. She heard the tones coming from the phone as he pushed the buttons. She laid her head back, closed her eyes and let the cold of the snow surround her.

"Hudson here. Get me an ambulance and a couple of squad cars out to the university. I'm behind the rec center. And fucking hurry."

*   *   *   *

David was frantic. How could he have lost her? She was right in front of him. Right in front of him! He saw her walk into that group of students that had come out of the science building, but when he got through the crowd, she was gone. No sign of her anywhere. He went to the professor's office where she had been headed, but he hadn't seen her. He contacted Smith and he hadn't seen her, either. He told Smith to get to the check point, just in case, and let him know if she was there.

David ran back to where he had last seen her and noticed a couple of books lying in the snow. He looked around and saw two sets of footprints leading to the back of a building. He followed the tracks and saw that they led into a back door. Just as he was about to go inside, he noticed a dark figure hunched over in the snow behind the next building.

He started towards the figure. It was a man, a man kneeling over something. Kneeling over a body. He felt the panic building up inside his brain. It was Megan's body. She was lying in the snow and there was blood....there was blood all over her and in the snow and all over....all over Hudson. Blinding fury filled him.

"No!" He screamed and leapt on Hudson's back, pushing him off Megan. They rolled through the snow. David stood up and pulled his partner to his feet, punching him two or three times in the stomach. Hudson kicked at him and then landed a punch of his own on David's right jaw. David lunged at him and they both fell into the snow again. Hudson elbowed him in the nose. A white flash temporarily blinded him as he felt blood beginning to pour out of his nose.

Hudson stood up stiffly and stumbled back over to Megan, putting his hands around her throat. The clicking sound of David pulling back the hammer of his revolver stopped Hudson and he slowly raised his hands and stood up. "You got it all wrong, buddy," Hudson said, turning to look at him.

Megan was lying lifeless in the snow and David could feel tears stinging his eyes. He aimed his gun right between his partner's eyes.

"Put the gun away, man," Hudson said calmly, his hands still in the air. "It's not what you think. Damn it, Stark, I'm gonna kick your ass."

"No, David," a tiny voice called out from behind Hudson. "No, don't." Megan was trying to sit up. She held her hands over her throat and blood was streaming through her fingers. "It wasn't him, David. It's not him."

Hudson turned and knelt down beside her. "Hang in there, kido, hang in there." He gently laid her back down and pulled his coat off, covering her with it.

Smith ran around the side of the building and rushed past David. "Oh, God," he said, looking down at Megan.

"I've already called for an ambulance," Hudson said. "It's probably too late, but get after those tracks. And whatever you do, don't step on any of them. What the fuck you waiting for? Get going!"

Smith pulled his gun and followed the footprints through the snow.

David just stood there, paralyzed, his arms at his side and the gun still hanging from his right hand. Realization slapped him across the face. Megan could have died and it was because of his negligence. He had let her down. He had promised to protect her. But it was Hudson who had saved her life. Hudson, his innocent partner. The man he just pulled his gun on and could have killed. He was the one who had saved her.

Fluffy white snow softly floated down from the night sky as David Stark slowly turned and walked away.

CHAPTER 9

▼

THURSDAY, JANUARY 22ND

*   *   *   *

8:15 a.m.

David placed a box on the top his desk and started putting a few of his personal items inside it. The other officers quietly went about their business, trying their best not to look in his direction. Banister had thrown him off the case and given him a two week's paid suspension, pending further investigation.

He was thrown off the case because of his relationship with Megan and he was suspended because of the way he handled the situation at the college last night. He knowingly put a civilian in danger, he didn't inform the department of the chance that The Cutter might show up there and last, but not least, he pulled a gun on a fellow officer.

Considering everything, Banister was easier on him than he probably should have been, but that was of little consolation to David. He had to hand over his badge and his gun for the first time in his career and it wasn't much less painful than reaching into his chest and ripping out his heart. This suspension would forever be on his record. The stupid mistakes he made on this case would follow him for the rest of his career. If he still had a career.

But getting thrown off the case and being suspended paled in comparison to the pain he felt from having lost Megan. She was going to live, but he had lost her. He was sure she wouldn't want anything to do with him now. He almost got her killed. He promised to protect her. But he had failed. Not to mention the fact, the bastard was still out there, free to try again.

True, they had a description of him and some blood and skin samples now, but they still didn't know who or where he was and that meant Megan was still in terrible danger. Several of David's fellow officers quietly watched him shake his head and walk out of the station.

He sat behind the Beretta's steering wheel, his head pushed back into the seat, trying to decide whether or not he should head to the hospital to see Megan. He longed to hold her in his arms. To tell her how sorry he was. How sorry he was that he wasn't there for her, that he wasn't the one who had saved her.

He called the hospital at least six times to see how she was, but couldn't quite muster up enough nerve to talk to her. He couldn't bear to hear her voice asking him where he was or why he hadn't protected her like he said he would. He had gotten out of bed twice last night, determined to go see her. Once he actually made it all the way down the stairs before turning around and climbing back up to his apartment.

He needed to figure out what to say to her first and, as of this morning, he still hadn't come up with anything. Nothing he could say would ever make up for his failure, the failure that almost cost Megan her life.

Of course, the longer he waited the harder it was going to be. All he had to do was start the damn car, drive to the hospital, walk into her room, look into those big blue eyes and…and beg for her forgiveness. The rest was really up to her. And he would just have to live with it.

David turned the key and headed toward the hospital.

*   *   *   *

8:36 a.m.

Megan woke up in a hospital bed and instinctively reached for her throat. It was bandaged and the pain was excruciating, but she was still alive. She squeezed her eyes shut and prayed, thanking God for sparing her life. The Cutter didn't usually make mistakes and she was thankful that this one time, things didn't quite go as he had planned.

A monitor connected to her finger and her chest, beeped out her vital signs and the quiet drip above her, announced that the I.V. sticking in her right arm was working as it should be. She found the bed controller hanging over the edge of the bedrail and pushed a button, raising her head.

She needed to use the bathroom, badly. There had to be one close by. The room had two beds in it, but she was its only occupant that morning. The walls were covered with light peach wallpaper scattered with little blue flowers all over it. An old T.V. hung against the wall opposite her bed and there was a sink across the room beside a closed door that she decided must be the bathroom.

Slowly, she swung her legs over the side of the bed, struggling to keep her white and blue polka dotted hospital gown from going up around her waist. She started to get up, forgetting about the wires connecting her to the machines behind her bed. The needle in her arm twisted as she pulled at it. "Ouch." She winced and yanked the monitor wires off her chest and finger then stood up carefully. A shiver ran through her when her bare feet hit the cold tile floor.

Rolling the I.V. stand along with her, she slowly made her way towards the bathroom door. Every beat of her heart throbbed in the wound on her neck and her head suddenly began to pound out its own objections to her getting out of bed. She became increasingly weak and the bathroom door seemed to be getting further away with every tiny step she made. The room began to sway and she felt her legs start to give way under the weight of the pain she was in. As if in slow motion, she felt herself falling to the floor.

Hudson walked in and caught her in his arms, just before she hit the ground.

"To the rescue again," she whispered and smiled at the man with the tan bandage across his right cheek.

"Just at the right place, at the right time." Hudson's wide smile brightened his otherwise sour face.

"I just wanted to see..." Megan touched the bandage on her neck with her fingers.

"Oh, it's not too bad. Could've been a lot worse."

"Have you seen David?" She tried not to sound as disappointed as she really was that he hadn't been by her side in the ambulance or by her bed when she woke up this morning.

"Not since last night." Hudson avoided eye contact with her as he helped her back into the bed.

"I know you must be angry with him...."

"Angry? Try down right pissed off."

"He…he really didn't want to believe it was you. There were just so many things…"

Hudson looked out the window at the enormous white snowflakes falling past Megan's sixth floor room.

"You would have done the same thing," she said.

"No," Hudson snapped at her. "No. *I* would have talked to him about it. *I* would have been a hundred and ten percent sure before I turned *my* partner in." He looked at her with hard eyes, but there was more hurt in his voice than anger.

"You gotta understand, when he found that blood in your car…."

Hudson shook his head. "Want to know whose blood that was?" He didn't wait for her answer. "Mine. That's whose. And he would have known that, if he would have just asked me. He would have known that I was waxing the car the other day and cut my finger on the can."

He looked across the room, studying the little blue flowers on the wall. "If he would have asked me, he would have known that I always work on the car when I'm missing Michelle." He blinked his eyes and gave Megan a weak smile. "Michelle was my wife. She died a little while back."

"Oh, I'm sorry. Is that how you keep your mind off it? By working on your car?"

"No. Actually, just the opposite. The car was Michelle's. Her father left it to her when he died about…oh, six or seven years ago. She'd been after me for years to fix it up, but I just never had the time. Never made the time. I kept promising her I'd do it as soon as I got freed up. But there was always another case, another reason to put it off."

Hudson swallowed hard and rubbed his forehead with his right hand, trying to hide the tears that were glistening in his bluish grey eyes. "The day I buried her, I locked myself up in the garage and worked on that old car for three straight days, until I had it running and looking like new." He smiled. "She would have really liked what I've done with it."

"You must have loved her very much."

Hudson bobbed his head a few times and chewed his upper lip. "It hurts real bad when you lose someone you love."

Megan watched the old man for several seconds before she attempted to change the subject. "Why were you at the college last night?"

"I was there looking for you. You see, Stark's a good kid, a good cop." He hesitated and looked down at the floor. "A good cop I'd like to smack up side the head right now, but…." He looked up at her and twisted his lips. "Well, he's got potential. I worked with his daddy a long time ago. His dad was a good man. Got killed when Stark was just a boy. And I...well I was sorta hoping to teach him the ropes as a kinda favor to his daddy."

"Anyway," he continued, "no disrespect, but I didn't believe a word you said about having dreams about this stuff. So I figured you must be in on it somehow. And I figured you must have been the one who turned him against me. Why else would he do what he did?" He got quiet and looked away.

Megan closed her eyes and shook her head.

Hudson looked back at her and smiled warmly. "Hey, kiddo. Don't worry. I'll forgive the son of a bitch. I just need to be mad at him for awhile, that's all. He just let his dick do the thinkin' for him...." Hudson cleared his throat. "Sorry. I didn't mean...."

He didn't finish his sentence. Apparently, he decided he meant exactly what he said. And she knew it was probably true. It would have been better if they hadn't become lovers. It was his feelings for her that made him jump to his conclusions about Hudson. It clouded his judgment. It pushed him into taking action before he was completely sure. Would he have done the same thing if it wasn't Megan who was next on The Cutter's list? No, he wouldn't have. He would have dug deeper, investigated further until he had all the answers.

"I'm so sorry." Megan looked at Hudson through the tears that were pooling in her eyes. "You're right. It *is* my fault. All of it. I should've stayed away from him. Let him do his job. I confused him. And I've screwed up everything. He probably hates me for what I've done to him."

Hudson shook his head. "In case he hasn't told you yet, he's in love with you, kiddo."

"Well then..." She blinked back a tear that was stinging her eye. "Where is he? Why hasn't he been here? Why hasn't he called me?" She searched his cloudy grey eyes for the truth.

Hudson glanced at his watch. "Well, right about now, I'd say he's getting his ass chewed out real good and no doubt he's already been thrown off the case."

"They can't do that. He's worked so hard...."

"He's too close to it now. Too close to you. A cop's gotta stay objective and you can't be objective when you're in love with a witness. Ahhhh." Hudson waved his hand, dismissing her worries. "He needed some time off anyway. Homicide's been a hard adjustment for the boy. He's use to helping folks. Helping get hooker's cleaned up and off the streets. Putting drug dealers behind bars and making the playgrounds safe for the kids. That kind of thing. Homicide don't help anyone. We just pick up the bodies and try to figure out who did it."

"You help the ones who might be next."

"Yeah, I guess so." Hudson forced a smile on his face.

"Well, if you see David, will you tell him that I'd really like to see him?"

"Yeah, you bet. But I'm sure he'll be here just as soon as he can. He's just got a lot goin' on back at the station. And speaking of work, I gotta get going. I just wanted to check on you. There's a police officer right outside your door and another one patrolling the hospital grounds. You'll be ok, so try and get some rest. You've been through a lot in the past week."

Hudson pulled the thin, blue blanket up to Megan's neck. "And I'll send a nurse in here." He held up the loose monitor wires in Megan's bed and shook them at her. "I'm just guessin', but I'll bet you need these.'

Megan tried hard to smile at the kind old man as fear began to creep its way back into her thoughts. "Do you think you'll catch him?"

"Oh, yeah. Just a matter of time now. They took some blood and skin off my ring. And now that we finally know what the son of a bitch looks like, every cop in Ohio is looking for him. Hell, we should have our man behind bars before dinner time."

He patted her on the leg. "David loves you, kiddo, I can tell. And not that anyone gives a shit, but I approve. 'Cause I can see it in your eyes that you love him back. And, well, that's good enough for me." Hudson smiled and winked at her again, before turning toward the door.

"Thanks," she called out to him. "Thanks for saving my life."

"All in a day's work, my dear." Hudson saluted and was out the door.

*   *   *   *

9:12 a.m.

When David pulled into the hospital parking lot, he saw Hudson walking to his red pickup truck. "Fucking terrific," he muttered under his breath. His knuckle's whitened as he strangled the steering wheel. This was all he needed right now. "My day just keeps getting better and better," he said and parked his car. He slapped at an annoying curl that had flopped onto his forehead while fighting the powerful urge to throw his Beretta into reverse and just get the hell out of town.

Hudson had seen him pull in was waiting for him when he got out of his car and closed the door. David stood there and watched him tap his right foot on the snow covered concrete. There was a tense silence that lasted an uncomfortable amount of time until finally, David couldn't stand it any longer and cleared his throat. "Um, I know I have some explaining to do....."

"Fucking understatement of the year," Hudson shot back.

"I don't know how you can ever forgive me...for...."

"I'm not sure I can."

"Can't blame you. I'm not sure I would forgive me, either."

"Damn straight you wouldn't."

David cleared his throat again and looked away. He had screwed up before, but nothing like this. Not anything close to this.

"That's why it's a good thing I'm a better man than you are," Hudson said. "I sure as hell am a better cop than you are." Hudson stepped toward him and punched him right in the face.

David's head flew back and he fell back against his car. "Son of a bitch!" He gingerly touched his lips, and then checked his fingers for blood. "Ouch. Did you have to hit me so hard?"

"Yes."

"I just wish you would've warned me first." David wiggled his jaw back and forth with his right hand. "Well, I guess I deserved that."

"You bet your sweet ass you did! *And* a lot more, if you ask me. But I'm an old man and besides, I happen to like that kid up there too much to fuck your looks up any more than they already are." Hudson shook his head. "I personally can't imagine what in the hell she sees in you. You're not much to look at, you live like a slob and you could use a hair cut. All I know is you must be hung like a fuckin' horse for someone as classy as that girl to even give you the time of day."

David shook his head and smiled at his partner.

"Listen, I know you'd like to go up there and see your lady friend. She'd like to see you, too. But I think I have something you might be more than a little interested in."

"Oh, yeah? What's that?"

"You had someone checking on the whereabouts of a Wayne Logan?"

David nodded.

"Well, they found him. And the fucker is living right here in Cleveland. And get this. He just happens to drive a 1985 *silver* Oldsmobile Calais. It's got Florida plates, so we weren't even looking for it. Oh, and wait. It gets better. He works for this little plastics factory off Superior, but just take a guess at what he does in his spare time."

"Taxidermy?"

"Give the man a cigar."

"You're fucking kidding me?" David jammed his fingers through his hair. "It's him! It has to be him!"

"No shit, Sherlock." Hudson shook his head slowly. "Damn, boy, how in the hell are you ever gonna get along without me?"

"Do you have an address for him?" David's head was reeling. This was it! All the questions were answered. All the pieces finally fit together.

"Yep, I just wanted to check on Miss Montgomery first and make sure the officer watching her room was on his toes. But tell me, kid, why were you checking on that Logan character? Did she dream it was him?"

David shook his head. "No. Logan is her father. Her real father. He doesn't know about her and until yesterday, she didn't even know about him."

"Holy shit."

"You said it."

Hudson tilted his head toward David's car. "Well, if you've got nothing better to do, what do you say we go catch ourselves a serial killer?" Hudson sprinted over to the passenger side of the Beretta and opened the door. He looked over the car's roof and impatiently motioned to David to get in. "You comin' or do I have to do everything myself?"

David slammed his fists down on the roof of the car. "I've been fucking suspended! No badge. No gun."

"You should've been fuckin' fired, you asshole." Hudson slid a black revolver across the car roof and David caught it with his hand. "Take it, I have an extra. Now, am I gonna have to walk there or what?"

Hudson got in the car and slammed the door. David looked at the gun, slid it into his holster and got in the car.

David suggested they call for back up, but Hudson would have no part of it. "Need I remind you, my boy, you're not supposed to be here? If Banister finds out you're still working the case with me, he'll have both our hides."

David had to agree with him.

"Besides, even though you are a fuck up, I like my chances with you a whole lot more than most of the other assholes I work with. Not to mention, it's your lead, kid, and you deserve to be the one to bring that psycho bastard down. Don't ya think?"

"Whatever you say. You're the super cop. I'm only the lowly sidekick."

"I'm glad you finally realized how things are." Hudson looked out the window as they sped towards Logan's apartment. "You know, it'll be kinda nice to show those high and mighty Feds a thing or two about detective work, don't you think? Let them keep looking for that twenty-something, overly intelligent, excessively privileged college student they've been looking for. We'll show 'em. That top-notch profiler of their's, don't know shit."

Wayne Logan rented one side of a duplex on 3rd Street. He had moved there about six months ago. He changed jobs constantly and paid cash for everything, making in extremely difficult to keep track of him. Aside from doing taxidermy, he was now working in a little factory that made plastic medicine bottles. He'd been there for a little over two months, but when Hudson called to see if he was at work this morning, the receptionist told him that he hadn't shown up yet.

David parked his car on the street, a couple of houses down from the duplex where Logan supposedly lived. They walked up the sidewalk. There was no sign of Logan's Oldsmobile in the driveway or parked anywhere on the street.

Hudson took the back of the house, looked in the detached garage and shook his head. David peeked into the side window, there seemed to be no movement in the house.

David knocked on the front door, his revolver pointing up. He knocked again, harder and louder. "Police, open up." Nothing. He kicked in the front door and heard Hudson simultaneously kick in the back door. "I'm in," David called to his partner.

"I'm in." He heard Hudson yell out. Then after a few seconds, he heard him say, "Nothing here."

David had his gun drawn as he slowly walked through the house, searching every room.

Hudson was standing in a doorway down the hall from him. "Hey, Stark, come here. Get a load of this." Hudson pulled a bottle of Tums from his coat pocket, shook out two tablets and threw them in his mouth.

David walked up behind his partner and looked over his shoulder. "Good God," he breathed out. All four walls were plastered with pictures. Pictures, newspaper headlines, articles and magazine covers about the women he had murdered and about the murder of Debbie Maxwell, Megan's mother. There were also some old pictures of a man holding hands with a pretty redhead and pictures of them kissing and a couple of cheesecake pictures of the redhead on a bed in a ruffled blue nightgown.

There were no less than three dozen candles all over the room and there was the faint scent of vanilla in the air. David walked over to a candle on the dresser and stuck his finger inside the jar. "The wax is still soft. Missed him by less than fifteen minutes, I'll bet."

Hudson walked up beside David, nudged him with his elbow and nodded toward the left wall. Taped to the wall was a collage of pictures from magazines cut up and glued together to make a woman. And at the top of the collage was a picture of Megan that had been cut from the front page of the newspaper. A lock of red hair had been taped to the top of her head.

David's stomach tightened and a sickening feeling washed over him. He longed to have Megan safe in his arms, but he knew he could help her more right now by stopping this sick bastard once and for all. Which was exactly what he and Hudson planned to do.

They searched the rest of the duplex, but no other evidence was found. No body parts, no taxidermist supplies, no black case, no yellow gloves. Nothing really, except some clothes, a few dishes and cups and in the fridge there was a Chinese take out box, a half empty pizza box and four Miller Light beer cans. The place was pretty normal other than the sick shrine he had set up in his bedroom.

Their next move would be to have Smith and Thomas watch this house, while they checked out where he worked. Maybe he was headed there himself. He could just be running late. After all, he had quite an eventfully evening last night. And if he wasn't at work, he should have a friend or co-worker who might know where he was.

They jumped in the car and headed to Superior Plastics.

*   *   *   *

10:02 a.m.

Megan was sitting in her bed, doing a crossword puzzle. She was trying to think of a six letter word for ill-humored when the door to her hospital room slowly opened. Megan looked up and smiled. "Oh, hi."

"Hey, I finally found you. I've been looking all over this hospital."

The man who came into Nancy's shop every Saturday to buy flowers for his fiancé walked through the door. He was dressed in a long white jacket. That was strange. Megan wouldn't have pegged him for a doctor. His hands were rough and unmanicured, like he made a living working with his hands. And the way he talked, she had been sure he was blue collar. Well, apparently the officer outside her door checked him out or he wouldn't have let him in.

"How did you know I was here?" She asked

"Oh, I have my sources." He smiled at her. "Here. These are for you."

"You are so sweet." Megan reached out and took the big bouquet of pink tulips he handed her. "Thank you." She lowered her face to the flowers and rubbed the silky bloom across her cheek. "They're my favorite."

"I know, you've told me."

A wrinkled old hand pulled a white cloth out of his jacket pocket and slapped the damp chemical-smelling material over her nose and mouth. She swung the tulips at him and tugged at his arm, but he held her head firmly against the pillow. The pink flowers fell to the white tiled floor as she lost the fight to keep her eyes open.

*   *   *   *

10:36 a.m.

Once they were back in the car, Hudson used David's radio to call the station. He wanted to let the chief know that they had definitely found their man. Within minutes, there would be an APB out on Wayne Logan. David and Hudson were going to check out Logan's work and follow up on any leads they found there. It was just a matter of time until The Cutter was in police custody and David could be by Megan's side.

"Hudson, where the hell have you been?" A woman's voice on the radio asked franticly, but didn't wait for an answer. "Do you know where Stark is? We've been trying his cell phone and he isn't answering."

"Shit." David looked down at the phone clipped to his belt. "I turned it off because I was going into the hospital."

"Um.....yeah...uh....I know where he's at," Hudson answered the woman and looked over at his partner, sitting beside him in the car.

"Well, we need to find him fast! That girl that was attacked last night, Megan Montgomery. She's been kidnapped from the hospital and Officer Stevens, Darrell Stevens, the one guarding her room.... he's dead, Hudson. Shot. The gun must of had a silencer on it 'cause nobody heard a thing. A nurse found his body in a bed in one of the empty rooms. They've already watched the surveillance tapes and a man, dressed like a doctor, pushed her out in a wheelchair through the patient pickup doors. Couldn't see them get into a car."

It took a second or two before the realization of what had happened slammed into David's brain. Wayne Logan had Megan. That butcher was determined to finish the job he had started last night. David could barely hear the rest of the conversation over the thumping of his heart, like a deafening drum beating in his ears. His stomach lurched and a lump found its way into his throat as the sick collage on the wall of Logan's apartment flashed inside his mind. Oh, dear God. He had let her down again.

*　　*　　*　　*

"Haven't seen him," snapped an old man sitting at a table busying himself by arranging brown plastic bottles in a cardboard box.

"You've already said that, sir." Hudson glared at Logan's less than informative co-worker. "Your foreman told us that you and Logan were friends and that you might know where he could be today."

"Wouldn't call us friends."

"Ok…." Hudson turned to look at Stark, pacing the floor behind him, and then back at the man again. "Well then, Mr. Thompson, why did your boss tell us that?"

"Went deer hunting with him a couple of times," the man said, not looking up from the table.

"Did Logan ever talk about places he likes to go?"

"Nope." He continued counting his little brown bottles and placing them in the box in front of him.

Hudson looked back at his partner and threw up his arms.

David exploded. He knocked the boxes, the man had just carefully packed off the table sending over a hundred little brown bottles flying onto the floor and bouncing off in every direction. He slammed his fists down on the table in front of the man and lowered his head to look him directly in the eyes. "I need to know if you have any idea where Wayne Logan may be today," David said through his clenched teeth.

"Well." The man grimaced as he stared at the vein popping out of David's neck. "You might try his cabin."

"And where is this cabin?"

"Bout forty minutes away, in LaGrange. Off route 301. Don't know the name of the street. Ain't never been there myself. He told me once he had a place in the woods where he stuffs those critters of his."

The two detectives were back in David's car a second later. "Well, I'm glad you finally got his attention," Hudson said, picking up the radio handset. "This is Detective Hudson. I need an address for a cabin in LaGrange owned or rented by one Wayne Logan. And I need it now!"

*   *   *   *

12:04 p.m.

Megan forced open her right eye, but it closed again almost immediately. It took several tries, but she was finally able to keep both of her eyes open. A dense fog seemed to surround her and she felt like she had to physically battle it just to stay awake. Her head pounded, even worse than it had in the hospital.

The hospital? Yeah, that's right. She had been in the hospital. She tried to reach for her bandaged throat and discovered her hands were tied behind her back. At the exact same time, she realized she was also gagged and tied to a chair. She was tied to a chair and sitting alone in the middle of a cold, dark room.

Where was she? What was going on? She had to force her drowsy brain to focus. Tulips. The man that had brought her the tulips. Her customer. That nice old guy from the flower shop dressed like a doctor. Was it him? Was he the one who held that rag over her face? Oh God. It was! Could he be…? No. No, that couldn't be right. She had known him for months. But why did he….? Why was he…? Megan couldn't fight it any longer and drifted back under the blackness inside her mind.

*   *   *   *

When she opened her eyes again, she was unaware of how long she had been there. She was still alone in the dark room, but this time she felt a hundred eyes watching her. Mallard ducks in flight and iridescent fish stared down at her from the wooden walls. On a small end table beside her, a stuffed raccoon, standing on his hind legs, eyed her suspiciously as he held an ear of corn to his mouth.

Scattered around the room were rabbits, squirrels and brightly colored pheasants, forever frozen in the midst of their daily activities, all watching her. Several massive deer heads looked down at her, their sympathetic big brown eyes warning her that she was next.

Megan struggled to free her wrists from the stiff nylon rope tied around them. She tried to stand up and found that her ankles were tied to the front legs of the chair holding her bare feet securely against the icy wood floor. She wiggled and tugged at her feet, but there was no give at all in the ropes around her ankles.

She decided it was best to concentrate on her wrists. The rope around them seemed to be a little looser and maybe, just maybe if she tried hard enough, she could free her hands and get out of there. She pulled and twisted her wrists against the ropes, feeling the coarse nylon dig into her skin.

After a minute or two without any success, she rested her sore wrists and looked around the small cabin. There was a half open door directly in front of her that led to a tiny bathroom. A dark red curtain was strung from the bathroom to the left wall which was bare except for a massive stone fireplace where puffs of smoke rolled slowly up from a grey pile of ashes behind the black screen. A green couch and two brown chairs faced the fireplace.

Behind her to the right was a small kitchenette with a little refrigerator, stove and sink. There was also a little round table surrounded by three chairs that matched the one she was tied to. In front of her and to the right a bench and a coat rack were against the wall, beside a thick wooden door. A door she was sure had to lead outside. Outside.

Seeing the door gave her the incentive she needed. She wrestled the ropes with newly discovered strength, but no matter which way she twisted, she could not free her hands. She heard a noise coming from outside and stopped to listen. It was a car, she was sure of it, and it seemed to be getting closer and closer until it sounded like it stopped just outside the door.

She tried to yell for help, but the scarf tied across her mouth prevented all but a few muffled yelps from coming out. She pushed her shoulder up to her cheek and tried to use it to pull the cloth from her mouth. She was on her fourth try when she heard the footsteps on the front porch.

Relief was soon replaced by dread when she realized that what she had first hoped to be her rescuer was, more than likely, her captor. Fear paralyzed her as the knob turned and the heavy wooden door opened quietly, allowing bitter cold air to rush into the room and encircle her.

A man, bundled up from the cold, closed the door behind him and stomped the snow off of his boots. He was carrying a black case. A black case that Megan recognized at once. Megan vigorously pulled at her wrists and twisted in her chair.

"Well, I see you're awake." The man's friendly southern accent seemed to betray the psychotic madman he was. He pulled off his brown knitted hat and stuffed it into his coat pocket. "Good," he said, removing his gloves and adding them to his pocket before taking off his coat and hanging it up by the door.

He sat on the bench and looked at Megan. A slow broad smile stretched across his face. "You are *so* beautiful." He removed both of his boots without taking his eyes off her, then stood up and rubbed his hands together. "I'm cold. How 'bout you?"

Megan looked at the man with unspoken questions in her eyes. He was acting as if he had invited her over for lunch. She didn't get it. This guy was a nice man. Not a cold-blooded killer. He had a warm and friendly smile, was probably in his late fifties, early sixties, with silver hair and beautiful deep blue eyes, the whites' of which glowed in the dark cabin. She had actually come to like him over the months she had known him.

He walked across the cabin floor and knelt down to work on the fire. Megan noticed a hand gun stuck in the back waistband of his pants. If she could only get free and get at that gun, she might have a chance to save herself. She pulled and tugged at the nylon rope around her wrists with such force, she felt warm liquid trickle down into her palms.

He stood and watched the fire for a moment and then held his hands out in front of it. "That's much better, huh?" He turned around to look at her and shook his head. "Would you look at your wrists?" He walked up behind her and inspected her hands. She felt him touch her and jerked away. He held his hand up in front of her face to show her the blood on his fingertips. "Look. Just look at what you're doing to yourself. Good thing I don't want your hands or I'd be pretty upset with you right now."

Chills ran up Megan's spine, causing the hair on the back of her neck to stand up, as he knelt in front of her and put his hands on her knees, the same old rough hands from her dreams.

She cringed and tried to pull away from him, causing him to laugh heartily. "Now, is that any way to act, you silly girl. I've been waiting such a long time for this day to come."

Megan turned her head and she felt his dry rough finger reach out to trace the outline of her ear.

"I was ok. Really," he whispered softly into her ear. "I was getting used to living without you. It had taken me twenty years, but I was finally getting use to it. Until…until that day last summer when I walked into your flower shop. You remember, don't you?"

He leaned forward and kissed her neck just above the bandage. "I couldn't believe my eyes. It was you. After all those years, it was you again. Back into my life. I kept trying to tell myself to forget about you, that it wasn't really you, but I couldn't." He kissed her cheek and then nuzzled his cold unshaven face against hers. "I just couldn't wait until the next time I would see you again. I came in every week, just like clockwork. Tell me you didn't know it was you I was there to see."

Megan could hear his words becoming heavier, more breathless.

He pulled the scarf away from her mouth. "Then, it wasn't enough anymore, just to see you. I couldn't get you out of my mind. I needed to have you."

She tried to pull away, but he held her face firmly to his and kissed her on the lips. He ended the kiss and his fingers gently explored her face. "I've been dreaming about this." He leaned forward and kissed her softly on the lips again, using his tongue to separate her lips, before pulling away slightly. "And to think, you were dreaming about me, too."

His hands found their way down to her breasts and fondled them for a second, then stopped. He put his hands back on her knees and slowly pushed them up under her hospital gown.

Megan's stomach heaved as she shifted away from his touch as far as she could and squeezed her thighs together. She could feel his breath, hot on her neck as he hooked his fingers under the elastic band of her panties and pulled them all the way down her legs, stopping at the ropes around her ankles.

"No. Please don't," she pleaded.

He ignored her and ran his hands slowly back up her legs to pry her knees apart. He pushed his body between her knees and she could feel him throbbing against her inner thigh.

"Please don't."

He lifted the hospital gown, looked down at her and shook his head. "That's been the whole trouble," he signed, lowering the gown back down over her legs. "No matter how much you look like her…," he took her chin into his right hand and studied her face, "you're just not Debbie. That's exactly why I had to do what I did." He let go of her face and stiffly stood up.

"Debbie?" Megan whispered the question.

He just smiled at her and shook his head. "You look just like her, in the face, but I use to tease her about how much I loved her strawberry pie. And I'm not talking about her cooking, either." He winked at Megan and walked around her slowly, looking her over. "She had bigger…." He held out his hands in front of his chest. "And a little rounder backside, too. She was taller than you are and she had the most beautiful green eyes you'd ever seen. I use to just get lost in them." He looked up at the ceiling and smiled at his memories.

"Here, I'll show you." He reached into his back pants pocket and pulled out a brown wallet. He flipped it open and smiled at what he saw. "See." He held out the wallet in front of her and showed her a picture. A picture of a woman who looked just like her mother.

"Perfect, isn't she? But that's ok, my darling." He folded the wallet up and shoved it back into his pocket. "Because I can make you perfect, too. As a matter of fact, it's taken five other women just to make you perfect. Hey, don't move. I wanna show you something." He rushed over to the red curtain and swung it open.

Megan gagged violently. A little stomach bile made its way up her throat, into her mouth, and she spat it out onto the floor. Her eyes watered as she dry heaved a couple more times. She couldn't breathe or scream or do anything but stare at the hideous thing he had laid out on his bed.

Pieces of skin were stitched together and stretched over a mannequin of a woman. The body was completely covered with skin except for the head, which was a plain ivory base waiting for Megan's face to be stretched over it. Something he apparently planned to take care of tonight. She didn't want to look at it any longer, but no matter how hard she tried, she just couldn't make herself turn away.

He jumped on the bed beside the nude body, waiting patiently to be finished. "See," he called out to her as he sat by his masterpiece, his legs outstretched and crossed. "She's almost ready." He patted the leg of the body. "Looks pretty good, huh? Well, it wasn't easy, I'll tell you that. Deb is one hard woman to duplicate. But I think I did a pretty good job. And now....now that I have your face. Well, everything will be perfect."

He smiled and looked at her from under his eyelids. "I can't wait until we can finally be together again. It's been so long." His voice cracked and he cleared his throat. He looked down at his work, caressed its arm and kissed its shoulder, before getting up off the bed.

"Oh, hey." He snapped his fingers. "I want to check something out before I get started." He walked over to a small dresser, opened up a drawer and pulled out a long red wig. "What do ya think? I had to make it myself. Couldn't risk anyone asking any questions. But I didn't do too bad, if I do have to say so myself." He held the wig up and admired it. "I just hope it fits right."

Debbie? Red hair and green eyes? And Megan looked just like her in the face? It couldn't be. But her mother's name was Debbie and she had red hair and green eyes. And that picture looked like her mother. Was this man Wayne Logan and was he building a woman to replace her mom?

Oh, God! That had to be it. She finally had the answers that had eluded her for so long. This was why she had those dreams. The Cutter was her real father. And she dreamt about Peter Logan all those years ago, because he was her brother.

The answers flooded her along with the sickening realization that she was the child of a madman and the sister of a cold-blooded murderer. She sat heavy in the chair, the answers like poison to her, rushing through her blood.

Logan walked to the front door, picked up his black case and carried it over to Megan's chair. He opened the case and rummaged through it, clanging his metal instruments together. "Now where are those scissors? Oh, here we go." He pulled out a pair of shears and held them up to the light. He stood up and walked behind her.

She felt the cold of the blades against her scalp and heard the tinny squeaking sound the metal blades made as they easily sliced through her hair and slid together. Tears began to work their way into her eyes as she looked down at the long brown strands of her hair on the floor and on her lap. When he was satisfied with his results, he put the scissors back into the case and placed the fiery auburn wig on her head, adjusting it a few times before stepping back to admire his work.

"My God. It's perfect. You *are* Debbie." He rubbed his chin. "Well, except for your eyes. But don't fret. I have them right here." He walked over to the end table and pulled out a drawer from under the forever feasting raccoon. Megan heard things rolling around in the drawer as he searched its contents. "Here! Here they are." He turned to her and held out two green eyes in his hand. "Perfect, don't you think?"

Megan wasn't sure, but she thought she might have blacked out for a second. She had tried to be strong, to remain calm and to stall for as much time as she could, but this was more than she could handle. This was it. Her time was running out. He was going to kill her right now and there wasn't a thing she could do to stop him. She hung her head and started to cry.

He put the two realistic looking glass eyes on her lap and they stared up at her while he brushed the long red hair away from her face and neck. "Don't cry, Debbie. We'll be together soon." He kissed her neck and then her lips. "Well, we best get started. I've got a lot of work to do." He reached into his black case and found his yellow rubber gloves.

Megan pulled at her arms with every ounce of strength she had left, but it just wasn't enough. "Somebody help me!" She screamed at the top of her lungs. "Somebody. Please. Help me!" She rocked her chair violently, tipping it over and crashing to the floor.

The green eyes rolled across the wooden floorboards and he raced after them. Once he collected his precious eyeballs from under the couch, he walked back to Megan and got down on his hands and knees in front of her. He lowered his face to the ground next to hers and lovingly stroked her cheek. "Hey there, it'll be alright." He pulled her chair upright and patted her on the leg. "It'll only hurt for a minute, I promise. Then you'll be Debbie and we can be together again. Everything will be perfect, just like it use to be."

"No," a whispered sob escaped her lips. "No, please don't do this. Don't do this."

He reached into his black case and took out his bone saw and laid it, along with his yellow gloves, on her lap. He turned her head and pulled the bandage off her neck. Taking a second to study the wound, he reached back into his case for a small thin knife and went to work.

She felt the cold knife dig into the incision on her neck as he began to cut through the stitches. She winced and cried out as the wound opened up and blood began to drip down onto her gown. She knew she needed to stop him now or it would be too late. He was killing her.

"Take your hands off me, you sick fuck!" She screamed.

He stopped what he was doing, sat back on his heels, and raised his eyebrows at her. "That's no way for a lady to talk. Debbie never used that kind of language."

"And she never loved you, either!"

"Oh, come on. What do you know about it?" He leaned forward and went back to work, pulling out her stitches.

"I know a lot more than you think, Wayne Logan."

He stopped again and looked at her. "How did you know my name? I never told you my name."

"Just look into my eyes and tell me, who do you see?"

Logan looked at her and pinched his eyebrows together. "You're just the girl from the flower shop."

"Did you ever stop to wonder why I was dreaming about you? Just look at me, Daddy! I've got your eyes!"

Logan quickly stood up and accidentally knocked the saw off her lap. "You can't be. I don't have a daughter. You're just trying to trick me into letting you go. Well, forget it. It won't happen, sweetheart. Nothing's going to stop me now. Nothing!"

"Want to know why I look just like Debbie? Because I'm her daughter, that's why. Yours and hers."

"No." Logan backed away from her. "It can't be. She would have told me."

It was working. She had to keep him talking. She had to stall as long as she could to give David enough time to find her. And he would find her. He had to.

"You were the biggest mistake she ever made," she continued. "Do you know she almost had an abortion because she hated you that much? But I am a part of her, too. That's why she went through with it. Because she hoped I would be like her, not you. And I am!" Megan puffed out her chest. "She made mistakes, but she was a good person and a great mother who loved me. And she loved Gene Maxwell."

"Stop it!" Logan clenched his teeth.

"They died in each other's arms, did you know that? And they're in heaven together right now and for all of eternity."

"I said, stop it!"

"And I'm sorry to inform you, Dad, but that thing you've created will *never* be Debbie. It will only be pieces of the women you murdered. Not Debbie! Never Debbie!"

"Stop it! Shut up!" Tears began to roll down his face.

"Debbie didn't love you. She never loved you. And that collection of flesh over there will never love you, either!"

"Shut up, shut up, shut up! Or I'll kill you right now, you little bitch!" Logan backhanded her across the face and then fell to his knees in front of her. He shook her ferociously, his fingers digging into the backs of her arms. "I swear it. I'll kill you, you fucking bitch!"

He let go of her arms and slapped her across the face so hard, it tipped the chair. She would have toppled over, if he hadn't grabbed her and slapped her again. Her face exploded with pain as she felt her jaw being knocked out of joint.

Logan looked at her, his eyes wet with unshed tears. "Why did you leave me, Debbie? I loved you so much. Didn't you know that? Didn't you know I loved you and still do?" He stared at her for a few seconds then swallowed hard. "I should kill you for breaking my heart and treating me like dog shit." He grabbed her shoulders and shook her again. "I should kill you, you fucking whore!" He drew back his hand and landed another harsh blow against her already throbbing cheek. "I should fucking *kill* you!"

Megan had to force her mouth to open so she could speak. "Maybe you should," she whispered. "Your sick perverted blood pumps through my veins, too. Maybe you should, so I can never become like you or your son."

He lowered his head and his entire body shook from the sobs that were ripped from deep inside his chest. "I didn't want to hurt anyone. But I was good when I was with you." He was crying so hard, she could barely understand him. "My life's been nothing but shit ever since you left me. I needed you, Debbie. I needed you back in my life." He stared down at the floor and cried for at least a full minute before he looked up and reached out to touch her bruised face with his rough old fingers. "You're right," he said calmly. "You do have my eyes."

Logan had tears running down his face when he pulled the gun out of the waistband of his pants and pressed the cold steel barrel under Megan's chin.

"You don't have to do this," she said, pain shooting from her jaw as her mouth moved slowly over the words.

"Yes...yes I do. Both of us have to die. It's the only way this can end."

Megan stared at him for a long moment before she heard the clicking of the gun's hammer as he pulled it back with his thumb. She squeezed her eyes shut. If she was going to die now, her final thoughts wouldn't be of her father, this cabin or the hideous body that rested on the bed across the room. No, her final thoughts would be of David.

She reached into her mind and pulled out a picture of him. His perfect body, that sexy tousled hair, the deep dimples chiseled into his strong face and those warm brown eyes searching her's for the answers she finally had. Her brain struggled to bring the image behind her eyelids alive. "Hold me," she begged him. "Hold me in your arms forever." She could almost feel the warmth of his skin against hers as he pulled her into his arms and she could even smell the spicy scent of his cologne as David lifted her chin with his hand and kissed her good-bye.

Bang! Megan jumped as the sound of the shot pierced her eardrums. Her image of David was gone. Now there was only black behind her eyes and a deafening ring left in her ears. She could still feel the cold hard barrel of the gun under her chin and the thick sticky wetness of what she was sure was blood, splattered on her arms. But to her surprise, she felt no pain. Was this what it was like to die?

She slowly opened her eyes. Logan was there, kneeling in front of her, still holding the gun to her chin and still staring right at her. No, wait. Not at her. Through her.

Bang! Another shot rang out. Logan's body jerked forward and fell onto her lap as the gun he was holding fell to the floor. The room spun madly around her.

She pried her eyes away from the hole in the side of her father's head and looked towards the door. A silhouette of a man was standing in the doorway, his back to the red and blue flashing lights that illuminated the dark woods outside the cabin. She couldn't see his face, but she knew him immediately. It was David. He had saved her after all. He had saved her. And not only from this nightmare.

She was alive! Her bruised and bleeding lips curled into a smile as relief washed over her. And as she sat in that chair, amidst the horror of that room, her heart was bursting with love. Love for the man who had just saved her life in more ways than one.

*   *   *   *

David stood in the doorway, unable to move. Megan was alive. He thanked God for that. But her nose was bleeding and the entire left side of her face was red with patches of dark purple on her cheek and jaw. Congealed blood crusted around the gaping wound on her neck. She was sitting in a chair. No, she was tied to a chair and wearing a long red wig that came down below her shoulders. Long chunks of her beautiful soft brown hair were lying on the floor all around her and her father's body was sprawled across her lap. Among the many stuffed and mounted animals in the cabin, a faceless mannequin, covered in human flesh from the neck down, was lying naked on a bed against the far wall.

David's head swam. The horror Megan must have gone through in the last few hours was unimaginable, but he had found her. Thank God, he had found her before it was too late. He had walked through that door without a second to spare.

Slowly, he crossed the room, his gun still aimed at the lifeless body on Megan's lap. He reached down and checked for a pulse on Logan's neck. "He's dead," David called over his shoulder to his partner, standing behind him in the cabin's doorway and silently shaking his head.

"He's dead," David whispered to the bleeding woman staring back at him with big unblinking, dilated eyes. He put his gun back into his holster. "Hudson, get an ambulance here, quick," he instructed without taking his eyes off Megan's bruised and battered face. "It's over. It's gonna be ok." He pulled Logan's dead body off of his daughter's lap and let it fall gently to the floor.

That's when he noticed it. Megan's underwear was down around her ankles. "Oh God," he gasped out loud, falling to his knees. "Oh, no. Oh, no." His eyes stung and he closed them against the onslaught of tears. Please God. Not this. Please don't make her have to deal with this, too.

His big hands shook as he reached for the white satin fabric and pushed it up her legs. "He didn't…He didn't…ra…" David couldn't even choke out the question as hot tears fell freely down his face.

Megan's chin quivered as she forced the corner of her mouth up and shook her head no several times.

"Oh, thank God." He pulled the red wig off her head and threw it at the man lying on the floor next to him. He turned back to Megan, her beautiful brown hair had been hacked off so short in some places, her scalp was visible. To keep her from seeing the shock in his eyes, he pulled her, along with the chair she was tied to, into his arms. "It's all over, Megan. You're ok, now. I'm here and it's all over." He needed to hear those words as much as she did. It *was* all over.

After several long seconds, he pulled back and looked at her. Deciding her forehead was probably the only spot on her face that didn't hurt, he leaned forward and kissed it tenderly. He took a knife out of his jeans pocket and cut the nylon rope, freeing her hands. Her wrists looked like hamburger, bloody and raw. He cut the rope around her ankles and unwound it.

"Can you stand up?" he asked her.

Megan nodded so he pulled her gently to her feet. She wobbled and he swept her up into his arms. She wrapped her arms around his neck and buried her battered face into his shoulder. David took one more look around the cabin before carrying the woman he loved out of her real life nightmare.

*   *   *   *

7:24 p.m.

Megan opened her eyes and saw David sitting in a chair beside her hospital bed.

"Hi there," he said, pulling his chair closer to the bed and smiling at her. She reached up to touch the dimple on his left cheek, but he turned his head and kissed her fingertips before taking her hand in his.

"Hi," she whispered back, not recognizing the raspy sound coming from her throat. She smiled and immediately winced from the pain that shot from her jaw.

"The nurse just gave you something for the pain and to help you sleep. You're going to be fine, but you need a few days rest. You've been through a lot." He kissed the top of her hand, just below the bandage that surrounded her wrist.

She had a bandage on the other wrist, too, and it reminded her of when she had been hospitalized, all those years ago, after tying to kill herself. But this time it was different, much different. This time she was bandaged because she had fought to stay alive, not the other way around.

She shook her head. "We've been through a lot." Something seemed different when she turned her head against the pillow and she suddenly remembered seeing her hair lying on the floor of the cabin. She reached up to feel her hair with her free hand and slapped her hand around her head. Her hair couldn't be more than a quarter of an inch long all over, maybe even shorter in some places. She squished up her nose. "How bad is it?"

"Well…" David narrowed his left eye and looked at her. "With a nose ring and a dog collar around your neck, you'd fit right in at a Marilyn Manson concert." He smiled and shook his head. "You're alive, Megan. Hair grows back."

She nodded and lowered her hand to feel the bandage around her neck. He was right. In the last two days she had a knife to her throat and a gun under her chin. It was only by the grace of God that she was still alive.

David stroked her forehead and bent over the bed to kiss the top of her head. "I thought I'd lost you." His voice cracked.

"Me too."

"I never, *never* want to feel that way again. I love you, Megan. I love you like I've never loved anyone before in my life." The words gushed out of him and he had to stop and take a deep breath. "Listen, I've got some vacation time coming to me. A lot of it. Let me take you away from here. Somewhere warm and quiet. Somewhere we can rest and you can heal and we can be together."

He bent over and carefully kissed her bruised, sore lips. "Marry me, Megan, and we can make it our honeymoon."

She raised her eyebrows. Was he crazy? They'd only known each other for two weeks and not exactly under normal circumstances, either. He knew her. As a matter of fact, he knew her better than anyone else ever did. He knew her deepest, darkest secrets and he still wanted to marry her.

As wonderful as that was, she hardly knew anything about the handsome man hovering over her, his dark sable eyes pleading with her like those of a little boy's. But there was one thing she did know for sure. She loved him. She loved him with her whole heart.

She smiled up at him as he waited patiently for her answer, but when she opened her mouth to voice her objections, he placed a finger across her lips. "Don't answer now. It's not fair to lay this on you right now. Especially with everything you've been through. But you have no idea how I felt when I thought…" David looked away and swallowed.

After a second or two he looked back at her with tears glistening in his eyes. "When I thought he killed you. Look, Megan, I have no doubt whatsoever that I want to spend the rest of my life with you. But, I realize you might need some time to catch up with me." He smiled and winked at her. "Well, I'll give you all the time you need. I'm not going anywhere." As if he had controlled himself just as long as he possibly could, he sat on the edge of the bed and gently took her into his arms and held her close to his chest.

The drugs were starting to take effect and a deep, peaceful sleepiness came over her. "I love you, too," she told him and put her hand on the side of his face.

"I love you, too." She fought her heavy eyelids, not wanting to lose the sight of David looking down at her, but eventually lost the fight and closed her eyes.

"Sweet dreams, Megan" she heard that sexy, velvety voice wrap around her as she drifted off, surrendering to the sleep that claimed her. And for the first time since her parents were killed, she truly believed that maybe, just maybe, the rest of her life could be filled with sweet dreams.

THE END

Epilogue

▼

May 15th

12:00 p.m.

The smell of flowers filled the air. White cotton ball clouds hung in the brilliant turquoise sky. Clevelanders were being rewarded for surviving another hard, cold winter with a beautiful and warmer than usual spring day.

Megan's white gown fluttered in the gentle breeze as she slowly walked down the aisle. Her short brown hair bounced weightlessly like some outward manifestation of the inner weight that had been lifted from her soul. She couldn't help but smile. And if she wanted to, she thought she just might be able to fly the rest of the way down the aisle. If there was a happier person on earth at this very moment, she couldn't imagine who it could be.

When she reached the end of the aisle, she stepped up onto the stage and a man in a black robe handed her a piece of ivory paper rolled up and tied with a tiny black ribbon. She took the paper and shook the man's hand.

Clapping and a loud whistle came from the crowd and her eyes followed the noise to see Sue, Nancy, David and Frank Hudson standing with their arms waving wildly. She lifted the paper over her head and yelled, "Yes!"

A rumble of laughter and applause erupted through out the crowd.

After the commencement exercises, Sue jumped up and down like a little kid. "Congratulations, girl. You did it!" She grabbed Megan and hugged her. "Hey, what a pretty necklace."

"Oh, thanks." Megan held the dainty gold heart tenderly between with her fingertips.

"A graduation gift from foxy over there?" She tilted her head towards David.

"No. It was my mom's."

Megan exchanged smiles with Nancy.

"I'm so proud of you, honey," Nancy said.

Megan wasn't sure if she was talking about her graduating from college or about how she had finally come to terms with the memory of her mother. Hate was heavy on the soul. It had taken a nightmare to teach her to accept Debbie Maxwell for the woman she was and to love her for the mother she was.

Nancy gave her a crushing hug and then wiped her fingers across her eyes. Hudson handed her a handkerchief from his coat pocket. "Thanks," she said, smiling at him.

"You're beautiful when you're happy," Hudson said, putting his arm around Nancy. He looked over at Megan and smiled. "You too, kiddo."

"Yes, she is," David said, handing her a big bouquet of white roses and giving her a kiss on the cheek. "Next time you wear a white gown," he whispered in her ear, "I'll be standing right beside you." He lifted her hand to his lips and kissed the finger that wore the diamond ring he had given her two months earlier. "I love you, Megan Montgomery."

"And I love you, right back," she announced, throwing her arms around his neck and kissing him.

"Hey," Hudson interrupted. "How 'bout we all go to Dad's for lunch? My treat."

"Oh, no you don't," Nancy said. "All they serve there is heart attack on a plate. And you know how your acid reflux acts up when you eat that junk. We need to go some place with a nice healthy salad bar."

They all laughed as Hudson growled and rolled his eyes.

0-595-34140-3

Printed in the United States
39311LVS00007B/76

9 780595 341405